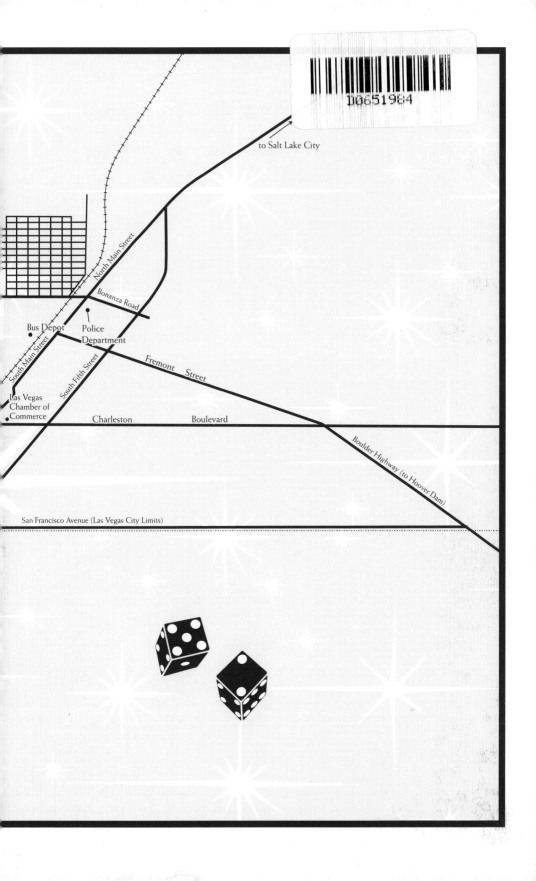

to Salt Lake City

North Main Street

Bonanza Road

Bus Depot

Police
Department

South Main Street

South Fifth Street

Fremont   Street

Las Vegas
Chamber of
Commerce

Charleston   Boulevard

Boulder Highway (to Hoover Dam)

San Francisco Avenue (Las Vegas City Limits)

The
IVORY COAST

Also by Charles Fleming

High Concept: Don Simpson and the Hollywood Culture of Excess

The IVORY COAST

Charles Fleming

St. Martin's Minotaur
New York

This is a work of fiction. Names, places, and incidents are the works of the author's imagination. Any resemblance to actual events, settings, or persons, living or dead, is merely coincidental.

www.minotaurbooks.com

Design by Susan Walsh

Library of Congress Cataloging-in-Publication Data

Fleming, Charles.
    The Ivory Coast : a novel / Charles Fleming. — 1st ed.
        p. cm
    ISBN 0-312-27464-5
    1. Las Vegas (Nev.)—Fiction.   2. Trumpet players—Fiction.   3. Casinos—
Fiction.   I. Title.

PS3606.L46 I96 2002
813'.6—dc21   2001048663

First Edition: February 2002

10   9   8   7   6   5   4   3   2   1

For Katherine and Frances

The
IVORY COAST

One

THE FIGHT BEHIND the casino was a nightmare. There was blood everywhere. One of Mo's men had taken a bad knifing. He had fallen into the pool and was thrashing around, clutching at the side, trying to get out. One of Haney's guys was stamping on his fingers. The water was going pink where he splashed in the shadow of the swaying palms. A big ape who worked for Haney had one hand wrapped in brass knuckles and one hand wrapped around another man's throat. He was putting the brass to that guy's face. Music pushed out of the casino like wind pushing sand across the desert.

To Deacon it was all a night at the movies: Haney's men and Mo's men, behind the casino. The big Starburst Hotel and Casino neon from the Strip side of the building blinked a red-gold-green over the desert darkness. A searchlight swept across his horizon, caught his gaze, and pulled it into the stars. The breeze blew hot. He was high and flying and he'd seen it all before. The fight scene. Take five.

It had started over a woman. Mo had sent two gorillas up to Stella's room to find out why she had missed the first set. The gorillas had returned with a report that Stella had a guy in her room—a colored guy. Mo was not asking what his lily-white lounge singer was doing with the colored guy. Mo told his men to give him the gate and get Stella up to his office. Like, now. And quietly.

That had been about eleven. By midnight it was out of hand. Who tapped Haney? Someone from inside Mo's organization. Haney was on it almost before it started. Four of his torpedoes came in through the front, dressed for business and moving fast. Before they had passed the registration desk, their black suits a blur against the turquoise and cream of the casino decor, they had picked up four of Mo's men as escorts. Someone was calling Mo on a house phone. Someone else

was calling security. The torpedoes were down near the lounge—
they called it "The Sunburst at the Starburst"—before Mo's men had
them outnumbered and surrounded. The ruckus itself started there,
just outside the lounge entrance. There was shoving and shouting,
and it was heated, but it was contained. It didn't have to be horrible,
yet. Haney was on one end of a phone line saying, "This is my town
and I'm not gonna tolerate any woman . . ." and Mo was on the other
end saying, "This is my hotel and I'm not taking any more of your . . ."
And a bunch of brutes who didn't even know why they were fighting
were getting the smell of blood into their tiny brains. The argument
moved out through the casino and off the floor and then spilled out
onto the pool area.

Deacon was finishing the second set. The Sunburst was full. Stella
still drew. Even if she sometimes took a powder mid-set and didn't
come back from her room, as she had tonight, Stella still drew. The
band had finished with a big-production version of "Night and Day."
Smoke and hush lay like a blanket over the room until right at the
end. Then the audience blew, and turned into applause. A lot of the
customers were on their feet and stretching and heading for the door
while they were still clapping. They would hit the pits in earnest
now, and start losing real money, and they were ready to go. It was
time for the Starburst to start collecting revenue.

Between solos Deacon had been sipping Kentucky straight bourbon
whiskey, straight out of a Coca-Cola bottle. He was sort of smoky
and blue inside when the set ended, low and mellow and quiet. He'd
put his horn away and stepped off the back of the bandstand, and
slipped out the back door of the club to grab a smoke.

The fight was on. He walked right into it. One of Haney's men
stepped out of the dark and threw him a huge roundhouse. Deacon
ducked and missed it and went into a shadow. He tossed the smoke
and scuttled away from the man with the big fists. Across the patio
six or seven more of Haney's guys, in black suits, were shimmering
in the seafoam-green light of the pool. Mo's guys were coming out
of the dark onto the patio and moving on Haney's guys like chessmen.
Overhead the searchlights crisscrossed a big V for *Vegas*. The air
crackled with neon hum and the scrunching of car tires on loose
asphalt.

In the shadows Deacon recognized Sumner, a sax player he knew,

and four or five other Negro guys from the kitchen. They were standing like statues, watching the fight, expressions of complete indiffer-
ence on their faces. Did it matter to them that the fight started over
a white girl boning a colored boy? Probably not. Deacon thought,
That's the only place to be in a fight like this.

But then the owner of the big roundhouse was behind him. Deacon
turned and crabbed down, and the punch whiffled over his head. The
big man's black shoes skidded on the concrete as he shifted his weight
to throw another. Deacon shot away sideways. Across the pool, he
saw one of Haney's guys draw a revolver.

All that Kentucky mellow evaporated. Everything evaporated. It
was so dry here that running water had to be pumped into the pool
at all hours to keep it from drying up. The lawn had to be sprinkled
all night long or it wouldn't get wet at all. For a moment there was
only the sound of the water hissing. Two more of Mo's men ran out
from the casino and then came the crump of someone's fist going into
someone's ribs.

Here came the big black shoes again, and the big punching guy.
Deacon slipped past the roundhouse again. He could see the man
who threw it clearly now. He was a vast brute, maybe a Swede, very
pale and not more than eighteen. He probably hadn't been in the
desert more than a week. Deacon had been beaten up by much bigger
guys, but they were always pretty good fighters. This lug wasn't. As
his punch came by, Deacon got behind it and pushed. The big guy's
shiny shoes gave out on him and he skidded down onto the ground.

Then a table crashed glass over the concrete decking. One of the
guys by the pool was Sloan, a bartender Deacon liked better than
most of Mo's men. He was wrestling down the guy with the revolver.
Then a burbling howl rose from the man in the pool who was getting
his fingers stamped and bleeding into the water. Sloan got the guy
with the revolver down, and he had his foot on the guy's gun hand.
Four shots went *blat! blat! blat! blat!* into the pool, where the water was
going pink.

Deacon went temporarily nuts. He threw two vicious kicks into the
pale guy on the ground and moved poolside. Keeping his left hand
low, guarding his horn-playing fingers, Deacon threw sharp right
punches at the finger-smashing man, who moved away from the pool
to defend himself. Deacon gave good, and got good, and went down

hard into a thatch of tiki lamps. So did the creep he was fighting—
another Irish cop, like Haney. Deacon thought he was called Harrigan
or Harrington or something. They both rose, soaked in lamp oil, and
squared off and started again. Deacon hit Harrigan hard, and he
bumped into a lit tiki torch and ignited. Harrigan shrieked and then
burst into flames—another Sunburst at the Starburst! Deacon shoved
him into the pool. The air seemed to sizzle for a second and—

And Deacon awoke.

His head ached. His right hand ached. Something was wrong with
his legs. Something was wrong with his bed, too. The sizzling sound
continued. Deacon opened his eyes. It was not his bed at all, or his
bedroom. It was a men's room. Urinals gleamed at him like rows of
teeth. Mirrors shone. Deacon was slumped into one of the shoeshine
chairs where, during the daytime, a guy named Fidget polished the
leather. The sound of water sizzling was a toilet running somewhere
at the back of the room.

How did things get so fouled? The night before had been fine—
not just okay, but fine. Cab Calloway's orchestra had been at the
Victoria for a week. Pearl Bailey was at the Sands. Sinatra and a bunch
of his crowd were rehearsing over at the Desert Inn. Someone had
gotten word out that everybody was going to be over on the West
Side, at Mamie's Black Bottom, after hours—and it was fine. A horn
player Deacon knew from his Chicago days was working with Cab
now, and he got him onstage for half a set. Deacon may have been
wailin' and he may have been failin', but then Pearl gave him a smile
that made his heart stop and he said, "Baby, this is *it.*"

There were lots of nights like that. Everybody was in Vegas.
Satchmo and Ella were in Vegas. Both of the Dorseys, Tommy and
Jimmy, were in town. Nat "King" Cole was headlining, playing weeks
at a time. Lena Horne. Eartha Kitt. Dinah Washington. The Treniers
were at the Starlite Lounge at the Riviera, and had been playing the
lounges longer than anyone but that nutty Liberace. Duke Ellington
had been coming since before they killed Bugsy Siegel.

The place was on fire, from the Strip to downtown to the West
Side. Especially, lately, the West Side. The Strip was happening, and
downtown was happening, but the West Side was where it really
cooked. That's where the colored folks were. It wasn't just Stella's

boyfriends who were getting run off the Strip. *All* the colored men and women were getting run off the Strip. The colored performers who were headlining the Strip could not get rooms on the Strip— not even at the hotels where they were billed as the opening act. Louis Armstrong or Louis Jordan might draw $25,000 a week head- lining the Sands, but they could not book a room there, or anyplace else. Pearl Bailey was headlining Wilbur Clark's Desert Inn—had been forever—but she had to enter the D.I. through the back door. She could not get a cocktail or a cup of coffee there, or anywhere else on the Strip. The colored entertainers could work, but after work they had to split. You might be the number one attraction at the Sands or the Dunes or the Desert Inn, but after work you were a Negro and you were *out*.

When the show was over, Sammy and Ella and all the rest of them had to make with the feet and get off the Strip. And when they split, they went to the West Side. They'd stay with friends, or in rooming houses or boardinghouses. They'd eat where their own peo- ple ate, and drink where their own people drank. And that was on the West Side.

And there were joints on the West Side where some of them went for the music. And those joints were jumping. There was Mamie's, and the little lounge at the Town Tavern, and the Victoria, and Slinkys Lounge. And now that Ivory Coast thing was coming. Deacon had never seen anything hotter.

Even by Vegas standards, the West Side was burning up. The whole country was burning up. The war had been over for ten years. The Depression was ancient history. Everybody was working. All those boogie-woogie bugle boys who'd gone into the army and learned to play reveille were pressing sheet metal or popping rivets or selling automobiles or life insurance now. Everybody was making dough. And everybody was spending dough. There was so much to buy, after the rationing and deprivation of the war. People were buying like crazy. They were buying houses and sofas and washers and dryers. They were buying televisions and record players. They were buying cars. Everybody was buying cars. Every joker in America was behind the wheel of his own pile of steel—his own private piece of highway heaven. And inside every one of those big American heaps there was a radio. The roads were lined with cafés, and inside every one of them was a jukebox. There was music everywhere you went—not just for the jazzbos and the rich folks. Everybody was getting some of it.

If you had a nickel, you owned the nickelodeon. If you had a car, you didn't need the nickel. The radio was on and it was free and everyone was listening.

The air was simply full of sound—the sound of music and the sound of commerce. All those jokers in their shiny Chevrolets and Chryslers were customers, and the car was the place to get them. Advertisers were pouring a fortune into radio, trying to talk every GI Bill into throwing some of his money at a Rocket 88 or a can of V8 or a can of Chef Boyardee. America was hungry and thirsty and hot, and there was a new kind of music for that. In Vegas, that music never stopped.

Drifting in and out of consciousness, Deacon was a jukebox, too. His head was a library of tunes, tumbling into one another, one riff rushing in on the next, horns and strings and rhythm sections all caving in on themselves. His fingers twitched over the horn parts, soloing silently as he rose and fell out of and back into the nightmare of himself.

His head played Charlie Parker and Gerry Mulligan. They were working the West Coast now, Mulligan with a new band that included this guy Chet Baker. Everyone told Deke he sounded like Baker, but better. Art Pepper was laying down amazing stuff in Los Angeles. Clubs like the hungry i in San Francisco and the Haig in L.A. were rolling it up every night of the week.

The music on the radio was mostly kid stuff. The McGuire Sisters had a big hit single in "Sincerely." Her nibs, Miss Georgia Gibbs, had a hit single with a cleaned-up version of "Dance with Me Henry." That knucklehead Bill Hayes was big with "The Ballad of Davy Crockett." Deacon would rather have been listening to Big Joe Turner sing "Shake, Rattle and Roll" or Ray Charles do "I Got a Woman."

America was still in love with Patti Page and Pat Boone. But for the jazzmen, the music was serious again, and the serious guys were making a real living at it again. And the guys in Vegas were making it better than anyone anywhere else. And on the West Side, at about three o'clock in the morning, when there was nothing on the Strip but men throwing dice and losing dough, the music was as good as music gets. All the white guys and all the black guys were jamming, and it was like nothing else in the world.

Now the Ivory Coast was coming. Mo was bankrolling it. That black boxer Lee was going to front the thing, just like that tired old Hollywood actor fronted Mo's Thunderbird. It was going to be a special place for all the Negro talent to get rooms and get meals and get happy.

It was going to be fine on the West Side, every night. Stella wouldn't have to bone so close to home when she got beige on her mind. And Haney would have to find a new excuse to send his goons in for the ass-whipping.

Deacon stretched one slacked and booted leg before him and groaned in pain, and tried to stand.

He was twenty-eight and long and tall, and dark and pale—black hair, worn long, over a long, sad face. High cheekbones. Strong jaw. Big black shiner over left eye. That hurt. Deacon squinted at the bank of mirrors across from the shoeshine stand. His dove-gray suit was badly wrinkled, and there was something wrong with his string tie, which was at half-mast and flying sideways. He still had his boots on. His wallet was still in his jacket.

The standing-up part wasn't going to work yet. Deacon rested back, closed his eyes, drifted off.

Later they had all been in Mo's office, shivering in the cold, upstairs at the Starburst. Mo, sleek and silver, said, "I don't like it and I won't have it. Figure out why Haney wants to be my headache, and do something about it." No one in the room had a clue whom Mo was talking to or what to do about Haney. Deacon was the first to leave. He took the elevator back down to the casino floor.

Fatty grabbed him just as he was coming off the car. He said, "I need a room."

Deacon said, "So get a room."

"No. Off the books. I need a private room, in the back. Your room."

Deacon said, "I was just going to sack out now."

"Don't," Fatty said. "I got this couple in from L.A. They're married, but not to each other. They need a place."

"Get them a room at the T-bird."

"That will take too long. I need the room now. I'll make it worth your while."

Deacon groaned and said, "Forget it. I need some sleep."

But Fatty had pulled him aside, out of the splash of the casino lights. He held something clutched in his left hand. He said, "Take this and disappear for three or four hours. A favor, Deke. Do it for me."

Deacon struggled and weakened and struggled and lost. He said, "I'll leave the room unlocked." He took the packet from Fatty and walked off.

Fatty said, "You oughta get some ice for that shiner, Deke."

He did not remember what happened after that.

Voices came and went down the length of the bathroom like horns calling through thick fog. One accompanied by clicking feet on the cream-and-white tile said, "Catnappin' in the middle of the day." And another, "Who is he anyhow?" And the first, "That's one of Stella's boys. Horn player they call Crush Velvet." "Crash Velvet now," the second said. "Haw-haw, you got that right." And again the flush. Deacon lifted his lids from the sound of swirling water, but the feet had carried the voices back down the tile.

Stella's boy. Mo's boy. Nobody's sweetheart. All the way awake now, Deacon saw that he was in the staff washroom, in the basement at the Thunderbird—sister property to the Starburst. He was not wearing a watch. Noon? Night? The fluorescent glare overhead told him nothing. He got to his feet and stood and went across to the line of sinks with the line of mirrors over them. Tall, thin men in black hair and wrinkled gray suits blinked back at him. The water was cool, and Deacon was hot, and Vegas was why.

It was Las Vegas. It was summertime. The hot sand blew and burned everywhere. Stella had extended their contract, again. Mo was not leaning on him too much, for the moment. The money was fine. Haney and his men were making it difficult to score, but Fatty always seemed to be keeping back something special for him.

And Vegas was cooking. The whole country seemed to be cooking. Ike was still in the White House. Everybody in America was working and saving and getting ready to have the American Dream come true. Deacon was shooting the American Dream every night.

And he was still in love with Anita. The thought made his chest ache. He threw cold water over his forehead and skidded it back into his hair, and kept on until the water dripped into his eyes and his hair stayed where he put it. The temperature in his head dropped a degree or two. His suit was a mess. Leaving the washroom, he found a cigarette in his pocket and stuck it in his mouth. The paper was dry and crinkled, and fired even before he got the Zippo to it. But it worked.

The Thunderbird kitchen was a vast metal madhouse. A hundred men or more, black and brown skins gleaming under their bright white cotton toques, were clanking pans and stirring pots and putting the edge back onto their knives. White men wearing red jackets and hoisting huge wooden trays came and went like clockwork soldiers. Lunchtime? The man named Sumner, the sax player Deacon knew from the West Side, caught his eye and called out, "Deacon! Give us a hand, man!" Fifteen other guys chimed in: "Yo, man. He'p us out!" Deacon said to himself, "How 'bout helping *me* out. Not much use while that big Swede was knocking me around the pool." But he waved and slid out the door between two of the men with trays. The kitchen clanged behind him and shook with laughter.

He ran directly into the steel-hard chest of a tall, wide Negro coming the opposite way into the chow factory. Deacon said, "Whoa, pony," and the Negro caught him in his arms and gave him a bear hug.

He said, "Crush Velvet! Where's yo' horn at?"

Deacon uncurled and said, "Worthless, I wish I knew. Every time I put it down I wind up in a jam."

Worthless grinned a line of massive ivory choppers at him and said, "Deacon, I been in a jam ever since the day I was born."

"And now you're poaching on Mo's kitchen staff?"

Worthless laughed out loud. He said, "Naw, man, I'm scoutin'."

"Stealing men like Jackie Robinson stealing bases."

"You watch if he don't carry that team to the Series," Worthless said. "In the meantime, anybody down here looking fo' suitable employment can talk to me about a job at the Ivory Coast."

"Mo's behind it."

"Mo's behind everything. But now Worthless Worthington Lee is gonna open a casino on the West Side and run Mo's cracker Jewish gangster self right back to Chicago."

Deacon said, "I'll tell him you said that."

Worthless was still laughing when Deacon got to the end of the hall. When he turned, though, Worthless had gone all serious and was leaning down and talking quietly to the sax player Sumner.

Deacon thought: *Working an angle. Every mother's son is working an angle. Mo runs the Starburst for the bad guys from Chicago. Mo secretly runs the Thunderbird for some guys from Los Angeles. Now Mo's the top-secret money for the casino built for Worthless and the guys from the West Side. And Worthless is sneaking around in Mo's backyard, looking for who knows what? Everybody gots a game. Except me.*

Deacon came up into the lobby and took a long, lazy draw on the cigarette. His eyes lidded down and the line of his jaw softened a little and, for the first time that day, he smiled. He went across the lobby. There was light slanting in from the front of the hotel. It was late afternoon, in Las Vegas, and Deke was up.

So was the Strip. The Starburst was newest among the newer hotels that had sprung up like cactus since the war. It was at the west end of the Strip, down the end of Las Vegas Boulevard. It was far enough away from downtown that it was in Clark County and not in the city of Las Vegas itself, which meant it answered to a different and entirely more corruptible set of lawmakers. That's why the Strip was there in the first place. The guys who were building Vegas up from the dirty little sandbag it had been since the 1920s wanted to do things their own way. They needed their own rules. But they also wanted to be near downtown, and the highway, and the bus station, 'cause that's where the money was coming from. So they decided to redesign things. One of the Chicago guys had said, "So, who decides where to put the city limits? Just move the line."

So it had been done. There were no rules down at this end of the Strip—no unions, no city cops, no congressmen, no history—and there was nothing for anyone to defend or protect. Nothing mattered but the money. And everyone was making tons of money.

Across the street, in front of the Starburst, uniformed carhops were moving machines off the driveway at the rate of about one a minute. Men and women recently married, or about to be married, and all dressed for success—Deacon caught a strain of Louis Jordan's "Reet Petite and Gone" in his head—got out of the cars and walked to the big swinging doors as if they were royalty arriving at Buckingham Palace. On the sidewalk a phony newsman with a Speedflex flash camera shot photos of the celebrities in attendance. There weren't any celebrities that afternoon, but that was okay. There wasn't any film in the camera, either. But it gave the honeymooners and the high rollers the impression that something important was going on—something more important than their losing lots of dough. It was good PR, as Mo would say.

It was working. The Starburst was hot enough that travel agents who were properly compensated were still recommending it to first-time visitors to Vegas, high rollers and honeymooners alike. After they got cleaned out—and just about everybody got cleaned out—the first-time visitors might become one-time visitors. But that was okay. Mo would have their money, and worrying was for tomorrow. And Las Vegas, whatever else it was about, was never about tomorrow. Vegas, Jack, was *today*. And tonight.

Outside the heat was vicious, inhuman and unnatural. A man did not even sweat. Deacon stood at the curb for a moment, drawing hard on the last of his cigarette and waiting for equilibrium to find him. Low in the sky, the sun was like a flat bronze disc—a big coin with the shine rubbed off of it. The sky around it was pale blue falling to dark blue as it neared the horizon. Soon it would be night.

The energy rose inside Deacon like mercury climbing a thermometer, and he was like a cartoon character at the movies, heating up and turning red and about to blow his top—"It's QUITTING time, baby!" Cars zizzed by in front of him, hot tires singing on the molten roadway. One sled with big balloon whitewalls complained at another and sounded its horn, but it went "Awww" as if the machine itself were too hot to bother.

Leaving the Thunderbird parking lot, crossing Las Vegas Boulevard to where the Starburst rose ahead of him, Deke threw down one boot and then another until he had a kind of walk going. Head first, determined, hot. A big black sedan blew by right behind him and shot dust onto the back of his legs as he pushed through the heat. Twin pylons supporting the vast Thunderbird sign—a Southwest Indian bird, wings ablaze, rising through fire—straddled the parking lot and shot into the air. He craned back to look as he strode under it, then dizzied and stopped. The odors of construction and boom—asphalt, pine, paint—should have filled the air. But they didn't. The air had no smell. There was no moisture for the smell to stick to. The mountains that rose pink and still to the west should have beckoned. But they didn't. They had the painted-on look of a movie backdrop. There was no texture of any kind. The heat and the breeze carried it all away, down to L.A. maybe. Down to San Pedro or San Berdoo. Down and out somewhere, but gone, anyway.

The shapes and colors of the Starburst—the hotel decor was supposed to capture the grandeur of the heavens and the speeding sleek shine of jets and rockets and airplanes—lifted off the pavement and shimmered, almost evaporating as they rose, and then refocused and became a hotel again. In this way the entire city would seem magical at night, when the shimmer came with falling heat and dark, when the whole place became chimerical and without gravity. It wasn't that much night yet. Deke and Las Vegas were just starting the day, so the day still had quite a lot of heft to it. Deacon shouldered through the front doors of the Starburst, gravity all over him again like weights on a deep-sea diver.

Dozens of men were already gambling. The sound of them hit Deacon, and the air-conditioning knocked him back half a step. He full-stopped, just inside the doors, as if he were under arrest, and lifted his hands in front of him to break his fall. He said, "Whoa, pony," out loud, and no one heard. The air was charged with jingle noises and the chatter of men at work, men concentrating very hard on having fun. A gravel voice belonging to a pitman said, "Boxcars!" and sixteen chumps with hats and cigars seemed to turn in unison. Deke went past there.

Theodore T. Behr, the Starburst/Thunderbird talent booker who was probably once known as Teddy Bear but in Vegas was called Fatty Behr, was standing near Reception, his eyes on the elevators, tapping his thigh with a rolled-up copy of the afternoon *Sun*. He was a tiny, grinning, pin-tidy man who always wore a polka-dot bow tie and a very expensive pin-weave Panama hat and an even more expensive light blue seersucker suit. ("Sure it is," Fatty said with that nervous laugh of his. "And I'm the sucker Sears sold it to.") His tight smile was pasted like makeup onto his tight, polished face. But right now his beady black eyes and his jumpy, jittery laugh were not for Deacon, who skipped Fatty's gaze and kept on going past Reception toward the back of the casino. Deacon had a shot of small panic run through him: *Where did I stash my works?* He remembered fixing and nodding off somewhere—no, not somewhere. He knew where. It was in that washroom in the basement—but he could not remember where he'd hidden the kit. He would need that later, but not now. Deacon pressed on.

Cocktail waitresses named Debbie and Didi and Diane and Diana slid past with their trays and their clickers and called to him, and he wondered for the eleventeenth time whether those were their real names, or whether they had real names anymore. Sloan said some of them hooked, off their shifts, and said they had different names for when they did that kind of work. Now they waved or winked with sidelong looks, and he winked back. Aileen the hatcheck girl smiled at him from behind Reception. So did the two blondes who worked the gift shop, California girls who might have been twins but weren't, named Alison and Amber, who smiled and pretended to blush. He mouthed a greeting at them—knowing that even had he shouted they would not have heard over the clatter of the slots and the jingle of the money and the voices that carried from the floor. No individual human sound was allowed to be heard.

Off the elevator and heading for the gift shop came the girl called Dot. She was a big-bodied brunette, gorgeous, flirty and full of possibilities. She was bare-legged and out of uniform and on the make, and she waved brightly at Deacon. He increased his pace and nodded his head and made a deferential gesture to her. *Another time,* he thought, *I will do something interesting with that. Not now.*

Deacon hit the pits going across the floor and got greetings from some dealers and stickmen. His feet in his boots and his legs in his pants were moving more in unison now. He was walking. He was having less trouble holding his head straight on his shoulders. His eyes could see. He could smile, even. There was ample opportunity, as he went. Everyone knew his name. Everyone knew everyone's name. No one knew much of anything else, and half the names were made-up names, but everyone knew everyone's name. Deacon kept moving across the massive casino floor, nodding and saying things like "Say, Ray," and "Howzit, Sammy?" and "Peter up!" at the guys he knew. He thought: *I bet I know a hundred different people in this town who smile at me and know my name. And if I was in trouble with the law, I'd rot in jail trying to raise fifty dollars' bail.* It wasn't a bad thing to think. Just another interesting fact to chew on.

Sloan was behind the lobby lounge bar. Deacon sat down hard and said, "Hey."

Sloan came mopping down toward him and said, "Little early for you. Or is it a little late?"

"It's both. Set one up."

Sloan started throwing things in a mixer, then fired a shot of rye into a water glass and set that down. Deacon took it away in a swallow, grimaced and said, "Again."

Sloan threw more rye into the glass. At the end of the bar a waiter stood humming, spinning his tray on one finger. Sloan said, "It's coming," and poured goop from the mixer into a big glass. He stuck a swizzle stick and a cherry in it and said, "You come out of that mess last night okay?"

Deacon put a hand over his right eye and said, "Except for the shiner. You?"

Sloan said, "I'm a little lumpy. Curly got cut up pretty bad. He's in the hospital."

Deacon said, "Best place for him. Give me another shot."

Sloan moved the tropical beverage down to the waiter, and over his shoulder said, "You hear Jimmy G is back in jail?"

"Jimmy G got to stop robbing banks."

"He's gotta stop now."

"He going up?"

"Vacaville. Keep him out of trouble."

"Gotta stay alive in fifty-five."

Sloan smiled and leaned in close. "Listen: I don't know this and I wouldn't know it and no one would tell me, and so I would not be able to tell you, but . . ."

Deacon drank down the rye, then gave him full attention.

"Mo the Man was looking for you last night. After the bust-up. He was dog-down mad, and it had your name on it."

"He say what it was about?"

"No-kee-dope. And I didn't ask."

Deacon nodded. He dug a five-dollar chip out of his jacket pocket and tossed it onto the bar as he kicked back from the chair.

"You got big eyes, Sloan. So . . . what's Fatty Behr upset about?"

"Female trouble," Sloan said, and laughed. "Not his own, of course.

It's Stella. She went missing last night, after the ruckus, and the word is she shacked up with some lucky fella."

"I know. Colored fella. That's why the big ruckus."

Sloan laughed and said, "No. After that. She found another guy and hotfooted it over to the West Side. Now nobody can find her."

"This was *after* that?" Deacon turned his gaze back toward the grinning Fatty. "Folks just can't stay out of trouble, can they?"

"Else we'd all be out of work."

"Speaking of which . . . What do you hear about that Ivory Coast opening up?"

Sloan laughed an unhappy laugh. "I hear they're gonna take two million dollars and hire every black-skinned bastard in town."

"Well, why not?"

"Why *not*? Why not is we don't need another casino. Why not is the Strip is already overbuilt. Why not is the last thing any of us need is a special place for *colored* people to go and have fun. But I forgot who I'm talking to: it's Deacon, the Negro's friend."

"Very funny."

"And what's worse is I'm not making a nickel on it."

"Raw deal, Sloan."

"That's a fack, Jack," Sloan said, then brought his voice back low. "Watch your six, Dee. Something funny is going on. And I don't mean Stella ebonizing the ivory and giving Mo a headache."

Deacon nodded going away backward, worrying about Mo. But there was no Mo visible. Going through the lobby, wondering where he had left his horn the night before, and where he had ditched his works, and whether Fatty left the room key in the room, and how he was going to find out, and what the rest of his day held, Deacon got weary inside. He thought, *Man, it is hard to live the way I live. And now I got Mo to worry over.*

Had it always been so hard? Ten years before, Deacon at eighteen had been just old enough to miss the Big One. He'd been drafted and served his two years in peacetime. Home had been St. Louis, but he had not lived at home for three years before boot camp. He'd skipped high school, gigging instead and chasing work where it led him. He learned to play his horn his way. In Kansas City one night, playing with a little big band to a gin-soaked crowd of white and colored

men and women who knew their music, Deacon had soloed and gotten a huge round of applause. After the show, he was sitting outside
the stage door, smoking a cigarette, when a raspy voice said to him,
"You the horn player?" He turned, and it was Louis Armstrong, and
Louis Armstrong said to him, "Stick with that thing, son. You got
talent."

Deacon had never looked back. Nothing about the straight world
appealed to him. He didn't even know guys who had jobs or families
or cars or houses. He didn't know anyone who had anything. Most
of his friends had a suitcase and a pawn ticket and a hangover. And
talent. Which sometimes got them fed. It wasn't regular and it wasn't
steady, but most of those cats were not ready for steady. Deacon was
not, either. The army had given him two years of regular, and that
was more than he wanted of it. He didn't mind the flophouses and
the all-night diners and the bus rides and the train platforms. He
didn't mind it as long as he was getting some work here and there,
and playing steady at the music he loved.

Chicago had been full of that. The work was very steady. He was
playing with Shep Shephard, and they were sharing the bill with the
Dorseys and Harry James and Count Basie and whoever else was
blowing through town. They were getting more applause than the
big acts some nights. The money was good and there was always
plenty of booze and plenty of girls. There was always a party somewhere, after the show, and he was always being invited to go along.
Most of the time he went. Most of the time it was fun.

Sometime in there some musician passed Deacon a marijuana cigarette and said, "Take a big pull on this." He did. It was very interesting. Pretty soon he was hanging around with more and more guys
who were smoking. Pretty soon he was hanging around with guys
who were shooting dope. Pretty soon he was shooting dope with
them. It wasn't a big thing with him. He could take it or leave it a
few months at a time. Some of the guys couldn't do that. They were
once-and-forever guys, hope-to-die guys, addicts who became addicts
the minute they hit the spike. Deacon thought that if he ever got
like that, he'd quit—but he knew that if he ever got like that, he
wouldn't be *able* to quit. So what was the point in worrying about it?

What was the point in worrying at all? Right now, it was a judg-
ment call: play like he did not know anything, and wait for the axe

to fall, or play like he knew what was going on, and move forward
to meet Mo halfway. He decided he'd better meet Mo halfway. It
wasn't like you could fool him, because you couldn't. So you might
as well face the music. Deacon came up out of the pits and headed
for the elevators.

The casino was half busy, but security was on. Deke counted four
plainclothes guys milling around. Most times of the day, that was
more than enough. Men could play and drink and chase women all
night long, and sweat and smoke and shout out loud, without any of
that turning into trouble. If it didn't turn ugly between one and four
in the morning, it wasn't going to. No matter how nasty it looked, if
security could keep the peace until one and then get it past four in
the morning without somebody getting hurt, it always turned out
okay. And it really took only a couple of guys, if they knew what
they were doing, to keep it in line.

That was only on the casino floor. What happened in the rooms
was different. Men and women wound up in unusual combinations—
the wrong man with the wrong woman, or the other way around, or
maybe three people doing what was usually done by only two. Sometimes it got ugly, or fatal. In one month alone, in just the two hotels
that Mo ran, Deacon knew about two guys who'd gone swimming in
the sky and one guy who'd put a hole in his head. All three of them
had gambled and lost and gone up to their rooms. The first two guys
had taken swan dives off the sixth floor, one in the Starburst and one
at the Thunderbird, one a week or so after the other. The third guy
had wrapped himself in Starburst bedsheets and pulled the trigger.
Sloan said he looked like a big red mummy when they found him,
soaked in blood but wound up tight. He had no idea what the two
fliers looked like when they hit the parking lot.

Some of the trouble couldn't be helped. People got excited, winning and losing hard, waiting to see which way they'd end up. That
made them tired, and when they were tired they behaved badly.
Sometimes the house would have to throw a player out. Just as often,
they'd give a guy a free room and a bottle of champagne. If he was
serious about his money, sometimes they'd toss in a chippie, just because the sap had lost too much bread and begun to think it was
something personal. Sometimes, Deacon had heard, the house would
even give a guy a little money—say, half a thousand to get home on,

if he'd lost twenty times that much—just so he didn't feel like a total chump.

He didn't believe that. Not even Mo the Man, who was a good man, who was the only good man Deke knew in the desert, not even Mo was that soft. Or that stupid. A guy who's lost it all, if he's a high roller, maybe you send him a bottle of bubbly and a piece of pie. The most he's going to ask for, if he loses it all again, is another bottle of bubbly and another piece of pie.

But once you start handing back money, there is no way it can end. Just like with losing. When a real gambler starts losing real money, the money becomes unreal. First, losing the money loses significance, and then losing the money becomes the entire point. It can't stop until the losing is over. And the losing is over only when the house says it is over, when the house says no to the marker and the checkbook and the Cadillac and the gold watch. If golden-haired children had financial currency on the casino floor, Deacon knew, Mo could open a brat farm. The Starburst Casino and Orphanage! There was nothing a gambling man wasn't willing to lose when it got bad for him.

It wasn't bad for anyone now. Half the men at the tables had just come in. They might have come directly from the airport. You could spot their wives, carrying pocketbooks and looking fresh and stiff, pulling idly at the slot machines, not really interested but beginning to get the idea. The other half were bedraggled. They were still throwing bones from the night before, out of habit and the fact that they had won a little and still had something left to lose. Some of them would leave the table before they lost it all. Some would still be here tomorrow morning.

Deacon hit the elevator bank and stood in front of the door that never opened. He stood and waited. Someone, somewhere above him, was watching and saying yes or no with his finger on a button. He waited. Yes or no. What difference did it make? Into his head rolled the new orchestration on "Tenderly" that he had worked up for Stella. His fingers twitched over the notes. It sang. It would sing. He could hear the whole band roll into it, and could even hear the places where the band would slack off a little and let him solo. Interesting thing, the brain. The elevator doors opened and Deacon stepped on. The sounds of the casino went away like bathwater down a drain as the doors closed, and he was swished up and away.

Thomas Haney was a small, pale man with watery, impossibly pale blue eyes, eyes so light that they made his face look transparent. He looked blind and weak. This was unfortunate. It made it difficult for him to make the impression he wanted to make. As the top cop on the Las Vegas Strip, Thomas Haney desired that other men—in fact, required that other men—treat him with deference. He turned evil when they did not. He was too small physically to inspire fear. But he had discovered in the service that he could intimidate other men with his eagerness for violence. As a soldier, he found that if he struck first and with a viciousness that the fight did not require, he could scare his opponent into defeat. As an officer, he found that if he punished a man far beyond what was acceptable to the other men, he could scare the other men into a kind of obedience. It wasn't respect. It was only fear. That was enough, usually, for him to get his way.

Standing now in Mo Weiner's outer office, with two of his biggest men standing guard beside him, Haney's blood pressure rose a point with every tick of the clock in his head. He had been waiting three minutes. He was angry, and he was getting angrier. In his mind he was going over the various things he'd like to do to Mo, and the various things he'd like to do to Mo's assistant, an ash-blond dish who sat now with her eyes on a fashion magazine. None of the things he wanted to do to either one of them was nice. They were all probably fatal. Haney would kill everyone if it was up to him.

Then his face reddened further: a tall guy in a rumpled suit came through the other side of Mo's outer office and didn't even slow down before going into the inner sanctum. The dish smiled at him, then said to Haney, "I'm sure it will be just another minute."

Deacon winked at Mo's assistant as he slid by, shivering. It was freezing here. It was always freezing here. Mo kept the place cold as a morgue. And quiet, and still. This was how Mo lived. It was dead cold, and silent, and it said "money." Everyplace else in Vegas was hot and loud. But here the temperature and the silence were like a bank statement. It told Deacon and Haney and everyone else that the guy inside has enough dough to burn the AC day and night, and he doesn't have to listen to anybody else's crap.

Inside Mo's private office it was colder still. The air felt thick and blue. Deacon went slowly across the carpet. Mo sat whispering orders into a telephone and pointing at a chair. Deacon sat. Beyond, airplanes from L.A. were landing at McCarran Field. Deacon watched without listening to Mo's phone call: it didn't pay to listen.

But then Mo was off the phone and speaking into his intercom. Mo motioned Deacon to stay seated.

"Just watch, and keep quiet," Mo said. "No matter what happens, do what I tell you. Do not say one single syllable. As a favor to me."

That was Mo: confident, not asking for a favor but telling you what you were going to do for him. As a favor.

He said, "This has nothing to do with Stella. Or last night. That's not what started the ruckus, in fact. This is about that kid we fired. The crooked kid who was dealing."

Deacon said, "I don't know anything about that."

Mo said, "I know you don't. Play dumb."

Then Haney was shown in. The frozen air in the room got tight. Haney was wearing his customary black suit, with a gray snap-brim hat. The two goons, also in black suits and wearing black fedoras, walked like bookends with him. The ash-blond secretary came in behind them. Mo said, "That's all for now, sweetie," and she pulled the heavy door closed behind her.

Mo stepped around to the back of the large oak desk that dominated the room, and stood behind it, staring at Haney. The small Irish cop blinked his invisible eyes on Mo for a few seconds and shifted from foot to foot, and seemed to consider sitting, and then didn't.

Mo spread his palms flat on the table before him and, without looking up at Haney, said, "What?"—not a question but an impatient demand for information. When Haney did not respond, Mo repeated it. "What? Out with it. You're wasting my time."

Haney said, "I'm wasting *your* time?"

"Yes. What do you want?"

"There's a little problem. You know what it is. It can stay a little problem or it can get to be a bigger problem," Haney said, glancing at Deacon. "Up to you. Alls I need is a little information and I go away. I can make it easy or I—"

"Make your point, Haney," Mo barked at him. "I'm busy and you're boring me. Make your play or scramble."

Haney grinned at the goon to his right and gestured at armchairs scattered around them. "Take a seat, fellas. This might take longer than we thought." He returned his attention to Mo, lit a cigarette, and sat down in front of the desk. Mo remained standing. Deacon could feel the power as it did not shift: the goons did not sit down. Haney had a weak hand, Deacon saw.

"I'm sorry to waste your time, *Mister* Weiner. I don't like coming over here. I don't like sending my men over here. I didn't like it last night—and by the way, I'm sorry about that man of yours that got cut up. But I'm here about something else. One of your dealers. The one who's in the hospital."

"Send flowers. What's your point?"

"Your dealer went to the hospital and he can't go home, *Mister* Weiner. Now it's a police matter."

"Show me a complaint, then, Haney. Show me a report."

"You know better than that, Mo. I don't have to show you a god-damn thing. It's you that's gotta show me some stuff. I want some cooperation from you."

"Then you're going out a loser, Haney, like everyone else."

Mo sat, even as Haney was coming out of his seat, his forehead creasing up with rage under his hat. He threw his cigarette onto the carpet and stood seething. The two goons, slower on the draw, moved forward a step, like pieces of machinery, but then stood, unsure, waiting. Haney took a step toward Mo's big desk. One of the goons put his foot out, daintily, and stepped on Haney's smoking cigarette.

And at that moment Deacon got it: Haney was the man from the photographs in Shipton Wells, the photographs the rat-faced man had in his overnight bag. Deacon felt the room slide sideways, and shuddered, and hoped no one was looking at him. His head screamed: *That's the guy! That's the guy in the pictures!*

Haney was busy with Mo. He said through his teeth, "Don't mess with me on this. Either I get the straight story from you or I'm gonna shut you down."

Mo smiled and said, "Cut it out. You're not going to do anything.

You run hookers, remember? You run dope. Those things don't interest me, so you don't interest me. Take your problem and go."

Haney had his hand inside his coat now, and the big goons were holding their hands down at their sides, ready to move.

Haney said, "Don't give me that crap, you Jew bastard. I was in Germany. I was in Auschwitz!"

Mo said, "On which side, Haney?"

Haney reddened. His blue eyes were so damp that he appeared to be crying. But he said nothing.

Mo said, "Sit down, Haney. You got no play." When no one moved, Mo said to the two goons, "Sit down, men. Relax." They sat, without looking at Haney. Deacon was impressed. Mo really *was* the man. He said to the goons, "Your boss didn't even tell you what this was about, huh?"

The men did not answer. Mo winked at Deacon, smiling now.

"I'll tell you what happened, Haney. You take it or leave it. But just so you don't look bad in front of your men . . . We caught one of our dealers cheating. Not cheating us, you understand. We'd never hire a dealer stupid enough to cheat us. No. This dealer was clever. He was cheating the customers! Cheating *our* customers! He was skimming what he stole for himself, of course, but that's not the point. He was cheating our customers. When we caught him, he wasn't even ashamed. He thought he was clever. He thought we should give him a raise or something, for being a smarty-pants." Mo laughed nicely. "I had this gentleman take him out and show him the error of his ways."

Haney's face was purple. He turned to his men, as if in supplication, and then said to Mo, "I don't believe you."

Mo laughed in his face. "No? What's not to believe?"

Haney said, "I saw the guy. I saw his face. I saw what somebody— Get up, you."

Haney was on his feet and coming toward Deacon, who started to rise. He checked himself and looked at Mo. Mo nodded. Deacon rose. Haney was at him. He said, "Let me see your hands."

He grabbed Deacon's thin wrists and stared at his hands, at his knuckles, then dropped them and said, "He ain't got a mark on him."

Mo laughed and said, "You've been in the desert too long, Haney. There's lots of ways to do what we did to that guy."

Mo laughed again, and this time it gave Deacon the creeps. It shut the room quiet, too. Haney looked at him. He looked at Mo. The two goons looked at their boss, and at Mo, and at Deacon, who gradually became the focus of everyone's stare. He stood, hands and arms limp at his side, watching Mo. He had no idea where any of this was going, but Mo was the only one in the room who could call it. There was no other power in the room. And Mo suddenly decided to call it off.

Mo said quietly, almost gently, "Haney, you amaze me. You run the Strip in your sleep. You miss nothing. You know what I'm doing before I do it. And yet you apparently heard nothing about this man's arrival. I sent for him as soon as I knew we had a problem with this crooked dealer. It was a problem that could not be solved, uh, *locally*. And you missed it all. And while I understand you feel put out about that, your behavior now is undignified. This is the man in question. I imagine you are armed. It doesn't matter. If I blink at him, this man will make sure that neither you nor your two men leave the room alive."

Nothing moved. All Deacon could think was, *Don't blink, Mo.* His eyes never left Mo's. No one, for a minute, made a sound.

Haney said, "Don't let it happen again. I can't let the Strip get a reputation for lawlessness. No matter who's breaking the law."

"Haney, I understand completely. We want the same thing. I can't let my casino get a reputation for cheating. No matter who's doing the cheating."

The air went out of the room. Deacon could see the relief cross Haney's men's faces. Haney himself seemed to shrink an inch. Mo was just Mo. He said, "And despite the unpleasant words, I am glad you brought this to me, Tom. It won't do for there to be bad feelings between us. We run this place, you and I and a few others, and we have to stick together, or the whole thing falls apart. So, thank you."

Haney and his men began to move toward the back of the room. Deacon did not move. Mo said, "I'll sweeten the pot a little, Haney, just to show you how bad I feel about this. How about my young friend makes a donation to your foundation?"

Haney said, "Make it a fat one. You owe me."

Mo said, "It'll be fat. I'll see to it."

At the elevator Haney turned and tried to give Mo a menacing look, but it was over. Mo waved like a schoolgirl, and they were gone.

He said, "Sit down, Deacon. You were brilliant."

Deacon exhaled hard and sat. He said, "What was that?"

"Nothing. Little thing. We had a dealer who was cheating the players. We showed him the door and he gave us some lip. So I had him taken out and taken care of. He'll be okay. It was just his face we did, mostly. The publicity angle, you know?"

Deacon shook his head and said, "No. I don't."

"Public relations. It's like advertising, but you don't pay for it."

Mo sat and folded his hands on his desk, as if instructing a slow child. "It's like this. If we got a guy cheating, and we get rid of him, what do we get? Nothing. We're back where we started. If we got a guy cheating and we have him arrested, what do we get? A headache, and maybe a reputation that we employ cheaters. But if we got a guy cheating and we make an example of him like this, and give him a beating, and get the cops involved, and then get the cops so mad that they almost arrest somebody . . . Baby, that's golden! It's all over town. Those two morons of Haney's are going to tell everyone they meet. You can't buy advertising like that! It says the Starburst is the cleanest house on the Strip. 'Did you hear what they did to that dealer they caught cheating? They practically killed the guy! They almost tore his face off!' That's working the publicity angle. That's how you gotta think, you want to get someplace in this town."

"Why me?"

"You could sell it. You don't look like a killer. You look nice, and clean—well, sort of clean, if you had not slept in your suit, which it looks like you did. It's even scarier to imagine a nice white kid like you cutting that guy all up. If it had been someone like Floyd—not that I'm saying it *was* someone like Floyd—well, that just makes sense, without being scary. You, it's different. Besides, you were here already. Saved time."

Mo smiled, indulgent. Lesson over. He said, "Now, is there anything I can do for you?"

"What's the foundation?"

"Do-good thing of Haney's. Orphans. Here."

Mo went into his jacket pocket and came back out with a one-hundred-dollar bill. He folded it, palmed an envelope up from his desktop, and put the bill inside. He said, "The address is over on

Bonanza. Marian will get it for you. I'd like it if you'd drop this over there the next time you're near downtown."

"Orphans?"

"Yes. Orphans. I know what you're thinking—what's a creep like that doing with orphans? Who knows? He funds this foundation for bastard kids. Personally, I think it's just a shakedown. But it's only a hundred bucks, and it keeps him quiet."

Deacon thought: *I can tell Mo, right now, or not tell Mo, or not tell Mo right now, about the photographs.* He thought, and chose . . . not.

He said, "That's all, then?"

Mo said, "That's all. So scramble, and let me do some real work."

Deacon rose and went to the door, noticing then—as he had before—that Mo never, ever shook hands, in greeting or in good-bye, and he wondered again why that was. He wondered why Mo was, why Vegas was, why everything was, and who the dealer was that got hurt. Mo was bent down low over papers as Deacon hit the door. He didn't say good-bye.

Downstairs again, after a moment of clear-headed recollection, Deacon remembered his horn and his works. In the case. With a hatcheck girl. His pockets yielded no claim check. But the horn case was there just the same. He grabbed it and was gone.

Two

WHEN HE HAD finished with Haney and then sent Deacon away, Mo mashed a button on his desk and said out loud, "Marian? Find Lee." He sat again and leaned back in his chair, inhaling and exhaling deeply, and analyzed the play. Haney would say nothing of this afternoon's unpleasantness. Haney's men would gossip it all over town. Mo would have to do something about the beat-up card crimper. He'd made his point, and there was no point rubbing it in. As for Stella . . . Mo would have to speak to her again about what she did on the side and ask her, again, to do it on someone else's real estate. And she would say she would, and then she wouldn't.

As for Deacon . . . He was smart enough to know the value of being used, and he would keep his trap shut. He had something else on his mind that he wasn't talking about. Mo worried over that a moment and then, out loud, though there was no one to listen, said, "Well done. A bad situation turned to advantage. I like that."

Over the past year or so Mo had got into the habit of speaking out loud to himself, even when he was not barking orders into his intercom. At first this embarrassed him, and he tried to stop, but then he had stopped trying to stop. He had always been a garrulous man. He liked to shoot the breeze now and then with a sympathetic ear. But there were no sympathetic ears here, and there was no more now and then. There was only work, twenty-four hours a day and every day just like the one before. Mo was alone, and Mo was surrounded by people he could not trust. He was surrounded by people whose lives he controlled, either because the Starburst or the Thunderbird employed them or because he could make or break them with a snap of his fingers. So, in effect, everyone around him was afraid of him. And this isolated him. It bought him only responsibility and the illusion of power and the impossibility of anything like friendship. No trust, no loyalty, no safety. No love. There were women and, well, so what? There were women. Lately even that didn't interest him. It was like food. If you cared about maintaining your health, you ate. But you didn't make a big deal out of it. Mo was like that now with sex. Maybe he was getting old?

Mo shrugged and said out loud, "I like that Deacon, though. Smart guy. Stand-up guy. Doesn't ask for anything. I like that." Then he mashed the button on the intercom again and said, "Well?" When the secretary finally responded, Mo said to the ceiling, "Have him meet me in the pro shop, in about ten minutes."

Mo slipped on his jacket, half of a silver-gray suit that was one of fifteen almost identical silver-gray suits that hung in his closet at home. Mo's hair had gone to gray during his first eighteen months in the desert. Women and haberdashers liked it, and liked the way it looked against this color suit. Mo's reaction: fine. He shot his cuffs, found a clean handkerchief in his desk drawer, and headed for the door. The hallway was silent and empty, but watched. (Mo's office was the only room in the entire facility that did not have an "eye in the sky" portal in the ceiling, through which the action below could be monitored.) Mo went to the hidden elevator door at the end of the hall—it looked to the untrained eye like a short length of wall with a mirror on it—pressed a button on the wainscoting, and waited. The mirror slid away and the elevator car opened. Mo pushed the lowest of the three available buttons, unmarked like the others, and after a short ride stepped off and into his basement office.

The room was just like the one on the second floor, but hotter. Mo hated the heat and kept his own office icebox cold. Here it was warm. It differed from the room two floors above in one other key way: there was a door out, at the back of the room. Only Mo and the room's designers knew about that. Mo went there now. He tapped a button hidden in the flocked wallpaper, and a door slid open. Mo went through it and was in the tunnel. The door slid closed behind him. After a brisk two-minute walk, Mo emerged through a similar series of contraptions and back entrances (the tunnel itself was a sewerage line, built by the city and then abandoned before it was ever connected to the main lines; Mo saw it on a blueprint and fell in love) into the lobby of the Thunderbird.

Mo was less well known at the 'Bird. He shot across the lobby and through the casino and out toward the pro shop without engaging anyone's interest. Had he been moving more slowly, he might have seen a dealer or two, bored at the table, look up with low eyes and note him passing. Some of the employees knew that Mo was involved with the hotel and casino. Some of the bright ones thought he was one of "Dashing" Bill Dawson's silent partners, backing up the genial cowboy with his wily Jewish business smarts. Some others thought Mo was connected, and represented Chicago's interests in the desert. No one knew the truth—that Dawson was nothing more than his patsy and his front, that he had no control and no power, that he was a has-been and a drunk and a failure as a man and in any other way you'd care to mention, that Mo chipping money to the Chicago guys was only his way of showing respect and maintaining order. Mo the Man was the man, the only man, behind the action.

Mo slowed as he went across the lobby, then stopped. The brick-red and ochre-yellow room, staffed with handsome men and women hurrying back and forth in brick-red and ochre-yellow uniforms, dizzied him for a moment. He picked up the pace again and moved toward the lobby gift shop. There was a blonde there with the most enormous breasts. Mo bought a good cigar and made a mental note to have the girl fired. A body like that was bad for business, unless it was onstage, and Mo didn't supply that kind of entertainment. Was she one of Fatty's broads? Maybe. Or she might become one, after Mo had her fired.

Mo got the cheroot going and gave Dawson a quick mental going-over. Dawson wasn't all bad. He had done what he could with his life, and the chips had not fallen his way; Hollywood was a rotten racket, and Dawson couldn't help being a drunk, and Mo couldn't very well front the Thunderbird himself. As it was he had more profile than he wanted. Killarney was the only one who knew the truth about the Thunderbird, and he had to: he did all the books for both hotels. Even that, even Killarney knowing as much as he did, made Mo nervous. Killarney was a good man, but still . . . He was a man, which means he was human, which to Mo was not quite good enough.

He turned his attention to the *shvartzer.*

Worthless Worthington Lee was waiting for Mo when he emerged from the casino twilight into the outside world. As his eyes adjusted to the sunlight—still vicious at 7:30 P.M., and it was Mo's first step outside in several days—Mo slowed his pace and moved across the patio toward the golf pro shop. He nodded to the old hacker who ran the pro shop and said, "Hiya, Bud." No more golfers were being allowed out at this hour, of course, because Mo wanted everyone on the casino floor, losing their money. Bud kept the shop open because Mo thought it looked better that way. By the same token, the lights would come on in the swimming pool as soon as it got dark out, even though the pool was closed from 6:00 P.M. to 6:00 A.M. It looked good. Besides, the *idea* of a night swim was far more romantic than any real night swim could ever be. The fantasy was always better than the reality, and Mo was selling fantasy.

Worthless Worthington Lee rose from where he was slouching in the pro shop's shadows and came uncertainly forward.

He was a sight, Mo thought. A real baby-frightener. He was a massive presence, incredibly strong still, despite his years, and in very good physical shape. He was like a big oil-black cat, an athlete made of hard meat and muscle. Mo also knew Lee was a shrewd thinker and a very tough businessman. There were few guys who made Mo think he could be outsmarted, and this was one of them. He was the closest thing to real power that the West Side had ever seen.

But he was none of that now, Mo saw. Worthless Worthington Lee, now, was a tired, slumping loser, shuffling and scraping, rubbing his palms together nervously, showing his gums when he smiled. He said, "How do, suh," and actually bowed his head. Mo had to laugh. He said, "Please! Worthless! Enough with the Stepin Fetchit. Let's take a walk."

The two men moved toward the green at the eighteenth hole, toward the setting sun, Worthless Worthington Lee managing to slump to exactly Mo's height as they walked. Mo sucked on his cigar until they were all the way onto the green. Across three hundred feet of grass two Mexican gardeners were splashing water around as the sun got fat and low and orange.

Mo said, "I gotta tell you, I like the way the whole thing looks. I think you and your guys are doing a terrific job."

Worthless Worthington Lee said, "Thank you, suh."

"I'm a little worried about being ready on time, and I'm a little worried about how much more money you're gonna have to spend

to get it ready on time, but I'm not even that worried about that."
Mo looked to see that he had the big man's full attention. He did.
He continued.

"I talked with Ronald yesterday and I've seen what his men have
cooked up for staff and dancers and costumes," Mo said. "Really first-
rate stuff. I'm very impressed."

Worthless Worthington Lee nodded his head and said, "Thank you,
suh."

"A lot of that stuff you couldn't get away with on the Strip, or even
downtown. But I guess it's okay for the colored crowd?"

"Yes, suh. 'At's the whole point. Gotta be somethin' that nobody
can see nowheres else. We cain't compete for headliners. Ain't no
Rosemary Clooney gonna play no Ivory Coast. So we gotta give the
folks somethin' else."

"You know best. I guess the law isn't going to care one way or the
other, as long as it stays on the West Side," Mo said. "What about
room reservations?"

"We booked, suh."

Mo started. "Not all the way?"

"Yassuh. All the way. Not a room left."

Mo said, "Now I'm really impressed. That's a lot of colored folks."

"Well, suh, we ain't got noplace else to go. Folks is rarin' for it and
ready. Been a long time coming."

"Yes. I'm sure it has."

The two men, moving slowly, had crossed the end of the eighteenth and were sidling over toward the fourteenth. The two gardeners, far away now, were on their knees trimming the grass around the
hole. In the late-afternoon sun, minus the Mexicans, it looked like
the postcards that advertised the hotel.

Mo was proud of the golf course. He had hired one of the really
huge names in golf, the absolute best in the business, and paid him
a fortune to come to the desert and design the course. At the last
minute the golfer, a WASP son of a bitch who should rot in hell with
the rest of his cashmere sweater knickerbocker pants Lincoln Conti-
nental country club pals, had decided that Mo's Chicago connections
might be harmful to his career. The *gonif* bastard had taken his money
and scrambled before the project was complete, chumping out Mo in

the process. Mo got the course, and the *momzer* golfer got his money, but Mo was never legally able to tell anyone who designed it. Or at least he wasn't able to advertise it on the postcards or the hotel brochures. Golfers knew. Mo knew. Worthless Worthington Lee didn't care. What was it about coloreds? Mo wondered. How come they didn't golf? Weird. They seem to excel at other sports, but they don't golf and they don't play tennis. Weird.

"Anyway," Mo said. "I'm pleased to see that the novelty value of the place is as high as I thought it would be. And you know I couldn't have done it without you. I think we're all going to make a lot of dough—more than you'll ever make on those deadbeat apartments of yours—and then some. And who knows? Maybe after it's over you can go legit and turn it into something real."

Worthless Worthington Lee said, "How you mean, 'after it's over'? You don't think it's gonna last?"

Mo cursed himself for his sloppiness. He said quickly, "Turn of phrase, Worthless. That's all. Of course, one day it will be over. You may be an old man then. I'm hoping that the Ivory Coast will become an institution in this town. I'm hoping that other hotels follow. I'm wishing on you the competition and the headaches and the ulcers that I've got. You should be so lucky."

Worthless Worthington Lee laughed an easy, indulgent laugh. He said, "I'se already an old man, and I'se already lucky. Don't wish me no mo' of either one. I cain't handle no mo' of either one."

"Good man," Mo said, and regretted it at once. He stuck out his hand and waited for what seemed an eternity for Worthless Worthington Lee to lift his own and shake limply. He showed Mo a mile and a half of pink gum. Then his smile went out like an electric sign turning off for the night.

He said, "The rest of the financial breakdown will be ready for Mr. Killarney first thing tomorrow morning. Was that your last question for me?"

Mo said, "That's right. That was the last question."

Worthless Worthington Lee gave him some more gums, then made them disappear. Mo thought: *This man could pick me up and snap me in half in a second. I wonder why, after all, he doesn't.* Then Worthless Worthington Lee said, "I be seein' you, suh," and turned and shuffled off toward the seventh hole, out across the desert, away from the hotel, as if he would walk all the way to the Ivory Coast, five miles distant in the gathering dusk.

When he was almost out of sight, Mo said aloud, "That is one strange *shvartzer*." He headed back past the pro shop, through the 'Bird lobby, down the tunnel, and into his own world again.

Deacon had gone straight from his meeting with Mo to his apartment, one of many airless warrens in the rabbit hutch of rooms that the casino provided for its employees. The buildings were directly behind the casino, and came at a price: the employees were required to bunk there and were required to pay for the rooms, at rents higher than they'd pay anywhere else in town. The room rate was drawn directly from their paychecks. It was just one more casino racket, another way the bosses chipped away, one more small advantage that, as the house, they had over the stiffs. And when the employees got off work, they were just stiffs—until they started work again.

Deacon had bathed and shaved and thrown on a clean shirt, and had gotten a friend in the laundry to take his suit down for a pressing. It was a beautiful, and beautifully tailored, Hickey-Freeman suit, left over from the days when he could afford to dress like a real sport. It didn't have a lot of life left in it. Deacon had his horn cleaned and cased and under his arm when the suit came back. He strode back into the falling desert night, feeling fresh and crisp, and with just barely enough time to get to the sound check.

These were unnecessary and mandatory. Stella and the Starburst management had pulled together a first-rate orchestra—not that tough, because everyone who did not have a rocket gig in New York or wasn't cutting sides in L.A. wanted to be here. Here was where the money was. Gleason, the Starburst's musical director, a fussy man who wore tight pants and a scarf around his neck, made no bones about it: the orchestra was sharp. It was a tight, jivey group of men who were happy to wait while Gleason or Stella fiddled over some detail, and tell one another jokes.

"You know why a cello is superior to a violin?" one asked. "Cello burns longer."

"What's the best way to play a banjo?" one asked. "With a hacksaw, man!"

"You know what's black and brown and looks good on a conductor?" one asked "A German shepherd!"

These musicians joked and smoked and didn't need rehearsing, except when they were introducing new material. The dancers were a mess and needed rehearsing night and day until they demonstrated that they could handle the old material.

So far they hadn't, but Gleason had lost the argument. For now there were daily, mandatory sound checks. Missing one meant getting your pay docked twenty-five dollars. Missing a second meant getting your pay docked a hundred dollars. Missing a third meant picking up your pay and moving on. Stella, who was blind without her glasses and yet refused to wear them in public, was the only one who ever did the docking. Gleason wouldn't report it. And so most of the orchestra could skip, now and then, and not be missed. Not Deacon. Stella always looked for him first when she made the sound check. The one time he'd been late, she knew about it. The one time he'd been missing, she screamed about it. She said if it happened again, he'd be out of work and blackballed on the Strip. Deacon believed her. She was a redhead and she was mean like that.

Most of the orchestra was already seated, in the big room that always seemed so cozy when the audiences came in but so vast and cold at times like these. Deacon slid in and sat, and glanced around to see if Fatty Behr was anywhere around. Not finding him, he looked instead for Gleason. He caught his gaze. Gleason rolled his eyes and tilted his head at his counterpart on the dance side, Andy David. (This was the same Andy David, the one who had won all the awards as Andrew David. His Broadway career was over and behind him. He had come west now "to rot in the desert," as he put it. Stella often said, "I'm going to *bury* him in the desert, the little creep.") Andy was languidly putting a hoofer straight on a set of steps he should have understood a month before. Gleason, who in fact was living with Andy but displayed a good deal of temper toward him while they worked, raised his baton and said, "Let's take it from there again . . . ," and the orchestra was with him. Deacon raised his horn, worked his fingers over the stops a few times, and then blew. For the next twenty minutes the orchestra worked that section of "Come Rain or Come Shine" sixteen times while the petulant dancer and his too-understanding tutor adjusted themselves to the music.

Deacon's head went lazing away as he played.

In the few months they had known each other, this was only the second time Mo had asked Deacon for a favor. The first had been the day after he hit town.

Deacon had come in from Chicago, after a very bad brush with the cops there, on the big dog. He'd made the run with less than a hundred dollars in his pocket, and spent $37.50 of it on the bus ticket. He'd found a room that afternoon right beside the Greyhound station, feeling—though it might have been his imagination—that someone had shadowed him from the arrival area to the cheap hotel where he'd bunked for the night. The following day, having rested and cleaned up, Deacon was getting ready to hit the union hall and begin making the rounds. The shadow was there again, but this time it came right up to him in the lobby of the hotel. It said, around a cigarette shoved into the corner of its mouth, "Mo the Man says you're coming with me."

Deke said, "No kidding. Is Mo the Man ever wrong about stuff like that?"

The punk grinned. He said, "Never."

Deacon glanced around. The punk had no apparent helpers, and Deacon thought he could probably outrun him. But he was tired, and Chicago had scared him some, and the name "Mo the Man" scared him fresh again. It was one of those names. You didn't talk about it, because no one ever talked about it, because everyone *knew.* If he wanted to see you and he sent a guy like this, it couldn't be good news.

So he said, "Okay." He parked his horn with the desk clerk. He and the punk went outside.

The heat was overpowering. It rose straight up from the desert floor in sheets, like rain falling up. There was no wind, and no sound, and no smell. There was just heat. Deacon followed the punk to the parking lot, where they got into an extremely shiny new Cadillac. The punk drove not to the Strip, as Deacon had expected, but straight out into the desert. When they were a mile or more from civilization—if, that is, you thought Las Vegas was civilization in the first place—he pulled the Caddy to the side of the road in front of a building that had once been a gas station. He pointed to it and said, "Mo's in there."

Deacon crossed fifty feet of gravelly dirt. The building was abandoned. There was nothing to indicate human forms had moved across the sand-blown driveway in years. As he stepped, Deacon thought: *Can't be cops. Could be Italians. Mo's not an Italian name. But if it is Mo from Chicago—that Mo the Man—it would be one of the Chicago Jews. And the Jews and the Italians are supposed to be working together in the desert. How much do I owe the Italians? How bad is this going to be?* He tried to look for the bright side, but couldn't find it. He felt the sun broil down on his head and said to himself, "Well, at least it's not hot."

He hit the door and swung it open. A natty little guy with silver-gray hair in a silver-gray suit sat on the counter next to an ancient cash register. He had a whimsical look about him and smiled when Deacon came through the door. He stood up as Deacon entered, and said, "Thanks for coming out. Here's the deal." He reached into his inside breast pocket and withdrew a snapshot of a guy with a face like a rat. "This is him. He's coming this way on the Greyhound from Chicago—just like you. We're not sure which bus. But it will stop in Shipton Wells. That's two hours east of here, right at the state line. There is a coffee shop there. You might remember it from last night. You're going to wait until you see him. Then you're going to talk to him. Tell him, 'Mo says go home.' If he says no, I want you to show him this."

Mo gave Deacon a second photograph, this one of a nice-looking family of four standing in front of an apartment building with palm trees and rosebushes around it. They looked too decent to have anything to do with the rat-faced creep in the first photograph. Mo noticed Deacon's hesitation. He said, "Don't ask. Trust me. If the guy still acts like he's not listening, take him out of the coffee shop and kill him. Take his body somewhere into the desert and leave it. Then come home."

Deacon nodded. He looked at the photos. The rat-faced man. The family. The apartment building had a little signboard on the lawn that read PARK PINES REALTY. He looked up at Mo, then out the front window of the dingy gas station office at the punk, who still leaned on the fender of the Cadillac.

He said, "How?"

Mo said, "How, what?"

"Come home how?"

"In the car. You'll take the car," he said, and indicated the Cadillac. "Can't you drive?"

Deacon said, "I can drive."

Mo smiled. He said, "That settles it, then. Take care of this, as a favor to me, and we'll be square. More than square."

Deacon nodded. Mo the Man was so shiny, so clean, and so very confident. Deacon didn't even want to ask what it was they'd be square about. Instead, he said, "Okay. As a favor to you. Plus I need some bread."

Mo laughed and said, "Don't push it, kid." He reached into his pants pocket and pulled out a small rectangle of paper that looked like a business card. It was, but blank except where someone had penciled in a telephone number. Mo said, "Call this number when it's done, up at Shipton Wells, and tell me it's done. We'll see about some money then."

"Okay."

Mo patted Deacon on the back as he went past and said, "Come on. You'll get started now."

At the curb the punk handed Deacon the keys to the Caddy. He and Mo stood watching as Deacon got in and started the big machine. They both waved as he pulled away like proud parents waving their boy away to college. Deacon drove in a straight line for ten minutes, until he was sure they could not see him anymore, before he pulled over and began to worry about what to do.

Mo had said, "Take him out of the coffee shop and kill him." Just like that. It was funny. Deacon had been around guys like Mo all his adult life, in the clubs and the bars and the gambling joints. But they'd never talked to him about what they did, or how they did it, or why they did it. He knew what, and how, but nobody ever said any of it out loud. He wished Mo hadn't.

Too late. For a fleeting moment, Deacon thought: *Drive to L.A., sell the Caddy to a chop shop, disappear. . . .* It wouldn't work. If Mo the Man got him in Vegas before he even got off the bus—which he had to do, if he got the punk onto him that fast—then he'd have him killed before he made Hollywood.

So he drove to Shipton Wells.

Gleason said, "Come on, you morons. Once again, *without* feeling . . . ," and the orchestra stopped and waited and started again.

Shipton Wells was not even a town. It was a Greyhound station—almost. It was a Greyhound ticket office, two Greyhound restrooms, and an outside area, under an awning, that passed for a waiting area. Across the two-lane highway were a Sinclair gas station and a coffee shop and a whitewashed old motor hotel that from the look of things had been boarded up longer than it was ever in business.

The gas station was getting all of the action when Deacon pulled the Cadillac into the coffee-shop lot and parked. There were two cars in line for fuel, and another two in the repair bays. A weedy kid in greasy overalls was moving slowly between the two cars getting fuel, hosing water into the radiator for one and checking the oil on the other. Two men who might have been driving the cars in the repair bays stood by, smoking. From the lot, Deacon could see past the freestone facade of the café, and past the coffee-shop counter into the dining area. There were no customers—not any customers—and nothing inside seemed to move.

It was one hundred degrees or more on the sidewalk. Deacon got out of the Caddy and moved slowly across the pavement to the bus station. Inside, a letterboard on the wall indicated that there were two buses arriving from the East that day. Both had gone through Chicago. One went through Shipton Wells at 4:35 in the afternoon, the other came through at 7:50. Hoping against odds that the coffee shop served cocktails, Deacon went out of the Greyhound shade and under the big sun and out of it again, letting the fly-specked screen door of the café smack shut behind him.

And there she was. Standing behind the cash register. Next to a glass case displaying slices of cakes and pies. In front of the door where the cook would come and go if he had any business doing that. Underneath a neon sign burbling electric green, affixed to a neon arrow, pointing away from the counter, that read COCKTAILS.

She was the most beautiful girl Deacon had ever seen. She was young, and had curly hair that was very dark brown, and had luminous skin that was brown, a very light brown, warm and rich and burnt, the color of coffee with milk. She was wearing a waitress uniform of beige and white. Her eyes, which were large and warm, regarded

Deacon with absolutely no expression. She might have been sleeping, or blind. Her lips, which were full and rich, were similarly inexpressive. For what felt like a long time there was no movement in the café. Deacon stood, listening to the echo of the screen door slam, staring at the girl, listening to the neon COCKTAILS hum.

When an eternity had passed, the girl smiled and said, "Good afternoon."

"Good afternoon."

"Ready for some lunch?"

"Yes. Or something."

"Take a booth. I'll bring you a menu."

Deacon nodded. He walked to the glass windows that overlooked the parking lot, and then remembered the bus station. Assuring himself that he could see that, too, he took a seat in a booth near the back. Then, realizing his back was to the cash register, where the girl would probably be standing, he got up and sat facing that way. He could see enough of the bus station, he reckoned. The bus wasn't due for two hours or more, anyway. It wasn't like there was much foot traffic outside, anyway. And the girl—

The girl arrived from behind him and leaned over the table, holding a menu and a glass of ice water, sweating huge droplets down its side, and set them down in front of him. Deacon smelled something that smelled like a bakery. Biscuits? Toast? The girl—

The girl said, "It's too late for any of the lunch specials, but I can probably get the cook to make something else if you don't see anything you like on the menu."

Deacon said, "What about a cocktail?"

"No," the girl said softly. "No. You'd have to go sit in the bar for that."

"How about a beer?"

"I could bring you a beer."

"Then I'll stay here and have a beer," Deacon said. "For now. Just the beer."

The girl nodded with what Deacon thought was a great deal of femininity and understanding. His heart melted. She turned away from him. He said, "What's your name? In case—"

The girl turned back and said, "In case of what?" and laughed. "I'm the only one here, except for the cook and the bartender. It's not like I'm going to lose you."

Deacon raised his hands from the table and said, "Sorry." But she leaned forward anyway, and smiled, and said, "My name is Anita."

"Anita."

"Folks who know me better call me Neeter."

"Neeter."

"I'll get the beer."

Deacon sat with the beer, wishing it were colder, nursing it until the parch went out of his throat, and then had another. He kept waiting for Anita to come back and spend a minute, talk to him, pass the time, something. She didn't. While Deacon smoked and drank his beer, the girl retreated to her position behind the cash register, where she stood, perfectly brown and still, in absolute calm, and looked out through the screen door at the parking lot and the bus station behind. As if she, too, were waiting for someone to get off the bus.

Nothing stirred. Then a tall, skinny kid wearing a white shirt and a black vest came from somewhere in the back of the café. He walked over to Anita, swaggering in a self-conscious way, carrying a coffee cup. He said something to Anita, who looked at him with drop-dead eyes. Deacon heard him say, "Aw, come on, Neeter. Give ol' Wally something special." Anita gave him the coldest imaginable look, but reached for the coffeepot and poured his cup full. He took the cup and left, giving Deacon a wide, suggestive wink as he passed through the room. Deacon wondered whether it was the cook or the bartender. Bartender, he'd guess, from the outfit. A kid he would greatly enjoy slapping. He went back to his beer. Anita went back into her reverie. Nothing moved for a while.

The first of the two buses came in not long after four-thirty. Deacon carried his bill to the cash register and said to Anita, "Thank you for the beers. I'd like to pay for them now, but I will probably be back in a minute."

Anita said, "Okay," and smiled again that smile of complete femininity and compassion. "You're meeting somebody on the bus."

"I think so," Deacon said.

"That's your Cadillac in the lot," Anita said. "I saw you come in."

"Yes."

"You supposed to meet someone and drive 'em out to your ranch?"

"No," Deacon said. "Not exactly. I'm staying in Las Vegas. I'm supposed to meet a guy and . . . give him a message, is all."

"Uh-huh," Anita said. The look of great understanding had gone, replaced now by one of either suspicion or something else that wasn't very nice. She said, "Long drive, just to give a guy a message."

Deacon watched her face and felt his heart sink. She was wise. She knew a bum when she met one. He had said too much, and he was acting like a fool. He turned and left the café. There wasn't anything to say. He couldn't be bothered with some chippie in some flyblown desert rathole anyhow. Deacon went through the hot sandy wind back over to the bus terminal.

A loudspeaker, an incredibly and unnecessarily loud loudspeaker, crackled nastily somewhere, and a grainy voice said, "Now arriving in lane six, the *Desert Wind*, from Chicago. Now arriving in lane six, the *Desert Wind*, from Chicago. Attention. Now arriving . . ." Deacon, the only customer standing in the station, listened to the broadcast two more times before the loudspeaker crackled back into silence. He felt he had all the available information pretty well memorized: Bus. Lane six. Chicago. A moment of extreme grumpiness came over him. He thought: *What the hell am I doing here? I could be in my hotel room, and probably having gotten a job today, probably having scored, definitely having a little fun, and instead . . .*

He had still not worked out what he would say to the rat-faced guy, if the rat-faced guy was even on the bus, if the rat-faced guy gave him any guff. He rehearsed again in his head:

"Mo says, 'Go home.' "

"No."

"No? Uh . . . please?"

Deacon had no heater. Deacon had no leverage. If the guy was a big guy, or armed . . .

Across the road the gas station looked empty. Deacon could see the pump jockey in the lube bay, working on some greasy part. Up the road, shimmering like a comet, came the big Greyhound. Deacon stood in a shadow and watched as it slowed and skirted off the highway, shooting gravel out from under the tires, and wheezed to a stop two lanes down from lane six.

Several men and women got off the bus. Deacon's heart went fast as their feet appeared in the bus stairwell and then turned into ankles and legs and then hit the molten asphalt. He felt for the mug shot tucked into his jacket pocket and thought again of the man's face. He wouldn't need to look at the snapshot again. He'd know. He stared at the bus, at the feet still falling to the pavement, wondering what business so many of them could have in a place like Shipton Wells. But everyone was getting off. The women, all of the women, went straight into the ladies' room. The men either idled by the bus, most of them smoking, or headed across the street to the coffee shop. Turning, Deacon saw now why the COCKTAILS sign was situated as it was, over the cash register by the front door. The men could see it—especially at night, Deacon guessed—as soon as they hit the asphalt.

Somebody was paying attention. Somebody who ran the coffee shop. Somebody who employed Anita. Probably a family member. Or a boyfriend. She had not been wearing a ring, he noticed. What in God's name was a girl like that doing in a joint like this anyway? In a town like this? It wasn't even a town. Pushing coffee mugs around a dirty counter for tips, flirting with guys like me . . .

Deacon's head ran on. Minutes passed. There was another announcement, repeated four times. Deacon walked onto the bus to make sure the man was not hiding there, checking the bathroom at the back of the bus, full of urine and body odors. Nothing. It was empty. He went outside.

Women poured back out of the ladies' room, looking no better for the break, adjusting their hats and sunglasses. Their high heels went across the pavement and back onto the bus. The men came after, the café screen door flapping closed behind them, flicking cigarette butts onto the slab floor of the station. Deacon knew the man he wanted was not among those who had gone across to the café. Now he sat and waited while the *Desert Wind*, bound for Las Vegas from lane four, made its exciting departure. Then it was gone, and there was nothing. Deacon went back across the street.

Anita smiled at him this time when he came in through the fly-specked screen door. And it was heaven. She said, "No luck, huh?" and Deacon shook his head. She said, "Another beer?" and he nodded. She said, "There's some in the back that are ice-cold. I'll get you one." And she smiled again.

The beer was ice-cold. There was a chunk of ice stuck to the label, which read CARLING BLACK LABEL. It tasted the way beer on a hot day is supposed to. Deacon slugged the first slug back and felt it roar, putting out forest fires the whole way. There was a bang at the back of the diner. Anita retreated to her place at the register. An angry brown-skinned fat man came through swinging doors, his eyes on fire, his thin hair rising wildly from his head. He said, in what sounded to Deacon like a Mexican accent, "How come there's no cold beers in the icebox?" Anita shrugged at him, then tilted the top of her head in Deacon's direction. The angry Mexican swiveled his head and took Deacon in, nodded at him, wiped a paw across his face, and nodded at Anita. He went away. Deacon could see the slack come back into Anita's posture, but not for a full minute of quiet after the man had gone.

When she drifted back over to his table, Deacon said, "Who's the fat guy?"

Anita said, "Just the boss." She smiled at him, this time with real, deep warmth, and said, "He won't come back for a while. Can I sit down with you?"

Anita slid into the booth, next to him, not across from him, and drew in close. She sighed and lay her head against his shoulder. Within a minute, Deacon felt her body go loose. She was asleep.

Deacon sat for a long time listening to her breathe. When he was sure she was really out, he reached for his beer and found it gone, then reached for his cigarettes and smoked the last of them. Then he sat. Nothing moved. The desert and the café and the fat guy with the angry eyes and the highway before them all were silent. There was the occasional *ding* of a customer pulling into the gas station, followed a few minutes later by the catch of a starter motor and the purr of a car getting back onto the road. Anita lay against him.

Thirty minutes later, it was a done deal. Deacon was ready, willing, and able. He was, officially, sent. He was in love.

The clock over the counter said 7:45. Deacon said, "Anita. Wake up, baby. It's time—"

And she was on her feet, hands fluttering to her hair, eyes frightened. Deacon said, "It's all right. You dozed off. No one saw."

Anita nodded stiffly. She said, "I'll get your check. That other bus will be here in a minute."

She presented him with the bill. Her eyes were distant. Deacon said, "I gotta do this thing. Then I gotta get back to Vegas. But then I'm coming back. Are you always here? Are you ever off?"

Anita smiled like a pro and said, "We're open seven days awake, like we always say, from midnight to midnight."

Deacon heard the crackle first, then the agonizing dry broadcast voice of the bus-station announcement. Over his shoulder he saw the big silver beast coming down the highway. He turned back to Anita. She was gone. Deacon glanced down the counter, through the short-order cook's window. Nothing. He went.

He checked the instinct to reach for the snapshot of the rat-faced man from Chicago. There would be only one nasty little man who looked like that, Deacon decided, if there was one at all. He slid through the ovenlike station as the bus came wheezing into its lane. The engine shuddered off. The side door jacked open, and the driver got down. Then there were two teenagers, who held hands down the steps and onto the pavement. One of them smiled and said, "Hot!" to the other. Deacon was reckoning to himself how many of the people getting off the bus would make the same idiotic observation. Then the rat-faced guy came down the two steps and started off toward the café.

He wore a brown suit too large for him and too heavy for the weather, and carried an overnight bag in his right hand. It looked weighted down with something, Deacon thought, because his right arm hung motionless as he walked. Deacon started off toward him, hoping to intercept him inside the bus station. When he saw he couldn't, Deacon slowed his pace until the man got outside, then sped up until he himself was right behind him. He moved quickly across the road, coming up fast as he headed toward the café.

The rat turned just as he hit the café steps. His right hand still held the heavy overnight bag, but there was a revolver now in his left hand. He said, "Move off, pal. Whatever it is you think you want, believe me, you don't want it bad enough."

Deacon smiled. He said, "Sorry, mister. My mistake. I thought for a second you were—" With a vaudevillian gesture, Deacon took the edge of his lapel and held his jacket open for the rat to see, then with his other hand took the pictures out of his pocket. He resumed, "I thought you were the man in this photograph."

He handed the picture of the rat to the rat. The rat colored and tensed, and Deacon, whose eyes wandered in that direction, saw his knuckles go white around the revolver. The man said, "How did you get this?"

Deacon smiled again and opened his hands, palms up. He said, "Mo says, 'Go home.'"

The rat said, "He says what?"

"Mo says, 'Go home.'"

The rat considered this for a moment and shifted the heavy bag. "He say anything about what I got for Haney?"

"No. He just said, 'Go home.'"

"Else what?"

"Else this," Deacon said, and showed him the picture of his family.

The rat went slack. The color drained from his face and then came back in its previous gray shade. He slowly shifted his weight down, until the heavy overnight bag was almost on the café steps, and then dropped it the rest of the way. He put the revolver back inside his coat pocket. He looked totally defeated.

He said, "Just like that. So, who's Mo?"

Deacon, surprised at this, said, "Mo is . . . Mo's the man."

The rat nodded. He said, "This was my only shot. Let me find out when the next bus is going, and I'll pack out."

Deacon nodded. The rat picked up his overnight bag, which now seemed altogether too heavy, and crumped slowly past Deacon, down the steps, back across the shimmering highway, into the bus station. Deacon checked the gas station. There was nothing moving down there. He followed at a distance: *Where was the guy going to go?*

The sun was going away, cracking over the horizon like a fat red egg. Deacon could feel the hot sandy wind picking up as the heat fell. He glanced into the café as he turned. Anita was standing behind the counter, staring out at nothing, the absent smile there again on her entirely perfect face. Deacon winced.

The sound of the revolver came to him while he was still trying to decide whether to follow the guy or go inside the café and wait for him there. Deacon dashed across the street.

Inside the bus station there was panic—people gasping and pointing and screaming. The sound seemed to have come from the back left side of the room. Deacon went there. Men's room. Closed candy counter. He chose the men's room.

There were two big brown shoes and what looked like the rat-faced man's brown suit pants sticking out from under the partition of the stall at the end. Deacon could see the corner of the heavy overnight bag. He knelt there and pulled at the bag—it was stuck, perhaps still held in the man's grip—until it sprung free.

No one, except maybe Anita, had seen the two of them together. No one, except Anita and the guy named Mo and Mo's punk assistant, could connect the two of them, even theoretically. Deacon took the overnight bag out of the men's room and went to the Cadillac.

The bag was probably bad news. Or it had bad news in it. But it was someone else's bad news. And someone else's bad news could turn into good news for Deacon. He snapped open the latch on the Cadillac and raised the trunk. He opened the overnight bag.

There was another pair of pistols, heavy dark pistols, sitting on top of an oil-stained rag, resting on a pair of pajamas and two freshly laundered shirts. Those in turn rested on two fat manila envelopes, which were on top of two canisters of movie film. Deacon opened one of the manila envelopes. It contained photographs. He held a snapshot up to the light.

What met him was grotesque in every way. It was a picture of a man doing something terribly unnatural to another man. And the other man was not a man at all, but a little boy—not more than five or six years old—dressed up to look like full-grown man. Deacon flipped through the stack of photographs. They appeared to be variations on the same theme. He choked back a wave of nausea, and closed the bag and the trunk on the Cadillac, and took the bag inside the diner.

Anita was gazing wistfully off into the distance. Deacon said to her, "I need a favor. I'll make it worth your while."

She turned her gaze at him and, as if looking through him, said, "Okay."

Deacon said, "Don't you want to know what it is?"

"No."

"Okay." Deacon saw her then—saw her age, and her weakness—and he had a second thought and held it just long enough to know it was there. He said, "I need you to hold on to this bag for me for a few days."

"Okay."

"It's best if you don't look in it. It's important that no one sees it."

"Okay."

"Keep it somewhere safe."

She said, "I said okay, silly. So, okay."

And she looked about twelve.

Gleason said, "Deke! For crying out loud, could you try and limit yourself to one tempo? Let's take it one more time from the break."

And then he really was back in Las Vegas. All that old stuff faded. All that stuff that had started everything came back to him and went away again, as if he were nodding down and going out. Deacon thought of Anita again as she was that first day, and would have laughed had the memory not made him feel so absolutely bleak. He said, "Sorry, man. Let's go again from . . . where?"

Gleason said, "Where indeed?" and the band swung back in.

The following day there had been a summons from Mo. The same punk that had followed him the first day in Las Vegas was back, with what might have been the same cigarette stuck in the corner of his mouth, this time knocking on the door of Deacon's room at the same cheap hotel and telling him he was wanted in Mo's office. It was early in the morning—too early, anyway, for a junkie trumpet player who slept all day and did two shows a night and then drank too much and fixed—and Deacon was irritated at being hauled out of the sack. He eyed the goon through half-shut eyes and said, "What?"

"Mo's office. Now."

"No."

The goon laughed. "No? That's a hot one. Come on."

"No."

The goon didn't laugh. He withdrew the cigarette from his mouth and smiled, showing the most amazing set of gapped teeth as he tried to think of a snappy comeback.

Deacon stopped him. He said, "Tell Mo what time it is, if he doesn't know. Tell him the guy in Shipton Wells is croaked. Tell him the guy in Shipton Wells will still be croaked in four hours. Tell him that's when I will think about coming to his office."

Deacon slammed the door in the guy's face. There was some pounding as he turned and went back into bed, but not much. It stopped and there was quiet again, and Deacon fell into sleep. Going down, it occurred to him, for the first time, that perhaps it was good if someone thought you were capable of murder. *The punk did go away pretty fast,* Deacon thought. And then he fell asleep.

An hour later he woke up and felt unnerved by his own behavior. Guys shouldn't go waking up guys in the middle of the morning like that. But guys got killed for a lot less than the way he was jiving Mo. Besides, he didn't have any idea how to go to Mo. He shaved and got dressed and headed out, then slowed down and went out for a bite, and had a beer and smoked ten cigarettes and read a paper and managed to kill almost three of the threatened four hours. Then he went to a phone booth, threw a nickel in, and dialed the number that was written on the back of the business card Mo had given him. A honey-voiced gal on the other end told him to come to the Starburst Hotel and Casino, on Las Vegas Boulevard, and ask at the reception desk for Mr. Weiner's office. He drove the shiny Cadillac there and left it with the parking-lot guys.

If the whimsical, silver-haired man had been upset by Deacon's slow response, he didn't show it. He didn't show anything. He might have been selling Deacon a sport coat or stock options or an insurance policy. He was still and cool and quiet—like his office. The Starburst itself was a vast explosion of color and noise and bright, brittle light, large and garish at a place where everything was large and garish. But upstairs, Mo sat quietly behind the desk in his long, dark office and smiled nicely as the punk brought Deacon in. The air was thick and cool. Mo rose from his seat and said, "Sit, sit. Drink?"

Deacon said. "Yeah. Scotch. Ice."

Mo nodded. A Negro in a white jacket appeared from somewhere in the shadows, bearing a silver tray with the stated drink on it. The punk faded. It was quiet. Deacon lit a cigarette and watched.

Mo said, "The thing in Shipton Wells did not go all the way according to Hoyle. The guy turned up dead in the men's room."

Deacon nodded.

Mo said, "The police are calling it a suicide."

Deacon nodded and tapped ashes from his cigarette.

Mo said, "It's not exactly a body in the middle of the desert, but they're satisfied. I'm satisfied. Is there anything you'd like to tell me?"

Deacon said, "No."

Mo smiled at him and shook his head slightly. He said, "O-kee-doke," and checked his watch. "There's someone coming in here in a minute you'll want to meet. Before she gets here, let me ask you again: Is there anything else you'd like to tell me before we conclude this piece of business?"

Deacon said, "No. There's just this."

Mo stood and watched as Deacon reached into his jacket pocket and removed the photographs of the rat-faced man and the little family. He stubbed out his cigarette and placed the snapshots on the desk in front of Mo, pulled a second paper out of his pants pocket, and said, "This is the ticket from the parking-lot guys, for your Cadillac."

Mo sat and said, "O-kee-doke." He mashed the intercom button on his desk. "See if Stella's around."

"I'm around." She had already come into the room, or had been waiting just inside the room, and moved now from behind Deacon. Everything smelled like perfume. Deacon heard the fabric of her nylons as she came into view. She was an expansive redhead, with an impressive bosom and a body that might have been really something ten years before. Now it was just kind of something, the kind that if you put it in the right dress and gave it the right lighting could still look like the real thing—from about the fifth row. With her eyes wandering over Deacon, she said, " 'Lo, Mo." She got closer, and her eyes got dreamier, and then she stopped. She said, "This isn't the guy."

Mo said, "Very funny."

Stella squinted, then pulled a pair of spectacles from somewhere inside the top of her dress and squinted again. She said, "This isn't the guy."

"This isn't the guy?"

"Mo! This is not the guy."

Mo stood and came around the desk and looked at Deacon with new interest. He said, "Excuse us for a minute, but there's been a mistake." He said to Stella, "You're sure?"

She said, "For Christ sake, Mo!"

And Mo said, "I'm sorry, Stel." Then, to Deacon, he said, "You two don't know each other?"

Deacon said, "No."

Mo said, "You're not old friends, from Chicago?"

Deacon said, "No. Got no friends in Chicago."

Mo said, "Oh boy. Then what are you doing here?"

"I'm a horn player."

"A horn player. Not a professional who does things for a living like you did for me in Shipton Wells."

"That's right."

"But you did that thing in Shipton Wells for me. Why?"

"You needed a favor. I needed someone to owe me a favor."

Mo whistled through his teeth and said to Stella, "So now I owe you a favor. What kind of horn player are you?"

"Trumpet."

Mo said to Stella, "Can you make room for a trumpet?"

Stella said, "I've always got room for a trumpet."

Mo said, "And we'll keep looking for the other guy from Chicago."

Stella said, "Sure," and gave Deacon a wink. "Until then, the position's still open. What's your name, until then?"

"Deacon."

Stella said, "Ha!"—and then stopped and stuck her eyeglasses on her nose again. She said, "Wow. Are you *that* Deacon, the Deacon from St. Louis?"

Deacon said, "Yeah."

"My, my. What in God's name are you doing here?"

"It's a long story."

"We've all got one of those, honey. Tell me part of it, someday."

Deacon finished his drink and left.

He was almost dozing now on the memory. And then Stella was there. She flounced into the main room like some redheaded chickadee—you half expected her to say, "Beulah! Peel me a grape!"—and said, "Hiya, boys. Let's swing a little." They did two numbers. Halfway through the second she focused on a 'bone player that was new to the scene—or rather she appeared to focus; without her glasses she could not have focused on Hoover Dam—and said, "Tell Gleason to give you ten bucks after rehearsal. Then go and get some lessons." Then she'd made her moment and it was over and she left.

Deacon realized, about two days after the Shipton Wells incident, that he had never made Mo pay him a cent for the job Mo thought he had done for him on the rat-faced guy. Mo would have noticed that. Mo would remember something like that. Mo would wonder, probably, why Deacon had not made him pay. If Mo had known anything about the overnight bag the rat-faced guy was carrying, that would be a problem. Mo couldn't know about that, though, or about Anita, or about where the bag was now. Deacon decided it would be fine. It would have to be fine. Until it wasn't, and then he would have to fix it.

Deacon packed up with the rest of the guys and went looking for Fatty.

Three

WORTHLESS WORTHINGTON LEE skidded off the fourth green, straight down into the sand trap and straight up the other side, and resumed his solid steps across the fairway. He was well pleased. Mo the big businessman had made a most interesting mistake, the kind of stupid mistake a smart man makes only when he has underestimated you. This put Worthless Worthington Lee in a very comfortable position. Mo was clearly embarrassed. If he moved quickly, and in the right way, Worthless Worthington Lee could make that valuable. Mo had said the money to stock booze into the casino's bars would have to come from Lee's side of the table. Worthless thought he could probably shift that burden back to Mo's side now. He could make Mo's mistake into money.

That was Worthless Worthington Lee's only real talent. He was good at taking other people's mistakes and making them into money. But it had taken him years to figure out how.

Physically he was built for the long hours of backbreaking mindless labor. And for years he had done just that. Then he had discovered the fight game. He had been given both a remarkably powerful build and a remarkable ability to withstand physical pain. Those had carried him a long way in boxing.

But that was not the same thing as having talent. As a fighter, he'd had none. Matched with men who were smaller, or weaker, or slower, or less powerful, or plain cowardly, he had won. Matched with men who were not, he had lost. Worthless Worthington Lee, despite being admired and even loved by some of the men in boxing, had never once won a fight that anyone couldn't explain afterward. And that was the definition of talent in the fight game. Real talent won the fights that no one could figure out.

But Worthless Worthington Lee was very good at figuring out how to make something financial out of nothing. It took a lot of living, and a lot of hurting, and a lot of wrong turns before he figured out where this talent really was—and the fight game, with its various allures, distracted him for more than a decade—but once he'd got it, he'd understood it. He thought, now, that all of that living and hurting would leave him alone for a while. He figured he'd done enough of both.

Worthless Worthington Lee had first come west as a chump. A mining company was advertising in his small Alabama town, where Worthless was chopping cotton like all the other colored folk. They said good workers were needed, for good pay and free housing and many other attractive benefits, at a place in the desert. He had never heard of it, but from the hearty, professional way the front men were canvassing the town, it looked pretty good. The company representatives were brusque, cheerless men in dark suits and dark hats who drove an expensive automobile around the countryside, pasting up bills that read GOOD WORK FOR GOOD WORKERS. Worthless and two of his friends, all in their middle teens, figured the front men were canvassing the entire South, so they jumped on board fast and were among the first to sign on.

A week later one of the three boys was in the hospital with heatstroke. Worthless's other friend was talking about running off. Worthless knew he had been duped by the company, but he didn't know what to do about it. The company was big and smart. Its men had canvassed only two towns in Alabama, not the entire state, and had still managed to bring more than 275 workers from the Deep South to the deep desert. The workers were there to build Hoover Dam. From the fall of 1928 to the fall of 1931, Worthless and the others built the dam. The one friend with heatstroke died in the "hospital," which turned out to be just another tent, not overseen by a doctor, where sick people were taken so they wouldn't interrupt the flow of work. The other friend had set out across the desert one night with a canteen of water and a loaf of white bread stolen from the mess hall, and was never heard from again. Worthless stayed on and helped complete one of the greatest engineering feats of all time. From the newspaper perspective, it was the Taj Majal. From the workers' perspective, it was the Great Wall of Death. They sweated and died and hurt and were hurt and cursed their bad luck and hoped only to survive long enough to get away.

Worthless Worthington Lee had survived. When the work was done, he took his money and himself to San Francisco. He put the money in a bank account, keeping back none at all for his own use. He was accustomed to being broke and doing without. The Depression meant nothing to him. He and his people had been Depressed as long as recorded time. Prohibition didn't meant anything, either. He'd been Prohibited before, too, and he didn't drink anyway. Worthless chased a construction job that promised a great future, but turned out to have no future at all and almost no present, across the San Francisco Bay into Oakland. It was there he met Flat Jack and got into the fights.

It was a very cold night on State Street. Worthless, who during that time was known only as Worthington or as Lee, sat with a collection of other hungry men on upturned apple crates at the mouth of an alley near the Greyhound station. It was a spot where people knew they could get workingmen, at any hour of the night or day, to do more or less any kind of work they needed doing. Worthless went to State Street to sit and wait when he wasn't working or eating or sleeping, for those were the only three things he ever did. They were the only things that needed doing. Some of the other men drank or chased women or got into trouble with the law, and when they sat on the apple crates, they talked about the heartache that brought them. Though they laughed a good deal about it, the appeal was lost on Worthless. It was like smoking: they all did it, and they all cursed it and were forever running out of cigarettes or matches or makings, and Worthless didn't understand why they didn't just give up the whole thing. But men don't make sense, Worthless knew. Or they do make sense, if you know how to look at it. He had heard a tent preacher go on one time about the "slavery of the mind and the slavery of the soul." And he had heard a man on the street, on Market Street in San Francisco, standing on the curb and screaming about the white man conspiring to tear the black man down by enslaving him once again with liquor and women and narcotic drugs. Worthless thought: *It's already done. We are men with appetites. We hunger. We are all enslaved from the start.*

A well-dressed black man was at the mouth of the alley late one afternoon in the winter of 1933. It was going dusk. Worthless had been working with a sanitation crew that week, rising in the dark and working from four o'clock in the morning to four o'clock in the afternoon. He'd drift back to the boardinghouse where he was sharing a room, clean up, take some food from the larder he kept under his bed, and come down to see about getting some night work. That night the well-dressed black man stopped his car and stepped into the alley and said, "I need a big nigger to take to the fights tonight."

A skinny-ass boy jumped up and said, "Am I big enough, sweetie?" and got a big laugh from everyone except the man doing the hiring.

Another man said, "What you want with this big nigger?" and a few of the fellows started up to their feet, sensing there might be some real work here after all.

The well-dressed man said, "I need a man for the fights."

"You gone fight him yo'self?"

"You gone pay the man or just beat on him?"

Worthless stood and said, "I'll fight."

And that was it. The well-dressed man had looked right past the other workers, nodded and pointed at Worthless, and said, "Come on, then. We ain't got all night." Worthless got into the car with the man, and they drove off. The man said, "My name is Flat Jack. I manage fighters. One of my boys got killed today, building that Bay Bridge. He fell. I need a man for the third card. We're going over to the Bayside Arena. You going to get yo' ass whipped by an Italian kid named Pezzo."

Worthless nodded and said, "Do I have to get my ass whipped?"

Flat Jack said, "No. You could whip his ass, I s'pose. Just don't die. I don't want two of my men to die in one day."

Worthless said, "All right. What time is the fight?"

Flat Jack said, "The fight is in twenty minutes."

"And how much you fixing to pay me?"

"Ten bucks."

"Then I'll do it for twenty-five bucks, or you can let me down right now."

Flat Jack slowed the car, and looked at his wristwatch, and looked at Worthless. He said. "You fight before?"

Worthless said, "No, suh. But I ain't no fool. I built the Hoover Dam. I ain't gonna let no Italian beat me up for ten bucks."

Flat Jack smiled an enormous smile. He said, "Okay, boy. What do they call you?"

"My name is Worthington Lee."

Worthington Lee was thrown into a pair of shorts that did not fit and a pair of gloves that were too heavy. When he first hit the Italian kid, it felt like hitting the side of a feather mattress. The Italian kid had smiled over his mouthpiece and thrown a fistful of lead into Worthless's face. Worthless roundhoused the kid as hard as he could, flat and hard on the ear, and the kid went down. That was in the first round.

At the bell Worthless said, "I can beat this boy."

Flat Jack said, "Beat him, then."

And so he did. The kid faded and fell in the third, and though he could have gotten up and gone on, he chose not to. Worthless had a win.

Flat Jack was happy. He paid Worthless his twenty-five dollars and asked him to come back the following night. For two weeks Worthless fought for Flat Jack almost every night. He won every single fight. Two weeks in, Worthless was on the second card, matched with a tough, experienced Polish fighter. Worthless got a big helping of him in the first round. At the bell he said to Flat Jack, "I cain't beat this man."

Jack said, "Don't start that. You go in there and kick his ass."

"No. I cain't beat him. He's too big and he's too fast."

"Don't pussy up on me, Lee. I got money bet on this."

"It don't matter. I cain't beat him."

There was the bell, and Worthless went back into the ring. And discovered again that he had an enormous capacity for withstanding physical pain. He knew this from the work he had done on the dam. He did not hurt the way other men hurt. Here in the ring he began to know this was true again. The Polish guy kept looking at him, after every substantial punch, surprised he was still there. Worthless just kept feeling farther and farther away from everything in front of him, as the Polack beat and beat and beat on him. Between rounds, Flat Jack cursed him and slapped at him and threw cold water on him and cheered him on. But it didn't matter. Worthless lasted all fifteen rounds, and lost the fight.

He said, in the locker room after, "I told you I couldn't beat him."

And Flat Jack said, "You're worthless."

The name stuck.

Flat Jack could have made plenty of money, Worthless always told him, if he had only listened. Worthless could virtually promise whether he would win or lose a fight if he got five minutes' experience of the fellow he was going to fight beforehand. He could watch a man work out in the gym, and know. But Flat Jack didn't listen. Or rather he did not listen when Worthless said, "I cain't beat that man." He always thought Worthless was jiving him, or planning to pussy out, or just choking. He'd say, "Sure you can. That man ain't no fighter." And Worthless would say, "I'm telling you. I can *not* beat him."

Afterward, Flat Jack would always tell him he was worthless. Pretty soon the other fighters and trainers started calling him Worthless. Pretty soon it stopped bothering him.

For five years Worthless continued in this fashion. He saw most of the West Coast. He got up to Seattle several times. He went into Mexico once. He saw country around Sacramento that looked like home. He saw country around Los Angeles—like the beach—that didn't look like anything he had ever seen. Flat Jack got crazier and crazier. Sometimes he'd fire Worthless after a fight and swear he was going out to find someone who could fight like a man. Worthless would just wait, and Flat Jack would come back in as if nothing had ever happened. He never, ever apologized.

But he started changing the way he played the game. One night, after Worthless had told him he could not beat the man he was scheduled to fight and Jack started yelling at him and calling him names, Worthless said, "Just bet the other way. Lay your money out the other way."

Flat Jack said, "I can't do that, Worthless. I have never bet against my own man."

Worthless said, "That's why you got no money."

So Flat Jack bet the other way, and won. After that he always bet the wrong way, when Worthless told him to. And pretty soon he started booking fights so that he could bet that way, matching Worthless up against shorter men or smaller men or weaker-looking men Worthless couldn't beat. That way Jack got better odds. And Worthless got a bigger beating. The fights lasted a long time. Worthless never got knocked out, and he almost never got knocked down. Every fight went fifteen rounds. Worthless began to be tired all the time. He had to drop all the daytime work. He was getting thirty-five dollars a fight, and Jack was paying his room and board, but with all the moving around, he was fighting only twice or sometimes three times a week. Despite his advice to Flat Jack and the amount of money Jack was making, Worthless himself never once bet on the other guy. He just couldn't.

But he saved every penny he made. Every time he got anywhere near San Francisco, he made a trip to his savings bank and put some more money in with his savings. His savings grew. But he was tired.

He and Flat Jack were sitting in a bus station in Yakima, Washington, watching the rain lash the fields. Worthless was a poor reader, but he read a newspaper every chance he could get. That day, he read a story in the paper about nickel mining in the desert. It was going on right around the place where he and the other men had built the dam. Concerns about the war in Europe were fueling speculation that America would soon be involved. That would put the war machine in motion. That would drive the price of metals through the ceiling. This made sense to Worthless. A week later, after he and Flat Jack had fought two more times heading south, once in Portland and once in some cold timber town near Mount Shasta, Worthless told Flat Jack he was leaving the fight game. Worthless took the bus into San Francisco, withdrew some money from his savings account, engaged a broker to purchase four hundred dollars' worth of shares in Cadminium Mining Co., and then began the bus journey back to the desert.

Nothing had changed. Worthless got a job managing a work crew—because he was the only one on the scene that day who had worked in the desert before—and got a bed in the same set of rumpled row shacks where he had bunked years earlier. The pay was better, but not by much, and the work was just as hard, but more dangerous. And Worthless was not as young as he had been, and the fights had taken a lot out of him.

But soon America did enter the war, and soon the price of nickel went sky-high, and soon Worthless Worthington Lee began to be worth something after all.

When he saw which way the wind was blowing, he went into the nearby community of Las Vegas, Nevada. He found a lawyer and got him to convert some more of his savings into some more shares in Cadminium. Six months later he used the same lawyer to convert some Cadminium shares into cash, and used the cash to convert some savings into some investments. Worthless Worthington Lee paid outright for five cinder-block shacks on the wrong side of town, the side of town where the black folks lived. It was 1943. A fortune in real estate, in this way, began.

And Worthless Worthington Lee came into his own. In 1955 he was forty-three years old. If you did not know him, it would have been easy to imagine him pulling out a big gold pocket watch and announcing the on-time arrival of the Texas and Pacific to Biloxi. It would have been easy to imagine him sitting down to a keyboard and tickling out a bluesy ballad in a bawdy house or standing before the congregation, leading the choir in a rousing spiritual. Worthless Worthington Lee, at forty-three, was a generic Negro. It would have been easy to imagine him doing any of the things that white folks thought black men did. This was part of Worthless Worthington Lee's success in the desert. No one paid any attention to him. He was able to shuffle and goof and shuck and jive to everyone's amusement, and then go about his business. Like everyone else's, this was the business of making money. It would have been difficult to imagine that Worthless Worthington Lee was a wealthy or powerful man. By 1955, though, he was.

It took Worthless twenty minutes to get off the golf course and across the sand and back to his little storefront office on Jackson Street. It was eight-thirty and the fullness of night had fallen. Jackson Street was beginning to hum. Folks were recovering. The tide of black workers leaving their jobs in the kitchens and basements and back rooms that fed the appetites of Las Vegas's white folks had ebbed. Now the tide would begin to flow the other way, and some of those same workers, now dressed a little better, would go out looking to have their own appetites fed. There would be card games and dice games over at Jeeter's. Worthless could smell chicken and ribs cooking in the street on that smoker that Roscoe John put up in front of Aggie's store. There would be big drinking down at the Houston Club and Smart Aleck. Worthless knew this because he owned the property where Houston's and Aleck's and Aggie's and Jeeter's customers did their business. He might as well own the sidewalk where Roscoe John parked his smoker.

Worthless threw the door closed behind him and shut the noise of the street away. He took off his jacket and sat heavily at the Formica kitchen table that served as his desk. There were scraps of paper all over the front of it, indicating business that still required his attention, and stacks of paper at the back of it, indicating business that no longer required his attention. He went into one of the stacks at the back and found a collection of memos and notes and contract details regarding the Ivory Coast Hotel and Casino. He pulled a pair of spectacles from his pants pocket and said, rather quietly, "Dina, honey?" There was no answer, but he expected none. He said, just as quietly, "Dina? Bring me a pot of coffee, baby." She was his wife, or at least she had lived around with Worthless long enough to be his wife. She was also a lush. She drank—all day, every day, and almost all of almost every night. She hardly spoke anymore. Worthless had loved her. There was not really anything more to it than that. He sat back in his chair and wiped his eyeglasses clean and waited.

Ten minutes later a dark, dusky shape emerged from the back room, shuffling in house slippers and a filthy bathrobe, carrying a metal coffeepot. Worthless did not look up. He said, "Thank you, honey. You go on back to bed now."

One of the slips of paper on his desk was his celebrity wish list. Over the past few months, Worthless had written down the names of the entertainers he thought should be there for the opening of the Ivory Coast. He had then begun the business of inviting them, which did not involve inviting them at all, of course, but involved putting the word out to his friends, his business partners, his business rivals, and everyone else that these people *ought* to be there when the Ivory Coast opened.

Louis Armstrong was on the list. So were Duke Ellington and Cab Calloway. And Lena Horne and Pearl Bailey and Nat "King" Cole and Della Reese. And Ella Fitzgerald and Dinah Washington and Sarah Vaughan and Harry Belafonte and Joe Louis and Hank Aaron and Jackie Robinson, Sammy Davis Jr. *and* those white boys he ran with. The Treniers. The Mills Brothers. The Nicholas Brothers. Everybody who was anybody who was Negro would have to be there. Or at least they'd have to have the chance to say no. Worthless added two more names now, those of a Las Vegas mortician he'd recently met and a black dentist who had recently opened an office below Fremont Street.

An hour and a pot of coffee later, Worthless had washed and put on a clean shirt and was moving back outside. Jackson Street was pumping. The smell of Roscoe John's lay like a London fog on the town, carrying with it Roscoe John's mysterious mix of spice and smoke. With it on the night air were sounds, too, as if the smoky smell enveloped the noise and held it close. Worthless pulled his office door closed behind him and went out.

At the end of the block a jug band had set up and collected a crowd. Across the street from there, coming out of Snuffy's, were several superior-looking females of the species, haughty broads in evening gowns and high heels that made Worthless wish, for a short second, that he was younger and hungrier and single. The impulse passed, and he laughed at himself and started down the block.

Miss Pringle was standing in the window of her beauty parlor, not having anything else to do but watch. Anybody who needed her services, and knew it, was done beautifying for the day and was now traveling in the opposite direction, moving toward becoming a mess all over again.

Worthless nodded and smiled his best businessman's smile at Miss Pringle—bony thing, he thought—and felt so full of love and concern that he wished he had a bowler hat to tip to her. He wished sometimes, at this time of his life, when he had his appetites mostly under control, that he was a minister or a priest, that he could walk down the street wearing the vestments or the backward collar and distribute good feeling and concern the way preachers sometimes do. Just walk along, letting everybody know that everything was going to be all right. As it was, he could do some of that as a businessman. He got to the end of the block, pausing to let pass a slow-moving car of Negro tourists with California plates, and stopped.

The Ivory Coast building was virtually complete. It had a big paper banner stretched across the front that read, GRAND OPENING! MAY 1955! IVORY COAST! Never mind that it was almost the end of May now and that there was still more work to do than could be done in the days left in the month. The sight of the building and the fluttering, dusty paper banner filled Worthless Worthington Lee with deep and nameless feelings. He stood now, viewing, and felt big and whole inside.

The facade itself persuaded the imagination to appreciate the grand historical glory of New Orleans and to sense the hot excitement of the people who lived there. At one end of the massive square building, a paddle-wheel motif suggested the riverboats and the water they sailed into the famed Louisiana port. A parkway at the other end of the building, where water would flow between weeping willows when the construction was complete, led the mind to contemplate the bayous and gave the place, Worthless hoped, a sense of mystery.

The other end of the structure, where the driveway entered the property and where the carhops would remove the patrons from their automobiles and show them into the big hotel/casino doorway, suggested the glamour and hysteria of Beale Street and the French Quarter. Cancan dancers in short skirts and garters would sway on the wrought-iron balconies that looked over the parking lot. Street musicians and bluesmen would play from the porches below. The purple and pink of the main facade and the looming fluorescent Ivory Coast logo would pitch a colorful shadow onto the entire corner of the community—his community, Worthless Worthington Lee's community. It would do for the Negro in Las Vegas what had not been done anywhere else in the world.

Harlem had it going on, Lee knew from stories. L.A. had Central Avenue. Chicago had the South Side. It was *all* going on. But this was different. This was about sex and jazz and good times, just like Harlem and Central Avenue and the South Side, but it was also about a new kind of freedom. This was not *also* for the Negro. This was *for* the Negro—for the colored man, first and last.

And this was Las Vegas, which was brand-new and full of possibility with every new day dawning. This was the desert, where nothing had changed in ten thousand years and where everything was possible. In the desert, nothing lasted—time and heat and the sun and the sand wore everything back to dust almost overnight. There was no history here. No one had anything at stake except Mr. Greenback Dollar Bill, just like Ray Charles said. And that ticket was going to start working for the Negro, here in Las Vegas, the way it worked all over the world for the white man.

The Ivory Coast would be the first thing like this the Negro had ever had. It was going to be *his*. It wasn't going to be colored-only, the way it would have to be in a place like Birmingham or Mobile. White folks could come and go if they wanted. Worthless knew that a certain kind of white man, and a certain kind of white woman, was going to be here the minute the doors opened. But this was for the Negro man and the Negro woman first. This would be their fantasy, their dream, their place of endless possibility. Whether to dance or dine or game or spend the night, whether to loll under the palm trees by the pool, while away an hour in the coffee shop facing the pink mountains, or to simply snug up in a room knowing they are safe and sound . . . This was the place. This was going to be the place, the only place, to be.

Worthless Worthington Lee exhaled a chest full of pride and slowly went on down the block, where he had some business with the boys at Jeeter's. He was going to go now and make them good and miserable. No good to keep them waiting.

Deacon had left the rehearsal and almost trotted to the hatcheck room, horn case in hand. He found there a new girl, a pretty one he had not seen before. He was about to flirt with her a little when she said, "Hey, Deke. Howya been?"

He was startled but he said, "Fine, baby. Swinging. You?"

She said, "I been missin' you a little . . ." and pouted.

"Keep this horn hot for me awhile, will you? I'll be back."

"Sure, Deke. You comin' soon?"

Deacon grinned at her and winked, and turned away—unnerved. He forgot more and more these days, including stuff he'd probably enjoy remembering. The girl was one cute piece, but Deacon could not remember where they'd met or what they'd done together.

He hit the casino floor and forgot her again. The place was jumped-up and rocking. You almost couldn't see carpet for the feet, nor tables for the heads. They were two deep at the back bar. The blackjack tables closest to Deacon's position had a double row of heads showing—six folks playing, six folks standing right behind them waiting for a place to open. Mo was making some dough tonight.

Deacon went circular around the edge of the casino, making for the front, and the reception area, where Fatty often planted himself. Deacon knew that Fatty had some sort of deal with Mo, some kind of arrangement whereby his salary skewed up and down based on the number of people the lounge and showroom were drawing in. Deacon also knew that Fatty did not trust Mo to give him straight numbers—which Deacon thought was small-minded and stupid, especially because Fatty let Mo know he felt that way about it—and that because of that, Mo had started fiddling the numbers just to rile Fatty up. So now Fatty had to stand at or near the front every night, watching the folks come in, counting the heads, figuring his cut.

Sure enough, Deacon found him near the elevators. He was wearing the seersucker and that very cool Panama brim shot back on his tiny head, and smiling that tense Fatty Behr smile. It vanished the instant he saw Deacon swing into view, then came uncertainly back, like a neon sign that had lost power briefly and was blinking back on. He said, "Dea-con," as Deke approached, and put out his hands, palms up, as some gesture of innocence or ignorance—I don't got it, I can't get it, and don't ask me.

Deacon didn't ask. He said, "Fatman. Howzit?"

Fatty said, "Everything is everything, Deacon," and his eyes went back to counting the house.

Deacon said, "What about it?"

"Now?"

"Yes, now."

Fatty looked at him sideways. "It's your funeral, man."

Deacon reached to shake Fatty's hand and palmed a twenty into it along with the shake. Fatty pocketed the bill. He said, "I thought I might be seeing you sometime tonight. You know my locker in the dressing room? On the upper shelf in locker one forty-five, three lockers down from the end."

Deacon said, "Thanks, Fatman," and was gone without looking at him again.

The dressing room was behind the kitchen, about halfway between the casino and the apartments where the employees lived between shifts. Deacon hit the dressing room. It was almost empty. Two or three kitchen guys were getting out of the checked pants and white blouses they wore and into street clothes. Deacon didn't know them, but nodded anyway. Across the room, behind them, was a pair of swinging doors that led into the other dressing room, the smaller, darker one that the Negro workers used. Deacon was not sure what other way there was to get into the Negro dressing room, but he had never once seen these swinging doors swing in or out. There was light visible now through the glass panels, but silence. Deacon checked his wristwatch. It was eight-twenty. No one was getting ready to go on or ready to go home, not at this hour. This was the beginning of the long night, and everyone was already where they had to be, and where they had to stay, until it was over.

Deacon found Fatty's locker, three from the end of the row, and shook the steel carriage lock until it freed. Inside, up, a shelf, a packet wrapped in a handkerchief, and home. Deacon pocketed the bundle and clicked the locker shut and was out past the three kitchen guys fast.

In his room he checked his watch again and found he had lost ten minutes in the journey. He reckoned he had about two hours left before showtime. Plenty.

He went to the bathroom and closed the lid on the toilet, and stood on it and stretched on his tiptoes. He lifted a ceiling panel away and pulled down a leather kit bag. He dusted off the toilet lid with his palm, and took off his suit coat, and sat.

He cooked. He tied off. He spiked. He nodded and he was gone, his head lolling over to one side and lowering and drifting and finally coming to rest, his cheek squashed flat against the cold tile of the sink stand. His last thought as he was going out was of Anita. He said her name and then he slept.

Worthless Worthington Lee could see that Jeeter was going to take considerable convincing. He could see that Jeeter, seated before him, his artificially straightened hair slicked back tight on his head, his shiny three-piece suit stretched tight onto his body, was simply not understanding things. Worthless had arrived half an hour before, told Jeeter to get rid of the customers in the back bar area, and said, "You sit on down, Jeeter, and let me tend the bar for a while." He'd made them both a cocktail, and had stood shining the top of the bar while he explained business, his own way, so that Jeeter would come around to his point of view.

It wasn't working. Jeeter sat in his chair backward, with his arms slung over the chair back, getting stiffer and stiffer by the minute. Everything Worthless said seemed to make it worse. Finally, when he could stand no more, Jeeter spoke:

"You one stupid nigger if you think I'm going to fall for that load a crap." Jeeter raised his buggy-eyed face and planted it on Worthless. *A brave man,* Worthless thought—*and too big a fool to be cool.*

"Now, now, now, Jeeter," Worthless said. "Don't jump up on me like that. If this was a load of crap and I was expecting a smart bidnessman like you to fall for it, then you right, I'd be plenty stupid. But that's not it. You missing the whole point. Let me explain it to you one more time, and if you still don't like it, I propose somethin' else."

Jeeter, satisfied that he'd made his point, nodded his head. Worthless polished the bar for a moment more, and started back in. "I am opening this club. It's going to have lots and lots of money behind it. And it's gonna have lots of money in it. You don't know who we got sponsorin' us. You don't know we got Big John Jefferson frontin' for us—but he is."

That caught Jeeter's attention. Big John Jefferson had been the heavyweight boxing champion of the world. Jeeter had heard, like everybody else, that Big John had gone a little soft in the head and was a bit of a nut or a bit of an alky, one or the other, but still. *Damn,* Jeeter thought—and then realized that probably Worthless Worthington Lee was lying to him about that anyhow.

"So it's all gonna be big, the only thing on Jackson Street worth payin' attention to," Worthless continued. "And everything else on Jackson Street is gonna go—one way or another. You, Jeeter, you are gonna go out of bidness. There is going to be no trade left over for you. Ain't no two ways about that. What I'm saying is, go out of bidness now. Close the dice games and the bar and the restaurant and take a vacation. In a month's time, we open the Ivory Coast, and I'll give you a job managing all the bars inside the casino. All four bars, Jeeter. Any one of them bigger than what you got here. And alls you got to do is go out of bidness now."

Jeeter said, "No. It's a load a crap, Worthless, and I see right through it. If it wasn't, you'd be making me a cash offer."

"I already told you, Jeeter, I got no money. Not any money at all.

I'd do it if I could. I'd buy you out right this minute and close this bar tonight. But I cain't."

"Then I ain't going," Jeeter said, and stood up from his chair. "You might want to be a big man, but it hasn't happened yet. You ain't got the weight to throw around, and I'm sick of you trying it on me. Now git, and stop bothering me with this casino crap. I'm a bidnessman, and I got a bidness to run."

Worthless sighed and stopped polishing the top of the bar. He thought for a moment, reckoning he had thirty more seconds to make some sense of this dopey-ass fool, and decided to make one final attempt.

He said, "All right, Jeet. You win. You made the call. One thing, though: if you gonna stick to that, and stay open, do yourself and me a favor. Don't go telling everybody how you throwed old Worthless Worthington Lee out of your club and sent his casino idea packing and made a fool of him."

Jeeter smiled, for the first time, showing one fat gold tooth in the front of his mouth. He said. "Why's that? Too hard on yo' pride?"

"No, Jeet," Worthless said. "Too hard on yo' health. You tell people you throwed me out of here, it's gonna make it harder for me to get them all behind the Ivory Coast—which, in case you ain't paying attention, is gonna mean tons of money and tons of jobs and tons of respect for this beat-ass community, which could, God knows, use a ton of all three of that. If you start telling people you put me down and shamed me out of here, and get 'em laughin' at me . . . Jeeter, I'm gonna have to come back in here and kill you."

Jeeter stopped and stared. He said, "What?"

Worthless said, "You heard me. I'm going to come back in here and kill you. It's as simple as that. Now you understand me?"

Jeeter did not, and Worthless saw it right away and it made his heart hurt. Jeeter got mad. He jumped forward two feet and said, "Get the hell out of my place, you tired old mother, before I smack you silly. Get out."

Worthless stood, towering over the little man with the gold tooth, and raised his hands in surrender. He turned his back on Jeeter and moved toward the door with heavy feet. The idea of killing Jeeter! The idea that he could threaten to kill Jeeter and make such little impression! What a burden it all seemed, sometimes. Worthless felt so drained that he simply forgot to say good-bye to Jeeter as he went out. He was outside on Jackson Street, and halfway down the sidewalk, his head full of good plans going bad, and barbecue smoke, and somebody else's music, and women in high heels and perfume, before he suddenly turned to thank Jeeter for his time. But of course Jeeter was gone and it was too late.

Worthless stopped feeling foolish. Jackson Street came back to life around him. He said, "Hey, Polly," to a hooker he know from New York who was new in town. "How you doin', baby?" And he moved on down Jackson, toward Roscoe John's smoker, thinking about his appetite.

Left alone, Jeeter congratulated himself on having shown the big man that he wasn't no sissy. He shoved a few chairs into place around the poker and blackjack tables, acting disgusted but feeling very proud. He had never been a strong man, but enough was enough. That damn stupid-ass Worthless, with his big stupid ideas about improving Jackson Street . . . Who the hell wanted a Negro casino anyway? All these shiftless mothers who came in and drank and gambled every night in Jeeter's place, well, they didn't have five bucks apiece and never would have. How you gonna run a big business off of people like that? Jeeter said out loud, "Cain't be done. It just cain't be done."

There was the click of a door closing, and the light in the barroom went out. Jeeter looked up in time to see nothing more than a big ham-sized fist slam into his face. Feet scuffled. There were two of them, and they were white—that was all Jeeter knew, and it was the last thing he knew.

Late the following morning Jeeter's people would finally bust the lock and get into the back barroom. They would find their boss, gold tooth glinting horribly, many hours dead. He would be stretched out on his back across a poker table, like a corpse at the morgue. His head and legs would be barely visible, hanging over the sides of the table. There was a piece of thin wire wrapped around Jeeter's neck and looped over his feet. Hog-tied, thus, and stretched like a piece of meat over the tabletop, he might have fought himself alive for several hours, arching his back far enough to breathe, before collapsing and strangling himself, and gasping and stretching and arching again and catching a little breath, before finally, exhausted, able to stretch no more, he had simply choked his own self to death.

Worthless, down the street chewing on a rib and waving at Roscoe John to please get him another napkin, never knew a thing about it.

Deacon, dozing in and out of a dream, was remembering. For days he let the hundred-dollar bill Mo had given him burn a hole in his pocket. Mo had not paid him for the run to Shipton Wells. He'd given him a job in the band, but the paycheck hadn't come across yet and Deacon had not asked for an advance. The hundred dollars was supposed to be a donation to that cop's "foundation" for orphans. But the little stake Deacon had brought from Chicago was almost gone. Deacon, going downtown, struggled the whole way with the idea of drifting into the Fremont, say, and using the hundred dollars to make some real dough. He was pretty sure he could pick a black-jack table and make some money with it. He was also pretty sure that he'd done enough gambling in Chicago to last any reasonable man a lifetime. Or *cost* any reasonable man a lifetime. It had almost cost him his, and if he had not left town when he did he might not have one to waste now.

When he got downtown he stepped off by the bottom of Fremont Street and kept on walking. The casino scene petered out. Soon it was just a tired old desert town again. Low buildings where men fixed cars or built furniture or rigged slot machines extended down either side of the street. Deacon caught Bonanza coming up on his left, and turned.

The foundation building was half a block in. It was another low, one-story job made of stucco and glass, but cleaner and quieter than those around it. There was a tiny square of lawn in front, and a tiny black man in overalls watering it with a hose. Deacon said, "Is this the orphan's foundation?" The black man nodded and jerked his thumb at the door. Deacon went inside.

Quiet. Not a single sound. Deacon went to a counter in front of him. He did not dare ring the bell and break the silence. Instead, he listened and looked. The walls were painted an institutional green, lime green like the jails and hospitals Deacon had been stuck in from time to time. There were two metal desks at one end of the front room, and a sofa and chairs at the other. But no people.

And then there was one. A tall, thin, very pale woman wearing thick glasses and her hair in a bun was suddenly there at Deacon's elbow. She wore a dark blue dress and high heels. Her eyes looked enormous. She said, "How can I help you?"

Deacon stared back. He said, "I have a donation to make."

"For the Children's Fund?"

"Is that the orphans' foundation?"

"We call it the Children's Fund."

"Well, here." Deacon fumbled the envelope with the hundred-dollar bill out of his pocket. The tall woman made it disappear. Her thin hands were suddenly empty.

She said, "We have a form we'd like you to fill out. So the children can write a thank-you note."

Deacon said, "No, thanks. I just wanted to make the donation."

"In whose name?"

"Put down your own, sister. I just wanted the kiddies to have the bread."

Deacon was backing toward the door. He felt something so entirely sinister in the room that his hands began to sweat. But the tall thin woman was smiling.

She said, "Of course. I understand. Let me thank you, then. For the children . . ."

Deacon was out the door so quickly that he bumped into the old guy watering the lawn. The man started and swung his garden hose around and shot half a gallon onto Deacon's leg before he could get clear. Deacon skittered back onto the sidewalk and went slowly down Bonanza and onto Las Vegas Boulevard and onto Fremont. Gamblers were going in and out of the casinos there. With the hundred dollars flown, Deacon had no reason to go inside. With one pants leg soaking wet, anyway, he'd only get a laugh if he did. He sat down on a bus bench and let the sun dry him out.

Across town, beyond the dusty downtown, out Las Vegas Boulevard, neon screamed. Blowing past in a big car a man would skirt the Nevada and the El Morocco and the Desert Spa, before coming down to the real action. The Desert Inn loomed on the left, and the New Frontier on the right. The Sands, and beyond it the Hotel Flamingo, rose like the city of Oz. Farther on, the Starburst and the Thunderbird were twin pylons of progress—unimaginably sleek and modern and cool, factories for fun, palaces of pleasure.

Mo sat behind his desk at the Starburst, shuffling receipts and nodding as Killarney spoke. The accountant, dressed like a finely tailored mortician in a very expensive black three-piece suit and wire-rimmed glasses, stood reverently waiting. Mo said, "This is it?"

Killarney said, "That's everything."

Mo said, "Sit, then," and Killarney did. Mo rose and paced. He said, "It isn't good enough. We've got to do something with the nighttime receipts. You know what's killing us?"

Killarney removed his glasses and wiped them with a handkerchief.

"I'll tell you what's killing us," Mo continued. "The dinner and the show."

Killarney stopped wiping and said, "We're selling out."

"That's what's wrong," Mo said. "That's exactly what's wrong with the whole economy of this place. The numbers are all upside down. Just like with the restaurants. If we succeed, we fail."

Killarney, who dreamed in numbers when he did not dream in lavender and silk and girls he would never have, sighed and said, "You're the one who's upside down, Mo. The restaurants are doing better business than they have ever done."

Mo slapped his hands down on the big oak desk and said, "And that's why it's not working. What's the average meal, now?"

"About six dollars. Not counting the bar bill."

"So, with the bar bill, about . . . what? Eight bucks?"

"Give or take."

"And at eight bucks, we clear what?"

"About two dollars. Two and a quarter, maybe."

"And that's considered good, right?" Killarney, consulted, nodded. Mo circled around the front of his desk and continued: "And the show? We're getting ten bucks a head for the show, and most folks are buying a few drinks, and we're charging a buck and half for the drinks, and we're clearing what?"

Killarney squirmed and said, "Harder to tell, Mo. It depends on the act, and how much the act is costing us and which orchestra they're using."

"But we're mostly losing money."

"No. When we're full, we're breaking even."

"No!" Mo looked triumphant. "That's the whole point! Even when we're full, we're screwed. We're getting killed on this stuff, and I never even realized it. I've been so busy worrying over the little stuff that I never even saw the big picture. I've been so busy worrying over Chicago and are they happy and is there enough left for me and what the hell am I doing with Dawson and the Thunderbird . . . I missed the whole picture."

"So . . . What's the whole picture?"

"We're playing this like chumps. We're selling people dinner and drinks and a show, and they're having a fine old time, and we're going broke—because they are not at the tables. Clearing two bucks a head for dinner? For crying out loud, I can make two bucks a head on the slots in half an hour. I can take two bucks off these chumps in ten minutes of blackjack, and five minutes of craps. That's why we took out all those damn poker tables—the money comes too slow. That's why we added seats on the roulette—the money comes faster. It takes one guy to run a blackjack table, so I don't mind that it's slower than craps, 'cause that takes four guys. But the restaurants and the nightclub are a disaster!"

"But that's what's bringing them here," Killarney said. "We book a big act, we book out for the whole week. You know that. We've proved that."

"But if we get them here and all they do is eat the food and see the show, we might as well leave 'em in Dallas. Except for the really high rollers, there's no point in having them here at all. We're going to have to come up with something."

Killarney relaxed. It wasn't going to have to happen tonight. He smiled. He said, "Well, that's your specialty. You go to work on this, and you come up with something, and I'll tell you how much it will cost and how much it will make, and Chicago will be happy, and you will be happy, and all the rest of us can go back to being happy. Done?"

Mo said, "Done. Now scramble."

Killarney scrambled. Mo sat. He said out loud, "How about making me a damned drink?" and a white-jacketed Negro appeared bearing a silver tray. His name was Oliver. He had been waiting just outside the door for forty minutes, standing with a tray, a small silver ice bucket, a heavy glass half-filled with scotch, and a siphon of soda water, standing at attention for forty minutes. By the time Mo had said, "How about—," Oliver had filled the heavy glass with soda water. He put the siphon on the tray, dropped three large ice cubes into the glass, and was walking. He was in the room before Mo finished his sentence.

And he was gone just as quickly. Mo stood with the highball, sipping it, forgetting to enjoy it. He set it down and left the room.

He did rounds. Several times a day Mo went like a lobsterman checking his traps across the great ocean of his hotel. Later he would do the Thunderbird. Now he cruised the Starburst.

Downstairs he went into the gift shop, where a bright-eyed blonde sold him a cigar. He stood across from Reception, lighting it and watching the men behind the counter. He moved with the lit cigar down through the pits, his cool eyes sweeping calmly across the blackjack, the craps, the roulette, and the banks of slots as he moved toward the back of the casino floor.

From there he took a broad carpeted stairway to the basement level. The gift shops were closing for the night. A few had lingering customers. All was quiet there. He knocked on a heavy door with peepholes in it and was given access to the casino security offices. Three uniformed and three plainclothes men snapped to attention, rising from their ashtrays and coffee mugs and cheap magazines to greet him. Mo waved the cigar and called some of them by name, never slowing as he moved through the back of the room to another heavy door, with another set of peepholes.

This one was slower to open. This was the money room. Six men in eyeshades sat counting there. Now Mo stopped. The big door swung closed behind him. The men glanced up, glanced back down, and continued. It was silent but for the ruffle of paper money. Bins of counted, wrapped bills were stacked on a table in the corner. Near dawn these would be packed into metal boxes on big rubber wheels— Mo thought they looked like the carts that ice-cream vendors used to work the streets—and moved out of the hotel. The men doing the counting came and went in four-hour shifts, patted down when they arrived, patted down when they left. Mo paid them very well, but he knew that did not matter. A dishonest man, a greedy man, no matter how much he was being paid, would not long resist the horrible magnetic attraction of all that loose cash. Mo had actually seen men begin to sweat while they counted—while they counted, say, their fifth or sixth pile of ten-dollar bills adding into the thousands. Mo or Killarney, who ran the money rooms, or Morgan, the chief security man, would fire a man for little more than perspiring or making nervous jokes in the counting room. It was like the submarine crews shadowing U-boats behind German lines during the war. One frightened man could demoralize an entire ship if he was left alone. Same here. One crook could make the entire counting staff crooked in a single night, Mo thought, if he got out of hand.

Tonight all was quiet. The smell of money, that indefinable, perfumey, sweaty smell of American money, filled the room. Mo puffed quietly on his cigar, watched another minute, and said, "You guys are doing a great job. First-rate. Chicago appreciates it. I appreciate it."

He said to Morgan, who stood silently behind him, "One and a half percent swaggo for the night car to L.A. You know the drill."

Morgan would prepare a steel lockbox of cash for the guys in Chicago. He'd get the swag into a car that would get it to Los Angeles, where it would get on a train and head east to some guys no one in Las Vegas had ever seen. One and a half percent was standard for the Starburst. So far, it had kept Chicago from coming out to check on things, and that was all Mo wanted. He said to Morgan, "Good and quiet down here. I like it."

"Thank you, sir. It's a good bunch."

Mo left them.

Upstairs, up a rear stairwell, Mo went through the kitchens. He had no business here, really, but like the gift shop where he got his cigar, it was a place to take the temperature of the hotel and the night. If there was something going wrong in the joint, even if it had not gotten big enough for him to notice yet, this was one of the places you felt it.

Example: One Friday night in the middle of winter, the winter before, Mo was making his nightly rounds and passed through the kitchen. A waiter he did not know was crying. Mo had never seen a waiter cry before. He stopped and put his cigar out, and watched the

waiter talking to one of the chefs. The chef looked unnerved. Mo
went to him.

He said, "What's going on, gents?"

The chef, who knew Mo, said, "Nothing, sir. Just a little problem
with one of the guests."

"What problem?"

"He's nuts, is the problem!" the waiter cried. "The guy is nuts! He's
got a gun, plus he slapped me and called me a queer!"

The man in question was a high roller from Denver. He had lost
a lot of money at the tables the night before. He was having a party
in his room and had ordered, along with some sandwiches and an
entire plate of pickles, a terrific amount of booze—bottle of rye, bottle of scotch, bottle of gin, soda water, tonic water, the works. He
had three times phoned down for ice. Then he'd ordered champagne,
and when the waiter got it to him, and upon request opened it for
him, he went berserk and started screaming. First he slapped the
waiter. Then he'd thrown the bottle of champagne at him and over-
turned the waiter's cart, then called him a queer and pulled out a
pistol.

Mo said, "Give me your jacket," and gave the waiter his own suit
coat. He told the chef, "Give me another bottle of bubbles. Better
make it the good stuff. Set up another cart."

The chef nodded to a second waiter, hovering, who shot off. He
said to Mo, "You're not going alone. Let me fade you."

Mo said, "Nah. I'll be okay. I'll be right back."

Mo pushed the cart onto the service elevator and went up to the
fifth floor. He rolled down the hall, past yards of gaudy flocked wallpaper, and found the room. The door was shut. Mo knocked and said,
"Room service!" When the door opened, Mo slid the cart in without
hesitating and went past a big guy in a bathrobe. He said, "French
champagne, sir. On the house. Compliments of the management."

The big guy grunted and jerked his thumb toward the bed. Mo
slid the cart over there, and pulled the bottle of champagne from the
ice bucket. "Shall I open this for you now, sir, with your permission?"
The big guy grunted and started scratching his ass and moving off
toward the bathroom.

There was a lump under the covers. There were two empty liquor
bottles on the bedside table. There was another turned over on the

carpet—rye, Mo would have guessed, for the room stank of rye. Mo pulled the cork, and held the bottle aloft for a moment, and with his free hand lifted the covers from the bed.

Under the covers, in a pool of blood, was a young woman. Mo saw dark hair, a bony spine, pale skin with a dark mole. Mo dropped the covers and said brightly, "Shall I pour now, sir, or would you like the champagne to chill a bit longer?"

The big guy called something from the bathroom, and flushed. Mo set the champagne down and checked the bedside table. A revolver was in the drawer. Mo took it and stuck it under his jacket. He called out, "I'll just leave it to chill a little longer, sir. And may I wish you a very enjoyable evening. Compliments of the management, sir."

Mo went out the door, leaving the girl and the cart and the stink of rye behind him. He got back to the service elevator and took off the waiter's jacket as he skidded down to the kitchen. He told the chef, "Don't send anyone else up there, no matter what." He handed him the revolver and said, "Wrap that in plastic and don't let anyone touch it. And get that crybaby waiter straightened out. I'll be back."

Mo called the cops. Ten minutes later he had Haney and four of his flat-footed plainclothesmen in the lobby. He gave them a quick rundown. He said, "The guy had a gun and I took it. He may not have another. Try not to shoot him on the property."

Haney had grinned, horribly.

The girl had been dead for more than twenty-four hours, it turned out, when Mo had spotted her under the covers. She had been molested, many times, within that same period. The big guy had blood on the front of his bathrobe, in fact, when Haney shot him. Then he bled his own blood until he bled to death.

Tonight the kitchen was quiet. A chef Mo had recently hired for the weeknight shifts was chewing on a toothpick, standing with his arms folded across his chest, looking down his nose at the carts as they went past him. Mo said, "Evening, Marcel. How's it?"

Marcel said, "Bone swar," with a Brooklyn accent. "It's going okay, Mr. Weiner. Good night in the dining room. Kinda slow otherwise. No room service."

"That's the way we like it, Marcel. We don't like room service. A guy eating in his room is costing us money. You keep up the good work."

Leaving the kitchen, Mo checked his watch and reckoned he had just enough time to hit the Thunderbird and make it back for the start of the first show. Stella had asked him repeatedly why he didn't come around to catch her sets anymore. He saw no reason to tell her the truth. Easier to show up. He'd hit the 'Bird, and come back. Maybe.

Across the hotel, in her room, Stella was powdering. A Negro maid stood waiting, armed with an arsenal of beauty products. Stella, wearing eyeglasses studded with rhinestones, peered at herself in the mirror, smiled, added lipstick, smiled, dabbed with a tissue at her teeth, smiled, added powder to a wrinkle coming off her left eye, smiled, and then said, "Get me something to drink, honey."

The Negro maid did not move, but something behind her stirred. There was a clink of glass and ice. In the dimmer recesses of the room, in the mirror, Stella watched a handsome young man, a very nervous handsome young man, tremble his hands over a cocktail. Stella said, "Scotch and water, honey," and watched the young man start over. He was wearing a sand-colored suit and hat that gave his skin the look of a burnished burl of redwood. Stella had scarcely ever seen anything so beautiful. She quickly removed her glasses, and smiled at the trembling young man, and said, "Make something for yourself, honey, and try to relax."

With that she lit a marijuana cigarette in a holder and inhaled deeply. She was the one who needed to relax, in fact. She was the one who in an hour's time had to entertain the people. She was the main attraction. She was the star. She was the star! It was thrilling to say out loud—but not in front of the maid, so she didn't—and if she smoked the marijuana and drank the scotch, she could believe that she was the star of something that mattered. It was a long way from Broadway, though. It was a long way from Hollywood. She knew she could never make the money there that she was making here—not anymore, anyway—unless she somehow went back to getting the parts that she had not, actually, ever been able to get. She never understood why. She had the looks, and she had the training, and she had twice the class of any of those broads. She paused over her drink, took another long pull on the cigarette holder, and totted them up:

Marilyn Monroe: talentless tramp. Jayne Mansfield: ditto. Doris Day: phony bitch. Shelley Winters? Elizabeth Goddamn Taylor?

The men were no better. Rock Hudson, for God's sake. Montgomery Clift? The little squirt James Dean? Who were they kidding?

It was simply embarrassing. That's entertainment? No! It was not! She said out loud, "I'll give 'em some entertainment. I've got a show to do." Then, more quietly, she said to the maid, "That'll do for now, dear. Let yourself out."

As the maid went, Stella rose. Her bare shoulders were like alabaster and she smelled of roses. She crossed halfway into the dim sitting room, and lowered herself into a soft armchair, and removed her eyeglasses. Then she held out her hands to the beautiful young Negro in the sand-colored suit, and said, "Come here, mister. Stella wants something . . . African."

Deacon awoke. He was still in his bathroom. He got a wobbly look at his watch, and it was almost nine-thirty. He pulled together his kit and packed it and stowed it, and tossed a little cold water on his face and stood dripping over the sink. He thought he looked good, kind of gaunt and greenish, kind of Halloweenish, kind of in-betweenish, and began to sing some kind of song out of those words as he got his suit coat on and moved off down the hall. He had fifteen minutes to pick up his horn and grab a drink. Or two. Depending. He had time. He'd coast.

The casino was hysteria. The jingle-jungle noises roared over him like a waterfall when he hit the main floor. The smoke was as thick as fog. The people were crammed in, moving like Pygmies. Deacon smiled indulgently, as at a naughty child, and moved on through the crowd. The smaller casino room was quieter, but not by much. Deacon waved at a familiar face at the roulette wheel, then instantly started wondering who that was waving back at him, and went on until he found an empty place at Sloan's back lounge bar. It seemed like a week, or two weeks, since Sloan had poured him those few hangover drinks. Deacon put the thought away. He was in the casino now, in the permanent twilight of the casino, where time stopped or moved but did not matter. It did not matter. He had a quick pair of scotches, on the rocks, letting the second burn down slowly like a fire running out of fuel. He tossed a five-dollar chip onto the bar.

Everyone else was already seated behind the scrim when he got to his chair in the orchestra. Gleason shot him a heavy eye. It had no meaning, but a little history. Early on, maybe the second week he was with the Starburst, Deacon had gotten ahold of some very powerful medicine. He'd scored from a guy he'd been told to meet near the old Hotel Apache, downtown, and had gone into the basement of that old building with the stuff. He'd tied off in the men's room there, spiked, nodded off in the stall, and not come back for a long while. When he woke, he had no clothes on. And it was twenty minutes to showtime. Deacon swapped his watch for the clothes he got off a lush that had just come into the men's room—giving up a perfectly good Hamilton for a pair of hunter-green corduroy pants and a dark green crushed-velvet shirt.

He played brilliantly that night. He was known to the band as Crush Velvet forever after. He replaced the swapped watch with a drugstore Timex.

Deacon winked back at Gleason, and sat unsteadily. But then he had his sides out in front of him, and the notes jumped and hollered from the page, and the song about being greenish and Halloweenish drifted off, and Gleason said, "All together, now . . ." and the orchestra swung into, what else, "Stella by Starlight." The scrim started to come up and there was a thundering of applause, and Deacon stood up for his solo and he went with it into the night.

Haney had fired up a fat Cuban cigar and was stretched out on the living-room sofa when the two gorillas got back from town. Haney heard them come up the drive, their big Lincoln scrunching on gravel. He said, "Make them wait in the front room, Willis." A figure in the shadows said, "Yassuh."

Haney lay back on the sofa. He was wearing a dressing gown of expensive Chinese black silk, tied around the waist with a sash, over milky white silk pajamas. On the record player spun a platter from the Sons of the Pioneers. The long, low desert house where he rested sat high above the city of Las Vegas, in the foothills ten miles to the west. Below him, if he cared to, Haney could see the twinkling of the

Strip. He sipped gingerly at a snifter of cognac, indulged himself with a cloud of cigar smoke, and rose from the sofa with a slight whine. A shadow moved through the dim light to the Victorola, and the music stopped.

The torpedoes stood in the front room with their hats in their hands, staring down the desert at the lights of the Strip. They looked huge to Haney, who usually did not have men of such size in the house. One of them, the pale kid who was new, stared at the wall in front of him. The other, the one called Harrigan, looked down at the carpet, and said, "We did the spook."

Haney said, "You killed him?"

"More or less. He's probably dead now."

Haney shook his head. "Was that necessary? Was it clean?"

"He wasn't willing to listen, sir. And it was clean. No fuss. No witnesses."

"You clip anything?"

Harrigan pulled a packet of folded bills from his jacket pocket and said, "We got this."

Haney took the bills and stuck them in his dressing gown. He said, "Two good birds with one stone. Money for the children, and that bum is out of the picture. Harrington, is it?"

"Yes, sir. Harrigan, sir."

"You know who the bum was?"

"No, sir."

"You care?"

"No, sir."

"All right, then. It's a good night's work. Make sure you log the extra time, and give yourself a half day off."

"Thank you, sir."

Haney left the room and listened for the Lincoln to skid the gravel going out the driveway. He said, "Willis? Freshen this." A black-skinned butler came from an adjoining room bearing a cut-glass decanter. He stopped at Haney's side to pour cognac into the snifter. He replaced the top to the decanter and said, "Shall I leave it?"

Haney said, "Thank you, Willis." The butler shot from the room. Haney cinched his dressing gown and rested back onto the sofa, and the music started again. The soft, urgent voices said, "Each day I face, the burning waste, without the taste . . . of *water* / C-o-o-o-l . . . *wa-*

ter." Haney sighed contentedly. The knock-up at the Starburst. The dealer in the hospital. That punk killer Mo had imported. The stuff with Worthington Lee. Jeeter's murder. Cash for the orphans. A skim for himself. In less than twenty-four hours. Plus, he'd had a haircut and a manicure, and been fitted for a suit.

The West Side murder bothered him a little. It was sloppy. Haney didn't like things to be sloppy. Sloppy was for the bad guys. In fact, it was often the difference between the good guys and the bad guys—because the good guys, the cops, were very tidy. Their mess didn't leave as many marks, which meant that when the good guys messed up—like tonight—it wasn't so easy to figure out what had gone wrong.

He didn't like the sloppy thing in Shipton Wells, either.

Haney had gotten the call from a highway patrol officer who was a friend. He had a stiff in a bathroom in the Greyhound station in Shipton Wells. He said he thought Haney would want to look at it. Haney didn't agree, but he went anyway.

Here's what he got: This guy with a face like a mole, or a rat, wearing a heavy brown suit, had sat down in the stall and blown half his face away with a police-issue .38. The numbers were filed off the gun. The stiff was carrying no identification. He had no luggage. The highway patrol officer had asked a few questions before he let the driver and the passengers go on to Las Vegas. He said the driver told him the stiff had boarded the bus in Chicago. He carried an overnight bag that looked like it was made of upholstery. A carpetbag. The driver didn't remember the guy saying a single word the whole trip. The bag wasn't on the bus. The driver hadn't seen the stiff get off in Shipton Wells, but since everyone had gotten off in Shipton Wells, he had not been paying attention.

But one guy, a pimply kid who worked at the gas station across the road, said he saw the rat-faced guy going into the café. The kid had come across to the bus station to buy a Coca-Cola and was heading back across to the gas station when he and the rat-faced guy crossed paths. The rat-faced guy had stopped just outside the café and had a short conversation with another guy. Then the rat-faced guy had gone back into the station, carrying that carpetbag. The kid could not remember what the other guy looked like. But he did remember that he saw the other guy, the guy from outside the café, carrying the rat-faced guy's carpetbag back out of the station a few minutes later.

Haney said, "You'd already heard the gunshot?"

The kid said, "No, sir. I'm deaf. I didn't hear anything."

Haney had looked at the body a bit more and then had gone across the road into the café. It was nothing to get excited about. The place was run by a fat little Mexican and his niece, a trim little beauty with big brown eyes and the kind of body you saw at the movies. The Mexican said he didn't know anything about any suicide. He went over to the station with one of Haney's men and looked at the body, and came back and said he'd never seen the guy before. The girl wouldn't go. She said the kid in the gas station told her the whole story, and she didn't want to know anything more about it. She was sure the guy had never come into the café. While Haney was talking to her, she turned away, quite suddenly, and started putting nickels in the jukebox.

Haney glanced over at the record player now and said, "Put on some Bob Wills."

"Yassuh," the voice of his butler returned.

Haney puffed at the Cuban. Messy business. Sloppy. He'd let the Shipton Wells thing go as a suicide, even though he didn't like the missing bag. But there was nothing on the wire about a felon with a face like a rat. Nobody was looking for the guy. And Shipton Wells wasn't even his jurisdiction. Haney had enough mess in his own backyard.

Four

THE NEWS OF Jeeter's murder ran up and down Jackson Street like a paperboy. Outside of Jeeter's own men, Roscoe John and Selma Pringle were the first to know. Selma was coming down Jackson Street early the next morning, ready to open her salon. Roscoe had appeared near dawn to do repair work on his grill, which the night before had given out under a slab of ribs at a spot that the rust had got. He had a sack of tools spread out on the sidewalk. Selma came slowly down Jackson Street, ready to open up and start sweeping up for the day. This was her problem with the desert: it was made of sand, and there were no trees to stop the wind blowing, and no matter how hard you cleaned on a Wednesday night, Thursday morning was dirty all over again. She had just expressed this opinion to Roscoe John, as she unlocked the door to her beauty parlor, when Roscoe said, "It's some kind of mess over to Jeeter's place, too."

It wasn't some kind of mess, exactly. The mess was cleaned up already. This was some sort of body. It was Jeeter's body, wrapped in a tablecloth taken from his own dining room, coming feet-first out the back door of the barroom and going into the open door of a waiting car. Roscoe John said, "Let me have a look at this, Miss Pringle. Might not be something for you to see."

He went across the street and conferenced briefly with the two young Negro men, both of them Jeeter's boys, who were moving the body. He nodded to them several times as Selma Pringle got her shop open and raised the blinds onto Jackson Street and watched, and then he came back across the street. He stepped up to Miss Pringle's shop door. He said, "Well, they killed that Jeeter. Hog-tied and killed him."

Miss Pringle gasped and put her hand to her throat, and said, "Heavens! Who would have *done* such a thing?"

Roscoe John thought for a moment and said, "Coulda been almost anybody, Selma. That little jackrabbit had a lot of enemies. It's some boys say it was Worthless. I say that's a load of bullarkey."

Selma said, "I don't believe a word of it."

By the time Worthless Worthington Lee heard the news, it was old news.

He and Dina had been through a rough night. She could not sleep. She rose and paced, then fixed herself a drink, clinking the ice cubes as she roamed around the little clapboard house and paced. This was not unusual. But the clinking ice cubes kept Worthless awake. He'd start to slip away, and then the clinking would rouse him; the clinking would go off into another room and he'd start to slip away, and then the clinking would come back. While the sun was up, Dina could hardly find the energy to get off the bed. At night she couldn't make herself lie down in it. Her belly was swollen as if she were carrying a child. Her breath came rasping and short. Worthless turned away from her and faced the wall and waited for the sun to come up. They both slept a bit sometime after five. By seven, Jeeter's death was officially big news.

Worthless knew it almost as soon as he hit the street. He had bathed and shaved and put on clean clothes—it was one of Worthless's absolute rules that he wear a laundry-fresh shirt and clean underclothes every single day of the week, without fail—and was going to walk downtown for coffee and breakfast at the Hotel Apache. He did so every morning, stopping first at the corner store to buy a newspaper to scan as he walked the half mile across the sandy streets that separated the West Side from downtown Las Vegas. He'd get his *Sun*, read the front page before the bottom of Jackson Street, and cover everything else before Bonanza Avenue dipped under the train tracks—officially marking the line between the good and the bad sides of town. Then he'd fold the paper, tuck it into his jacket, and continue his stroll.

This day something was wrong, and he knew it at once. Sumner, that dark, dark boy he'd hired out of the Starburst kitchen for his own Ivory Coast, was rolling slowly up Jackson Street in an old Ford, practically idling, looking for some kind of trouble. A boy Worthless did not know was driving. Sumner pointed his chin at Worthless and said, "Hey, killah."

Worthless smiled, confused, and said, "Hey, boy. Ain't it past yo' bedtime?"

Sumner showed his teeth and said, "Soooo-wheee, piggy-piggy-pig. Soooo-wheee." The Ford idled on. Worthless was thinking about marijuana, and pills, and wondering why a boy like Sumner would be acting that kind of fool.

Then he was in Garcia's store and grabbing his *Sun*. Garcia, a Mexican who was so old, and whose shop had been on the West Side for so long, that people forgot he was Mexican, said, "Good morneen, and tha's fifteen cents." Worthless put down a quarter, like every morning, and Garcia slid back a packet of Wrigley's spearmint gum, like every morning. And Worthless noticed that the old man's hand was shaking. His woman stood behind him, a look of grave concern on her old Indian-brown face. Worthless said, "Morning, Miz Garcia," and left them.

Roscoe John was waiting for him outside Garcia's store. He pulled Worthless aside and said, "You need an alibi, I'm behind you all the way."

Worthless, a bit unnerved now, said, "Alibi for what?"

"For snuffing Jeeter."

"Jeeter is dead?"

Now Roscoe looked shocked. "You didn't kill him?"

Worthless said, "Of course I didn't kill him. Are you crazy? Who would kill a little thing like Jeeter?"

"Lots of folks would."

"Well, sure. But, who *would*? I sure as hell wouldn't."

Roscoe looked disappointed. He said, "I thought it was you. Now nobody knows."

"We'll find out. And we'd better get a funeral going, too. I don't think Jeeter had no folks, did he?"

"Nobody that'd admit it, anyhow."

"That's enough, Roscoe. Man's dead, we gotta be nice about him now. Where did he die?"

"Right there, in his place."

Worthless went there. Inside, the two men that had carted Jeeter out of the nightclub were mopping something thick and red off the floor. The carpet was stained dark. It was the very room, and the very table, where Worthless had argued with Jeeter the night before.

The two men started and jumped away from their work when he came into the room. Worthless said, "I'm sorry about your boss, boys. Can you tell me what happened?"

Only one of the boys responded, and only by shaking his head very slowly from side to side.

Worthless said, "Have the police been here?"

The same boy shook his head.

Worthless said, "We got to call 'em."

Twenty minutes later three of Lieutenant Tom Haney's best men screamed into the West Side, siren blaring, and skidded to a dusty, noisy halt in front of Jeeter's. The siren cut a horrible swath of sound through the early-morning still. That was the point. Haney told his men to use the siren, always, when they were going into the West Side. He thought it unnerved the Negroes, and he liked having the Negroes unnerved. Some men thought that your happy Negro was your manageable Negro. Haney didn't think so. A happy Negro was a Negro who was going to get himself in trouble and make trouble for someone else, too. Haney's experience had shown him that the scared Negro was far easier on his police force.

Holbrook, his brother-in-law, always said, "Just keep them in their place." Haney said, "Yes, and keep them *down*."

Today there were only Worthless and the two young men inside the bar for the siren to unnerve. The small crowd outside dispersed as soon as Haney's men rumbled out of their car. Worthless sat at the table he had shared with Jeeter the night before, and waited. He told the two young men, "Be still. Just tell the truth. Nobody can't hurt you if you tell the truth."

Bill Dawson greeted the day on his hands and knees. It was not a pretty sight. But it was the only way for him to do what had to be done. First he awoke. This was ugly. Though he made every effort and had spared no expense to minimize the horror, there it was. He awoke. The room was very dark, and still. The curtains were thick and velvety. The carpet was thick and velvety, too. The upholstery was plush. There was no sound. Dawson pushed the covers aside, and slid to the floor, and began to make his way across the carpet.

His head throbbed from deep behind his eyes. His guts churned.

His chest trembled. The room swam before him. He could scarcely breathe. He knew that when he died, he would die exactly like this— a coronary, a stroke, something, while crawling on his hands and knees to the bathroom.

Once there, as the texture changed from deep plush pile to stiff, frozen marble, Dawson skidded on his pajama knees to the toilet. The lid was up. Dawson raised his aching head over the edge of the bowl, resting his chin on the porcelain, and vomited violently. When he was finished, he gripped the edge of the bathtub, pulled himself up, steadied himself against the sink, and reached for the large tumbler that rested there in an ice bucket. It was a heavenly mixture of tropical fruit juices and tropical booze—white rum and dark rum over pineapple, coconut, banana, and orange—that his man prepared for him every single day of the week. Dawson lifted it with his two anxious hands and drank it down.

He had begun his day in exactly this way for at least the past ten years. The ritual had started when he was still making movies in Hollywood. It had continued after he came up to the desert. For the past seven years, as co-owner and president of the Thunderbird Hotel and Casino, Dawson had found that the ritual was one of only three or four things he was required to do on a daily basis. It was the only one, he felt, that he *should* be required to do: without it, nothing else would exist at all, and doing it, he felt, demanded almost more of him than you could reasonably expect of a man. But he was a man of his word, by God, and a man of honor. He had made a deal, and no one was ever going to say that Bill Dawson went south on a deal. By now, anyway, his man would have prepared a second tumbler of tropical heaven, and it would be waiting for him in the other room. Thus fortified, Dawson slid out of his pajamas and into a bathrobe hanging from the back of the bathroom door and went back into the bedroom to continue the morning ritual.

Bill Dawson, once known as "Dashing" Bill Dawson, had been a very big Hollywood star. He had started as a teenager, having run away from his San Luis Obispo ranch home before completing high school, riding and currying horses for Mack Sennett and the silents. He wasn't like the drugstore cowboys who dressed in boots and chaps and hung around in front of Schwab's and didn't know a bridle from a dog biscuit. Bill Dawson knew horses and rode better than Roy

Rogers. So he'd done some background riding for Sennett. Then he'd doubled Gene Autry on a Western. Then he'd signed on with a group that made serials, and for several years got steady work as a bad guy. But he had a falling-out with one of the producers—as was often the case for him in the early days—and lost that job. The best work he could find, for a while, was at the stables in Griffith Park. This turned into the big time. He became friendly with the wife of J. Allan Sargent, who was then a top man at Metro. She hired Dawson to train her polo ponies. He gave her all his attention. Then he met J. Allan and, after a night of muscular embraces in Sargent's stables, began to give J. Allan all his attention. J. Allan rewarded him with a contract at Metro.

Within months he did not need J. Allan Sargent anymore. Metro cast him in *Prairie Song* in 1933, over Sargent's objections. He didn't want Dawson away and on location. Sargent was overruled. And Dawson was a sensation. He was big and handsome, with wavy black hair and cornflower-blue eyes. He had a deep, commanding voice. He had originally been cast as the *Prairie Song* tenderfoot. On the third day of principal photography, the director told him to report to costume and get refitted to play Corporal Hall, the second male lead. He took the bigger part and wore it well, and got terrific notices from *Variety* and the *Herald Express*. Before the picture opened, Dawson had already done two others. Within a year he was a star.

Dawson rode the next ten years like a bucking bronco. The studio arranged dates for him. His social calendar was a whirl of the Mocambo and Ciro's and the Brown Derby. There were premieres to attend. There were pictures to make. There were endless photo shoots, making publicity stills for Metro's movies. There was fan mail to answer.

And there were men. Dawson was discreet. He'd drive down to Palm Springs or up to Lake Arrowhead. He'd sail to Catalina. He'd have someone drop by the house—a sprawling ranch-style home, with no ranch and no ranchers, that he bought in Beverly Hills—but always quietly and alone. Did the boys at Metro know? Probably. They knew everything. Did they care? Maybe. But no one ever said a word to him. He went on the dates, sat for the publicity stills, and allowed the publicity men to tell the reporters whatever they wanted about his latest conquest or his newest girlfriend or his plans to marry or where he was planning to buy an engagement ring or . . . whatever they liked. Dawson never even read it. On the odd occasion when someone actually asked him a question—it happened sometimes at Metro parties, after a premiere or something, when someone's wife who did not know any better would say, "I'm just so tickled to hear about you and Susan Stambler!"—Dawson would smile and twinkle his blue eyes and say, "Why, ma'am, you *embarrass* me." Women, for some reason, found this charming. And Dawson had discovered that if you could charm their wives, the men were very easy to handle. He kept his mouth shut and his nose clean and his private business private.

But he could not handle the drinking. Dawson had never even seen booze until he was in his very late teens. His folks did not drink. No one in the Sennett organization drank. Nor did anyone on the serials. It was not until he was at the Griffith Park stables that he began to see it. Some of the older stable hands kept bottles hidden in the stalls. They'd go for them, shakily, at various times during the day, skulking in and out and keeping it to themselves. Dawson thought they were pathetic. One afternoon a boy he thought was very handsome, a Mexican groomer named Perez, more or less made him take a swallow of rye whiskey. It burned, and Dawson choked and hated it. But it did something to his head that he liked. For a long time he was not sure whether it was Perez or the booze that excited him.

With Metro came social drinking, and he found out it was the booze. Dawson just loved drinking. With two highballs in him, there was nothing he could not do. He was taller and better looking and wittier and more masculine. His deep voice deepened. He was calm and at ease. Executives like J. Allan Sargent did not scare him, and executives' wives did not embarrass him. Dawson became himself. Every once in a while, once every four or five months, if he was not working and had no reason to exercise extreme caution, Dawson would go overboard—sometimes figuratively, and sometimes literally. He'd get those two highballs under his belt and he'd be *gone*. He'd get on the phone. He'd start making plans. Soon he and a friend were off to the desert or the mountains, or headed up the coast to some-one's place in Malibu, or down to Long Beach to someone's boat. And off they'd go, drinking and driving or drinking and sailing or drinking and flying, once or twice. It was an absolute ball, and Dawson loved it better than anything else. To be with a guy he really liked, a man he really admired and who really moved him, to be off adventuring, drinking like men and pushing a big car down the road or piloting a big boat through the water . . . Man, that was *living*.

Unfortunately, it often did not end as well as it began. About once a year or so, Dawson would wind up someplace he should not be, or did not want to be, or could not remember getting to, or could not figure out how to get away *from*. He'd wake up in a cabin by a lake, alone, and have no clue what lake it was or how he got there. He'd wake up in a hotel, with some scabby kid, and have no idea who the kid was or what hotel he was in. There would be foggy pieces of the night before, like postcards from someone else's vacation, but no real memory. And often what he did remember he did not like. A fight. An argument with a waiter. A frustrating moment with a boy. Something misunderstood and then a fight, and then tears. And then . . . a wretched morning like this one.

He'd find a phone and call Metro, and they'd get one of their studio cops to figure out where he was and go fetch him. No one ever said a word about it later. Each time, Dawson would swear this was it— this was the last time, he was going on the wagon, he was taking the pledge, he was *done*. For a few weeks he'd stay dry, and then for a few weeks he'd drink like a gent, and then . . .

Dawson finished the second tumbler of juice and booze and crossed back into the bathroom. His man had come in from the front room while Dawson was guzzling and dancing along memory lane, and started the shower. The bathroom was steamy, and as he dropped the robe and slid under the scalding water, the mirror over the sink showed a big man, still fit, past his prime but just barely. As he did every morning, Dawson said to himself, "Gotta get back into the saddle. Getting flabby. Do that today, maybe."

He had not actually been on a horse in years, if you didn't count publicity stunts for the hotel. Which was why he was in Las Vegas. Which was why he left Hollywood. By the early 1950s the drinking was pretty bad. He wasn't getting the best parts. He wasn't getting the second-best parts, either. He'd rail at his agent, and he'd rail at the guys at Metro. Dawson was bigger than that shrimp Alan Ladd and could've done *Shane* at a walk. He was better-looking than Mitchum by a mile, and a better actor than Burt Lancaster or Kirk Douglas by a mile. He had everything they had—except the career.

Wasn't he "Dashing" Bill Dawson? Evidently not. One day a Metro guy said, "No. You *used* to be 'Dashing' Bill Dawson. Now you're just another rummy. We're not renewing your contract."

The desert thing had been a fluke. Dawson had put away quite a bit of money. (One of the good things about being a rummy, he found, and maybe the *only* good thing, was the economy of it. He had no energy for hobbies. He never married or had kids. He never bought anything and never really went anywhere. He did not collect art or polo ponies or sports cars or speedboats or antiques. He owned only the one house, and it was paid for years ago. The money just accumulated.) Dawson and a friend who was an agent had gone up to Las Vegas to see this kid at the Flamingo. He was a new client for the agent, a young and very handsome singer that everyone said could be the next Sinatra. Onstage he was captivating. Offstage, as soon as he opened his mouth, Dawson knew the kid had no chance. He lisped and minced and was such a homo that Dawson almost burst into tears. All that talent! What a waste. He patted the kid on the hand and said, "You got great pipes, boy. You're going right to the top."

That night, after the show, Dawson found himself shut into a corner at the Flamingo's Stage Bar. It must've been three o'clock in the morning. Dawson was past half-crocked. An exceedingly well-dressed man with silvery gray hair and a silver-gray suit was nodding his head at everything Dawson said, and nodding at his friend the agent, too. Dawson heard himself saying, "Sick of the movies anyway. Been thinking about sticking some money in the ground up here. Yours could be just the place."

The following day, late in the afternoon, the silvery-gray gentleman, who it turned out was a very big piece of business in Las Vegas, was in Dawson's suite of rooms at the Flamingo with a couple of lawyers and a ton of paperwork. His name was Mo Weiner. By dinnertime he and Weiner had become co-owners of a beat old joint called the Thunderbird. Dawson was just about officially broke, too, when it was over. A week later he sold the house in Beverly Hills and moved into a suite at the Thunderbird. He had never, not once, looked back.

Out of the shower, standing in a world of steam and silence, Dawson moved to the sink and found the third tumbler of tropical heaven, which he knew his man would have brought in and set there while he showered. It was there. Dawson drank but a sip now. The two he'd already had were at work. His brain was coming back on. His body, cleansed of the previous night's poisons and now replenished by the juices and the shower, was his own again. He was ready for the day. He guessed without looking that it was two o'clock or so. He would be required directly after breakfast to sit with the hotel manager and sign papers and authorize purchases. He would be required at sunset to get on a horse and stand with it in front of the hotel and wave to arriving guests. He would be required at ten o'clock to go onstage to introduce the evening's entertainment. And he would require, in order to accomplish this, a vast quantity of alcohol. And at least two changes of very expensive Western clothing. Stepping out of the bathroom, he said, "Davenport: Dress me."

Deacon had stayed up late the night before. He had not intended to. He had intended to get racked around midnight, right after the second show ended. He had intended to knock down eight hours or more before rising. He wanted to get out to Shipton Wells, and he didn't want to be dragging.

That hadn't happened. The night had gone badly. His head had throbbed, the shiner seeming to actually shine under the hot bandstand lights, from the smacking it took by the pool. He was hot, too, under the lights, as if it were the noontime sun and not part of the perpetual twilight of the Starburst. The crowd was good. The band was strong. He had a tumbler of Kentucky straight bourbon whiskey underneath his seat. But it wasn't working. Midnight came and went. He was vibrating like a tuning fork.

All he wanted was to get off the stage, get quiet, get some sleep, and get out to the desert early in the morning, to make the drive to Shipton Wells and see Anita. While he was trying to think up a story to tell her about the black eye, the black eye seemed to get worse.

He was still trying to figure out what to say about the photos in the overnight bag, too, in case she asked. And she'd have to ask, if she'd looked in the overnight bag. And she'd just about have to look in the overnight bag. So far, though, she hadn't said boo. But she was quiet like that. It didn't mean she didn't know something. It meant she was a bit of a moll: she knew how to keep her eyes open and her trap shut.

And for how long? Deacon experienced the physical sensation of chest pain when he thought of her alone at the café. Was that love? It was something like love. So were some of the other things he was experiencing. For example, other girls didn't interest him much. For example, he thought of Anita first thing in the morning and last thing at night. For example, anytime anything interesting happened to him, he immediately imagined telling her about it. For example . . . he could make up examples all day. And they took him no nearer to knowing what to do about Anita.

Deacon got away from the stage and stowed his horn, then went back out to the lobby and had a double in the lounge. The buzzing in his head got louder. He gave it one more double, and went searching for Fatty Behr.

Finding him proved difficult. The small, slender supplier of the stuff that made Deacon sleep was nowhere. Deacon moved slowly past the points where Fatty ought to be, saying hello to people who could not help him, saying hello to people he did not know. Not in the lounge bar. Not in the lobby back bar. Not in the nightclub, emptying now that the music was over. Not in the pits, busying now that the night-club was closed. Deacon slid through the reception area. No.

Outside there was a commotion. News cameramen were popping flashbulbs on the Starburst driveway. Deacon saw Mo, beaming like a proud papa, off to the side. The flashes caught Deacon's eyes and made his head hurt. There was a great flash, several pops all at once, and then the big Starburst front doors swung open with a whoosh of desert heat and outdoor noise.

She was a big star already and getting bigger. She had done the fight picture with Lancaster and Douglas two years before, when the credits had read, ". . . and introducing Dorothy Baines." Nobody had to introduce her after that. She had made two or three comedies and renegotiated a contract or two. Now she was a star, taking top billing over guys just a little smaller than Lancaster and Douglas. On her arm as she blew like a zephyr into the Starburst was Steve Carter, the big-bicep muscle boy from RKO. He was a real actor, though—

that's what his talent agent and publicity man kept telling the studio—and the gossip sheets said he was playing house with Dorothy Baines, and she had said she wanted him for her next picture, and he was about to get his shot. Alexander Freidrich had cast them both in his next feature, a sort of murder mystery that was a remake of a Frank Capra comedy that itself was already a remake of a drama Lewis Milestone had made out of a Booth Tarkington short story.

Freidrich, the director, coming through the door behind Baines and Carter, wearing sunglasses against the midnight glare, appeared to click and calculate as he passed. A whippet-thin young man in a black suit stood close to him, whispering as Freidrich nodded with interest.

Behind them all was Mo, cool and gray in his muted silver suit, like a pool of bright still water in the night. He shot Deacon a quick glance, then went back to the man at his side, a squat, ugly man in a dark suit and heavy black eyeglass frames who was studying the damp end of an unlit cigar. Mo took the man's elbow and pointed at something in the back of the room. The man gazed without interest.

Then Fatty was there, coming silently up behind Deacon and slipping a small packet into his hands. He said, "Heard you were looking for me, chief."

Deacon said, "Yes. I wanted to get—"

"You got. Now git." Fatty smiled, but the tone was dismissive.

Deacon said, "What's with the stiffs from Hollywood?"

Fatty kept his eyes forward and said, "The fat guy is the head of Monolith Studios. He wants to make a casino picture. The guy in the shades is the director. He wants to make the casino picture, too, and Mo wants him to make it at the 'Bird. He's willing but he needs convincing, if you get my meaning. He likes redheads, with freckles all over, and he likes 'em in high school, and he likes two at a time. You know any redheads?"

"Not from high school."

"Then beat it. Word is that's what Dorothy Baines likes, too. More redhead chickies, and young, too. I'm busy."

Fatty went off. Mo turned the squat studio man toward the tables. Freidrich had his two stars going down into the pits, where heads were turning and the action was slowing.

Deacon ran smack into Stella.

She was overdone in turquoise, a color that did nothing for her, and there seemed to be more of her than ever. Her breasts looked enormous, and her hair rose and coiled like a wild animal. She had a lorgnette around her neck. She lifted it and peered at Deacon, and said, "Hey, honey. Borrow me for a minute, will you? I need a date."

Stella took his arm and slid into him. She got her mouth close to his ear and said with hot breath, "I want to go over to the West Side, and none of Mo's mooks will take me. Will you take me?"

Across the room, going down across the pits, Mo was holding the studio guy's arm and guiding him toward their future. The bimbo and her leading man trailed, with the director and his skinny aide-de-camp pulling up the rear. Mo raised his eyes, at that very moment, and caught Deacon squiring Stella.

And Stella said, "I know you'll take me. 'Cause I know you have a car. And I know you don't want Mo to know what you've been getting from Fatty."

Deacon stiffened. Stella patted his arm and gave him a damp smooch on the cheek, squeezing his arm just a little tighter. She said, "You're a hype, baby. Mo wouldn't understand. Guys like Mo, they don't understand. But *I* understand. So, whatta ya say?"

He said, "Sure, Stella."

Stella's eyes closed when she smiled. She gave him another smooch and said, "Get a car. I'm going to go get beautiful. I'll meet you in front."

The sun had gone down and the last bus had come and passed hours before. The light had faded. The heat had fallen. Now it was quiet and dark in Shipton Wells. Anita stood at her post by the door, looking out past the empty bus station, listening to the *ding!* of a car leaving the gas station and wondering how long she had. Customers came and went at this hour, fewer tonight, probably because it was not a weekend. The boss said she had to be ready, no matter what time it was, when someone came through the door. So there was always a pot of fresh coffee. There was always a pitcher of ice water. There was always a kitchen stocked with everything you needed to make everything on the menu.

But she had a hard time staying awake for it. She was the only waitress and the only cashier. The boss was too cheap to hire anyone else except Wally the bartender, and all Wally did was come in at night and pour drinks and clean up in the bar, and her uncle hardly paid Anita anything to start with, but he insisted that somebody be there at that door the instant a customer came through it. Anita had tried catnapping in the booths. She had tried catnapping at the counter. She'd even convinced her uncle to put a cot in the storeroom. For a week or more she had caught up with her sleep there. But her uncle got frisky and started bothering her, and Wally was always making fresh remarks, and it got to where she wouldn't go near the cot until she was afraid she would pass out unless she got five minute's rest. And then one night she did not wake up when a customer came through the door. The guy started shouting for service, her uncle got to him before she did, and that was the end of the cot.

Now she stood at the door, almost dozing, dreamy. The knotty-pine walls gleamed around her. A Coca-Cola clock over the counter said it was eleven-thirty. There was an Artie Shaw song on the radio, which she kept turned down low under the counter. It was kind of slow and romantic. She felt kind of slow and romantic. Anita pushed a lock of wavy brown hair off her biscuit-brown forehead, and sighed. Deacon was coming in to see her from town in the morning.

She honestly did not know what to do with that boy. He had been up three times already since they met. He brought her nice things— really nice things, things that cost a lot of money and things that showed her that he was really thinking about what she'd like to have. He'd brought her a beautiful Pendleton car coat with raglan sleeves, to go driving in. He'd brought her a new Capehart radio so she could listen to music she liked while she stood behind the counter. He'd brought her a little RCA Victor record player so she could listen, in her room, to some of the music he himself had recorded. It was jazzy and kind of kooky. But she hardly ever got to go stay in her room, 'cause of the boss and this nasty café.

The music changed and some guy was talking about air condition-ers and she started humming "Some Day My Prince Will Come." Deacon was a sort of prince. And she was maybe some kind of a Sleeping Beauty, under some kind of a spell, waiting to be awakened. She knew that he was in love with her. Or she thought that's what it was. He got this serious faraway look on his face. It wasn't like her uncle or the men she met in the café. They knew what they wanted, and she knew what they wanted, and that made it simple: either you gave them what they wanted, and got what you got in return, or you did not give them what they wanted, and suffered the consequences.

She'd been living around men, like that, since she was twelve. Her parents had died, long since. She had lived with her grandmother forever. But her grandmother got old and stopped making sense and couldn't take care of herself. One of her mother's sisters had come to take the grandmother away, to put her in some kind of a home. That left Anita. She already looked four or five years older than she was. Her mother's sister, who had always lived in Phoenix, did not really know how old Anita was—only that she'd been there, with the grandmother, for longer than anyone knew. She said, while she was getting Anita's grandmother's things together, "You know we're selling the house. Where will you go, *mi hija?*" And Anita had said, "I got a fella."

An hour later she was alone, for the first time in her life. She stayed for a week in the house, on her own, until the real estate agents told her that they needed it empty. She packed two small suitcases—one of them more for the things she expected to get than the things she already had, because she had almost nothing—and went to the Greyhound station.

She had a plan, sort of. There were two places in town she knew she could go. One of them was to a man who ran the pharmacy. She had done part-time work in his store. He had made his interest in her abundantly clear. She knew she could get something from him. She didn't know how, really, but she knew enough to know that it would happen. The other place was the house of a man named Morales, whom she had always called Tio Tony. He was not an uncle, Anita thought. Her grandmother never referred to him as her *tio*. But other people did. He had been related to Anita's mother somehow—a cousin or a boyfriend, or something. Growing up on the border, with all the comings and goings of a small town like Calexico, Anita had seen Tio Tony over the years. He ran a café in town, and he always had a car, and he had a snappy black pencil-thin mustache that Anita thought made him look like a movie star—like Leo Carrillo or one of those Mexican actors. He always found a way to get her alone and ask her embarrassing questions. Once he had put his hands on her, down there, and once he had taken her hands and put them on him, down there. She understood.

The Greyhound station plan did not work out. She hoped some nice man would take notice of her, then take an interest, and then take the time to listen to her story. It was a sad story. She could make it sadder. The right man would understand and take her in. Anita had big ears, and she'd been around high school boys a bit and knew what that meant. She didn't mind. She was scared of being alone and not having a place to stay. So she sat in the Greyhound station, watching and waiting. Several buses came and went. Families and single men and women, and women on their own with children, came and went. Anita was invisible. No one seemed to notice her at all.

Until it was dark. Then two policemen came in and had a quick chat with the guy behind the ticket counter. One of the cops stayed there, and the other one came over to where Anita had sat for the entire day. He was actually the older brother of a girl that Anita had gone to school with, long before, when she had still gone to school. She couldn't even remember the girl's name, but she remembered her face and remembered that she had older brothers. This one said, "Good evening," without smiling, and put his hands on his hips. He said, "I'm only going to tell you this once. Buy a ticket and get on the next bus out of here, or get on your feet and get out of town walking. I'm coming back in an hour and if you're still here, I'll arrest you on a vag charge and lock you up. Understand me?"

Anita nodded.

She went to the pharmacy. The man that ran the place was in the back room. He was very pleased to see her. She told him a little about what had happened, and he was sympathetic. He said, "My girl, what a terrible day you must have had! You should have come to me immediately. Let me just tell the boy that we're leaving. We'll get you something to eat and someplace to lie down."

The pharmacy man had taken her to his house, a dusty bungalow on the edge of town. He'd fed her soup. He kept telling her how unwell she looked. He kept saying, "Why you poor *thing*." He gave her two pills that he said would make her feel more comfortable. They made her feel very sleepy, which he said was natural, after what she had been through. Then through sleepy eyes she watched as he gave her an injection, in the thigh.

When she woke up she was no longer a virgin. The pharmacist explained in medical terms why there was bleeding and told her it would not happen ever again. That night he gave her another shot. This time she did not bleed. Within a week or so, without ever knowing exactly how she knew it, Anita knew what sex was.

A month later she took that to Uncle Tony. They'd left town together. She had been with him ever since. He still had the pencil-thin mustache. He had gained a lot of weight. Anita dreamed of doing terrible things to him—with a butcher knife, with a hammer, with a big automobile.

She dozed now, on her feet. Deacon. Deacon. Someday her prince would come. In the morning, her prince would come, bringing presents across the desert, like a wise man traveling alone to see the baby Jesus.

But when he came he would have that look in his eyes. It wasn't the look that her uncle got, once a week or so, when he came looking for her. It wasn't the look the pharmacist used to get. It wasn't any of the looks she got from the men who came into the café—the looks that said "How much?" or "What a tramp!" or "What a piece!" (There was even a look, and it was the one she hated most of all, that said, "Now isn't that a *shame*." She got that from priests and very old men and sometimes from women.) Anita knew, from practice, what all of those looks were and where all of those looks went.

With Deacon she did not know any of it. He was dreamy and sweet and he brought her stuff and he told her she was the most beautiful girl he had ever seen. She knew he'd seen a lot of girls, but from the look on his face, she knew he meant it when he said that.

But he never touched her, except to give her a kiss on the cheek when he arrived and a kiss on the cheek when he left. Someday my prince will come, she said. Sure, but he won't like girls.

The gas station went *ding!* again. Anita straightened up and looked out the door. There were two men pulling into the café parking lot. She knew that Wally would be out back, leaning against the café wall, smoking one in an endless string of cigarettes, and that she'd have to go fetch him if the men wanted to drink a cocktail. The very idea of seeing him, of having to speak with him, made her feel weary. She'd go out. She'd say, "You got some business." And he'd pull his big horse lips back over his big horse teeth and say something like

"How about you and me doing some business?" And she would smile, or frown, or remain blank, and it did not matter at all. If she were slow to retreat, he'd laugh and try to smack her on her bottom. This left her with ugly thoughts. *With a big cleaver,* she thought, *as his hand is coming out to smack me, if I cut down hard and the knife blade is moving fast . . .*

Anita patted her hair and waited for the men to come into the café.

Going down into the pits, steering Albert Sherman through the maze of blackjack, craps, and roulette tables, Mo was thinking, *Sherman. Sherman. What kind of a Jew is called Sherman?* The mogul on his arm might have been a lot of things in his life, but he was certainly never not a Jew and he was certainly not a Sherman when he was a baby. A Schumann, maybe, or a Schumacher, but not a Sherman. Mo could think only of the Union general that burned Atlanta. In the world where Mo grew up, a self-respecting Jew would not be called Sherman. He might change the name, but not to something like Sherman. But maybe that is the sort of name you need if you're going to run Hollywood. A Northern goy capable of destroying an entire city?

This guy didn't look capable of destroying anything bigger than a baloney sandwich. But he had an interesting cold-bloodedness to him. Mo was pretty good at gauging the rise and fall of temperature in a man, pretty good at reading appetites. Sherman didn't have any appetites. He was just chewing on his cigar and taking it in. Mo had heard that some of those Hollywood guys got into some pretty high-stakes poker and pinochle and bridge. This guy wasn't one of them. A real gambler, watching other gamblers, gets itchy. That will tell. But this guy might have been watching old ladies knit. And he wasn't looking at the broads, either. He was calculating something else. Money, Mo thought. That's all that's left.

He said to Sherman, over the rumble and jangle of the room, "I'm surprised we haven't seen you up here before."

Sherman shrugged and said, "It's not my kind of thing. But you're having a lot of success with it." Sherman surveyed the room around him. In view were perhaps two hundred guests—playing, moving through the tables, waiting for places at the tables, sitting at the lobby bar or the lounge bar, wandering past Registration, standing and smoking cigarettes in front of the gift shop. Sherman said, "Pretty busy night for you?"

Mo said, "What, tonight? This is dead. This is a Thursday, though. And it's early. By midnight there will be three to four times this many people here. Nothing happens in Vegas until midnight."

Sherman said, "That's impressive. And it's all a cash business. I like that."

An hour later Mo had found out that Sherman liked to eat, too. Mo had two men from the kitchen prepare a huge meal for the mogul, a meal of prime rib and Yorkshire pudding and champagne. He ate while Mo sat with a scotch and water. They talked business. Mo played Sherman like a Stradivarius.

Sherman said, "I may take a little convincing, if you know what I mean, but I think we can make an arrangement to shoot the picture in one of your casinos."

Mo said, "I'm happy to do some convincing. Whatever it takes, for here or at the Thunderbird. It'd be good for business, and I'm happy to consider making the appropriate concessions, or contributions. And I think it will make a colorful setting for your motion picture."

"We're shooting in Technicolor, you know."

"Wonderful! Too bad nothing can be done with the Ivory Coast. What a set *that* would make!"

Sherman said, "What the hell is the Ivory Coast?"

Mo said, "It's new. It's not open yet. It's going to be the hottest, raciest casino in the country. For Negroes only. Off-limits to white folks, unfortunately."

"The hell it is!" Sherman roared. "You can't make anything off-limits! That's against the damn law. I want to see it."

It was done.

It was easy. People, in fact, were always easy. All you had to do was listen to them. What they said might be complicated and what they did was often complicated, but people themselves were pretty simple. They would always tell you what they wanted if you could stand to listen to them long enough. And once they told you what they wanted, they were yours.

Mo had learned this in Chicago. Because his family was what his family was, Mo never got too far away from the family business. And the family business was crooked. But Mo had finished high school and gone to college, where he had received a little education and a lot of panache and polish. After that, no one could think of sending him around on the usual stuff. So the family, along with several of the other families, put Mo in charge of a string of restaurants and nightclubs around the city. The hub of it was Allen's Steak House, on Riverside Drive. The city pols, the ward heelers, and the bigwigs all went there to eat and drink and carouse. The cops, never. Mo got a reputation for getting done what needed to get done. If a guy needed to get another guy a broad, Mo served. If a guy needed to set up a high-stakes poker game, Mo served. If a guy needed to buy a dealer or a couple of players to rig that poker game, Mo served. And he did it all with remarkable aplomb. No one had to tell him anything. No one had to say, "I need you to fix a poker game so we can rob this guy," or, "I want a big blonde with a big chest who will do anything I ask her to do." Mo understood, from listening, when a man said something like "There's this guy in from Seattle that wants a game" or "I bet a broad like *that* could be a lot of laughs." And he made it happen.

Later, after Capone had wrecked Chicago and gone to prison and the family was falling apart and looking for new places to put its business interests, Mo had taken the money west and stuck large amounts of it in the desert. It wasn't officially the family business anymore. Mo wasn't officially in the family anymore. He had broken with them, during the war, when he had gone into the service. With Capone having ruined the rackets, the family, Mo's father in particular, had insisted that Mo stay out of the fight and stay home. With the family's political connections, this was as easy as a phone call. Mo wouldn't make the call. He said to his father, "Shame on you. You know what the Krauts are doing over there. Shame on you." And he walked out.

His father, who believed that family was first, last, and always, never spoke to Mo again. That was the only time in his adult life, in fact, that Mo could not listen and know what someone wanted. His own father, and he had no idea what the old man wanted.

By the end of the war, Mo was gone. Chicago was history. He was a retired officer and a veteran at thirty-five years old. He had invested smart. He had a lot of dough. Bugsy and the others were setting up in the desert. Mo waited, organized, planned, and schemed. In 1950, only four years after Bugsy opened the Flamingo, Mo opened the Starburst. Two years later he was remodeling and reopening the Thunderbird. Now he had the Ivory Coast coming. And he was going to get all the free publicity in the world for it, out of this short, squat, stinky, cigar-chomping creep from Hollywood.

He said, "I can make this happen for you, Mr. Sherman."

Sherman grinned past the cigar and said, "Call me Sherry."

The week before, Deacon had been to the hospital to visit the dealer he had allegedly beaten to a pulp. His name was Fitzgerald, and he was in Valley View Medical. Deacon had not gone on his own. It was none of his business, and it didn't interest him. But one morning Mo had caught him sitting at the lobby back bar. He was nursing a whiskey and soda, the last in a series of many, many cocktails he had consumed. He'd been with a couple of girls from Santa Barbara at the beginning of the evening. They were friends of a sax player he knew from Los Angeles; they'd come in for some high times and gambling, so they'd looked him up. They were stale and dull, a couple of over-worked broads in too much makeup, and he'd ditched them after an hour or so. Then he'd hooked into some characters from the Starburst band, and they were headed over to the Desert Inn. Once there, someone had said, "This place is strictly for garlics." And they'd all agreed and piled back into someone's car and gone over to the West Side. LaVern Baker was there, at Mamie's, singing "Jim Dandy" and going wild.

Deacon had stayed over on that side of town until after dawn, then crawled home to the Starburst lobby bar. Now he was just fizzing down, getting back down to size, when Mo sat and ordered a tomato juice.

He said, "Put some Tabasco in it, will you?" When the bartender turned away, he said, "I need a favor."

So Deacon went to the hospital.

It was hard to see the dealer inside his bandages. His head was a big cotton wad, with eyes somewhere in there. Deacon wouldn't have known him even if he'd known him, and he didn't think he did.

He said, "Hey, pal. How's it going?"

The dealer said, "Mmmmph-war."

Deacon said, "That's good. Mo and the folks at the Starburst wanted me to drop by and see how you were doing. And give you this. It's a little cash. And the hospital bill is taken care of. Mo feels pretty bad about what happened. He blames himself. He doesn't want there to be any hard feelings. Or any gossip."

The dealer rolled his eyes, and said, "Ar-kor."

Deacon said, "That's good. As long as we all understand each other. Mo says maybe he can fix you up with some work when you graduate from this place. He'd like you to look him up—first thing, when you leave here. What he doesn't want is for you to go around town look-ing for work, or even talking to people, *before* you go see him. You get that part?"

The dealer nodded his head.

Deacon said, "Good. And I'm sorry. This thing musta hurt pretty bad."

The dealer nodded again. His eyes, piglike inside the bandages, looked wet.

Deacon said, "Yeah. It was that guy Floyd, huh?"

The dealer stopped nodding. His piggy eyes now looked scared.

Deacon said, "Forget it. I'm just blowing. Remember what I said about visiting Mo. It's the only smart play you got."

The dealer nodded again as Deacon was going.

Deacon got back to the Starburst near noon. He'd been up and running, one way or another, for more than twenty-four hours. He knew he should go see Mo. He didn't have the strength. He shot back to the lobby bar, but Sloan had clocked out. A midday bartender whose name Deacon didn't know fixed a disapproving eye on Deacon as he sat and slumped.

He said, "Can I help you?"

Deacon said, "Whiskey and water. Not too much water."

The bartender said, "You sure about that? You look like you might've had enough."

Deacon said, "Save the sermon. Make the drink. Or don't. But don't talk to me."

The bartender shrugged and made the drink, and overcharged him. Deacon made a mental note to get the jerk fired when he spoke to Mo. He guzzled the drink, stiffed the bartender, and went to his room and slept.

When he awoke—with not enough time to shower, shave, dress, eat, and make the rehearsal—he made time to go see Mo. He'd forgotten about the bartender. Mo wasn't in his office, anyway. Deacon told his secretary to tell her boss that Deacon had taken care of the thing with the guy. The secretary didn't look as if it would ever occur to her to ask for more information. She smiled and said, "I sure will."

Haney arrived at his office at the police station after midnight. This was true every night of the week. No matter what else was going on. Haney had usually, as he had tonight, hit two or three spots and looked into two or three things. He'd been out since mid-afternoon, one of his men driving while he made his rounds. He'd get a haircut or a manicure first. Then he'd get a late lunch. He might visit the foundation offices if there was a donation to attend to. Then he'd be on the phone to the station house. At dusk he usually began his police business.

Tonight that had included seeing two casino managers who wanted to make donations to the foundation—at least one of whom was hoping Haney did not know, or did not ask, about the broads he was working in his rooms at the hotel connected to his casino. This was an empty hope. Haney had put several of the broads onto the job in the first place, and no one in Las Vegas moved a chippie anywhere without him knowing about it. He was also going to visit a jewelry store that had gotten robbed and, after dinner, make a stop on the West Side to see about this character Jeeter.

Cops had been sitting on the place all day. Haney had seen photographs of the victim. He had read statements from witnesses. It was pretty tidy police work, in the end. He visited the crime scene, too, just to say he had and also to make sure that the work that preceded all the police work was also tidy.

It didn't matter. There was nothing there to connect anybody to anybody. There was a dead nigger on the West Side. Holbrook would be pleased.

Haney's office looked like a crime museum. There was a big, wide desk with all the usual desk stuff on it in the middle of the room, with a pair of matching leather club chairs facing it and a pair of matching cabinets against the wall. The decor was strictly cops and robbers. The walls were covered with cop mementos, each exhibit a testimonial to Haney's history as a policeman.

In one black-framed box on the wall was a foot-long, serrated hunting knife. Below the knife was a small black-and-white mug shot of a bright-eyed Negro. Below the photograph was written, "Rodney Sweet used this knife to behead his wife in June 1947." Below that, the word EXECUTED.

Next to that box was another one. In it was a wrinkled, yellowed severed ear. Below the ear was a publicity photograph of a brassy blond showgirl. Under her photograph was written, "The ear Loretta Wallace cut off Allie Skink for ransom money in August 1951." Next to that: EXECUTED.

In other boxes were bloodied vials of prescription pills, rusty straight razors, nooses, knives of every description, and many pistols. There were gleaming German and Italian handguns, American Smith & Wessons, a pair of pearl-handled Colts, and a few crude handmade weapons fashioned out of pot metal. Each weapon was set next to a photograph of its owner or victim. The word EXECUTED appeared often.

Haney came into the room hatless and raging. There was a new assistant D.A. coming over, a guy named Filcher. He had been given the Jeeter murder. Without consulting Haney, he had sent two of Haney's guys to pick up a retired boxer named Worthless Worthington Lee. They had grabbed Lee and stuck him in the tank, and Filcher had already spoken to him. Haney was furious. Coming into the room, he told one of his guys, "Go get that rookie bastard and bring him here now. Then we'll talk to this Lee."

Haney knew Worthless, or knew enough to think he knew Worthless. Big nigger, old boxer, made some dough investing in the mines and real estate, and now he's going to open that spade casino. (Haney had already joked to his men that the decks of cards they'd use at the tables would all be in one black suit. Spades. No hearts or diamonds or clubs. His men had not laughed.) He knew Worthless played it pretty straight over on the West Side. He didn't run hookers or dope. He wasn't looking to run hookers or dope into this new joint. As far as Haney knew, he was on the up-and-up.

Unlike that little creep Jeeter. He was a whole different story. He was already into hookers and had been trying to get in on the dope racket. He had not listened when he was told that this was a terrible idea, that the dope racket was all sewn up already, and that there was no room for another guy running broads. Jeeter had told the two men who went to talk to him about this that they'd better mind their own business and stay out of his. He said he wasn't interested in Haney or Haney's ideas about broads or dope on the West Side. He said he wasn't interested in making any damn contribution to Haney's damn foundation, either. He said, "Now get out of my club, or there's gonna be trouble."

Haney, remembering that, said out loud, "You got that right."

The D.A. was young and tall and smooth. He came into the room wearing a suit that cost five times what a cop earned in a month and a superior look that gave Haney a stomachache. Filcher was . . . what? Irish? The kid didn't look like a Mick. Kraut, maybe. Or mutt. Nobody was what they appeared to be anymore, anyway. Used to be you could see a guy and hear his name and know what the story was. Now . . .

Haney said, "Filcher, is it? Sit."

The young man smiled and turned his back on Haney to look at a photograph of six dead men slumped over a blackjack table, the blood from their head wounds pooling on the felt. He said, "Isn't *that* charming? I'm surprised you get any work done in this room. But then you start rather late . . ."

Haney said, "Get used to it. You want to see me, this is when you see me. State your business."

Haney sat and flipped open a folder on the West Side killing. Filcher smiled and, daintily, sat on the arm of one of the leather club chairs.

"It looks pretty straightforward. The deceased argued with the suspect the night before his murder. A business disagreement. The suspect threatened the deceased. Open-and-shut."

"Eyewitnesses?"

"No."

"Prints?"

"Nothing yet."

"You got nothing."

"We might get a confession. I understand you have a pretty good track record in that department."

Filcher smiled that smile again. Haney wanted to puke. What a punk! Still, useful. Imagine a fresh D.A., here in his office, promising an open-and-shut case and almost telling him to extract a confession. What a world!

He said, "I'll have a go. He looks like a pretty tough customer, though."

"I'm sure you'll do just fine," Filcher said.

Filcher rose from the arm of the club chair, smoothed the front of his suit, and then snapped the crease back into the front of his trousers. "And if not, I'm sure you can simply plant some evidence or obtain some eyewitnesses or pervert justice in some other similarly expedient way, eh, Haney? Isn't that the way you do it here?"

"Get out," Haney said.

Filcher laughed a high musical laugh as he left.

Haney said, "Let's go down and see this guy."

Worthless Worthington Lee had been in jail before. Not much, but enough. It did not frighten him the way it had when he was younger. He'd been in the tank three or four times on the vag, before he took up boxing, and he'd been arrested once after a guy he'd fought had died, a day later, after Worthless had left town. Once, he and all the men who sat waiting for work in the Oakland alley had been swept into paddy wagons and taken downtown. Worthless never knew why.

This time he knew why. Everyone said Jeeter this and Jeeter that, and it all had his name on it. Jeeter must've told ten people that he'd been threatened. Worthless felt like a big old fool. There was people you could threaten and people you could not threaten. If you didn't know which was which and you guessed the wrong way, it was a world of trouble every time. And Worthless had not known and he'd guessed the wrong way, and here he was. He was calculating: *If I call a lawyer now, I look like a bum and these cops are gonna get sniffy on me. If I stay in here overnight and make a call in the morning, Dina's gonna be on her own and that means trouble. If I call Levy now, or Adamson, they can get me off this hook by nighttime. But not for a murder . . .*

Haney came down the hall with two plainclothes cops and two more in uniform. The detective gave Worthless the creeps. He was small and pale and had incredible eyes—blank almost, as though they were made of water, or mercury. They made Worthless nervous. He liked to look a man in the eye. He didn't want to look at this man at all. He'd seen him around, and he didn't like what he saw. Haney's men threw open the cell door, and the lieutenant came in and sat down.

He said, "Spill it."

Worthless said, "Mister Haney, I got nothing to spill."

Haney said, "Come on."

Worthless said, "I got nothing. I didn't do nothing, and I don't know nothing, and I got nothing to say."

Haney smiled and said, "Sure you do. You just need a little warming up."

It was after one o'clock. Deacon had waited forever for Stella to get herself beautiful. She'd left him in the lobby and gone upstairs. Deacon had gone to see about a car. Then he'd used Fatty Behr's stuff and done what he had needed to do. For the past thirty minutes, he had sat nodding and grinning, slumped down in one of Mo's big old gangster cars in front of the Starburst. It was a Buick, a brutal black monster that sounded like thunder. Now he sat with the motor off, his hands in his lap and his eyes roaming around the skyline. The lights of the Starburst rose like fireworks and left smoking shadows as they passed crisscrossing above him. Headlights and taillights strolled hand in hand down Las Vegas Boulevard, carrying carloads of revelers. Music filled the air, Someone's radio was playing Prez Prado's "Cherry Pink and Apple Blossom White." It made Deacon think of the way Louis Jordan and his Tympany Five did "Caldonia." He squeezed off a salvo of that in his head. "Caldonia! Caldonia! What makes yo' big head so hard?"

Then Stella was there, a cloud of scent blowing in on the passenger side of the car as two doormen escorted her into the big black car. Deacon roused himself and fired the thing to life and let it roar for a minute. Stella eyed him with interest. The engine screamed. Stella said, "You want to take your foot off the starter, big boy?"

Deacon lifted his foot and the car quieted down. He dropped the clutch and eased the Buick out onto the Strip, and headed for the West Side.

Stella said, "So very hot and dry here tonight," as if that were a new idea. Deacon did not answer. It had been hot and dry here for a while, he reckoned, and that probably was not going to change. She said, "I mean, more so than usual, even." And Deacon said nothing some more. Stella said, "Quiet, too. Cat got your tongue?" Deacon smiled and tried to say, "Meow," but it came out more like "mmmmyo." Which did not make any sense, but it shut her up.

Without thinking about it much, Deacon got the car over past Bonanza and skidded down under the railroad tracks and turned up Jackson Street. A block on, there was life. From one block of sandy desert to the next, there was suddenly a crowd. Folks were on the sidewalk and spilling into the street. Neon blinked. Horns blared. Deacon drove up past two or three joints where in the past he had gone to drink and jazz it up. Tonight he was guessing Mamie's Black Bottom would be more like the right place.

It was. There came from the front door two snappy young men. One got the door open for Stella, and the other came around for Deacon, who pressed a five-dollar bill and the car keys into his hands. He said, "This is Mo's wagon. Don't bang it up." The kid looked like he knew what that meant.

And then the front door was open and a cauldron of red-hot jazz spilled out onto the sidewalk. Deacon took Stella's elbow and steered her inside.

Must've been thirty couples on the dance floor. Another sixty couples were jammed around little tables. Rows of heads and hats stood two deep at the bar and lined up along the walls. The air was sweet and smoky and hot like a steam room. From the little raised bandstand came the sound of Benny Carter's "Slow Freight," the way Carter used to do it with Coleman Hawkins. A waiter came swooping by with a tray of drinks over his head. Another came right behind. The second one said, "Cocktails moving. Get *out* my way." Deacon squeezed Stella's elbow a little tighter and leaned down to her ear. He said, "I see a little spot down on the right side, there," and began steering her. He knew she could not see a thing without those glasses of hers—even if the room had been lit, even if the smoke cleared, even if the joint were not jammed full of bright black faces. Deacon saw that theirs were the only white ones in the room.

Someone said, "Say, Crush!" as he passed. Deacon turned and got a wave from a drummer whose name he did not remember. With him was a singer he knew named Natalie Something, who was really a waitress at one of these West Side joints but had a wonderful voice. And at the table next to them, now that he looked, Deacon saw a pair of horn players, brothers from San Francisco he'd jammed with some other night. One of them raised his hat slightly and grinned, while his brother cocked his hand like a pistol and started firing.

Deacon got them to an empty spot, which then turned into a seat at a table, and then turned into two. They sat. The swoopy waiter came around and took a cocktail order. Deacon pushed his hat way back on his head and opened the front of his sport coat. The music sounded like heaven. That go-round of music ended, there was some wild applause and a shouting out for something, and the band started in again.

Onstage were the Five Dollar Bills. The original Five Dollar Bills had all been cats named Bill, including the leader, whose name was Bill Williams and who was called Double Bill. He was the only Bill left in the band. Whenever he was in town and Deacon showed up, he'd ask Deacon to come and jam a little. Bill called him Chet. Deacon was not bothered by this. Being mistaken for Chet was not so bad. Being mistaken for Chet as a player was not so bad at all. He'd corrected Double Bill the first two or three times, and then he'd let it go. Double Bill always wanted him to jam, and he was a beautiful player. And if sometimes he said, "Give a little hand for Mr. Chet Baker," when Deacon sat down, well, so what? He wasn't going to embarrass Chet Baker any.

Tonight it was three guys Deacon had never seen before who came up to the table. Two of them leaned down to Stella and one to Deacon. That one said, "Bill says why'n't you come and play a little?" Deacon said, "I got no horn, man." And the guy said, "We get you a horn. You come up after the next number?" And Deacon had looked at Stella. He'd planned on asking her if she minded. One look at her face answered the question. She was batting her eyelids and squeezing the hand of one of the other two guys. Deacon said, "Sure, man. You say when."

They said when a little while later. Double Bill leaned into a microphone and said, "My friend from the Starburst orchestra, the man they call Deacon, the man with the horn they call Crush Velvet, come on up here *now*." There was a little scatter of applause, a little hint of recognition. Deacon saw, too, a little hint of "check out the white boy," but maybe that was only his imagination. You heard so much of the other side of that—"Get that nigger out of my nightclub," say—that it was hard not to imagine it swinging both ways. Not tonight? Not tonight. He hit the stage and someone handed him a horn, he said hello to the guys there, and then Double Bill said, "How about 'A Foggy Day' in A?" and the drummer clacked three times on the side of his snare and they were off.

Deacon tried to do several things at once. He tried to listen and he tried to play and he tried to keep his eye on Stella. The music was bigger than the rest of it, though. He did not keep his eye on Stella. Or, not for long. Somewhere in the second chorus he started hearing the music better, and he closed his eyes, and he soloed a bit, and then he watched Double Bill do the most amazing things for a verse or two, and then the trombone player took off for a bit, and then it came back around for the coda, and Deacon was smiling like a fool and he suddenly realized that Stella was not where he had left her and had not been there for some time. Then the song ended and there was a lot of applause and someone shouted out, "Crush Velvet Deacon," and Double Bill said, "That's right," and gave him a big smile, and Deacon thought, *And so what? Let Stella be Stella . . .*

It didn't wash.

He found her about thirty minutes later. He worked the doorman and he worked the bartender and he worked some of the guys in the band. Finally he put together a few facts: Stella had been sitting with a man named Robinson, and they might have left together, and there might be a set of bungalows about three blocks from Mamie's that did a pretty brisk late-night hot-pillow business. Deacon fortified himself with a double and set out.

The night was dry and still, and the stars seemed not even to twinkle. They shone, close and clear. Deacon got moving up Jackson Street. It was two o'clock, and things were quieter. The nightclub run by that guy Jeeter was closed. The bar across the street from it was doing big business. The man that sold ribs and chicken had taken his cart home.

Deacon found the bungalows. They were stucco jobs set at the back of a gravel parking lot. Each one had a yellow porch light. None had light coming from inside. There did not appear to be a manager's bungalow or a registration office. Deacon stood in the middle of the gravel lot, listening. Coming from one bungalow at the back was a high-pitched whine. Deacon moved toward that. As he got closer, the whine began to sound human. And then it sounded female. And then it sounded like a whine of pleasure. Deacon got very close, standing almost on the bungalow porch. A voice he knew was Stella's said, "Oh *God*. Oh *Jesus*."

Deacon sat on the porch and lit a cigarette. Stella moaned and called for her maker. Deacon smoked. Stella thrilled. Deacon waited. It was half an hour. Nonstop whining and moaning. It was another half an hour. Nothing but that voice: "Oh *God*." Deacon smoked. His watch said three-thirty.

That was enough. Deacon rose and knocked three times on the bungalow door, and said, "Stella. It's time."

There was silence, and then a new moan, a low moan that might have come from Stella's partner. A full minute of silence followed. Then the door flew open and Stella was there, smoothing her dress, smashing her hair into shape. The bungalow was dark behind her. She pulled the door closed.

She said, "Did I bring a pocketbook?"

Deacon said, "No."

Stella said, "Okay. Then how 'bout taking me home?"

It was half past four when Deacon hit the sack. He told himself that he would sleep for three hours, rise, and then run to Shipton Wells and Anita.

Some hours earlier they had moved Worthless from the cell to an interview room upstairs. It was a blank, white room with a metal table and three metal chairs, two on one side, one on the other. There was a two-way mirror on one wall. There were two metal ashtrays on the table. The linoleum floor was stained and chipped. Worthless thought he could make out bloodstains on the walls as well. But this might have been his imagination. It was two o'clock in the morning. He had not eaten any supper. He was tired.

Haney and his men had come and gone several times. They had asked the same questions several times, and several times had made the same threats. Worthless was their man for the Jeeter killing. They knew he was the man for it, and they had the stuff to make it stick. If he told them the truth, they could make it better for him. They could make it an argument, with Jeeter pulling a gun or a knife, and it could wind up second-degree murder or even manslaughter. If he did not tell them the truth, they could make it worse for him. They could make it premeditated, and Worthless running Jeeter out of business so he would have the West Side to himself, and it could wind up first-degree murder and the electric chair.

It wasn't working, but by midnight Worthless was beginning to get scared. He was thinking, *Well, why not? No witnesses, looks like. My alibi is a rummy old broad who doesn't hardly know her own name. Jeeter being dead is good for my business. These white cops are willing to say anything they need to say to close me down. I'm big and Jeeter was little and I used to be a fighter. And I got money. A big nigger with money? If I was a white man in Las Vegas, I'd call it first-degree murder.*

Worthless had some angles to work, but he didn't like them much. He could bring Mo in. That might embarrass Mo, might even mess up Mo's business, which was none of Worthless's business, but that would be very bad for Worthless's business. He could get, through Mo or on his own, a hotshot trial lawyer. Maybe. But a court trial would take months and, even if he got off, would wreck everything about the Ivory Coast. Levy and Adamson were both smart men, and they could probably do anything that could be done, once it got to a trial. But it was sort of all over by then. Someone would drag Dina into court. Worthless did not think he had the stomach for that. He crossed his arms over his chest and let his head drop. Maybe a minute or two of sleep.

At two-thirty Haney's stooges came back into the room. The lighter of the two, a curly-haired fat guy, said, "Lieutenant Haney is getting plenty tired of this, Lee." The other guy, a dark-haired guy with a nose pressed flat against his face, said, "He's *plenty* tired. He's mad as hell, too. I think it's time for you to fess up. Otherwise, I think this is going to get ugly. You are going to get hurt, and bad, nigger."

Worthless decided then. He said, "Tell Lieutenant Haney I got something to say to him. I got to say it to him alone. Tell him I'm ready."

The two cops left in a hurry. Worthless composed his thoughts. He would have to do this with Haney all by himself. He would have maybe fifteen or twenty seconds. He'd have one chance. If he got it wrong, Haney would probably kill him. If he did not get Haney alone, the other two cops would kill him. If Worthless did it in front of the two cops, though, Haney would *have* to kill him. What if the other cops were watching through the two-way mirror? Worthless would have to risk that Haney was smart enough to see this coming. He'd have to risk that Haney was smart enough to protect himself.

Haney came in. He looked tired. Red eyes. Hat gone. He smelled of tobacco and something else—scotch maybe, or cognac. He looked calm, though. He did not look afraid. He came into the room and left the door open behind him.

Worthless said, quietly, "You'd best close the door. What I got to say is only for you."

Haney grinned at this. He said, "Really? You've got a secret?"

Worthless said, "It's the only way I can tell the truth and finish this."

Haney said, "All right, then." He stuck his head out the door, smiling, and said, "Man says we got to do this private-like. You boys throw the switches off and give me a minute. If it gets violent, you come on in and rescue the big nigger."

Haney sat in one of the metal chairs across from Worthless. He looked amused. Worthless was very frightened. One chance. One way out. The slimmest of chances it would work.

He took a deep breath and looked down at his shoes. Then he dragged his gaze off the floor and looked straight into Haney's eyes. He said, "I know about the orphans and your foundation. I know what it does. I know what *you* do. I told one other person, case anything happened to me. I'm sorry, 'cause it's none of my business, and I don't want to make it any of my business. But I did not kill that boy Jeeter."

Haney kept smiling for a bit. The smile tightened, then sickened, then went away. He had his eyes on Worthless's eyes the whole time. He did not look away. A little color came into his cheeks. He was very still. Worthless felt light-headed, tight-chested. He could hear Haney's wristwatch ticking. It was like listening to the count, like lying flat out on the canvas and watching the lights swing and sway above him, and the referee standing over him, and the crowd like a calliope. Then Haney's face snapped shut. The light went out of his eyes.

Haney stood and went to the door. He opened it and leaned out, and the two cops came right to him. He said, "Cut him loose," and left. Only then did Worthless begin to sweat. His face was suddenly bathed. He rose unsteadily to his feet. The two cops stared at him. One moved down the hall after Haney. Worthless heard him say, "I told you to cut him loose. So cut him loose."

Thirty minutes later he was back on the West Side. Coming up Jackson Street, his head and feet aching miserably, he almost stepped on that boy Deacon, who was sitting on a cinder-block wall outside of Mamie's Black Bottom. Worthless said, "Hey. What you doing on my side of town?"

Deacon said, "Just doggin', Worthless. You know about a joint along here somewhere that a man can take a woman with no one asking whose woman she is?"

Worthless said, "That be Angel's place, I imagine. It's up a block and over a block that way. But you look like you on y'own."

"I'm solo, Worthless."

"Then you got to go to Aunt Betty's."

"Whussat?"

"Aunt Betty runs the high-end joint. That's where the *white* women at. Cost you a couple a bucks, but they say it's worth it."

Deacon shook his head and said, "No, man. I'm not *looking* for a woman. I mean, I'm looking for one, but it's one I was with before, y'see."

Worthless said, "I see. Well, maybe it's like I said. You got to go to Angel's place. You gotta take a woman with you, though. Angel don't supply no women."

Deacon laughed and said, "I *got* the woman, Worthless. I just lost her for a minute."

Deacon went up the road. Worthless walked on, and then he was back at his own house and inside and getting his shoes and jacket off. He did not think he had ever been this tired, even after a fight. Maybe after working the mines. Maybe not even then. This felt worse, for sure.

Dina was pacing, the clink of her glass like a bell tolling. She mumbled at Worthless as he came into the kitchen, and he said,

"Yeah, it is late. I got held up with this thing. Now I guess I'm gonna take a bath."

Dina mumbled again and shuffled off. Worthless heard the bath-water start running, and started thinking "What if?" What if what he knew about Haney wasn't true? What if Worthless was the only man Haney would have to kill to protect his secret? What if Haney had not believed Worthless had told someone else? What if Haney had said, "Who did you tell?" Worthless, feeling shaky and empty and very lucky, got undressed and went off to the bath. He eased into the hot water and listened to Dina clink back and forth across the living room.

Five

THE MAIN MEN of the town met monthly in a private ball-room off the Strip, in the basement of the Overland Hotel. The meetings had been going on for years. Holbrook and Seligman had started it. In about 1949 they had held a secret breakfast meeting. Their sole topic of discussion was Marquez, the Mexican who had made a bucket in uranium and now was planning to open something he would call the Zanzibar Hotel and Casino, at the far western end of the Strip. Seligman was outraged. Holbrook had said, "He's got a pile of dough, and he's serious." Seligman had said, "I don't care. The last thing we need is a bunch of Mexicans running around our town. You've seen Tijuana. All that racetrack and bullfight crap. And those donkey bars." Holbrook said, "That's not what he's planning to do here." Seligman said, "That's not what they planned for TJ, either. It just happens, with Mexicans. They're not like us. This Marquez has got to go."

Seligman had won the argument. He had a group of toughs fire-bomb the Zanzibar and beat up some of Marquez's men a week before it opened. But Marquez was heavily insured. He made a fortune off the fire. And a week later three brown-skinned men who were never identified, never caught, and never seen again marched into Seligman's office at the Trocadero. They shot his receptionist, two security men, his personal assistant, and a room-service waiter who was serving coffee. All five of them died as Seligman watched. One of the killers smiled at him while putting a final round into the waiter's back.

The second meeting was between Holbrook, Seligman, and Marquez. It was held in the basement of the Overland Hotel. The walls there were flocked and the furniture was red velvet. It looked like a bordello, which, in fact, years before, it had been. Grotesque chandeliers hung from the ceiling. Holbrook thought of dancers with short skirts, and the music of the can-can rang in his head.

The meeting had been held more or less monthly since. In time came other men, all of them hotel and casino owners. Mo Weiner was invited to join six months before the Starburst opened. He had his bona-fides from Chicago, and people in the desert knew his people there. Before and after him had come men like Hackberry and Truxton, Williams and Houck and Prewitt and Wingate.

They were the men who had built the city in the desert. When Holbrook and Seligman had first come to town, there was no town. Las Vegas was a dusty sandbox. It was 448 miles to Reno, and 290 miles to Los Angeles—almost the definition of the middle of nowhere. There was a Union Pacific train station. There was Greyhound service. There was no airport. There was no Nellis Air Force Base, so there was no atomic-bomb testing. There was no Bugsy Seigel, so there was no Flamingo and no gangsters. Downtown's Fremont Street had a few casinos and hosted the annual Helldorado Day—the city's chief claim to fame—which included a rodeo, a beauty pageant, and a beard-growing contest. It was strictly Hicksville. Not even the electricity from Hoover Dam stopped in Las Vegas.

That all started changing in the forties. The Air Force put the base there, at Yucca Flats. Suddenly there were servicemen who wanted to spend some money on the weekend and were looking for illicit ways to do it. Then Roy Rogers and Dale Evans made that movie *Heldorado*. (The censors made them change it from *Helldorado*.) Then the El Rancho Vegas opened up, offering rooms at four dollars a night and desert horseback riding in the moonlight and outdoor breakfasts and barbecues—and gambling. The Hotel Last Frontier followed shortly after. Then Bugs and the Hollywood crowd showed up. Holbrook and Seligman had wandered in and started making money, and stayed and became rich.

The silver-haired, sixty-year-old Holbrook was the unelected but undisputed dean of the organization. He was not the richest or the oldest, or the biggest or the most powerful. He was certainly not the smartest. But he'd got there first, along with Seligman, and compared with his squat, simian, blunt-fingered colleague, he was tall and urbane and senatorial. When Seligman spoke, men argued. When Holbrook spoke, men listened and tended to agree. Even this cantankerous group of men, none of whom saw one another socially outside these breakfast meetings, and any one of whom would have gladly attended any other's funeral, listened and tended to agree. That was partly because Seligman always called Holbrook on the telephone, early on the morning of the breakfast, and told him exactly what he expected him to say. And it was partly because someone had to lead and someone had to keep the peace, and Holbrook could do it. His brother-in-law was Thomas Haney, the police lieutenant who was the law in Las Vegas. That made Holbrook seem even more senatorial. A phone call from Holbrook to Haney, a thumbs-up or a thumbs-down, could mean the difference between staying open and shutting down. Staying open was how you got rich and stayed rich. And rich was how you exerted power.

After preliminary comments concerning a few city council matters that required attention and a reminder that details of the breakfast meeting not leave the basement of the Overland Hotel, Holbrook said, "Gentlemen, I give you Pinchus Seligman."

Two of the casino operators looked at each other and said, "Pinchus?" The others gave the man their attention.

He said, "We got a problem developing on the West Side. We've talked about it before. I thought we had a way to make it disappear. It didn't disappear. I'm talking about this Ivory Coast."

There was a little buzz around the table.

Seligman said, "I'm talking about the *shvartzer* boxer who's building this casino for niggers only. Like we discussed a few months ago, I thought we could make it tough on him if we just took everyone we knew and squeezed 'em by the nuts a little—the banks, the insurance people, the drivers, the liquor guys, and so on. It's not working. The *shvartzer* has got lots of dough, from somewhere, and he's buying his way through everyone we know."

Houck, a small, hostile man with a bristle-brush haircut, said, "I don't understand the problem. It's a casino for the coloreds. Who gives a rat's ass about that?"

Prewitt, Houck's immediate neighbor on the Strip and a man who hated Houck passionately, said, "Perhaps Mister Houck, being *Canadian* and all, hasn't seen what the Nigra can do to a place. We got 'em in Dallas. We *know* what the Nigra can do to a place."

"But it's the West Side," the casino veteran Wingate said. "It's a mess already. It's always been a mess."

Prewitt said, "That mess'll spread. The Nigra is like the kudzu vine. You let it in, it will take over."

Seligman said, "It's already in. That's the point. This guy has got the money, and he's buying the muscle. Alls I want to know is, where is the money coming from?"

Mo Weiner was very aware, at that moment, of who was and who was not looking in his direction. No one appeared to be looking in his direction. Or rather there were eyes looking around the room, sweeping one to the next, as at a poker table, but no one was stopping and resting on him. He decided to stare at Houck. No one liked the Canadian. Maybe suspicion ought to fall there.

Houck said, "I'd bet on Dawson."

Marquez laughed and said, "That old rummy? Are you kidding? He's barely keeping open himself. How could he afford to bankroll someone else?"

Wingate said, "You know who's behind Dawson. There is plenty more where that comes from."

Marquez said, "Those hardballs from Los Angeles? You guys don't really believe that, do you? Dawson got no connections. Believe me, I *know* Los Angeles. Dawson got no friends in Los Angeles."

Houck said, "It doesn't matter. We got to do something about this Ivory Coast."

Mo saw his moment. He said, "I say let it open and see what happens. I think it's going to be very good for us all."

There was silence around the table. Seligman, who dreamed of the day he could spit on Mo Weiner's grave, said, "How do you figure that?"

Mo said, "We've all got these colored people working for us. They're running our kitchens and the laundries. Without them, we got no cooks, no busboys, no maids, no dishwashers, no janitors, no groundskeepers. Without them, we have to find someone else to do all that crap. Who are we gonna get? We can't afford to pay white people to do the work. So, the colored people got us by the balls—if they ever wake up and realize that."

The group stared.

Mo said, "So far they're not awake. It's quiet. But you know what's happening in Alabama and Mississippi. That's what's going to happen here. Not right away. But it's coming. The Negroes are angry, and they're right, and if we don't give them some kind of a break they're going to kill us all."

The group stared. Seligman started to speak. Mo raised his hand.

He said, "So, we appease them. Give them a place to drink and dance and listen to music. Give them a place to gamble and to *lose*. Give them a taste of that. You know what's going to happen. They'll like it, because everyone likes it, and they'll want more of it. They'll play, and they'll mostly lose, and they'll need to make more money so they can play again. They will need their jobs, more than they need them now. They'll need *us*, to keep on playing. And when they lose, and when they get mad about it, they'll be getting mad at one of their own people—this *meshuggener shvartzer* with the Ivory Coast. I think the very worst thing that can happen is he opens the joint and then can't make it go. Then the darkies will want to come and gamble on the Strip."

Houck said, "And goddamnit, that will never happen!"

Holbrook said, "That will never happen."

There was no further discussion. The men agreed. As the meeting broke up, Seligman said to Mo, "I think you're full of it."

Mo smiled, indulgent, knowing that would irritate Seligman, and said, "Pinkie, you worry too much."

Seligman said, "I worry just the right amount. And I'm worried just the right amount about this nigger casino."

Mo said, "You could wind up being right. But the cost of being right, right now, is too high. You wouldn't have Holbrook's backing."

Seligman said, "How do you know?"

"Because of his brother-in-law," Mo said. "Haney wants this casino. He wants the coloreds staying on the West Side. He wants them kept down where he can control them. This is going to help him. Colored people on the Strip is his nightmare."

"Colored people on the Strip is *everybody's* nightmare."

"Really?" Mo regarded Seligman with disgust. "There are lots of people who think Jews on the Strip is a nightmare. If the tide in Europe had turned a little differently, maybe everybody in America would feel that way."

"You're wrong, Mo. The average American Jew is too smart to fall for the casino crap. The average American nigger . . . All he wants is tight pussy, loose shoes, and a warm place to take a dump."

"That sounds like a weekend at *your* place."

Seligman was on him almost too fast. Mo ducked the first one and got tangled in the second, but got his head down into Seligman's chest and buffaloed him forward. The blows rained onto his back until Marquez and Wingate pulled Seligman away. He was red in the face and had a line of white spittle on his lips. He was rendered, for the first time in anyone's memory, entirely speechless.

It was noon or later before Deacon finally got to Shipton Wells. He pulled Mo's big new Cadillac around the side of the Greyhound station, up close to the freestone facade of the café. There was not an inch of standing shade anywhere. The sun fell straight down like a knife blade. There were no buses or passengers at the station. Deacon sat with the car windows down for a minute just listening to the heat and silence.

Deacon had not been in the desert long enough to know the temperature automatically, the way desert veterans did. They were always saying things like "Ninety-five, at least, I'll bet" or "Just a hair under a hundred, I'd say." To Deacon, it was hot and dry and as empty as outer space. Deacon had known the hot damp of summer in New York and Baltimore and Atlanta—that gummy, languid, liquid heat that made everything slow and sloppy. This heat was not that heat. This heat was without texture. It did not cling or cloy. It did not make Deacon think of screened porches and mint juleps and night-blooming jasmine. It made him think of electricity and vacuum tubes and experiments in sensory deprivation. The Cadillac door slammed. Nothing moved.

Inside the café were four tables of diners—three couples and a family of four. Coming through the door, Deacon did not see Anita. His heart sank at the sudden thought: What if she was not here? What if there was some other waitress? What if Anita had gone, and he could not find her?

Then she came through the swinging door from the kitchen, carrying a tray of breakfast food and headed for the family in the booth. She was carting pancakes and French toast, and eggs and bacon and juice. She glided as if she were carrying a single slice of bread. The tray emptied itself. Anita raised her head in his direction, and flicked a dark curl off her forehead, and smiled. Deacon went weak, and took a booth near the door.

It was almost ninety minutes before the joint was quiet. Two of the couples had been drinking beer, and it took them forever to get tanked up enough to get back into their car. Another family, this one a group of beat-up Okies with hardly a full set of teeth between them, came in like whipped dogs and sat in the back. They studied the menu for ages. The father of the group, whose face was tanned the same color as the knotty-pine walls, drank water while his children and their mother ate sandwiches.

And then they were all gone and Anita was sitting with him. He'd had several cold beers. His head was soft now and quiet. Anita saw that look on him, that mellowy, kind of stupid look that some men get when they've been drinking. Her uncle did not get that way. He got red in the face and hot in the eyes and dangerous. The pharmacist, however, had been like this. He got soft and kind of sweet.

Deacon was always sweet. She didn't understand him. He came, and sat, and drank beer, and looked all moony at her. He'd ask her questions, about the restaurant, about her uncle, about the customers, about what she did at night. She told him a little bit of the truth. Then Deacon would tell her, but only when she asked, about what he did, about the casino and the nightclub and the band.

Deacon said, "How about another one of those cold beers?" She looked puzzled, but she got up and went away from him and headed for the bar. His heart sang, watching her. She was so delicate, and so strong. She was so gentle, and so fierce. She was everything. Sometimes she looked at him and he could feel the most amazing power—a hot-blooded, full-bodied, fully equipped *woman*. He would catch fire inside. And then sometimes she looked at him and she was an absolute child, lost and afraid and defenseless. The fire would die and smolder.

It smoldered now. She came back with the beer, using her skirt to wipe the top and exposing a length of delicious brown leg. Deacon had not been with a woman in a long while. His head was goofed-out from chasing Stella around last night. He heard her voice again saying, "Oh *God*," and it heated him. Anita slid into the bench and scooted the bottle of beer across to him.

And he said, so suddenly that he surprised himself, "I really want to go to bed with you."

She stared. Nothing moved. The heat was appalling. The radio she kept under the counter, the good one he had bought for her that she took to her bedroom every night, was playing something soft. Anita smiled and put her hand over Deacon's.

She said, "Now?"

Deacon said, "Now. Right now."

Anita laughed and said, "Right in the middle of the day?"

Deacon said, "Right now."

She rose and took his hand and led him through the back of the kitchen. The Mexican cook was not there. Somewhere distantly another radio was playing. Deacon felt the booze rise in his head. Anita twitched ahead of him, the white bow of her apron strings bobbing like a butterfly. They went out through the back screen door of the kitchen, into and across a dirt parking lot. There were six cabins in the back, freestone buildings like the café, in two lines of three. Anita moved quickly across the dirt lot to the cabin at the farthest side on the left. She went up two stone steps and jerked the door handle, and the door swung open.

It was very dark inside, and stale. Deacon knew the motel rooms never got used, because the Mexican who Anita said was her uncle did not want to pay anyone to clean them and did not get customers often enough to make it worthwhile keeping them clean between guests. Her uncle let them sit. This one had sat a long time. Deacon could feel the grit of sand under his feet.

Anita went quickly across the little cabin and shut herself into the bathroom. Deacon pulled off his suit coat, and sat on the bed and kicked off his shoes. He lit a cigarette. He desperately wanted a drink and wished he had thought of bringing a bottle of beer with him, at least. Off in the distance, muffled, he heard the Greyhound bus station P.A. system announcing the two-thirty from Chicago.

Anita came back into the room. She was naked but for a pair of bright white underpants. She held her hands over her breasts. Her curly hair was down now, tumbling over her shoulders. She took two steps out of the bathroom and stopped. Deacon had never before in his life seen anything so beautiful or heartbreaking. He slid up on the bed, and pulled the covers back slightly, and nodded at her. Anita came across the room and sat on the bed. Her eyes were full of fear. Deacon patted the bed and urged the covers back a bit more. Anita slid in. Deacon pulled the covers up to her shoulder, lay down next to her, and stroked her hair. When he felt her go slack, he moved closer to her, and put his hands on her shoulders, and put his lips on the back of her neck, and kissed her there.

She wasn't ready.

He said, "This is what I want, Anita. You are everything that I want. But I don't want it like this. I love you, and I want it the right way."

Anita buried her face in the bed and began to sob. She thought, *He* loves *me.*

Worthless Worthington Lee had gotten a couple of hours' sleep after leaving the police station and had started his day as he had every day before—up early, cleaned and dressed at home, down the street for a paper from the corner market, and over to the Hotel Apache for coffee and breakfast. It was ten-thirty, though, before he made it back to his office at the Ivory Coast.

The construction was running behind, but it was running fast. The main room was complete. The main ballroom was complete. The registration area and the two lobby bars were complete. The ground-floor restaurant was nearly complete. The guest rooms were coming along more slowly. Three of the planned eight bungalow buildings out beyond the swimming pool, each housing four suites, had been finished. The annex building, where another fifty rooms would be, was further behind. Most of the activity today was there. Worthless counted sixteen men in overalls scampering this way and that as he came through the front gate, crossed the parking lot, and went into the front reception area.

Inside it was hot and smelled of sawdust and paint. The carpet, in the main rooms, had gone down the day before. It was gold, bright gold, the color of wheat ready for reaping—the color of gold money—with patterns of red and blue shot through it. His designer had told him that blue-and-gold and crimson-and-gold were the colors favored by the most prestigious American universities. That had been good enough for Worthless, and now it looked fine. He felt ashamed to walk over it with shoes on. At the back of the room, where some of the gaming equipment was being installed, he found Sumner talking with two workmen. He said, "Sumner. Catch me in the main ballroom." The two men went there.

The ballroom ceilings were high and arched. There was a raised stage at one end and the floor dropped by degrees to meet it. High at the back, low at the front, with a pit for the orchestra and a dance floor crowded over now with tables, the ballroom was Worthless's own design, created with a view to maximum entertainment value and maximum traffic ease. Worthless did not want anyone to come in and sit down and stay any longer than necessary. He wanted them on the tables. But if they were in the room, he wanted them to have a first-class experience. Workmen were installing the tables now. Worthless told one of them to bring coffee and cream for two. He said to Sumner, so black that he almost disappeared in the darker ballroom, "Tell me what you got while we watch this guy do his stuff."

Sumner took a notepad out of his pocket. Worthless had asked him to calculate liquor purchases. As he started spreading note pages on the table in front of him, Worthless called out, "Anytime you ready, Mr. Peet."

The curtain onstage parted and a small, dapper black man in a white linen suit peered out. He said, "Mr. Lee! You snuck up on us! But we're ready. Girls!"

The curtain parted still farther. Surrounding Peet were perhaps forty or fifty women, young and black and fine. Sumner drew in his breath and said, "Damn!" quietly. Worthless said, "Damn *right*, damn. That's some womanhood." Peet waved to someone offstage and turned back to Worthless. He said, "This is group one. We'll watch them do a half a number. We'll need to pick six."

The girls hurried into a kind of line. Music started, from a record player offstage. Peet said, "Now, girls!" and the women began a rudimentary series of dance steps. Kick, lift, kick, turn, kick . . . Worthless had no idea what to look for. Peet did, though. After less than a minute of music, he said, "That'll do!" He ran off the stage, forward to Worthless. Close up, his age was apparent: he was only, maybe, twenty-two. He smiled nervously and turned back to the stage. He said, "I don't know your choices, of course, but I think this. Number four from the left, excellent. Three over from her, fine. Last girl on the very far right, fine. Four down from her, again to *her* right, also very good. The rest are hopeless. What do you think, Mr. Lee?"

Worthless smiled and said, "We agree, Mr. Peet. How many more groups are there?"

Peet said, "Well, we need forty girls. I'm doing them like this, in groups of fifteen. I'd say we have about a hundred."

Worthless thought he'd swoon. A hundred women, like this! All looking for work in his establishment. He regarded the collection of women onstage. They looked anxious, and bored, and some of them were just achingly beautiful. They were light and dark and black and beige and one of them, even, blond. He said, "All like this?"

Peet said, "Well, not all as good as this. I put some of the best ones in the first group."

"But they all look like this?"

"*About* like this, yes. And you understand, of course, these are not the *main* dancers. The *main* dancers are already here, on salary, hand-picked from places where they were already working, all around the country. I brought most of them here already. These girls are just the line dancers."

Sumner said, "Damn," again.

Worthless said, "Amen, brother. Let's see the next group, Mr. Peet. But you do the picking. You doing fine on your own. Don't mind us. We're just gonna watch."

Worthless sipped his coffee, watching tiny Peet go away. He had seen photographs of the main dancers. Like his headwaiters and the section managers, they had been recruited from all over the country. The search was huge, and the searching was tough—because there were not that many colored people with the kind of experience re-quired working anywhere you looked. Worthless had hired several men to do the scouting and the hiring, and they had raided some of the country's biggest hotels and nightclubs and private clubs. They'd raided waiters from the Pullman cars. They'd cruised Harlem and Cen-tral Avenue in New York and Los Angeles for dancers and singers and musicians. The only thing they couldn't get him was dealers. Nowhere you went in the world were there any Negro blackjack dealers, or boxmen or pitmen for craps, or croupiers for roulette. Worthless had a group of white dealers right now, schooling some colored men. He might have enough time and enough recruits, by opening night, to employ black men only. He might not.

But he was going to have enough dancers. He was going to have too many dancers. The girls posed now, onstage, like prize cats. Worthless was wondering how many of the more beautiful ones might stay on as cocktail waitresses if he asked them nice. Peet dashed into them, saying, "Sorry, dear . . . not your day . . . sorry, dear . . ." as he went down the line, and some of them looked crushed. Worthless made a note to himself: *Ask someone to start asking the girls, the minute they come away from the audition, if they have other work in Las Vegas. If not . . .*

Sumner said, "Here's what it looks like to me," and started pushing numbers across the table.

Worthless thought, *I can do the math. I can look at the women. But I can't do the math and look at the women at the same time. Is that gonna be a problem for me? Can I do this every night—look at numbers, look at the girls, and not get strange?* He said to Sumner, "This looks like too much gin to me. People really drinking that much gin?"

Sumner said, "Yes, they are. It's a summer drink. A hot drink, you know? They drink that gin fizz and that Ramos fizz and all that other fizz. They drink that gin and tonic. Lots of that stuff you use gin. Lots of folks won't be drinking bourbon and scotch, if it's too hot."

"Okay, then. I'm gonna make an order tonight, I think. These liquor boys are being real funny with me."

"They scared of the big bosses."

"What you mean?"

Sumner looked at another line of women coming onto the stage. This group was finer than the last one. Sumner said, "I heard the big bosses been trying to think of ways to run you off 'fore you get started. Putting the heel down on the liquor people was one way they thought of doing that. They figure if you cain't get booze in here, then you cain't keep no customers, and you go out of business 'fore you get started."

"That's good thinking," Worthless said. "Why'n't they do that?"

"Liquor boys said no go, is what I heard," Sumner said. "Liquor boys want yo' money, same as everybody else. Plus I think maybe Mo put the word on 'em to leave you alone. Plus I think some of the big bosses like the idea of a bunch of liquored-up niggers anyway."

"How come?"

"Easier to handle. Easier to beat on, if there's trouble. And they don't know trouble up here in the desert."

"They ain't gonna get no trouble. It's gonna be folks drinking and dancing and having a *good* time. Else I close this place down. I'm too old for trouble."

Sumner laughed and said, "Yeah, I see the way you too old for trouble, from the way you looking at them dancers."

Worthless laughed and said, "I'm like an old coon dog. I been chasing it so long without catching it, I wouldn't know what to do with it if I *did* catch it."

"I 'spect some of them girls would show you what to do . . ."

Worthless looked at Sumner—so fine and black and strong. He said, "I saw you one morning a while back, rodeo-riding a car around with some bad-lookin' boys. What was that all about?"

Sumner dropped his eyes. He said, "Aw, that was just funnin' around."

"It looked like something more than drinkin'," Worthless said.

"Naw. Just funnin' around."

Worthless looked at Sumner looking at the ground. *If he was my son,* he thought, *I'd keep asking until he told me the truth. But he's not my son.* Worthless said, "That's fine, Mr. Peet. I'll check back with you later in the day."

Deacon woke first. He had been asleep only a few minutes, he thought. Anita slept beside him, far from him, deep and away. Deacon listened to her breathe, felt desire rise in him again like the tide, and got off the bed and away from her. He lit a cigarette and peered out the window, through the dust and across the short stretch of desert back to the café.

There were no cars in the lot. It was quiet. He could feel the heat radiating from the windowpane. The sky was so crisp and blue it hurt his eyes.

He had told several women in his life that he loved them. He had told each of those women he loved them in several different ways. At different times, though the words were always the same, it had meant different things. Sometimes it had meant "I'm sorry." Sometimes it had meant "I am leaving you." Sometimes it had meant "I really want you to love *me*." Sometimes, most of the times, in fact, it had meant "I really, really want to have sexual intercourse with you *now*."

It had never, except when he was pretty far gone with the bottle or the needle, meant "I love you." With Anita, when he had said, "I love you," he actually meant "I love you."

What a mess. He stood with the cigarette burning down, wondering what he was supposed to do next. He saw images of Bogart and Alan Ladd and Dick Powell, hard guys who never let a woman get to them, who always walked away with a wince and a grin, who always got the last word and always ended up alone. But that was the trouble. Deacon was already alone. He did not want to end up alone.

But this? He flicked the cigarette onto the floor and sat down on the bed. Sometimes Anita looked about twelve years old to him. She looked about that now. Once, weeks before, as he was walking with her from the café to her cabin, Anita had suddenly gone girlish and taken a few skip-steps in front of him. He thought, "How can I make love to her?" She *was* kind of grown-up, in a lot of ways. Deacon guessed he would not be her first, from the way she carried herself, and the way she behaved with other men. Still . . .

On that day, that skip-stepping day, when he'd got her back to her cabin, she'd said to him, "Does the big bad man want to give the 'ittle bittle girl a 'ittle bittle kiss?"

Deacon said back, "No. And don't ever do that to me. You're not old enough to baby-talk."

Anita had looked crushed, and Deacon at once regretted saying it. Her face had hardened, and in her eyes she went away from him.

She said, "I'm sorry, old man. You probably just want to pick up your little handbag. I'll get it."

Deacon said, "No. Leave it."

Anita turned away from him and went into her cabin, saying, "I'll get it."

He followed her inside. There was a rustle in the closet. She was throwing dresses and coats out over her shoulder as she dug for the bag. She said, "I'll get your little bag. I'll give you back your little bag. And you will take your little bag and you will leave here and you will not come back."

Deacon was behind her then. She had her hand on the bag.

He said, "Stop that."

She said, "I don't want you coming back here."

Deacon took her and pulled her to him and hugged her close. She was sobbing. He said, "Yes, you do. You want me coming back. And I am coming back."

She said, "I want you to."

Deacon had kissed her then. She didn't kiss like a girl. She kissed like a woman. She pressed herself into him and he felt her breasts and her body and the heat of her. He caught the heat, and his brain caught fire, and he kissed her deeper still. She sobbed. His fever waned. They put the bag back into the closet and went back into the café.

He lay on the bed now and ran his hand over her forehead. When she stirred, he said, "It's time, baby."

Anita stirred and smiled, catlike, and rolled onto her back. She arched and stretched and opened her eyes to him. And he was in love all over again. He kissed her again, long and deep and wrenching, and said, "I need to throw some cold water on my face."

She said, "On *something*, I guess," and he left the room.

An hour later Deacon had drunk a bourbon highball and two cups of coffee. The sun was low and the sky was crisp and deepening into dark blue. A busload of pilgrims from the East had just pulled into the Greyhound station. Anita stood with him in the parking lot, watching them, weary in her eyes. Behind them, in the café, the Mexican watched, and saw. Deacon noticed him there. He took Anita's arm, avuncular in his very posture, and said, "I'd like to find a way to bring you into the city for an evening. I'd like to play for you. You think there's any chance of that?"

Anita said, "My uncle has been talking about closing down for a night, actually. He's got something wrong with him, a goiter or something, or a cyst. He says he has to go into the hospital for a night for them to do something to it. He says I got to stay here on my own, that he's got some friend who is going to come and cook. I already told him I won't do it. Lord, look at them all getting off that bus."

They both looked across the street at the Greyhound as it spilled Midwestern galoots onto the hot asphalt.

Deacon said, "Tell your uncle that we talked and that I said you can't be here on your own with this friend of his. Tell him I said you got to close for the night. Or that I'll hire him somebody to cover your shift. Tell him I'll cover the money."

Anita, wide-eyed, said, "You'd do that?"

Deacon said, "Sure, I'd do that. Maybe I could drag you into Vegas that night to listen to me play."

Anita said, "Wow. That little handbag of yours must be filled with solid gold."

Then the Greyhound passengers were coming across the lot. Her uncle shouted, "Anita, dammit! *Andale, pues!*" and she was going away from him.

Haney lay back in the big claw-foot bathtub, engulfed in the rising steam, and closed his eyes. It was peaceful, like this, the only peaceful time he ever got. Every night at this hour, he had his man run him an extremely hot bath, and put a record on the record player, and make him a highball drink, and put the drink and a packet of Turkish cigarettes and a book of matches on a little table next to the bathtub. And Haney would undress and lower his perfectly pale body into the perfectly scalding water, and light a Turkish cigarette, and sip the highball and listen to the Sons of the Pioneers, or Gene Autry, sing about life in the West. It was not life in the West as Haney himself experienced it. It was a better life in the West than the one he knew. It did not contain casinos or prostitutes or crooked politicians or dead Negro nightclub owners. Or police lieutenants. It contained instead pinto ponies and sagebrush and tumbleweeds and untrammeled, un-sullied women and simple, stoic, quiet men. Haney did not know any people like the people in the music he liked. He did not know any West like the one in the music he liked. It didn't matter. He liked the music. He drew on the Turkish cigarette and blew smoke at the ceiling and considered the evening ahead.

Bob Wills and His Texas Playboys were singing.

The last of the daylight was gone by the time Haney rose, pink and wrinkled, from his tub. His man had come in at eight o'clock and said, "Trout?" and Haney had said, "Sure. Why not?" Now Haney dressed and went to the dining room, where, alone, he ate his fish.

Half an hour later he was in his black car, dressed in his black suit, moving across the dark desert. He said to his driver, "Let's go over to the West Side. I want to see that Ivory Coast again." The two gorillas in the backseat grunted in assent.

Jackson Street was winding up. Roscoe John's smoker was working. Billows of gray and white effusion blew the smell of roasting sausages overhead. Standing in her doorway, Miss Pringle fluttered a scented hand at the smoke and then, when it did not shift direction, slid her beauty-parlor door closed against it.

On the sidewalk in front of Garcia's store, three sharp cats from Los Angeles, wearing long coats and pointy shoes and straightened and pomaded hair, argued about how to spend their evening.

One of them said, "I don't care about eating. I can eat anywhere. This is *Las Vegas*, man. I want to *gamble*. I want to do some *gaming*."

Haney, pulling to the curb in the long black automobile, caught the last of this. If he were an anxious man, this is where his anxiety would live. It would rest on exactly this kind of bad nigger—from out of town, lacquered up, liquored up, and looking to gamble, just like these boys. The crime rate in L.A. was far worse than in the desert. The cops down there had let the Negroes get loose. The coloreds had got jobs in the aircraft factories, and had bought houses with their GI Bill loans, and had turned South and Central Los Angeles into their own private jungle. That Central Avenue—and Haney knew this because he had seen it with his own eyes—was worse than Harlem. Negro restaurants. Negro bars. Negro nightclubs. Negro *radio* stations, for Christ's sake. There was Negro everything, wide and deep everywhere you looked.

There was Negro crime, too. Mostly, and thank God for that, the Negro committed his crimes against the Negro. The men fought one another. Even the *women* fought one another, which Haney found strangely more terrifying. The men fought with knives and guns and broken bottles and furniture and pipes and wrenches and every other damned thing you could think of. Luckily for the policeman, the Negroes mostly used the weapons on one another.

The only trouble with that, Haney believed, is that once the Negro began enjoying that criminal behavior, once he got a taste for the violence, he would stop worrying about who was the victim of his behavior. The Negro might hurt his own today, but it would be *our* people tomorrow.

Haney said to the driver, "Those guys can't help us. Ride on, but slow."

The driver reengaged the automobile and pulled slowly up the curb. Haney studied the faces. He needed a certain kind of man, a certain kind of Negro man, and he had to be young and with a certain something about him. He'd need a little of that jackrabbit in him, a little spark of—

"That's the one," Haney said. "Stop the car. Let's get that little boy in the green sport coat."

Haney and the two men slipped out of the big black car and moved swiftly to the corner. A slim young black man in a green jacket, matching green hat, and black sunglasses was standing at the corner. But not for long. He saw Haney and the two big gorillas get out of the car and move toward him, and he was off like a shot. He got to the next corner, only, before the two gorillas were on top of him. They muscled him back to the corner, off the curb, and into the car, mashing him into the seat between them while Haney slid into the front.

Haney said, "Check his pockets."

The man struggled, but Haney's men found four paper packets of marijuana in his jacket pocket, and two paper packets of pills tucked into the sweatband of his hat.

Haney said, "Okay. Get us out into the desert."

The black man said, "Who the hell do you think you are?" The gorilla to his left, without a word, hit him so hard in the face that he passed out.

Haney said, "That will hold him for a minute, anyway."

When he came to, the young black man was lying on his back, staring up at the desert sky and the face of Lieutenant Tom Haney. His legs were spread and his feet were tied to the front bumper of the big automobile. His hands were tied together, over his head, and roped to something he could not see behind him. Haney was grinning.

He said, "Good morning. Tell me what you know about the Ivory Coast."

The young man said, "I don't know anything about the Ivory Coast. It's gonna be a casino for colored people."

"Who's behind it?"

"That boxer Worthington Lee, man. Everybody knows that."

"And who's behind him?"

"Nobody, man. He's it."

Haney seemed to consider this for a minute. Then he kicked the young man in the testicles.

Haney stepped back and said, "Let me ask you that again."

The young man said, "Stop! I don't know. I just know he was a fighter. He owns lots of property around the West Side, man. I don't know anything else about him."

Haney kicked the young man in the testicles again.

He said, "Let me ask you that again."

Stella was about halfway into it when a knock came at the door. She shook the young man off of her, and hissed, "Get into the bathroom!" She got up off the bed and found her peignoir. The knock came again. She called out, "Coming!" She knew it could only be Mo. Stella at times like this always kept a housemaid posted, sitting on a chair outside her door, and no one but Mo would be allowed to knock. Anyone else, if it was an emergency, the maid herself would come in and make an announcement. So this had to be Mo.

Stella did a quick ruffle over her hair in front of the vanity. Through the bathroom door she could see her young gentleman caller, staring wide-eyed from where he stood in the shower stall. Stella put a finger to her lips and then shook it at him, and inspected herself briefly. The mirror said she looked terrific—lily pale, but with fire in her cheeks, her green eyes alight with desire and her red mane a tumble of passion.

She opened the door, and Mo said, "Jesus, Stella. You look horrible. We gotta talk."

"Now, Mo?"

"Now. Maybe you'd fix me a drink?"

Stella said, "Sure, Mo," and went to a sideboard. The maid always set things up there nicely for her. There was ice in the bucket and fresh soda in the siphon. Stella mixed a strong scotch and soda and added ice cubes. She thought the air smelled fairly obviously of the marijuana that she and her young man had smoked. She felt gauzy and nice, light and gay, as if Mo were a social caller and this were nothing more than a friendly visit. She wished she could introduce the young man, whose name was Joseph. She longed to call him Joey and to show him to Mo. "Joey, this is Moey," she would say. She stirred the drink and giggled. It would be nice if he worked out, this Joey. He had very good reefer, and he was very large and sexy. Unfortunately, she needed that part more often than she needed the reefer. She bought the marijuana only once every two weeks or so. She needed the lovemaking every day, it seemed. She stirred the highball with a wistful sigh.

"Stella! What about it?"

Mo broke her reverie and brought her back. She went across her suite with the drink in hand. Suddenly it was just a room and she was just a tramp and Daddy was very angry with her. She stood by the bed, pouting.

Mo said, "Sit, please. And thank you for the drink. Jesus, but this room needs cleaning, Stella. It smells like the monkey house. I want to talk to you about the second show."

"Sure, Mo. What about it?"

"I want to cut it. I've been worrying over ways to get the crumbs out of the lounge and into the casino, and to keep them in the casino a little longer. One of my ideas is to put on a free feed at midnight. That will keep some of the cheapskates up past their bedtime. Or at least it will keep them here, or bring them back here, if they are thinking about wandering down the Strip or into downtown or whatever."

"Jeez, Mo. A free meal? What'll that cost?"

"Not too much—or not too much compared to what they'll do for me at the tables. And at the slots. I'm going to put in more slots, too."

"I think you should put in more tables. More roulette."

"For you, I would, Stella. But most of these crumbs are not you. I got roulette and blackjack and craps and poker already for the folks who want that. But that's for the gamblers. And it eats up a lot of real estate. Only so much room for tables. And it eats up salaries, too. Four guys for each craps table. Two guys for roulette. No guys for slots. I need more slots for the people who aren't really going to gamble—the wives and the girlfriends, you know. The old folks who don't have as much to play with, or who are afraid to lose. That's the future of this casino, I think. The high rollers will be the icing on the cake for us, forever. But the nickel-and-dime crumbs are going to be the cake. We have to make more room for the crumbs."

There was a slight rustling. Stella's eyes shot to the bathroom. Mo's eyes followed hers there. Stella fluttered her hands to her hair and said, "What does that have to do with the second show?"

Mo said, "We got to get them back onto the floor sooner. We've got to make the show shorter and less interesting. That's the problem. It's going like gangbusters now. It's a great act. You look up and down the street, and you see all these juggling acts and magic acts and novelty acts. I'm *proud* that we don't have any of that crap. This is a real old-fashioned *show*. It's a great band, and you've really been sending them."

"So what's the problem?"

"The problem is, I'm not making enough dough on it."

Mo could see the young man's face peering past the bathroom door. He was embarrassed for Stella. Hiding colored boys in her room. Sneaking them into the hotel, repeatedly, after Mo had begged and pleaded and threatened and ordered. . . . She was like some pathetic junkie, with this black bone thing of hers. She probably couldn't help it. Did she try to help it? She seemed sincere when she said she would try. "I *swear*, Mo. This is the last time. I *swear*." There was never a last time, though. Or there was always a next time.

Mo said, "Get out here, boy. Now."

The young man came trembling from the bathroom. He was wearing one of Stella's nightgowns, a fluffy froufrou thing with ruffled sleeves and a high collar. He came a step onto the carpet and stopped.

Mo said, "Come on, now. Come out and mix yourself a drink or something."

Stella said, "Mo, this is Joseph."

Mo said, "How ya doing, Joseph. Nice to meet you. Go on and have a highball."

The young man went fast to the sideboard. Mo heard his hands nervously clinking ice into a glass.

Mo said, "The first show runs an hour now. Let's run it an additional fifteen minutes. Let people stay a bit more, drink a bit more. That would run us up to ten-fifteen or so, right? Then we start the second show at eleven sharp. Go half an hour and stop. No encores. Lights on at eleven-thirty. That way, some of the crumbs will hit the pits.

Some of them will go stand in line for the free eats. Some of them will go to bed. A lot of them will hit the slots, though, instead of waiting in line for the grub. Then some of them will eat and have a cup of coffee and want to start over."

The young man stood by the sideboard, sipping his drink. Mo regarded him with sadness. What a dreadful place to be! This room, this broad, at this hour of the night, and her boss roaring in and him hiding in the bathroom. He probably wouldn't be back, which was good. For this reason alone, if for no other, Mo could not wait for the Ivory Coast to open. Stella could do this stuff on someone else's time, and on someone else's turf.

Mo rose and said, "Stella, you will notice I have been extremely nice about something. I won't be, the next time. You know how important you are to me, and to this establishment. It's not important enough to risk closing down. If it happens again, I'll throw you out myself. And you know that no one else in Vegas will give you a shot if I do."

Stella gave him her most baleful, tragic look. Without her glasses on, though, she could not see if he was buying any. He did not sound like he was. On his way to the door he said, "See you around, Joseph. But not around here, ever again, or I'll have you skinned."

An hour later Haney and his two gorillas were back on Jackson Street. Haney told the driver to turn left.

The Ivory Coast was half a block off Jackson, down a wide, dirty boulevard that, a block again farther, dipped under the train tracks and officially left the West Side. That was the demarcation. That was the line that, Haney feared, he and his men would not be able to hold. He saw it as a military challenge. Mount a pair of machine guns at either end of the railroad bridge. Post snipers below. Dig in at the top of the rise where the street dropped down toward the bridge. He'd order his men to wait for the first wave as it came down the boulevard. Wait until they'd hit the crest and were dipping down to cross under the tracks. Then ambush and attack. Pause. Wait. Repeat.

He realized suddenly that he had positioned his men, in his mind, backward. The way he had set up the ambush, his men would be on the Negro side, defending the West Side, against imaginary hordes of invaders from the East. They'd be firing on the white men then.

The young black man they'd taken out to the sand had not been very helpful. Through bleeding lips he had insisted that Lee was operating alone, as far as the money went, which was preposterous but the best they could get from him. He had also told them, though, that Lee had a wife who was a drunk—which Haney had not known—and that Lee was very friendly with Mo Weiner—which Haney had not known—and that Lee did not drink, chase skirts, or smoke reefer. This last was interesting only because the young man was a specialist, it turned out, in the sale of reefer. Haney realized, once again, that if your instincts are good and you follow them, you will *always* get something useful for your trouble.

The young man had not come out of it so well. Haney had been frustrated with his inability to have answered the question he most wanted answered. And he wanted to show Lee that he meant serious business. So Haney had gotten the driver to start the car and back up slowly while the young black man was still tied to the bumper at one end and to a Joshua tree at the other. He'd had one of his men stuff the young black man's necktie into his mouth first—because who, really, wanted to hear *that?* Instead, they had listened to the big car purr, to the black man moan, and then to the mushy *snap* of his shoulders and hips popping out of their sockets. Haney raised his hand then and said, "Enough." They'd thrown the wailing black man into the trunk.

Now they lifted him back out of the trunk. He had passed out and was as limp as a plate of spaghetti. Haney said, "Follow me, and bring that with you. Hang on to him until I say so."

They were ushered in by a handsome, dark-skinned black man Haney thought he'd seen working over in one of Mo Weiner's joints. The man stared at the limp bundle the two bodyguards carried. Then, without asking, he guided Haney and the thugs across the lobby, across brand-new red and blue and gold carpeting that looked expensive, down into what would be the pits, where men were assembling tables for craps and blackjack, past a bar and lounge area, down a long hallway and through steel swinging doors into the bright, fluorescent-lit cavern of the kitchens.

Worthless looked up from a conversation he was having with one of the cooks, standing over a huge gas range that had just been fired up for the first time. The cook was holding his hand eight inches or so above a stack of bright blue flame and nodding his head enthusiastically. He said, "That's why they say, 'Now you cookin' with *gas.'* " He looked up at that moment, and the light went out of his eyes.

Worthless turned to follow his gaze and then said, "Why'n't you take off, Herman." Herman did.

Haney pointed to the floor in front of Lee, and the gorillas dropped their load there. Haney said, "Throw some water on him." One of the gorillas grabbed a soup pot from a hook and filled it with enough water to douse the man's head. He shook awake as if from a nightmare and began to scream at once. He thrashed, but nothing seemed connected to anything else. He writhed on the floor and looked to Lee like a broken puppet.

He said, "Who is he?"

Haney said, "He's your future. He's what you're going to turn into if I have any more trouble with you."

Lee said, "You ain't had no trouble with me yet. You ain't *going* to have no trouble with me."

"Shut up," Haney said. "Keep your blue-gum, nigger mush-mouth shut."

The man on the floor moaned louder still. Haney flicked his eyes at the gorillas. One of them threw a heavy foot into the man's face. He went out again.

Haney said, "This boy was carrying enough marijuana to light up half of Jackson Street. He won't be back with it. Someone else will, though, and if I find him in your establishment, I will kill you both. And I'll kill your rummy wife, too. Fact, I might start with her."

Lee wavered slightly, just slightly. Haney caught it. He thought, *Bingo.*

Haney said, "I will start with her. It's bad enough this place is opening. If you don't keep it quiet, and keep it clean, and keep decent white folk out of here, I will turn your world into a nightmare. You understand me?"

Worthless nodded.

Haney said, "I think you *do* understand me. I won't say any of this again."

He said to the gorillas, "Leave that. Let's go." And they went.

Worthless called out, "Herman? Sumner? We gonna need a doctor for this old boy here. Start off by running up to Miss Pringle's salon. Get some Mercurochrome for his face. Sumner, you call the doctor."

The two younger men ran off. Worthless Worthington Lee sat down on a milk crate and put his head in his hands.

Deacon had not got away from Shipton Wells until seven-thirty or later. It wasn't dark yet when he got back onto the narrow two-lane blacktop leading away from the Greyhound station. The road ahead was a dark strip of asphalt running down across the desert, a razor-straight scar on the sand, marked into the distance with power poles.

The car hummed like some great electric dynamo. It was Mo's newest—a big beige-and-tan Cadillac Eldorado convertible—and it was a beauty to drive. The seats were leather, hand-crafted and imported, they said, and smelled like a brand-new glove. The engine was supposed to be 270 horsepower. Mo had torn an ad out of *Fortune* magazine and showed it to Deacon. It read, "Even in the distinguished company of other Cadillacs, it is unmistakably the 'car of cars.' " Mo had said, "Read that," and chuckled. "Now I *have* to buy one." So, of course, Mo had bought *two*. When Deacon had asked to borrow the car for some personal business, Mo had said, "Sure. Do a shakedown on that Eldorado. Let me know how it rides."

By the time the Eldorado had cleared the mountains, it was dark. Coming down the other side, the top down and the wind whipping by him, he got the full effect of Vegas at night. It rose and shimmered in the distant blackness like the city of Oz.

But it was only Las Vegas. He had the city lights for an hour as he motored the Cadillac heavily westward. Two cars passed, leaving town. Nothing was going his way, before or behind. He was thinking about Anita, and how to get her into the city with him. Maybe he could get her a job? Not at the Starburst, and not at the Thunderbird. Mo was too smart and too suspicious, and too legal: he'd know what Deacon was up to right from the start, and he'd probably figure out that Anita was underage without even asking how old she was. So . . . what? Deacon would have to park her somewhere. And that would require a little do-re-mi. Maybe the Ivory Coast? Maybe Worthless would like a pretty hatcheck girl? And, because it was the West Side, wouldn't worry too much about her age?

In the meantime, Deacon had the more immediate problem of just getting Anita out for an evening. He was thinking maybe he'd try to find a girl from the Starburst to cover Anita's shift at the café. There was that Dot, one of the girls who worked the gift shop. She had been a waitress at the Thunderbird before coming across the street to the Starburst. She was very flirty, and very pretty, and very willing, he thought. He would ask her to do him a favor on the Shipton Wells thing. He could make it financially interesting. She might want it made interesting in some other way. That he could not do, but maybe he wouldn't tell her that straight up. If he could spring Anita for a night, he'd let Dot think what she wanted. She was a grown-up, from the look of her, and could probably take care of herself. With that body, actually, she could probably take care of a platoon. Deacon found there was some residual fire in him, something left over from the few minutes alone with Anita in the cabin. The sight of her, coming toward him across the room, the perfect nut brown of her, the swell and arch of her, her long, lean legs and those perfect white panties, and her hands cupped over her full breasts, and her hair curling down around her face and over her shoulders . . .

Deacon shuddered and the big Cadillac slid slightly into the east-bound lane. He righted the car, and rolled the window down farther. If only he could grab a cold shower now, on the road. If only he could score now, and fix, on the road. If only he had a highball, or even a cold beer. He had half an hour left to drive, he reckoned. Then to ditch the Caddy. Then to get to his room and shower and change. Then to find Fatty before it got too late. Maybe go down to Sloan's bar and get a couple of drinks in him, and maybe get a bottle of Kentucky bourbon to tuck under his seat, to tuck into his horn, to tuck himself into the music. All of that—he checked his watch—with only an hour to go before "Stella by Starlight." He revved the Eldorado and hummed on across the desert floor.

Six

MO WEINER CAME down from his suite of rooms at the Starburst Hotel and Casino—silver-haired, silver-suited, and suave—two hours after the decent people of the world had finished breakfast and started the day. He had half a grapefruit, two slices of unbuttered toast, and a pot of black coffee—as he did every single morning—in the Starburst coffee shop. The waitress was always nervous. The hostess was always nervous. Even the busboy was nervous. Mo did not know what to do about this. For a long time he had tried to be friendly, act natural, and make friends with his employees, just as he would make friends everywhere else in life. But he had stopped trying after finding that he repeatedly failed. He was the boss. Employees were obliged to mistrust or fear the boss. Mo had stopped caring. Though he did tip more heavily than was appropriate. Today, like every day, his check read twenty cents for the coffee, ten cents for the toast, and fifteen cents for the grapefruit. A regular customer could get a whole breakfast for not much more than that. The Starburst Hotel and Casino offered several space-age breakfast meals at very competitive prices. The Astro included three hotcakes, two eggs, hash brown potatoes, and coffee for seventy-five cents. The Super Astro, which was the same meal with a tiny sirloin steak thrown in, cost $1.50.

The trick was the coffee. The Starburst did not serve a cup of coffee. The Starburst served a *pot* of coffee—a little pot of piping hot, fresh coffee for everyone that ordered java. It was a point of pride with the Starburst coffee-shop waitresses. They were not smart enough to know that this was smart pricing. Coffee cost the house next to nothing. A cup of coffee and a small pot of coffee were virtually the same product. But while you could still get a single cup of coffee in other places for a nickel, at the Starburst your piping hot *pot* of coffee cost twenty cents. That was a profit of about eighteen cents on every customer who ordered coffee. Not much, but this was how casinos like the Starburst made rich men out of their owners. A little here, a little there, chipping away on every small margin they could find.

Mo left two bucks on the Formica tabletop and went out. He noted, as he went, that the carpet near the coffee-shop entrance was fading. It caught a lot of afternoon sun. It would have to go. He also thought the space-age uniforms his waiters and waitresses wore had begun to look tatty. Or maybe he was getting tired of them.

Maybe it was the competition. The Strip was on fire. Mo worried. Going across the lobby and up the elevator to his hypercooled offices, Mo walked the Strip in his head.

When he had started doing business in the desert, there were only the El Rancho Vegas, the Hotel Last Frontier, the Flamingo, and the Thunderbird to contend with. Despite Bugsy Siegel and his gangster friends, it was all pretty homey stuff. The oilmen and the ranchers from Texas and New Mexico and Arizona came to town with their wives. They liked a show and they had plenty of dough. They enjoyed winning but they could afford losing. There was no rough stuff. The relationship between the casino operators was collegial.

The Flamingo's big cylindrical Champagne Tower and the Thunderbird's huge rising Navajo birds made other hoteliers nervous, at the start, because they were so grand and seemed to threaten change. Change did not come, though. It was business as usual, only more so.

Then Wilbur Clark had opened his Desert Inn. Milton Prell had built and opened the Sahara. Then in 1952 the five-million-dollar Sands had opened. The stakes went up. It wasn't just a few cattle ranchers and oil barons anymore. Now it was gamblers, and gangsters, from New York, Chicago, San Francisco, and Los Angeles. The big friendly family feeling went away. Soon the big empty vistas of sand that stood between the casinos became casinos themselves. From Fremont Street heading west on Highway 91 it was nothing but boomtown.

Las Vegas was hot, but it wasn't warm anymore. This crowd liked music and dancing and gaming. It liked excitement and big-name entertainers. For years audiences had been delighted by performers like Pearl Bailey, and the Mills Brothers, and Liberace, even Sophie Tucker. It was a small-town crowd having fun doing small-town stuff. Then the Sahara and the Sands started bringing in people like Marlene Dietrich and Lena Horne. Stars like Bob Hope and Bing Crosby came in for golf tournaments sponsored by the Desert Inn. The Flamingo brought in Harry James and Count Basie and even Jack Benny. The Sahara brought in Louis Prima and Keely Smith. The biggest names in show business were coming to the desert, bringing huge audiences and commanding huge salaries.

And then there were the floor shows. There was the "Dancing Waters" extravaganza at the Royal Nevada. There were the feathered dancers of the Painted Desert Room at the D.I., and the Ramona Room at the Last Frontier. The Starburst had put on its own "Constellation of Beauty, Galaxy of Girls" show, at a cost of many hundreds of thousands. Gone, within a few years, were the cowboy clothes. Now the men wore dinner jackets in the casino, and the women high heels, furs, and jewels.

There was more money to be made, but it was tougher to make.

Now the stakes were going up again. The Riviera, the Strip's first multilevel hotel, with its nine towering stories, had opened in April. The hotel had the Strip's first elevators, too, and the largest lobby of any hotel in town. The owners had hired Liberace to open the nightclub and the Treniers to open the lounge. A week later the Royal Nevada had opened, with its ridiculous Indians, in costume, greeting guests. A week after *that*, the Hotel Last Frontier had closed and the Hotel New Frontier had opened, right next door.

Next now the Dunes was opening—and the owners had Frank Sinatra in their hip pocket. Farther down the Strip, huge construction projects that would become the Tropicana and the Stardust were opening giant holes in the ground. The already dusty desert was like a vast, sand-blown building site. Everywhere you looked, signs read DINING! DANCING! GAMING!

Mo, going into his office, said, "Money! Mayhem! Murder!" His outer office assistant, who knew better, did not even look up from her work. She said, "Coffee?" and Mo said, "Thanks."

The midnight meal was a brilliant plan. Mo was well pleased. Shortening Stella's second show, too, was smart business. But Mo had no illusions. Business was going to get very, very rough over the next couple of years. Even if his customers could remember that they stayed at the Star-*burst*, and not the Star-*dust*, and even if some of the marginal joints like the Bagdad or the Zanzibar went south, the size of the pie was not increasing as fast as the number of people who wanted their slice. The T-bird, he thought, would be the first to go. He did not know why anyone stayed there, anyway. He found the rising-phoenix motif garish and tacky. In fact, he hated all that Old West look, all that cowboys-and-Indians crap—all the beaded belts and turquoise and stitched shirts and string ties. That Gene Autry crap. That Roy Rogers crap. That Sitting Bull crap. Mo laughed to himself. Sitting Bull crap. It was *all* crap. Only in Vegas would the Indians and the cowboys get friendly enough to do business together. It would be like the Germans and the Jews doing business. The Hotel Auschwitz? Hotel Concentration Camp and Casino? Enjoy spartan Jewish living with a touch of German decadence! Stay in a real stalag while you and your friends "concentrate" on having a good time. It's a gas!

Mo said out loud, "Get Killarney over here for me, will you?"

Then he went back to thinking about money. He was, more than anything, scared. The problem was: too much money, too fast. There was too much money being made, and too much new money coming into town. That much money attracted the wrong people. It was going to draw more of the hard guys.

That's what had happened to Mo in Chicago. He and his family had worked around the edges of the law, running everything from numbers to gambling to girls. Mo had overseen interests in construction, heavy equipment, and trucking and hauling. With Prohibition, the trucking business boomed. Mo moved naturally into bootlegging, moving crates of hooch between the East Coast and the Midwest. After a while, when Prohibition didn't go away and didn't stop the flow of alcohol, Mo decided the real money was in the cargo, not the trucks. Soon he was importing whiskey across the border from Canada.

So were lots of other guys. The money was huge. And the more money there was, the more guys where were. The more money they made, the more money they wanted. The big guys got bigger. The little guys got out, or got taken out. Mo tried to stay out of the worst of it. When the game got serious, he got serious. He bought out a couple of competitors, then bought out the equipment and manpower that belonged to a couple of competitors who did not want to be bought out. Around him other men were using different means to achieve the same ends. Guys who did not step aside were gunned down. Guys who did not step aside for Capone, particularly, were gunned down. By the time of the St. Valentine's Day Massacre—as the newspaper boys termed it—Chicago was a very unhealthy place for a guy like Mo to live. He lived. He stayed. He lost many, many men. His men took out many, many men. In the end, by the time the feds ran Capone off to prison in 1931, Chicago was a graveyard. Prohibition ended. Prosperity turned the corner—heading *this* direction, for a change. But Mo had lost his stomach for the whole thing.

He wasn't interested in surviving a bloodbath like that again. But that's what he saw coming. Bugsy Siegel and the Flamingo were nothing. Bugsy was a piker. The Flamingo was a footnote. Now that the Dunes was going up, with that kind of scope and that kind of money behind it, everything thing else would go up.

Mo had kept his people in Chicago quiet with a very slight rake. They had no idea how little of his action they were getting. If they had, they would let him know—with bullets.

But with all the new hotel construction, though, and the headliners opening in everyone's lounges and nightclubs, and people like Walter Winchell and Hedda Hopper filing stories and doing radio spots from the lobbies of the big casino-hotels, that was all going to end. Chicago would want a bigger bite. And their cousins from New York and New Jersey and Los Angeles would not be far behind. All those nice friendly fellas from that nice monthly breakfast meeting were not going to be so nice and friendly anymore. There was going to be blood on the desert. Mo did not want it to be his.

The Ivory Coast had to open, and open big. That was Mo's out.

Fatty Behr had never learned to drive. In Boston, where he spent his childhood, no one knew how to drive. Even the men who owned automobiles did not know how to drive. During the Depression only rich men owned automobiles, and they usually employed drivers. Later, after the war, average Joes started owning automobiles. They thought they could drive, even when they could not. Some of them had seen jeeps at Omaha Beach and Okinawa.

Not Fatty. He'd dodged the war on a medical 4-F. And he'd never felt obliged to learn to drive. He'd spent most of his professional life, if you could call it that, in New York. No one drove in New York. He'd knocked around San Francisco, but no one drove there, either. Now, in Las Vegas, it was a bit of a challenge. Living and working in between the Starburst and the Thunderbird, as the entertainment director, he had no need of wheels. Any business he conducted, he conducted in the hotels. He'd run across Las Vegas Boulevard two or three times a night. If he had to run downtown for something, he'd get one of Mo's guys to drive him in one of the Starburst or Thunderbird cars. Same with making runs to the airport. There was always a way to avoid driving.

Except for Haney. Haney was the problem. Haney would not come to the Strip to do the business they did together. And Haney would not meet downtown, either. It was always out of town. It was always private. Once, Fatty had brought a driver, and Haney had gone insane-y. Barking insane nuts.

It was early in their acquaintance. In fact, it was Fatty's first big buy. He had been told that a certain man would meet him at a certain time in a coffee shop adjacent to Hoover Dam. He was told to come alone and bring cash. Fatty had collected the cash and packed it in a suitcase. He had not come alone, though. He'd borrowed a car and a driver from the Hotel Cairo, where he had recently talked himself into a job as a talent booker. He and the driver left Vegas for their appointment. They arrived at Hoover Dam and parked, and entered the coffee shop at the visitors' center right on time. It was nine o'clock at night, and the visitors' center was closed, and the parking lot was empty. But the door to the coffee shop swung open, and Fatty and the driver went inside.

Fatty almost fainted when he saw Haney sitting there. He knew Haney was the cops. He knew Haney was bad cops. He would have gone back out the door, but Haney had two goons with him and they stood up when he came in and braced him and his driver. One goon pushed Fatty gently down into a seat. The other goon pulled Fatty's driver away from the table.

Haney said, "I told you to come alone."

Fatty said, "He's just the driver."

Haney said, "I see two guys. That means you're not alone. You're gonna do business with me, you gotta learn to listen. I say alone, I mean alone. Do you have the money?"

Fatty opened the suitcase. Haney eyeballed the bread. He looked across at the driver and said, "Give me the keys to the car." The driver, a mumbler by nature, reduced now to complete silence, slid the car keys across the table. Haney nodded at one of the goons, who took them and left.

There was silence but for the distant rush of water. Fatty was thinking he'd have to come back another time, during daylight, to see the great Hoover Dam. Architectural wonder. Engineering magic. All that, and a coffee shop. We live in the age of miracles.

He heard a car trunk slam. The goon returned, and set the car keys on the table again.

Haney stood. Fatty was surprised to see that he was not a big man. Most scary men were big men. Haney was just scary. He headed for the door, and everyone followed. He said to the mumbler, "What's your name?"

The mumbler said, "M-m-morris."

Haney laughed. He said, "M-m-morris, you're coming with us." He picked up the car keys and gave them to Fatty.

They all went outside. The goons moved Morris the mumbler toward their car, a low black sedan without police markings on it, and shoved him into the backseat. Haney said to Fatty, "The stuff's in the trunk. Next time, come alone. Get back to town."

Fatty said, "But . . . I don't know how to drive."

"Learn fast," Haney said.

Haney and the goons spun out of the parking lot, spitting gravel behind them. Fatty never saw Morris again. He was certain Haney had killed him and buried the body in the desert. In fact, Haney and his goons had driven Morris to Shipton Wells. Haney had given him a hundred dollars and said, "If you come back to Las Vegas and I see you, I'll kill you. Now go." But Fatty never knew that. It took him six harrowing hours to get back to town, jerking the car in and out of gear, wrecking the clutch and chopping gears out of the transmission and boiling over the radiator twice. It was four in the morning before he pulled into the Hotel Cairo parking lot. The car was ruined. He had missed two shows. The owner fired him. But the stuff was in the trunk.

After that, Fatty always borrowed a car and drove. Though he still did not really know how. Today, under a baking summer sun that seemed to turn the road to rubber, he was pushing a big sedan south on Highway 91. He had left the Strip an hour before. There was supposed to be some sort of roadhouse.

Haney and his men got there first. They parked behind the low ranch-style roadhouse building, leaving one man with the car and another trailing Haney as he went in through the kitchen. Moving slowly, poking his toe into crates of onions and potatoes on the kitchen floor, Haney sniffed the air and threw a critical eye on the short-order cook, who stood over his smoking grill, smoking an unfiltered cigarette and returning Haney's baleful gaze.

Haney said, "Where's the boss?"

The cook said, "Who's asking?"

Haney winked at the man who followed him into the kitchen. The man promptly whisked a copper skillet off a hook on the wall and swung it full force into the cook's head. The cook tumbled over sideways, swore, and righted himself.

Haney said, "Where's the boss?"

The cook hooked his thumb at the door.

Haney said, "Thanks."

In the front room four faded cattlemen were drinking beer in a booth. The room smelled of french fries. The owner, an old rummy Haney had not seen in years, sat at the counter with a cup of coffee and the end of an old, vile-smelling cigar. He looked up, then jumped up when he saw Haney. The policeman pushed him back down into his seat and said, "Relax, Flynn. We're not here for you."

Haney and his goon went to the booth at the far back. Haney sat facing the door. He said to the goon, "Get us something cold to drink. And make Flynn get rid of those cowboys."

Fatty pulled in fifteen minutes later. He parked in front but saw Haney's gorilla out back, sitting in the black sedan parked there. Outside the car the heat was vicious, the sun pounding down like a great hot hammer, pounding the anvil of the desert. Fatty wiped his forehead with a handkerchief and went out of the blistering light into the roadhouse darkness.

Some corny tune was playing on the jukebox. A guy was singing about a tumbling tumbleweed. Haney was seated near the back. Fatty went there and sat down.

Haney said, "Afternoon."

Fatty said, "Yes."

Haney said, "In addition to our usual business, I have a separate item to discuss with you. It concerns this Ivory Coast joint on the West Side."

Fatty was surprised. He kept that to himself. He thought of Morris the mumbler, and his bones baking under the desert sun. He said, "Yes."

Haney said, "Spooks don't bother me. But spooks with money make me nervous. Spooks with money and narcotics make me *very* nervous. I don't want there to be any narcotics on the West Side."

"There's narcotics there now. Not mine."

Haney said, "I know that. And I'm gonna stop that. But I want to know—and I want *you* to know—that you won't be bringing anything in after I close that down."

"Whatever you say."

Haney said, "I say no narcotics on the West Side. Not to anyone— not even to your white dope fiends. Bad enough we got them here at all. But it has to stop there. A Nigra who's drunk is a Nigra I can handle. A Nigra on dope . . . well, that's an animal. A wild animal. I won't have it in my town. What about the broads?"

Fatty said, "What about them?"

"You handling them? Or is it that man Deacon?"

"Deacon? And the Ivory Coast?" Again Fatty was surprised. Haney was asking him? About Mo's guy Deacon? Fatty said, "I don't know anything about the broads on the West Side. I thought Aunt Betty had that all sewn up."

"Betty's not my problem. I'm talking about girls outside, and girls in hotels."

"That's not my department. Everything is being done by that boxer Lee. He's making all the calls. I don't know about Deacon."

"What do you mean?" Haney turned his ice-blue eyes on.

Fatty took a moment. Should he sacrifice Deacon? He said, "Deacon's just a horn player."

"Just a horn player?" Haney stared. "Isn't he one of Weiner's tough guys?"

Fatty took another moment. Maybe Haney had Deacon already. Was there any value in protecting him? Or in protecting Mo? He said, "Actually, I think you're right. That would explain a lot. I see him in places where just a horn player wouldn't be."

Haney grunted, satisfied. Fatty had said what Haney needed to hear. Mo is leaving everything up to Lee. So, Mo is in. It's Mo's money.

Haney's brother-in-law, Holbrook, might find that a useful piece of information.

For himself, Haney was reassured that the guy Deacon was involved, too. Else, why would Fatty tighten up and try to lie to him about it? Even lying, Fatty was useful.

Haney said, "Pretty tough working the Starburst and the Thunderbird at the same time, huh?"

Fatty said, "It's a nightmare. Impossible. Everyone wants everything, all the time, and all at the same time. Between running the acts and keeping the customers happy—you know, the dope and the broads and the hooch and the room arrangements that no one is ever supposed to know about—it's a nightmare."

"Lucrative, though, eh?"

Fatty smiled. "It's not so bad, at the end of the day."

Haney said, "If you want the Ivory Coast concession on the hookers, let me know."

Fatty said, "Well, thank you. I'll keep that in mind."

"And keep it to yourself. I have a feeling this West Side situation is not going to be healthy for several people. You don't want to wind up on the wrong side of things."

Fatty went back out of the dark roadhouse into the blazing Las Vegas afternoon. Inside his car the air was molten. It took him an hour to get back into town. By the time he did, his hands were shaking so badly that he was almost tempted to dip into his own inventory. Instead, when he got back to his room, he took a pill. No good to get going on the needle. That was the way to wind up on the wrong side of things, as Haney had said, at the end of the day.

Deacon grabbed Dot in the gift shop. She was dusting the glass animals with a big feathered thing. Deacon came through the door and said, "Bet you could tickle almost anybody with a feather like that."

Dot turned on him, smiling. She said, "Want to give it a whirl?"

"When's your day off?"

"I'm off Sunday and Monday."

"You got plans for Sunday?"

Dot squinted her eyes at him and faked bashful. She said, "Not yet, I don't."

"Then here's some plans for Sunday, and for Monday. I need a favor. A friend of mine needs help running his café. One shift, maybe eight hours, on Sunday night. I'll make sure the bread is right."

Dot had stopped looking bashful. She said, "You want me to work in a coffee shop?"

Deacon said, "I need your help, Dot. This friend of mine . . . well, it's a long story. I'm asking you, as a favor. Just Sunday night. Then, Monday night, you and me'll get into a little trouble. Do something atomic."

Dot was smiling again. She said, "You know Spike Lee is over at the Copa Room."

Deacon said, "I got the Copa in my back pocket. You want to do that, we're sitting front-row center. Eating lobster and drinking champagne. If I can count on you for Sunday."

Dot said, "Sure thing, baby."

Deacon reached over and ran his thumb up the feather duster until he got to her hand. He said, "I'll pick you up Sunday, right out front, around noon. Then Monday we'll tie one on."

Deacon left her dusting the glass animals. He was thinking, *Who the hell do I know at the Copa? Nobody. Maybe Sloan has an in. Or the fat man. Or Mo? Can't ask Mo. No . . . could ask Mo. But then would have to explain to Mo. Don't want to explain to Mo. Or anyone. What the hell am I doing?*

He hit the pits going away from the gift shop. The joint was alive, though it was only four in the afternoon. Men and women in hats were smoking and drinking and throwing dice and drawing cards and laying bets as if time had no meaning. Which, of course, in the casino, was exactly the point. Maybe that was the appeal. The casino made time stand still. It made time go away. It did for the average man or woman what only music and dope did for Deacon: it made the whole crazy Ferris wheel stop, right at the top. You could see and you could

breathe and you were alive and yet you were not afraid. Then the
Ferris wheel came down and you had to get off. And then you got
on again. For these bums, though, the ride could get expensive. Lose
little, lose big. Or, maybe, win.

Normal people got the ride from winning. The real gamblers got
the ride from winning or losing. It didn't matter which, as long as it
was winning or losing *big*.

Deacon got the ride both ways—making money, with the music,
and spending money, with the dope.

He went up to Mo's office.

Mo was sitting, sleek and silver, at his desk, and he welcomed
Deacon in, waving at a chair, offering a cigar and a drink, patting
Deacon on the shoulder. Deacon said no to the smoke and yes to a
whiskey and water. He sat and lit a cigarette. Mo listened, and said,
"Sure, Deacon. I'll set it straight with Stella. Or I'll have Fatty set it
straight."

"That's fine, Mo. I just need to take care of some little business."

Mo, twinkle-eyed, said, "You'll need a car, too. I'll let someone in
the garage know. But you're killing me with the gas on this Shipton
Wells thing."

Deacon winced. *Of course Mo would know. Why in the world would he
not know?*

Mo said, "I haven't met the young lady. She must be something
special."

"It's not like that, Mo. It's not what you think."

Mo twinkled some more. He said, "If you say so, my boy."

Deacon winced some more. He said, "It's really not like that. She's
. . . she's just someone I'm trying to help out."

Mo twinkled. He said, "I understand. And it's none of my business,
anyway. As long as it's not against the law, or as long as you don't
get caught, you have my blessing. Whatever it is, it can't be half as
bad as what everyone else in this godforsaken town is doing."

"It's not."

"Then we're square."

Deacon thought about that idea, and finished his drink.

He said, "Actually, we're not quite square. I think maybe you owe
me some dough from that original Shipton Wells thing."

Mo smiled. He said, "*Do* you? I wonder if you could be right about that."

"There was supposed to be some cash."

"There was supposed to be a guy you were gonna send back to Los Angeles or make disappear in the desert, too. That's not what happened."

"The guy disappeared himself. Same difference."

"No," Mo said. "*Not* same difference. He didn't disappear. You left the body. You involved the cops. That could have been an enormous problem for us. It wasn't—but it could have been, because you did not do what you were asked to do. That's part of why you never got paid."

Mo waited. Deacon smoked, and said nothing.

"That, and you never asked to get paid," Mo said. "Which I always found very interesting."

"I was pretty shook up over that guy shooting himself."

"No," Mo said. "You weren't shook up. It was something else. I knew that morning, that first morning you sat in this office, sat *right there*, that there was something going on. You didn't want to tell me what it was. Do you want to tell me now what it was?"

"It wasn't anything. It isn't anything now."

Mo smiled. He said, "Okay. Take the car. Visit your chippie. You change your mind about what happened with the guy from Los Angeles, I might change my mind about the dough."

Deacon went out mad. Mo had him, and he knew it, and he enjoyed it, and Deacon hated that. "Visit your chippie." Mo said that to anger him. No other reason to say it. Nothing to do with Anita. Just a way of getting at Deacon. Mo wanted to rile him. Which meant that if Deacon got riled, Mo won. Deacon went out past Mo's front office assistant, forced a smile, and hit the elevators. Did Mo watch the eye-in-the-sky monitors, ever? If he did, he'd see a whistlin'-Dixie Deacon going away from him. The whole world loves you when you're happy. Deacon got Satchmo singing in his head, the sound like maple syrup pouring over gravel: "When you smilin', oh, when you smilin', the whole world smiles witchoo." The elevator bell rang. Deacon turned back on Mo's assistant, who had been watching him from under her lowered lashes. He said, "You know something? You and me are going to get *friendly* one of these days." She blushed furiously. Deacon stepped backward onto the elevator car just as the doors slid shut.

Bilious Bill Dawson strolled uneasily through the lobby of the Thunderbird Hotel. He did the walk same as every day. He'd done one-third of his daily service to the hotel, inking his signature onto a stack of purchase orders and paychecks. Then he'd had a swim and a few highballs, and gone back to bed. He'd slept through the hottest part of the day, then dressed for the evening in hand-tailored denim jeans, a hand-stitched western shirt that sparkled with sequins, a ten-gallon hat and matching kid gloves, and very expensive hand-tooled cowboy boots and belt. Silver spurs hung from the boots. Silver pistols hung from the belt. A silver star, bearing not the word SHERIFF or MARSHALL but the word DAWSON, gleamed over his heart. In his left front pocket was a roll of the dark-red-on-dark-green Thunderbird Casino's twenty-five-dollar chips. This was part of Dawson's duty as the president and resident celebrity at the Thunderbird: he was expected to hand out forty of them, every night, to lucky casino guests. In the hottest of the summer months this job was agony. The hat and belt and boots and gloves weighed seventeen hundred pounds in the heat. The spurs jingled like the gates of hell. Dawson ached with the pressure of the very air, and the pressure of the hotel guests staring at him as he clinked past them, as they wondered if he was somebody and, sometimes, decided he was not.

He went out now across the lobby, jingling all the way. Some evenings he couldn't get this far without some female screaming out, "It's Bill Dawson!" Other nights he got all the way to the front door and got outside and got on his horse and wondered whether anyone looking had any idea who the hell he was. Dawson wasn't sure which he preferred. His ego liked the first scenario. His fragile constitution preferred the second. If he could get to the horse and get on the horse, and get back through the lobby to the back lobby bar, he could get a highball. If he started conversing with some guests, he could get another, or two. If he continued in this fashion, he could hand out all forty of the luscious little chips before ten o'clock. Then they'd give him a fine lovely big tumbler of his tropical heaven, and he'd go out onstage. He'd tell two jokes and sing half of the words to "Carry Me Back." It had been the hit song from his most popular cowboy movie, *Out West Again*, and had somehow become his unofficial theme song. Onstage, he'd half sing, half talk the words, "At the end of the day / If you love me that way / Carry me back . . . / To the land that I love / Where the setting suns go / Where the desert winds blow / Carry me back / To the land that I love." Some of the women in the audience would be in tears before he was through. If there were some in the front row, and they were sweet and old, Dawson himself would begin to cry. By the end of the day . . . he would be in tears, and barely able to choke out the last "land that I love." Then he'd straighten up and wave a big wide farewell at the audience and say, "Cowboys and cowgirls, please say howdy to Tex Kino and the Wilson Sisters!" Or whoever it was. Some nights, he'd know before he got to the name of the band that he'd forgotten the name of the band, and he'd say instead, "Cowboys and cowgirls, please say howdy to . . . my pardners, and enjoy the roundup!"

And he'd leave the stage and throw himself back into that tumbler of fine tropical medicine. He'd usually go directly to his suite. Sometimes, if someone from the old days was in town, he'd go to the lobby bar and have a chat and a few more drinks. That invariably ended with some hotel employee saying, "Carry me back, my ass. Help me get this old drunk up to his room, will ya?"

Not tonight, though. Dawson had received a phone message that afternoon from Mo Weiner. It said, "Meet me in the lobby bar at ten-fifteen." That was pure Mo. No explanation. No apologies. Just "meet me." Dawson knew from experience that it was something important. Mo never socialized—not ever—and would be coming around at that hour to discuss business only if it was something urgent. The very thought made Dawson weary.

It was probably something to do with the extra checks he'd been signing. For the last two years, almost every day, there was a Thunderbird check written out by the Starburst-Thunderbird accountant to a name Dawson did not even know. He'd asked Killarney the third or fourth time what the check was for. Killarney had said, "Just sign it, will ya?" And Dawson had signed it. Was it Killarney's skim? Someone else's skim? Or legitimate expense? Dawson did not know, and did not need to know, and did not care to find out. He was doing his job, which was signing the checks. Writing them, and keeping track of them, was someone else's job.

But now Mo was onto it. Dawson remembered dimly the plot of a picture called *Silver Spring Serenade*. He'd played a good-hearted cowpoke who inherits a silver mine from an old guy whose life he's saved. Turns out the guy has a daughter, and the cowpoke agrees to run the mine with her. Pretty soon the cowpoke, who can barely read or write, is signing bum checks so the girl can skim the profits off the mine. Turns out she's being blackmailed. When it all goes belly-up, the cowpoke is left holding the bag.

Dawson could not for the life of him remember how the picture ended. He knew the cowpoke came out okay, because he *always* came out okay in a Bill Dawson picture. He wished he could remember *how* though.

When he got to the lobby bar, using all the strength he could summon, he said to the bartender, "Give me a little pot of black coffee, will you?" The bartender looked surprised, but did as he was asked.

Dawson lit a cigarette and sat down to wait.

Worthless Worthington Lee stayed up almost all night. He'd spent the afternoon meeting with Ivory Coast people. He was one week from opening, and there were ten thousand details to resolve. He felt he had, today, resolved one thousand. When evening came, he began meeting with the people who would assemble Jeeter's funeral. Food and drink and flowers and music. Worthless had made all the arrangements with the funeral home itself the day before, and the grave site at the cemetery was prepared. By three o'clock in the morning, Worthless had organized all the musicians. Most of them were sidemen playing at the Strip casino lounges. They came, after work, at Worthless's invitation. All of them, to a man, agreed to come back at noon to march down Jackson Street in Jeeter's name.

Worthless was back up and moving at eight o'clock. He said good morning to Dina, who had been up shuffling around later than he had, and left the house. He got his paper at Garcia's. He walked down

Jackson Street, underneath the tracks, out of the West Side, and had his breakfast at the Hotel Apache. He was back on Jackson Street and then in the Ivory Coast at ten o'clock. Everything was in place. Jeeter's casket would be carried from his bar, down Jackson Street, left on Bonanza, and straight into the Ivory Coast. His closest friends would get into the hearse with the casket and go on to the cemetery. Everyone else would eat and drink and carry on in the Ivory Coast ballroom—almost 100 percent completed now. This would be a fine send-off for Jeeter. It would also be a fine introduction for the Ivory Coast. Worthless liked killing two birds with one stone. This way, he would get to just about every important colored person in Las Vegas. They'd see the hotel, they'd drink his liquor and eat his food, and they'd come back.

At noon precisely, the doors to Jeeter's barroom opened and the six pallbearers carrying Jeeter's box came into the street. More than a hundred people were waiting there, the men in fedoras and the women carrying fans, all baking under the midday heat and throwing flat shadows straight down at their feet. Twenty-five or more musicians waited with them. When the pallbearers appeared, the horns began a mournful dirge—Worthless, who had no ear for music, thought it sounded like "St. James Infirmary"—and the procession began to move up Jackson. Within a block, the tempo had lifted. Something that sounded to Worthless more like "The Darktown Strutters' Ball" poured forth. One old lady said, "Hallelujah, brothers." By the time they got to Bonanza, the tempo had snapped up even further. The band sounded like it was playing Dixieland—awfully lighthearted for a funeral, Worthless thought, but very nice just the same. When the procession swung into the Ivory Coast parking lot, as previously arranged, the band began to play standards. "When the Saints" was first, of course. Thirty beautiful colored girls in tight bodices and frilly petticoats appeared on the second- and third-floor porches above the entrance, dancing and swinging those can-can steps. The crowd, which in the four-block walk had swelled to at least two hundred, swarmed through the front doors of Worthless Worthington Lee's hotel and casino, across the lobby, gasping and calling out with pleasure and surprise, and into the main ballroom. Onstage, an entirely separate band of musicians struck up. The curtains parted. The audience burst into applause. There, onstage, under one gorgeous red baby spot, was Louis Armstrong, ol' Satchel Mouth himself, horn in one hand and handkerchief in the other, shining under the lights and smiling like Satan. The crowd went wild. Worthless Worthington Lee's heart swelled. Satchmo, whom Worthless had never met but whom he had called upon the evening before and begged to perform for the late Jeeter's final moments, stepped up to the microphone and began to earn the one thousand dollars Worthless had offered to pay him for his time. He said, his voice hoarse and rasping and beautiful, "Ladies and gentlemen, this one is for Mr. Jeeter." The band swung into "West End Blues."

The Ivory Coast, in that minute, was born. Worthless knew, right then, that it was all going to happen. He'd gotten word that about half the celebrities on his wish list were planning to attend the opening night. He'd gotten word that a whole bunch of *other* celebrities wanted to attend, too. There had been calls from people representing Cary Grant and Jack Benny and Tallulah Bankhead and Spencer Tracy. Someone from Sinatra's office had called. He'd told them all the same thing. Sunday night, last Sunday night in May, May 29, come on in. If only half of them showed up, Worthless thought, he was a guaranteed winner. If only . . .

Jeeter's coffin, meanwhile, had gone out the kitchen doors and into the back of a waiting hearse. No one but the driver accompanied him to the cemetery. Jeeter was buried there without further ceremony.

Mo had come in so quietly that he had joined Dawson and ordered a drink almost before Dawson knew he was there. The movie star turned and . . . there he was, nodding his order at the bartender and surveying the casino around him.

Mo said, "Nice crowd tonight, Bill."

Dawson nodded.

Mo said, "You're going out of business."

Dawson gasped. He said, "We're going out of business?"

"Not 'we,'" Mo said. "You. I'm selling the Thunderbird."

"But why?"

"It would take too long to explain, Bill, but trust me—it's the smart play." Mo smiled with entirely believable affection. He said, "You'll be taken care of. You know we've been siphoning off a little cash for

the last two years or so. It's all banked. You will be pleasantly surprised, I think, at how it adds up. And the siphon is going to get
bigger."

"Why?"

"The 'Bird has to be losing money. It has to be losing money fast,
and in a way that makes it look like bad management. Otherwise, we
can't sell it. Unfortunately, the bad management will have to look
like your fault. You'll never get a job like this one again. But you
won't need one. If you take the dough you get out of here and put
it someplace smart, you'll be okay. You might be able to buy back
that ranch you pissed away."

Dawson signaled the bartender to take away the coffee and bring
him a cocktail. The bartender, though, looked at Mo. Mo nodded.

Dawson said, "I don't like it, Mo. Why does it have to look like
my fault?"

Mo smiled and said, "Because you're the patsy, Bill. You've always
been the patsy. It's nothing personal. Someone has to be it, and
you're it."

"But I built this casino, Mo. I *am* this casino."

Mo took a deep breath and exhaled deeply, surveying the room,
quieting his mind. Dawson was pathetic.

Mo said, "No, Bill. You didn't build the casino. We needed a
front. You had a clean name and a clean reputation, and you were a
little bit famous a long time ago. I don't think you brought in any
business. I don't think you drove away any business, either. But you
want to keep it in perspective. We protected your investment, and
gave you a place to stay and a job to do, and gave you a staff to
keep the booze flowing. Pretty good life for an old lush, don't you
think?"

Dawson stared and blinked.

Mo said, "Pretty good life. And no reason for it to stop. You'll take
enough dough out of here to set yourself up exactly the same way,
on your own. I'll even see to it that you get the same man to be your
valet. Or you can try and hang on here. Either way, the Thunderbird
is going down."

"And I'm left holding the bag," Dawson said. "Just like in *Silver Spring
Serenade*."

Mo looked blank.

Dawson said, "The bad guys try to leave the cowpoke holding the bag. But that's not the way it ends!"

Mo said, "If you say so, Bill. But that's the way *this* one ends. Don't chump yourself out of a good thing. Ride along, and you'll do fine. Buck it, though, and you'll get buffaloed. You can't win."

Dawson nodded, defeated.

Mo said, "That's the way. You'll find the money makes a big difference."

The little radio hummed and glowed in the fading light. Anita lay on a bedspread of chenille, feeling the heat fade, feeling her energy fade, resting between shifts. It was late afternoon, the time between the two buses from the East, and she had told her uncle, "I don't care if anyone comes. I got to lay down." Let him serve some coffee. It was his place, anyway. Wally would be on duty in an hour or so. She went to her cabin.

But now she heard no wheezing bus stop, no slam of doors, none of the skidding of tire on gravel that meant customers. She heard nothing but the radio humming, and under it the sweet, muffled sound of Artie Shaw or Harry James or some bandleader like that. She thought of Deacon, of how his horn would sound, of his face as he played.

Sleep did not come, though. She watched the light fade and felt the heat go, but sleep did not come. She rose from the bed and went to the closet.

In the corner, underneath a hatbox that did not contain a hat, wedged between two suitcases that held no suits, was the overnight bag that Deacon had asked her to keep for him. She drew it out of the corner and into the closet doorway. There was just enough light to see—if you had seen it before and knew what it was.

There were two reels of film. Anita had opened one, once, and held the tiny frames up to the light. She had not been able to make out the images at first. Then she'd looked inside the paper folder underneath the film reels. There were photographs there. She could make out those images very easily.

They were horrible, the most horrible thing she had seen ever.

There was a man, and he was having sexual relations. And she could not even have made herself say, out loud, the rest of it. She'd shoved the photographs back into the folder and then looked at the second reel of film to see if it contained the same thing. It did.

The images frightened Anita deeply. She wanted to weep or wail or find the man in the pictures and kill him. He was beastly and horrible, worse than any man, worse than the men she had known. What he was doing to the others . . . It was the worst thing she could imagine. In fact, she could not imagine it, not really. It was inhuman. It was—

The cabin door swung open and threw light across the bed and into the room. Anita started, then froze. Her uncle stood in the doorway, adjusting his eyes to the light, and then came into the room. He said, "Oh, there you are," and sat on the bed as the cabin door slowly shut behind him, bringing the dusk back over the room.

He said, "It's gonna be busy tonight. I got a feeling. You wanna rub my feet for me?"

Anita said, "No."

He said, "No. Not you. Nothing for your poor *tio* who takes care of you."

Anita, with as much silence as was possible, closed the overnight bag and slid it across the closet floor, back between the two trunks. It slid with a *ssshhhh* sound. Anita sat looking at the floor, praying for her uncle to continue thinking about his feet.

He said, "What's in the bag?"

She said, "Nothing. It's just an old bag."

"I need a bag like that for the hospital."

"This is just a nasty old bag."

"Lemme see it."

She said, "How 'bout I clean it up for you, make it nice?"

He said, "Yeah, okay. *Man*, my dogs are dying."

Anita pushed the bag into the back of the closet, and rose from the floor. Her uncle was spread-eagle on the bed, his hands clasped behind his head. His goiter had gotten bigger. It stood out like a big white egg on the side of his neck. The doctors were going to cut it off. She wondered what they did with it after that, and what it was like to cut someone with a knife. She thought her uncle looked frightened. She thought he looked like a fat gingerbread cookie. If she had a big knife, she would cut him in half and serve big pieces of him to the people in the photographs.

He said, "Whyn't you ever be sweet to your old uncle anymore, Neeter?"

Anita moved close to the bed, and said, "You ain't being expecially sweet to your old Neeter, either."

Her uncle's eyes snapped open. He said, "I can be sweet. You know I can."

Anita said, "Well, then . . . How 'bout giving me a couple days off?"

Her uncle grunted and said, "I'll think about it. Maybe when I go in the hospital. Maybe."

"Wally could watch over things. Or you could close for a night or two."

"Close the café? Never. And Wally . . . you know Wally. He's an idiot. He can barely pour a drink." Her uncle lay back on the bedspread. "But I'll think about it. Maybe you gotta trade me something for it?"

Anita said, "Maybe *I'll* think about it. Now get out of my cabin so's I can get ready for this big crowd of customers you say is coming."

Her uncle groaned and rolled back off the bed, and shuffled his feet to the door. He had a look on him. Anita knew the look. It told her that she could do anything she wanted with him and get anything she wanted from him, if she did just the right thing at just this right moment. Like what she used to do with him in the hammock. Her stomach rocked violently. She said, "Get out, now."

When he was gone, she went trembling back to the closet. She wondered again what in the world Deacon had to do with the horrible man in the pictures. She prayed it was blackmail, or some similar angle. And she prayed that the man in the pictures was rich and important and that Deacon would get all kinds of money from him. And she hoped Deacon would hurt him, bad, once he was through.

She took the film cans and the folders out of the overnight bag. She took an old shirt off a hook in the back of the closet, and wrapped the cans and the folders in it, and shoved it all into the bottom of the empty hatbox. She felt in the lining of the overnight bag, as she had before, just to make sure. There was nothing but the vile pictures. She took the overnight bag into the restaurant with her.

Later that night, when the thousandth customer had finished his coffee and said good night and gone out to the car that would take him away from Shipton Wells and back into a life that was actually worth living, as Anita scrubbed maple syrup and ketchup and dried milk from the counter, her uncle crept in. She smelled the booze on him before he got to her, and spun on him. He had that dazed look from the cabin, still, but now he was drunk, too. He said, "Nita, baby," but she was ready. She reached through the short-order window and grabbed a carving knife. She said, "Get away from me, you pervert."

Her uncle, surprised, stopped in his tracks and tried to focus. He said, "Now, wait, Anita, *baby*. . . ."

She waved the knife at him and said, "If you touch me, I swear I'll cut it off."

He cursed, something under his breath and in Spanish, and turned from her. Anita put the knife away and finished mopping the countertop. He left. From somewhere in the back of the joint came a crash, like the sound of tin cans falling. She heard him curse again, in her head, calling *her* something sexual and angry. Calling *her* that. Pervert.

Deacon had been onstage for what felt like hours when they signaled his solo. He rose unsteadily and felt his chair scoot out from under him as he stumbled up. Someone said, "Whoopsie daisy," and Deacon turned in the wrong direction and grinned at someone who wasn't there.

He was at Mamie's again. It was two or three o'clock in the morning. There had been the usual two sets at the Starburst. He'd found Fatty, and gone back to his room and fixed. That was supposed to have been it. But then he was somehow in the lobby bar, and then he was somehow with these two men and a woman from Los Angeles who wanted to see something hot, and then they were not at the Starburst anymore. He did not remember the people from L.A., or how he got to Mamie's, or even who got him up onstage.

But the song was "Tenderly." He was standing up, cradling his horn. The room was dark and close and lovely. Deacon planted his feet wide on the floor, and began. He blew, and it came out all smoky and foggy and soft. Not cold, though. It was a hot fog, a warm smoky feeling like a San Francisco afternoon in the summer. Deacon closed his eyes and saw the Golden Gate Bridge, and beyond, and the wind brushing the waves on the bay. He blew big, wide smoke rings of sound, fat blue notes that rose and hung in the air and drifted. As he played, he could feel them hover and collect and move around the room. They were smooth and gentle as clouds. He touched the music with a lover's hand. A mother's hand. His mother's hands. His lover's hands . . .

Anita.

When he opened his eyes the crowd was clapping and no one was looking at him anymore and he tried to sit down but the seat had gone away. He sat and kept sitting and there wasn't anything to stop him, so he kept going until he was sitting on the floor, still playing, crowding notes together until they formed a chorus—ba dat da DAH da, ba dat da DAAAAH da, ba dat da DAH da DOT! Then the song was over and Spooky or Smokey or Slappy or whatever the guy's name was who ran the band was saying, "Ladies and gentlemen, Crush Velvet, Deacon and his blue horn . . ." and people were clapping and Deacon smiled and raised his hand up and waved from the floor.

Seven

DEACON WAS GOING across the casino floor, wondering whether he could keep down any breakfast, when he heard someone call his name. He turned. A bellboy wearing the Starburst uniform dashed up and said, "Telephone call. Take it at the desk."

Deacon said, "Yeah," into the phone, and found Anita there.

"I've got the afternoon and evening off. My uncle feels really bad. He says he's closing for the night."

"I'll see if I can get a car."

"No. The bartender guy is going to drive me. I'm going to come in to Las Vegas."

"O-kay. Lemme see . . ." Deacon was thinking: *Where? What? How to get this done?* He said, "How well do you know your way around?"

"It's my first time."

O-kay. Deacon thought another moment, and said, "Have him take you to the Greyhound station. It's downtown, right near Fremont Street."

"I can't come and see where you work?"

"No, honey. You can't come here. I'll meet you at the station at about . . . two?"

"All right." She sounded lost and small.

"We'll do something fun."

"All right."

Deacon put the phone down and found a buck for the bellboy, who had stood by, waiting for a tip. Deacon said, "Here, kid. You obviously need this more than I do," and went out the front of the Starburst.

The sun was high and hot, and Deacon didn't have his shades on and he wasn't wearing a hat. He decided to forget about breakfast.

Instead, he flagged a cab, and stood with his eyes blocking out the sunlight until he heard the car roll up and stop in front of him. He slid inside and said, "Take me over to the West Side. Over on Jackson Street."

Tom Haney rose that morning filled with gratitude. It was good to be running the police, in this town, at this time. It was good to be the lieutenant. It was hardly like police work at all. He rolled in late, rolled out late, rose when the mood suited him, ate and dressed well, and left the donkey work to the donkeys. Somewhere else in this city, at this moment, someone who worked for him was door-knocking some bum, trying to get a lead on a stolen TV. Someone else was sitting in the station-house basement, thumbing over stale, sweat-stained rap sheets, trying to figure out what happened to the stuff in the evidence locker. Someone else was getting the manager to open the door to an apartment or a back hotel room that hadn't been opened in a week or more, lighting a cigar and holding his nose as he went inside, choking back the smell of clotting blood or rotting food or vomit or semen or something—some stinking remains of some crummy crime.

And Tom Haney was having toast and coffee at home, while his man drew him a bath and laid out his clothes.

He had done all those other things. He'd been some other lieutenant's donkey, and he'd done all the donkey jobs. He'd washed revolting stains out of the backs of police cars. He'd door-knocked women to tell them their sons and husbands were dead. He'd had to beat the truth out of men too scared to tell it, and sometimes had been forced to beat them pretty bad. He didn't have to do that anymore.

Because it was early, he'd go see his sister. He had a little money accumulated, "collected" in the course of police business, for the foundation. He'd get that over there today, see how things were going, see what needed doing. Sometimes he found that the very thing the foundation needed to keep going—a new typewriter, some new carpeting, stationery supplies, a coffeepot—was available for free if Haney just asked. He'd simply say to someone who'd got his tit in the wringer on some stupid misdemeanor, "I tell you what I'd really appreciate your doing, while we wait for the paperwork on this thing to get down to the courthouse. I'd sure appreciate your sending a little coffee percolator like that over to these friends of mine. . . ." Nine times out of ten, the thing would get done just like that. The tenth time it wouldn't, and that guy would find the paperwork got to the courthouse just the same way as the guy who donated the coffeepot. So far, nobody'd ever had a lawyer mention it in court.

Today, driving out of the hills and into town, Haney reminded himself to remind himself later to start a background check on that guy Deacon. Something was fishy there. Might as well find out now, before the fish started to stink.

By two o'clock Deacon had not figured out yet what to do with Anita when she arrived. He'd collected and ditched several plans. They were all good plans, but they all involved things that he did not think would be smart things for Anita. Deacon sat at the coffee bar, watching the buses come and go, thinking, *She's not old enough, and she's not white enough. And this is a dopey-ass situation to be in.*

Then a car drew up at the curb and she got out, and he forgot all about that. She was wearing a white print dress with a little pattern of yellow stripes, and a matching white hat, and her legs were bare. She leaned into the car to say something to the driver, then turned and stood with one hand on her hip and the other hand shading her eyes as she looked around the station. She was, simply, as beautiful a girl as Deacon had ever seen. He stood up and almost ran to her.

Thirty minutes later he had walked with her down Fremont and over to Lassiter's, which was a little steak house where Deacon thought no one would give him any unnecessary guff. Fremont had already knocked her out. She stood underneath the big winking cowboy sign for the Pioneer and just laughed and laughed at the guy the locals called Vegas Vic. She said, "He's smoking a cigarette. He's *waving*," just like she was the first person who ever noticed that. Deacon took her through the lobby of the Westerner, which was the classiest of the casinos downtown, and then through the Las Vegas Club—"The House of Jackpots"—so she could see the gleaming rows of slot machines. She wanted to throw a coin in and pull the big lever. Deacon said, "Naw. That's for suckers. Let's go get us a steak."

He was thinking: *We'll both wind up in jail if I don't get you out of here but quick.*

The guy at Lassiter's gave them a look, but only a look. Deacon ordered for both of them, and got her a soda and got himself a Carling. Anita was like a little girl. She kept asking him questions— Did he ever go into those casinos? Did he gamble? Did he play poker or craps or blackjack, or what? Did he ever win a lot of money? Did he ever *lose* a lot of money? How much? Did it cost a lot to stay in a place like the Horseshoe? Or the Hotel Apache? Was that where the rich people stayed?

It was as easy as giving candy to a baby. She just loved it all. She was glowing with it. Deacon kept thinking, *If it was nighttime, I'd know what to do next. If it was dark, and not so bright outside, we could go down Fremont like any other couple. If it was late enough, we could go in and have a drink and pull on a slot and . . . just like folks.* As it was, every time he thought about the next thing to do, he decided it was the wrong thing to do.

Then he thought about the Ivory Coast. He said, "Hey, I got a good idea. There's this friend of mine that's going to open up this big joint. How about we go and see him about getting you a job?"

"A job?"

"Sure. He's going to open this big hotel-casino. He's going to need all kinds of people—waitresses and receptionists and cigarette girls and who knows what all."

"I hardly know how to wait tables."

"Don't worry about that. I talked to him already. He said to drop on by."

The guy in Lassiter's was still giving Deacon that look when they left. Deacon said, "I know what you're thinking, man. I never saw a girl this beautiful before, either."

Anita socked him on the shoulder as they went out the door.

Deacon had been to see Worthless the day before. Worthless was surprised to see him come through the door. It was daytime, for one thing, and he didn't usually expect to see guys like Deacon in the daytime. And the Ivory Coast wasn't open yet, so he couldn't imagine what business Deacon would have with it. Worthless figured that guys like Deacon were exclusively in the business of playing music, drinking juice, smoking reefer, and chasing skirt. And none of that happened during the daytime in a casino that wasn't open yet.

But Deacon came breezing in, loose and easy, and Worthless stopped worrying. He said, "Crush Velvet, you are out of bed and looking mighty chipper today."

Deacon said, "Clean livin', Worthless. I quit drinking and smoking."

Worthless said, "Is that *so?*"

"Yep. Right before I went to bed last night. Then I started up again this morning."

Deacon lit a cigarette and watched Worthless laugh. He hated doing stuff like this, and didn't know where to start. He gazed around at the workmen coming and going, brisk black men carrying tools and supplies, black women moving back and forth. It was as busy as a train station. But Worthless was looking at him kind of funny, from behind that laugh.

Deacon said, "Looks like you're getting close here."

"Yes, indeed. I think we might make it."

"Looks good." He gestured at the main room and the men and women working there, and spied a familiar face. "You got that boy Sumner here all the time, too."

"Yes, we do. There he goes now."

"Don't work him too hard. Leave him some energy for that saxophone. You know he's something special with that thing, don't you?"

"Well, I heard that. I'll try not to bust him."

Deacon nodded and stepped over to a cocktail table to put his cigarette out. Across the room, Summer had stopped his work and was staring over at Deacon and Worthless as they talked. Deacon was getting more uncomfortable by the second.

He said, "So I got this thing I need to ask you about. I got this friend. A sort of girlfriend. Her name is Anita. She's . . . she's just this amazing . . . But the thing I need to ask you is: I might be trying to see if there's anyplace where she could, you know, if someone—I'm trying to get her a job."

Worthless laughed out loud. He said, "Deacon, is that *all?* I thought you was gone ask me to marry you. Of course I'll see this girlfriend of yours about a job. What's she do?"

"Man, you gotta meet her to see. She doesn't have to do anything.

She can just stand there and stop a clock. She's just . . . something else, man. You gotta meet her."

"Well, then, let me meet her. And if I can do something with her, I will."

"Worthless, thank you. I'm picking her up in about an hour. Can I bring her around here after that?"

"Sure. But let me ask you this: is she a white girl? 'Cause I am not hiring that many white folks."

"Worthless, you gotta see her. I don't know what she is, exactly. She isn't a white girl. Or she isn't *just* a white girl. She's too beautiful to be just anything."

"She mulatto?"

"Or something. Half of this, half of that."

"Quadroon? Octaroon?"

"Nectaroon. Nectarine. You'll see her. She's out of this world."

Worthless said, "I see she means a lot to you, anyway. Bring her around. I'll see what I can do."

Haney was always struck, when he had not seen her for a while, by the physical oddness of his sister. She was so tall and so thin, and her eyes were so big, that she looked hardly human. She looked like Olive Oyl. She looked *worse* than Olive Oyl. On the other hand, the fat, sloppy Holbrook was no Popeye. So maybe they made a match. The idea that a person like Cora and a guy like Holbrook could mate, for life, was almost impossible for Haney to imagine. At least they could not have kids. The offspring would be horrible to look at.

There were no offspring at all around today. Haney knew without asking that they were not in the building. He could smell them— smell the talcum and the milk and the other baby smells—and he knew without even looking that today they weren't there.

In the back he found Louise, his sister's assistant, tidying up a playroom. She turned, startled, when he came striding in, and said, "Why, Mr. Haney. I didn't hear anybody come in the front."

"You need a bell. You used to have a bell. What happened to the bell?"

"I don't know. I'll ask Johnnie about that."

"Who's Johnnie?"

"He's the older gentleman who takes care of things around here."

"I'll talk to him. Where is he?"

"Well, he took your sister and some of the children over to the hospital. It's time for some of them to get booster shots."

"Tell her I stopped by, will you? And get that damned bell fixed. You need to know about it if someone's coming in that front door. Could be anybody. Could be a thief."

"But all we have here is the babies, Mr. Haney."

"A thief won't know that until he's killed you all. Get the bell fixed."

Louise shuddered. Haney smiled at her and said, "Good day," and went back out the front door.

The car was hot and sticky inside. Haney wondered for the hundredth time what Las Vegas would be like without the goddamn heat. It would be about perfect. But of course it would be different. Probably kept all kinds of creeps away, that heat. Kept all kinds of businesses away. He jammed the air conditioner on high and sat with the car idling while he waited for the thing to cool, then pulled the car slowly around toward downtown.

Off Fremont, just as he was turning the corner onto Las Vegas Boulevard, goddamn if he didn't see that guy Deacon turning the opposite corner, going the opposite way. Haney jammed the accelerator down and spun all the way around the block, and came back down Fremont from the other end.

And there he was, across the street, coming straight up Fremont. He was walking with a very pretty brunette, a slim girl wearing a clingy white dress and a big white hat. She looked like a cool drink of water. And that Deacon was walking along with her like some schoolboy, shuffling along like a lovesick kid. Haney slowed the car and stopped it just under the huge Vegas Vic sign, just in front of the Pioneer. The two of them were walking easy, not going anyplace, passing time. Lovebirds. Haney smiled. If he could figure out who the girl was, he would have Deacon's tit right in the wringer. Without even knowing why he wanted it there, he found the idea satisfying. Knowledge was power. Power was everything. Haney liked power. He uncradled the radio microphone and buzzed up the station house. He said, "Get Harrigan. Tell him to leave the station immediately and come over to the north end of Fremont Street and look for my car. Tell him to make it snappy and keep his big Mick mouth shut."

The heat and the big lunch and Anita were making him almost dizzy. Dizzy Deacon. He walked with her up Fremont, almost melting with desire, hanging on her words as if they were coming from heaven. He knew she was saying nothing—chattering about her uncle, and the creep named Wally, and the customers, and how tight folks are about tipping—and still it was like music in his ears. The whole scene was magic. The street glittered like ice. The tourists moved in slow motion. Vegas Vic waved and smoked and said, "Howdy." A black car was parked across the street from them. The man inside must have been baking like an Idaho russet. Anita said, "Maybe the casino people know how to spend their money. The café people are so tight, you can hear their pocketbooks squeak when they open them."

Deacon said, "We'll ask my friend about that. Look here. They're putting up a banner for that Helldorado thing." He pointed to where some workmen with a ladder were stringing up signs from the lampposts. "That's this parade thing they have here. They get covered wagons and Indian dancers, and they have floats and all that. There's a beauty contest, and a beard-growing contest. Maybe you could win something."

"I *hope* you mean in the beauty contest."

"Well, I don't know. I've never seen you first thing in the morning. Could be a big beard-grower, too. Maybe you could win both those contests."

Anita socked him on the shoulder again. His heart had never felt so full. He said, "Let's go around the corner, to the Apache, and see if we can get a cab. Too hot for all this walking."

Harrigan found Haney at the top of Fremont, the big black sedan idling with the air conditioner going full-blast. The Irishman jumped in and slammed the door and sat in the cold for a second. Haney said, "I want to get a line on this character. He works for that bastard Weiner, over at the Starburst. He's up to something fishy, and I want to know what it's all about. We're going to pull around the corner here, and you'll see him walking along with his girl. I want to know what they do and where they go, and I want to know who she is, too. See what you can find out."

Harrigan said, "Right."

Haney pulled the sedan around the corner, onto Las Vegas Boulevard, then turned around in an alley and went back to Fremont. They caught up with the couple there. Deacon and the girl were standing in front of the Hotel Apache. Deacon was pulling a bill out of his pocket and handing it to one of the carhops. Haney said, "Looks like they're getting a taxi. Better jump."

Harrigan went out. He was thinking, *I could have stayed in that nice cold car, and we could have tailed the taxi that way. But no. Now I got to jump out into the heat and ankle myself over and stand in the heat and wait in the heat until this monkey gets a taxi over here, and then get into a hot taxi and try and follow them.* He went without a word.

Haney watched Harrigan's broad Irish back going down the street. He thought, *What a great thing, to be a big, stupid, simple mug like that. Never asks a question. Never has a clue. What a nice, easy way to live. Just happy, doing his police work, never wanting more from his life than a pat on the back and a pint of Four Roses.* He switched the air conditioner down a notch—it was arctic in there—and drove back around to the station house. It was almost lunchtime.

Going off Fremont in the taxi, Deacon slid his arm around Anita and sat back deep in the seat. He felt her slacken. As she watched downtown go away, her eyes lost some of their luster. Deacon said, "Hey. What's the matter?"

"Nothing. I guess I just thought it was bigger."

"What was bigger?"

"All this. Las Vegas."

Deacon laughed and said, "But that's just a little bit of it. You just saw the downtown part of it. You didn't see the Strip."

Anita brightened again. "There's more to it?"

"Lots more. You ain't seen nothin' yet. Especially 'cause you haven't seen it at night. That's when it shines."

"I wish I could stay tonight."

"I know. Here's the Ivory Coast."

The facade was almost complete now. Something that looked kind of like the streets of New Orleans and the Vieux Carré, and sort of like the prow of a sailing ship, and kind of like a wedding cake rose from the sand and asphalt. Palm trees swayed, fronds fluttering, in the afternoon wind. The parking lot was like a big black lake without boats on it. Deacon paid the cabbie and said, "Let's go find Worthless."

They did, inside, sitting with a man in white overalls staring at a page of blueprints, which he and the man in overalls had spread over a bar in the casino area. Anita took his hand and squeezed it hard. Deacon squeezed back, then let it go. He said, "Come on, now."

As he approached, Deacon heard Worthless say, "I say we got to have it, the fire department code say we got to have it, and the blueprint say we got to have it. So, where is it?"

The man in overalls was scratching his head, and pondering. He said, "I'm sure there's a good explanation for this. And you got company."

Worthless turned. Deacon watched his eyes come to him, then move to Anita, and stay there. Even in the poor light, blinking after the glare of the taxi ride, Deacon could see Worthless's reaction. His eyes stayed on Anita until Deacon said, "Hey, Worthless. This is the gal I was talking to you about."

Worthless moved away from the bar and left the white overalls there. He said to Anita, "Welcome to the Ivory Coast. My name is Worthington Lee. You must be . . . ?"

She said, "I'm Anita. Some folks call me Neeter. Or Anita."

"I'm some folks. I'll call you Neeter. It's a pleasure." He took her small hand in his two big ones, then gave Deacon a professional sort of smile. "Hey, Deacon."

Deacon said, "Anita would like to have a talk with you about some employment."

"I understand that," Worthless said.

"So, maybe I'll let you two talk a while, and then I'll—"

"You come back later," Worthless said. "We'll just get to know each other a little. And you come back."

Worthless took Anita's hand again and began to steer her across the casino. She went without a backward look. Deacon nodded at the man at the bar wearing white overalls, who said to Worthless, "You want me to just wait here? I'll just wait here. I'll just sit here and not do anything. I'll just wait until you're done, and sit here and not do anything at all. I think I'll just sit here."

Worthless wasn't listening to him, anyway. He and Anita went all the way to the far end of the casino, Worthless gesturing here and there with his left hand and holding Anita's hand with his right.

The white overalls said, "I'll just sit here while you get your ashes hauled by the nice little piece of black—"

"That's enough," Deacon said.

The man in the overalls regarded Deacon with cold, dull eyes. He said, "Oh. She's a friend of yours, too?"

"That's right, man."

"Okey-doke. Then I'll just sit here and not say a goddamn thing."

"That's the ticket," Deacon said. "You wouldn't want to get a big ass-whipping, from me and from Worthless and from several other guys, just because of some comment you made about a girl you don't even know. Right?"

The man in the overalls said, "Right," and turned back to his blue-prints.

Deacon wandered across the casino, out into the lounge area, and back to the nightclub. The place was huge, and it was beautiful. There was a comfortably large stage, fronting a sea of dinner and cocktail tables. Seating must be six hundred or more, Deacon was thinking. Big new red curtains. The smell of turpentine, or paint. Ashtrays already on the cocktail tables. Deacon lit a cigarette, and imagined the view from the stage. This would be a good room.

Out the side door of the nightclub Deacon found some men scurrying around a food prep area. He went through swinging doors and into a kitchen. There were more men there, all black, most of them in white, scrubbing and polishing, sharpening knives, running a stone over the big griddle. One of the guys was Summer, from the Star-burst. He was coming forward with two big blades, swinging them like a Turk swinging scimitars. He said, "Dee-con. How's it going, man?"

"Hey, Sumner. It's going along. How 'bout with you? How's this joint doing?"

"Doing good. Who's the pony you saddled up for Worthless?"

"She's a friend of mine. Trying to get her a job."

Sumner laughed. "Well, that shouldn't be too hard. Depending on what kind of job she wants."

Deacon said, "It's not like that, man. She's just a waitress, or a hatcheck girl, or something like that."

A couple of black men working with pots and pans stopped and started giggling. Sumner winked at them. He said, "Whatever you say, Deacon. I can see you working it."

"No. I got no angle on this one."

"You the operator."

"I'm no operator."

"I hear you a long-distance operator. Got girls in Chicago and El Lay."

The men with the pots and the pans laughed out loud now. One punched another on the arm. Two more men carrying rags stopped to listen.

Deacon said, "Not me, man. I'm no operator."

"You operating now, baby. Bringing in a girl for Worthless. That's *operating*. That's the love doctor. Operating."

Deacon said, "Aw, cut it out."

"*Cut it out!* It's a love surgeon. The love doctor is in, and it's an *emergency*."

Sumner's small audience laughed and moved off.

Deacon said, "You finished?"

Sumner nodded and said, "I'm sorry man. I just jiving you around some."

Worthless had taken Anita around the casino floor and shown her the nightclub and the coffee shop and the restaurant and the place where the gift shop would be—if the idiot builder got his blueprints straightened out—and was guiding her now down the hall that led to the swimming pool and patio. She seemed impressed. But it was hard to tell. She was quiet. Very quiet, in fact, for such a pretty girl. She wasn't quiet like she knew she was in charge. She was quiet like she was just watching and waiting and listening. Like she wasn't entirely there and was taking notes for later. Worthless did not know when he'd seen a prettier girl. She looked the way he remembered Dina looking when they first met. Not that she looked like Dina. That wasn't it. But looking at her made Worthless *feel* the way he felt when he first looked at Dina. As he stared at her, a voice in his head was saying, "Tsk, tsk. An old dog like you." But he kept staring, and guiding.

He said, "Out here is the swimming pool. We gone put another snack bar—like a snack *shack*, you understand—over there. Folks can get a cold soda or a bag of potato chips or a little sandwich without having to get dressed and go to the coffee shop."

Anita nodded and said, "You'd better put some water in the pool first."

Worthless laughed louder than he should have and felt the afternoon sun blaze down on him. He had not been outside during the middle of the day in many days. The heat made the patio seem very unappetizing to him. But in the light the girl was even more beautiful. He said, "Let's get back inside, where it's cool. I want to show you some of the guest rooms."

Anita said, "Don't you think we should find Deacon?"

"There's time for that, now. Come on over this way."

There was a shape ahead of them down the hallway going toward Reception. Coming in out of the light, into the darkened hall, Worthless couldn't read the face that went with the shape. But he tightened up inside just the same. The shape did not look like good news.

It belonged to a big, red-faced man in a black suit, who was moving methodically down the hallway palming doorknobs. He looked up when he heard the patio door swing closed, then turned and faced Worthless and Anita. He said, "Who's the boss man here?"

Worthless smiled a big gummy smile at him and said, "Well, thass me, suh. What can I do fo' *you*?"

"You can get over here and show me the . . . the . . . occupancy permits. And the permits for your elevator."

"Well shucks, now. We ain't even *got* a elevator."

"Then get me them occupancy permits. Police business."

"Sho' nuff. Gimme about two minutes." In a lower voice, he said, "Anita, you wait here. I'll find Deacon."

Anita stared at Worthless as he went away from her, transforming, just like that, from a proud, strutting cock of the walk to a shrinking, shuffling Bojangles. She turned her look on the cop, who returned the stare without any expression. When Worthless had left, he said, "Where's your boyfriend?"

"What do you mean?"

"The white guy. The guy you came in with."

"I don't have any idea what you're talking about."

The cop said, "Get an idea. I'll ask you again. Where's the guy you came in with?"

"I don't know who you mean."

Anita moved all the way into the lobby area that fronted the reception desk. She sat there, praying that Worthless would return or Deacon would reappear, or something.

The white policeman said, "I'm not going to ask you this too many more times."

Then Worthless was shuffling back toward them. He said, "I got them occupancy papers, suh. But I declare I'm confused. Ain't these papers for the fire department?"

The white man said, "That's right. So what?"

"Well, ain't you with the *police* department?"

"I never said that."

Worthless gave the cop a long look. He said, "Well, no, suh, I guess you didn't say that."

"Where's the man that came in with this chippie?"

"Man that came in with this girl?"

"You heard me."

"Lawd, suh. I didn't see her come in with no man. She juss drop by to speak with me on some personal business."

The white cop said, "Personal business, huh? Personal business. I like that. I'll be around. If I find out that personal business involves prostitution, I'm coming back here like a hurricane. I'll blow your house *down*. Get me?"

"Yes, suh."

The white cop looked at Anita again and said, "I'll be watching you."

Then he left them. Worthless said, "Nothin' worse than a policeman without work to do. Let's go see can we find that Deacon."

On the ride back to the Greyhound station, Deacon had told Anita to hush up and wait until they were alone. He nodded at the driver, winked at Anita, and said, "Not yet."

Then they were back at the station. The sun was low in the sky, and everything was painted orange and red. The station was busy. Men and women getting ready to leave town milled about, many of them wearing the defeated look of men and women going away broke. Deacon lit a cigarette and said, "Okay. What happened?"

Anita told him about the white cop, and about the tour she'd gotten from Worthless. She said the last thing Worthless had told her, just when they'd spotted Deacon sitting in the front bar in the casino, was, "We'll have to talk another time about a little job for you."

"But he said you could have one?" Deacon asked.

"Not exactly, but I think I can. I think he liked me."

Deacon laughed. "I *know* he liked you—if that's the right word. I've never seen him behave that way with anybody. You knocked him out."

"That policeman is what knocked him out. He turned into a little kid. He acted like his daddy had caught him playing with matches."

"He was playing with you. Playing with fire."

Anita smiled up at him. He gave her the smallest possible kiss on the cheek. She pouted at him and said, "That's all the kiss I'm gonna get from you?"

"That's all the kiss you gonna get from me *here*. When I get you alone, I'll kiss you all over, till you tell me to stop."

As he turned from her, Deacon felt her shudder. There was still no car for her at the curb. It was going on six o'clock. He had a sound check.

He said, "I gotta fly. You think this Wally character is going to be much longer?"

Anita shrugged. Her pout returned. Deacon said, "I'm sorry, baby. You know I would stay with you if I could—all night, if I could. Maybe if this thing works out for Sunday, we'll have a whole night together. I'll show you everything there is to see."

"And what do you think about that job?"

"It's in the bag. I'll make it happen. I promise. And I'm gonna go now."

He gave her a tiny kiss again, and was gone.

Harrigan had stood, across the Greyhound station, watching the whole thing. He stood now, watching Deacon go. He had changed his mind, six times or so, about what was going on. When the guy left the girl there, he changed it again. The guy was either her pimp, or her boyfriend, or just a friend, or a business partner of some kind, or maybe he was some combination of two of those. Because he acted like all those things, sort of, and none of those things. Harrigan checked his watch. Haney would be in the station, wanting a report. The girl was sitting alone. She was minding her own business, watching the road like she was waiting for someone. She was *not* working. Harrigan was about to give up and go in when he saw the girl hop to her feet and run across the station floor. A tall, gangly kid wearing a loud sport coat was waving to her from just outside the building. *The boyfriend,* Harrigan thought. But then the girl got to the curb, and she dodged the kid's embrace and instead just got into his car. Harrigan said, "Typical," under his breath, reminded again that all women, always, are bad news. Look at this one, playing two sides against the middle. Clear as day, and Harrigan didn't even know the little tramp's name.

When Deacon and the girl had gone, Worthless went over to the bar. A kid he'd hired out of the Starburst, a kid named Fidget, was polishing glasses. Worthless said, "Make me a little bourbon highball, will you, boy?" And the kid, who'd been a shoeshine man at the Starburst and had never tended bar before, said, "A bourbon highball coming up."

Worthless sipped at the drink, clinked the ice cubes around in the glass, and thought about Dina, clinking around their house all night long. He suddenly felt sorry for himself. *Why,* he thought, *did all this happen to me? Why did all this happen to her? We been good people. We been decent, God-fearing, righteous in the ways of the Lord. Why us? I look at a girl like that Anita—a girl so young and fresh and sweet, and not yet bruised up by her life—and I remember Dina when she was young and sweet, and I got to ask myself what in God's name did I do wrong? Played it as straight as I knew how. Always did the* right thing. Always tried to be good *man.*

Worthless, watching Fidget work while he wondered what had gone wrong, noticed for the first time that the shoeshine boy had no fingers on his right hand. He said, "Say, what happened to yo' hand, man?"

Fidget stopped wiping glasses and smiled up at Worthless. He said,

"A d-dog bit off my f-f-fingers. When I was a boy. The h-h-hand come out all right, but it wadn't anything they could do about the f-f-fingers."

"You do good work, just the same," Worthless said. "I'm glad to have you over here."

Fidget said, "Thank you, sir," and went back to cleaning glasses. Worthless set the drink down and stopped feeling sorry for himself. He thought: *Well, why me, indeed? Why do I get to run this big casino? Why do I get to eat regular and have a roof over my head? Why do I get to have all my fingers? Why me?*

That black boy Sumner was coming out of the kitchen, yanking along with him another young man that Worthless had hired to run the staff of waiters. Sumner said, "There you are. We got a problem." With that, he muscled the young man forward by the scruff of his neck and hurled him toward Worthless, who caught the smaller man in his arms and pushed him slowly away.

Sumner said, "This man is stealing from you. Skimming off you, and you ain't even open yet."

Worthless said, "Well, what is it?"

"Skimming, man. He signing in deliveries that ain't complete."

Worthless eyed the young man. His name was Johnson or Lincoln or Jefferson, or some president. Worthless said, "That true, boy?"

Johnson or Jefferson stared at the ground and kept his mouth shut. Sumner kicked him on the behind and said, "Go on, now." The young man remained silent.

Worthless said, "Well, if you ain't gone say it ain't so, then I'm gone guess it is. So . . . git. Don't come back."

Sumner said, "That's it? You gonna let this thieving bastard steal from you and just walk away?"

Worthless said, "That's it. Now git, before I change my mind."

The young Johnson scampered for the front of the building without looking back.

Sumner said, "You ain't even gonna call a cop?"

"We had enough cops here for one day. Don't want no more cops here at all. And that boy couldn't have done much damage, anyway. Best to find out he's a crook now, and get rid of him. I'm glad you took care of that."

"That's all right."

"Now you better show me what we missing." Worthless put his arm out and wrapped it around Sumner's shoulders, and walked with him back into the big kitchen.

"And tell me what you know about that gal of Deacon's."

Eight

DEACON MADE THE Copa Room connection through Fatty, who, naturally enough, knew someone who could make it happen. Fatty promised to make that guy make it happen. When Deacon pulled a twenty from his wallet, Fatty said, "Save that for the Copa guy. And you'd better make it two Jacksons."

Deacon made a note to make it two Jacksons and said, "What about the other thing?"

Fatty said, "See me Friday."

That had been the middle of the week. Next Deacon had gone to the gift shop and hooked up again with Dot. He'd dropped another Jackson there, pressing the bill across the glass countertop at her and saying, "Get yourself something nice for Monday. Meantime, I'll be around Sunday, late morning. Say, noon?"

Dot said, "Noon."

He'd dropped a sawbuck on the guy who kept Mo's cars shiny, too, to make sure one of the machines would be gassed and good to go when he was ready. Sloan was back there in the garage, eating a sandwich and sipping Coke through a straw. He said, "What are you fixin' up to do, Deacon?"

Deacon said, "Nothing fancy. Just need a car."

Sloan said, "Man *got* to have a car."

Deacon said, "Man got to drive."

Sloan said, "Got to go someplace."

Deacon said, "Only way to go."

Sloan sucked on the straw, and said, "You gone."

Deacon tipped Sloan a hat that wasn't there and went away. He slid up to the front of the Starburst. The guy who delivered Mo his

Cuban cigars was just leaving. Deacon said, "Hey, man, you heading down the Strip or up?"

The man said, "Going down Fremont way."

Deacon said, "Carry me?"

"Hop in."

Twenty minutes later Deacon was on the second floor of Gorman's. It was Las Vegas's only "nice" store for ladies. All the women bought their nice things there. Deacon wanted to buy something nice for Anita. He had no idea what that meant. But he'd thought about it. He didn't know her dress size or her height or her weight. But he knew exactly where the top of her head brushed his face, and how wide her shoulders were in his arms and how small her waist was in his hands. After some monkey business with a saleslady named Berta, which involved Deacon clasping several of Berta's fellow shopgirls around the shoulders and waists until they could all agree on a size, Deacon was looking at three cocktail dresses and one evening gown. One of the cocktail dresses was a seafoam-green affair with chiffon. Another was fire-engine red, and had a matching hat. The third was basic black. Deacon did not know what Anita had in her closet. But he could see her in the black and knew it was right. He said, "Wrap it up." And Berta said, "Are you sure you don't want a girl to go with that?" and three of the shopgirls, who were hovering, laughed.

Deacon took the big black box with a big white bow out to the boulevard and thumbed a ride back to the Starburst. He was hoping he would not see Dot coming through the back side of the casino and have to explain the package. That would have cost him several more Jacksons, and he was already wondering where he was going to get the ones he'd need for Sunday and Monday nights. But he did not see her, or Sloan or Fatty or Mo. He slid up to his room unobserved, and parked the package in the closet.

Fatty had said wait until Friday. For Anita, he must wait until Sunday. For now, he decided to wait until dark. He lay down on the bed and rested.

Worthless had told the two contractors the same thing twelve or fifteen times already. Now he said it again. They stood in front of him in the reception area of the Ivory Coast—or rather of what

Worthless hoped but did not really believe would *become* the Ivory Coast—and listened while he told them again: "If this place is not ready on time, both you boys are in serious, serious trouble. I won't answer for my own behavior. This is the last warning I'm gonna give you. If the doors don't swing open Sunday night on a business that's ready to do business, both y'all better be dead already."

The two men nodded and went away. Worthless groaned.

It would never work. It was never going to work. It never had a chance of working. There was no point in worrying now whether it would work or not. Worthless went looking for the electrical contractor.

Making the call to open Sunday had been the roughest decision Worthless had ever made. The pros and the cons were many, and they multiplied every time he started thinking about it again. Every argument against opening on a Sunday had an equally powerful argument *for* opening on a Sunday. And every argument *for* opening on Sunday had its equally powerful argument against. When the arguing was done, Worthless came up with this:

1. Nobody ever planned anything for Sunday night, so no one could have other plans.
2. Many of the town's colored folks had Sunday night off already.
3. The kind of folks who had to worry about going back to work Monday morning weren't the kind of folks he wanted in his casino anyway. Not on opening night.
4. Sunday was the Lord's day. It was go-to-church day. Folks who worried about such things could come on a Sunday night with a clear conscience, ready to start sinning all over again.
5. What the hell?

Worthless was expecting every kind of calamity. In restless sleep, night after night, he saw his worst fears realized. One night he presided over a vast and empty Ivory Coast—spotless, silent, totally void of all human presence. Another night a mob of angry white men stormed the Ivory Coast and took Worthless and poor Mr. Peet outside for a necktie party. Another night the Ivory Coast was packed wall-to-wall with young women. They all looked like Dina had looked when she was a young woman—which is to say they looked a lot like this new girl Anita—and it broke Worthless's heart.

By the Wednesday before opening, he was exhausted. He felt like he was staggering around the canvas in the seventh or the eighth round. He was able to keep going only because he knew it could not last beyond the fifteenth. He fought until he heard the bell, every day, and then he collapsed in the corner. Then he got up and did it again.

Haney had been in again. Sumner, whom he'd removed from the Starburst and made entirely his own, came in now and said, "That cop is here again."

Worthless crumbled a little inside, and said, "Tell the lieutenant to come on back."

Sumner said, "Naw. He says you got to come out with him."

Haney was waiting on the sidewalk, pale and cool, dressed all in black like always, and looking like the Grim Reaper under the noonday sun. Two of his goons stood behind him, leaning against a black sedan parked at the curb. Worthless listened but could not hear the sound of the motor running, which relieved him. At least they weren't taking him out to the desert. . . .

Haney said, "Walk with me. Down to Jeeter's place."

Worthless said, "Yassuh. I right wid you," and shuffled toward him.

Sumner spat on the sidewalk in disgust. Worthless said to him, "You sit tight and keep an eye on things for me, boy."

Sumner said, "No. I'm coming."

Haney regarded the two of them. He said, "Sure. You come, too. Raleigh, isn't it?"

Sumner swallowed hard and said. "Roland."

Haney said, "Ro-land. Roland Sumner. Upitty name, isn't it? You come, too."

Folks on the street stared as they passed—Garcia sweeping in front of his shop, and Miss Pringle drawing back the curtain in her front room. At the curb, where he was just setting up for the night, Roscoe John paused as he rubbed spice into a butt of pork, and whistled under his breath. He said to himself, "I *knew* ol' Worthless was the man killed that Jeeter." Worthless passed them all without staring back.

The place had been kept locked since the morning of Jeeter's funeral, when they'd loaded the casket into the hearse. Now it smelled like an old beer hall—old booze, old cigarette smoke, stale bad breath, and lousy perfume. Something was going rotten in the refrigerator, too. Worthless thought of the big walk-in freezers at the Ivory Coast. *How long would a man last in there,* he wondered, *before he started to smell like this? How long did a man last in the ground, before he started to smell like this?* Haney's gorillas stepped into the shadows at the back of the main room. Sumner faded into the back, too. Haney himself took a seat at the bar. Worthless stood, hands at his sides, pained.

Haney said, "We have some interesting leads on the killing of the nigger Jeeter. I imagine you've heard some interesting things, too?"

"No, suh," Worthless said. "I ain't heard nothin' about nothin' about Jeeter."

"Mmm-hmmm," Haney said. "And *you* had nothing to do with it."

"No, suh," Worthless said.

"But you are going to help us figure out who *did* have something to do with it."

"Me, suh?"

"That's right." Haney looked around at the room, at the carpeted floor, and just now seemed to notice the odor. He wrinkled his nose and said, "You're going to be in the center of everything. You're going to be hearing everything, and seeing everything, on the West Side. You will be king of the West Side. You'll have your queen. What's her name? Diana?"

"Dina."

"Die-na?"

"Yassuh."

"Dina. Like a dinosaur. Dina Saur. Like Dinah Shore!" Haney laughed. It was an ugly laugh. Worthless pulled his lips back over his teeth until it looked like a smile. He had hardly ever wanted to hurt someone the way he wanted to hurt Haney.

"Yassah."

"Heh-heh," Haney finished. "You know, we all want the same thing out of this Ivory Coast. You want to make a big splash and attract all the right people and avoid the bad elements. So do I. I want a high-class establishment here on the West Side, for the colored people. What I don't want is a whorehouse for white folks. I don't want fraternizing. It's called miscegenation, and it's white men and colored women together, and I won't have it. That and narcotics. I just won't have it. Is that clear?"

"Yassuh."

"And if there's some element, some bad element, that's causing you problems, you need to let me help you with that," Haney said. "We have a new assistant district attorney. His name is Filcher. He's very eager to take care of Jeeter's killing. If you've got a problem with someone, we could kill two birds with the same rock. Make it look like this person you have a problem with was the man that did Jeeter, if you see what I mean."

"Yassuh."

Haney regarded Worthless. This was a guy who had fought dozens and dozens of men in the prize ring and who had a zero-knockout record. This was a guy, he had to remind himself, who had said, "I know about the foundation." He had looked, that night, like a scared, shaking spook who'd just got religion. Now he just looked like a scared, shaking spook. Same guy. Haney thought, *I will never understand niggers.*

He said, "I'd like to take that killing off the books. Not that any-one's clamoring to have it cleared up, you understand. That guy Jee-ter—no one cares who did him. Still, it's messy, and I don't like to leave things messy. So we're looking for the right guy. You got some ideas, you can tell me about them. And that goes for you, too—wherever you went."

Haney glanced around until he spotted Sumner, sitting like a block of ebony, at the back of the room. "Step out of line, it could be you. *Roland.*"

Sumner didn't even blink. Worthless felt a rush of pride. Sumner was not a boy anyone was going to push around. But Haney must have been joking. He didn't seem to notice Sumner, now that he'd threatened him.

He said to Worthless, "There's another little thing going on. Man was on the way from Los Angeles or Chicago to deliver some material to me. Personal material. He got ambushed out around Shipton Wells. He never made it to town. And I never got the material. You hear anything about that?"

Worthless's head was buzzing like it had bees in it. A million angry bees. This white man, this white *policeman*, looked scared. Nothing spelled trouble like a scared white policeman.

Worthless said, "No, suh. Ain't heard nothing about that."

Haney said, "But you'd tell me, if you did."

"Yassuh. Surely would."

"Good. Unhealthy, for you not to. Very unhealthy."

Worthless nodded. First a scared policeman. Now a scared policeman making threats. Next, of course, was a scared policeman making good on the threat.

He said, "Yassuh."

Haney smiled. "At the end of the day, for me, it's all a question of narcotics and chippies. I don't want 'em over here. If I find out you got 'em in your Ivory Coast, we're going to have big problems. Otherwise, I'm going to be your best friend on this thing."

Worthless pulled his teeth back into a grin, again, and felt pure hate come up in his throat. He croaked out, "Yes, *suh!*" and stepped forward with his hand out. Haney stared at it with disgust and shook his head.

He said, "Let's beat it, boys." And they were at the door and gone.

Sumner slid forward. He said, "We are going to have bad trouble with that man."

"We got trouble *now.*"

"What's the 'personal material' crap?"

Worthless said, "The Lord only knows. Now, let's get back on this thing and not let them cops cost us any more time."

It was like a little game they played. Anita had decided to look at it that way. In the late afternoon, when her uncle was very tired, during the lull between lunch and dinner, he would sometimes lie down in the living quarters attached to the café. He would rest for fifteen or twenty minutes. Anita would pray that he fell asleep. Often he did. Sometimes he did not. Then he would call out, and she would go to him.

As happened today. She was cleaning the coffeemakers. It was Friday. There would be lots of late traffic, from people running to Las Vegas for the weekend. They would want lots of coffee. The café and the bar were empty. Wally would not be on duty for another two hours. Her uncle had still not agreed to give her Sunday off. He hadn't said no but he hadn't said yes, either. And she imagined he was just as aware of this as she was. He said, "Neeter? Bring the baby oil!"

It always started with a massage. Her uncle lay in a rope hammock strung taut between two posts. Anita dragged a chair over next to it. He was lying facedown in the dim light, almost snoring, his breath heavy and unpleasant-smelling. Anita sat. She pulled her uncle's shirt up, and then removed the cap from the bottle of baby oil. She splashed a little into her hands and began to massage his shoulders.

Within two or three minutes he began to moan, and to squirm. Anita moved her hands lower and began to massage his middle and lower back. His moans increased. Anita pushed the waistband of his trousers lower and used her thumbs to work the flesh around his hipbones. He would groan, and wriggle. Anita sat straight in the chair, her knees together, her posture perfect, her strong hands working over his lower back.

Then she stopped. Practice had shown her how to finish fast, and the way to finish fast was to stop, right now, and wait.

If there was something Anita particularly wanted, she would ask him for it just before she touched his thing. He would always, but *always*, tell her yes. Only once had he changed his mind after, and told her he would not give her the extra money she wanted. She had waited until the next time he called for a massage. She had rubbed his shoulders and his middle back and his lower back, oiled her hands slowly, and then left the room and walked out of the building and across the road into the Greyhound station. She had heard him shouting her name while she calmly sipped a Coke in the empty, barnlike space. When he finally came stomping across the street, red-eyed and hysterical, Anita knew she had him. She said, "Maybe you'd better give me the money first, and then go lay down again." Her uncle had flinched as if she'd slapped him. Then he'd reached into his pocket. She had gone to him again in his hammock. It was the last negotiation of that kind they'd ever had.

This time, she waited until he was almost twitching with desire, and said, "I'm gonna need to take that Sunday off when you go in for your goiter."

Her uncle grunted.

"You gotta say yes," she said. "Deacon's got someone lined up. Another girl."

Her uncle grunted.

"You gotta say yes."

"Okay. Yes."

Anita slowly removed the cap from the bottle of baby oil. She poured a bit more of the clear liquid into her palm. Then, noisily as possible, she smeared her hands together and rubbed the baby oil around. By now, her uncle was electrified. Anita counted another twenty. She then reached both hands under the hammock. There, sticking through the rope, was his pointy, drooling thing. Anita counted to ten, then clasped it in her oily hands. With one slow stroke now, or two, she could finish. Her uncle moaned horribly, and the hammock shook, and with it shook the posts. The entire cabin seemed to shudder. Then it was done. Anita rose and went to the sink, and turned on the hot water. When it was warm enough, she rinsed and washed her hands. She left the room without looking at her uncle again. She knew, from practice, that he would sleep for twenty minutes, then rise and clean himself and the mess on the floor. Then he would come back into the café and never say a word about what had happened.

Tonight, while he slept, Anita finished cleaning the coffeemaker and then scoured all the pots. She thought, weary to think it, *I am ready for this part of my life to be over. I am ready for the next part to begin. Sunday night must be something* special.

"I assure you, Mr. Dawson, the pleasure is entirely *mine*."

Dawson smiled his Hollywood cowboy smile and shook the skinny assistant district attorney's hand. He said, "Well, ain't that nice."

But Filcher was not finished. He said, "I'm *serious*. This is like a dream come true."

Dawson smiled some more and signaled the bartender. He and the skinny D.A. were in the lobby bar. Dawson had on his western outfit. He had just done his turn in front of the hotel, on horseback, and had given away about half his "welcome chips," when one of the registration clerks had brought this character forward and made the introductions. All strangers made Dawson nervous. This guy Filcher made him particularly nervous. He said, "Just lemonade for me," and turned his attention back to Dawson.

"You're almost the whole reason I'm out West in the first place," Filcher said. "I just can't tell you what an impression your movies had on me. Particularly the earlier ones. Like *Sagebrush* and *Three Rode Out.*"

"Those are my favorites, too," Dawson said. The bartender was taking forever with his drink. Out of the corner of his eye he saw the idiot fighting with a can opener and a can of pineapple juice. He said, "Max! We're parched over here, pa'dner."

"And *California Cantina.* I was just a little boy when I saw that. I remember looking at this big, strong, masculine man and thinking, 'If only *I* could be like that.' You played a sheriff. That's what sparked my interest in law enforcement."

"Is that so?" Dawson said, working hard to keep his voice steady. Here at last was the drink. He said, "Mud in your eye, son," and drank off two-thirds of the boozy tropical beverage. "Let's have some more of these, Max. Long's you got that damn pineapple juice open."

Filcher said, "I never told anyone. Might have sounded a little strange, you know? I became a prosecutor because of this big sissy Hollywood cowboy."

Dawson stiffened and said, "How's that, son?"

"You remember the sheriff was a coward at first, and then has to do the manly thing after his deputy gets shot."

"I'd forgotten. But you're right. We shot that in Santa Barbara, y'know."

"It's such an honor. When Lieutenant Haney told me you owned the Thunderbird, well, I had to come right over. I've only been in town a month, you know."

"Is that a fact?" Dawson asked, desperately wishing this was over. He had about twenty more of those "welcome chips" to dump before he could go back to his room and lie down. He pulled four from his pocket and slid them across the bar at Filcher. "Maybe you'll come and see the show. I sing a little, tell a couple of jokes. The orchestra is something else. Maybe you and your family can stop by tonight."

Filcher said, "Family? I don't have a *family.* What do you think?"

Dawson thought, *Ah. He's one of the boys.* With that, he relaxed. He did not know how it happened, but it did. Word got out somehow that he was not like the other Hollywood stars, that he was different. Discreet as he was, word got out that he liked young men. And sometimes he'd meet a young man, like this one, who knew. He never said a word, of course, and made a particular point of avoiding anything intimate with them, unless they were very good-looking, but his heart softened to the young man just the same.

Dawson said, "Bring some friends, then. It's a fine show."

"I won't miss it. In the meantime, I just have to ask you a couple of things. I hope you don't mind if I squeeze a little business in."

Dawson smiled his friendly smile now. It was smaller than the cowboy smile, but more appealing. He said, "You go right ahead on. Max! Let's have that next round!"

Filcher leaned forward and clasped his hands together on the bar. Dawson could smell the soap on him now and see clearly the comb marks in his perfectly groomed little head. He wasn't bad-looking, not at all. Dawson wondered what it would take to get him up to the room. Probably nothing at all. "You know, I've got some terrific old movie posters upstairs." Or, "I bet *you'd* look swell in cowboy clothes." Those lines had all worked, at one time. Instead, he gulped at the drink Max set before him.

Filcher said, "I hear business has been a bit rough for you and Morris Weiner recently. I hear the rake is down considerably. I also hear you and Mo have been skimming pretty steady for a while—maybe skimming more than is smart."

Dawson said, "It's not me. I have nothing to do with the money at all."

Filcher said, "Please, Mr. Dawson. May I call you Bill? Bill, please. I *really* don't want to hear it. My point is this: the Thunderbird is going up for sale soon. You're looking for a buyer stupid enough to believe that the casino could be a big moneymaker if it wasn't being managed by an old boozehound like you."

"Now, you just wait a minute," Dawson said. "You're talking to Dashing Bill Dawson."

"Not anymore," Filcher said. "I'm talking to Three-Dollar Bill Dawson—as in queer as a three-dollar bill."

Dawson rose and said, "That's enough."

Filcher pushed him back down. He said, "Keep your shirt on, Bill. That *is* the plan, isn't it? Sure it is. So, my point is this: you know the old creeps who run this city, all the casino operators, who meet once a month for breakfast? I need someone in that room for me. So I need to steer this hotel to someone on my side. I can do that, and you can still sell, and you can still sell at the right price. Or you might be able to stay on board with the new owners, whoever they turn out to be. But I need to steer it, so that I get someone in that room. If you can't find the buyer you want, or you decide to stop skimming and take the hotel off the market, we'd need to think of something else. I *still* need you in that room."

Dawson, stricken, said, "I've never been invited."

"So get invited."

"But how? Mo is the one that goes."

"And I can't crack that egg, can I?"

"Crack Mo? Never."

"That's right," Filcher said. "But you I *can* crack, right? We have an understanding."

Dawson said, "Well, sure. I guess we do. You and me . . . we understand each other. We're kinda like family."

Filcher said, "What do you mean?"

Dawson smiled his big smile again. He said, "Well, maybe more like cousins. Kissin' cousins, maybe. Fellas who understand each other."

Filcher stood up and stuck a five-dollar bill on the bar. His smile was ice. He said, "You pathetic old fairy. Fellas who *understand* each other? Don't kid yourself. But think about what I said. I need to be in that room, and I think I can find a way to make you be the guy who's in it for me."

Dawson could only nod.

Filcher, going, said, "Kissing cousins! See ya, cuz!"

The district attorney's laugh, as he was going away, was horrible. Dawson put his face in his hands for a moment, then called out, "Max! Send a cocktail down here."

Mo was in his office with Killarney when the phone call came in from Hollywood. Killarney rose to leave. Mo motioned for him to stay. He said, "This won't take long," and picked up the receiver.

A female voice said, "Please hold."

Then it was Albert Sherman on the line. Mo said, "Hello, Sherry," and "Mmmm-hmmm," and "Is that so?" and then, after listening a long time, "You have him meet me here at three o'clock, Sherry, and we'll take care of the rest. Consider it done." Then, after listening again for a while, he said, "Bye," and hung up.

"That's settled, then," he said to Killarney. "That Hollywood studio guy is sending a crew up to film the opening of the Ivory Coast. He's going to make a movie about it or a movie that takes place in it, or something. Good publicity, don't you think?"

Killarney said, "Fine."

Mo said, "It's pure genius. He came up to film the Thunderbird, you know."

Killarney said, "That's one of the things we need to discuss. Dawson is balking."

"He doesn't want to go?"

"He doesn't want to go at the rate we've offered him."

Mo rose and walked to the window and looked out. A plane was landing at McCarran. Cars lined the Strip. Life was good.

He said, "Leave it to me. I'll get him hooked up with the guy Sherman, from the studio. We'll distract him with that. Make him think Sherman's an investor or something. I'll get him to sign and I'll get him out."

"Good luck. Now the bad news."

"Let's have it."

"No one is going to go above two and a half mill for the 'Bird."

"I don't believe it."

"Then *you* go meet with the money guys," Killarney said. "I'm telling you, everyone laughs if you say three million."

"Then we're talking to the wrong people," Mo said, and came back around to his desk. He picked up a Cuban and bit off the end of it. He said, "No one will gamble in an empty casino. No one likes to sit at an empty table. What can we do to get some people to sit at *this* table?"

"Like who? Everyone's already been invited in."

"How about Marquez or one of those pirates?"

Killarney looked shocked. He said, "Marquez wouldn't pay a nickel for the Thunderbird."

Mo said, "Sure he would. Marquez would take the 'Bird in a minute if he could get it at the right price. So let's put the word out that we're hurting and that the price is falling, and let them figure out how far and how fast it's falling. One of them is bound to make a bid. Once we've got one of them in, we can get a couple more. Then we'll start them in against each other."

"And then what?"

"And then I don't know. Either one of them gets it, or someone we haven't met yet comes in and sees the action, and he gets it. Maybe one of these Hollywood guys, or something like that. Who knows? Maybe Dawson still has friends we don't know about."

"That's a desperate idea."

"I'm a desperate man. Now . . . are we finished?"

"We're finished. Especially if you can't get a fish for the Thunderbird. With all we've laid into the Ivory Coast . . . I don't even like to think about what happens if it doesn't open up right."

"Then don't think about it," Mo said, and smiled as he lit the Cuban. "Just sit back and enjoy the ride."

Deacon would probably not have gone on his own. It was late. The second set had run long. He was tired. There was nothing left of the Fat Man's stuff. Fatty had promised more by Friday. Now Friday was here, but Fatty was not.

Then Sloan appeared out of nowhere. He said, "Hey, boy. We going to the West Side."

Deacon said, "I got no wheels, man."

Sloan said, "Man don't need no wheels. Got me a Buick Century. We gonna fly."

Deacon thought about it for just one moment and said, "Then let's fly."

It was a sharp ride, big and shiny, and it smelled brand-new. Deacon lit a smoke and said, "This is that four-door job."

"Check it out," Sloan said. "It's got that Dynaflow just like the Roadmaster. Just like the Riviera. And no centerposts. You roll all the windows down, it's like flying around in an airplane."

"Who'd you steal it from?"

"Lady I know got her big daddy to buy it for her," Sloan said. "And the lady can't drive."

"Nice daddy."

"Gone daddy."

"You drive it."

There didn't seem to be much happening on the Strip. Sloan cruised Fremont, too, and it was quiet. Some cat he knew was standing in front of the Hotel Apache. Sloan tooted the horn and then wagged his finger at the sidewalk, but kept going. He said, "How about taking me across the tracks?"

Deacon said, "Sure. Where?"

Sloan said, "I don't know, man. Where you go. I never been over there."

Deacon said, "Then let's go. Drive on."

He guided Sloan up to Bonanza and across to Jackson, saying as they passed, "That big building there is going to be the Ivory Coast."

Sloan stared. There were black people everywhere on the street. Deacon pushed him on a few blocks and said, "Pull in over there. We'll check out Mamie's."

Sloan stared some more, and got quiet. He was nervous about leaving the car. He was nervous about carrying his wallet. He was just plain nervous. Deacon said, "Nothing's going to happen to you or your car or your wallet—except you got to take some money out of it, and spend it, 'cause I'm broke."

A couple of guys Deacon had last seen jamming with Spike Mulligan were onstage with two more guys that Deacon did not know, one of them strumming a guitar and all of them blowing hard. Deacon waved at the man behind the bar and steered the big-eyed Sloan to a table. He looked like a salmon, pink in the face, gasping and staring around, trying to smile.

When he got his drink and paid for it, he quieted down some. The band was first-rate, doing a thing that sounded like Django Reinhardt. Deacon said, "Coleman Hawkins used to solo on a Django Reinhardt thing just like this."

Sloan said, "I got no idea what you're talking about. Where's the women at?"

Deacon waved his hands around and smiled. The women were everywhere. But none of them were white women. They stayed an hour listening to the quartet hammer around. Sloan had three more drinks, and got smiley and sloppy-looking. All the women in the room appeared to have dates, but Sloan was drooling at them just the same. There was a tall black woman, wearing a fur coat and surrounded by attentive men, and Sloan couldn't stop staring. Deacon didn't know her, but he guessed she was hot stuff from out of town—a singer he didn't know yet out of New York or Chicago or something.

Sloan said, "Get a load of that broad."

"What's about we leave?"

"Yeah. We too cool for this joint."

Going out the door, Deacon bumped into that jet-black man Sumner from the Starburst. He said, "How come you're not playing, man?"

"I'm going on now. Hang around and sit in with us."

Deacon said, "I gotta fly. Next time?"

"Next time."

On the street, Sloan said, "Where's the next place? How 'bout getting us some live ones?"

Deacon said, "Jeez, I don't know. Kinda late for that stuff."

Sloan spat out a nasty laugh and said, "Man, it's *early*. I wanna have some fun."

"Let's walk around the corner."

Three blocks away, down at the end of a quiet, residential street, was the house that belonged to Aunt Betty. Deacon had never been inside. He had his doubts now, as he and Sloan turned the corner and made their way along in the dark. *Bound to be expensive,* Deacon was thinking. *Probably have to use Mo's name to get in. Sloan likely to make a big scene and embarrass the hell out of everyone.*

There was a man on the sidewalk in front of Aunt Betty's. He was on his hands and knees, and he sounded like he was crying. Sloan said, "Get a load of this," as they approached. Deacon said, "Shhh." When they were very close, they heard the man shout up at the dark house. He said, "Aunt Betty! Aunt Betty! I ain't been *serviced* yet."

The house stayed dark. There was light from some upstairs windows, but the windows did not open. Deacon said, "Let's blow."

They were back on Jackson Street. Sloan had somewhere on the walk back pulled a hip flask out of its hiding place. He'd offered Deacon a slug and then drunk the rest of it down. Now, with women off his mind, he was going down fast. Sloan was sloppy-drunk and red-eyed. He waved across the street to two women who were going down the sidewalk. They looked like cleaning women who'd just got off work. Sloan said, "Hey, baby! What's happenin'?"

Deacon decided it was past time to get Sloan off the streets. He said, "Come on. It's dead over here. Let's go check the action on the Strip."

They found their way back to the big Buick and got in. Sloan made a big thing out of opening all four windows and demonstrating the magic of no centerposts. The wind blew in on them as they drove down Jackson and onto Bonanza and left the West Side. Sloan drove the big boat down and under the railroad tracks. The car weaved a little.

Sloan said, "Look at this thing shimmy. Dynaflow my butt."

Deacon said, "I think that's bourbon-flow."

"I am the Roadmaster. Of the Century."

"You're drunk."

They were halfway to Fremont Street when the police car appeared. Sloan squinted at the rearview mirror and said, "We're cooked, Deke. We got cops."

Deacon said, "Pull over. Pour 'em a drink."

Sloan pulled to the side of the road. The red light on top of the police car shone like a beacon. The cops turned their spotlight onto the driver's side of the car, flooding it with white light.

Sloan said, "It's those sons a bitches from the other night at the Starburst."

Deacon turned to look and was blinded. He said to Sloan, "Go easy, sport."

A voice that Deacon did not know said, "Where you boys going?" and Sloan said, "Got to put out the fire at yo' mama's house, Jim." Deacon slumped down in the seat.

The car doors flew open and Deacon was yanked out by a pair of very big hands. On the way out he saw the face of the big pale Swedish-looking kid he'd fought with outside the Starburst that night. Then something hard hit him in the side of the head and he went down.

Sloan was saying, "Take it easy. I'm *joking*. We were going to your *wife's* house. She said her deadbeat, flatfoot husband—," and then there was the sound of someone hitting him hard. He went over onto the pavement, where he lay long enough for the policeman to give him a boot to the face. Sloan cursed, and the cop did it again.

Then they were cuffed, and sitting on the car bumper. Sloan had blood all over his chin and looked dazed. Deacon thought he might be hurt bad. But the spotlight from the police car was still incredibly bright and he couldn't see into Sloan's eyes, so he wasn't sure. He wasn't sure of anything, actually. His ears were ringing. There seemed to be no traffic on the boulevard.

The cop who was not the big Swede said to Deacon, "On your feet." Deacon complied. The cop said, "Roll up your sleeves." Deacon didn't move. The cop shone his flashlight into Deacon's face and yanked up his shirtsleeves. He said, "This one's good. Put him in the car." The big Swede took Deacon by the elbow and yanked him toward the cop car and shoved him into the backseat.

The other cop told Sloan to stand up. As he was rising, the cop dropped his flashlight. Sloan kicked it with his feet. The ray of light coming from it skittered and spun madly. Deacon heard Sloan laugh. The cop leaned down to pick up the flashlight, and Sloan went for his gun. He was laughing wildly and not managing the gun very well with his hands cuffed, but he had the revolver up and was training it on the cop, who stood holding the flashlight down low. Deacon heard Sloan say, "How now, brown cow?" And the big blond Swede shot him.

There was one big boom from his revolver, just at Deacon's right ear. Sloan fell over backward onto the Century. There was the *ping* of bullet on bumper as the shot from the cop's gun went through Sloan and into the back of the car. Sloan slumped and fell into the dirt and dropped the policeman's gun. Then he was gone. The big pale kid, standing right next to Deacon, whispered a curse. Deacon did not even turn to look.

The Swede conferred briefly with his partner and got behind the wheel of the cruiser and started it. He left his partner by the side of the road and drove back down Las Vegas Boulevard, toward downtown. Deacon turned to look back at the Century, and Sloan, but the patrol car was moving away fast and Deacon could not see anything behind him in the dark.

At the station, the Swede told the desk sergeant, "Narcotics. Use, and possession. Murphy says don't book him yet." The desk sergeant nodded. Another cop took Deacon down the hall to a room containing a single desk and two metal chairs. He said, "Stay in here," and locked the door behind him. Deacon sat in the metal chair and smoked one cigarette. Then he put his head down on the metal table and went to sleep.

Mo came down from his office and slid onto the casino floor about one o'clock. One of his men had called and told him that Haney and three detectives were there. Mo didn't see them. Mo went around past the reception desk and the gift shop, and into the pits.

It was a busy night, for a Thursday. The tables were nearly full. Hats bobbed over the craps tables. The blackjack tables were busy. There seemed to be more women than usual playing. But maybe that was just Mo feeling restless. He noticed sometimes that all he noticed was women. Then he usually got a woman, and then he noticed that he stopped noticing women for a while. Tonight, though, it appeared to him that there were simply more of them about. Maybe Lili St. Cyr or one of the other big strippers was dancing someplace close and the men had left their wives behind. . . .

A pitman working the roulette table gave Mo the high sign. When Mo got to him, he said, "That police lieutenant cruised through here about fifteen minutes ago. He was working fast and looking for someone, and he didn't stay long."

"He say who he was looking for?"

"No. But he didn't find him."

"Or her."

"Or her."

Mo glanced around. The noise, which he seldom even noticed, seemed to him harder than usual to bear. Sometimes it was like the rush of water over stones, or the sound of waves on sand. Tonight it was all sharp edges and shrill voices. A lady shrieked. A jackpot siren went. A boxman said, "Coming out!" from the craps table, and the men there shouted at the dice, "Come on, seven," and "Any craps!" and "Be good, baby!" and "Go, shooter." Mo's stomach turned over once and flopped back down.

"Keep me posted," he said, moving on.

The kitchen seemed quiet when he got there. So did the hallways and the counting rooms. Would he even know, he wondered, whether something was going wrong? How would he know? Would it be deathly still? Would everyone be jumpy and have sweaty faces? If it was an inside job, and the joint got knocked over, would he know afterward that he should have seen it coming?

Morgan was inside, watching over his boys like a mother hen. The three plainclothes security guys were reading and smoking. The three men in uniform, Mo guessed, were doing the floor. Mo nodded to the plainclothes guys and said, "Evening, men. All quiet?"

"All quiet, sir. Busy night, looks like."

"Lotta counting ahead, I'm afraid."

Morgan unlocked the inside door. Behind it, the six silent men in eyeshades worked slowly through the piles of cash. Paper whiffled. None of the men even glanced up as Mo came into the room and circled the big steel table on which they were working. He said, "Evening, boys," and got no response. Had anyone answered, Mo thought, Morgan would probably fire him. Mo moved back past the door and out. He said to Morgan, "Same as usual. One and a half percent swaggo for the night car to L.A."

"I understand, sir."

"Good man."

Mo took a back elevator up from the basement. It landed him in a hallway leading away from the casino, down to the guest rooms. *If I were a thief,* he thought, *I might come down this way. I might drop quietly down into the basement. But I'd have to have guys inside, even with a quiet approach, to get away with any real money. I'd try to hire guys who were . . . what? Guys who needed money? You'd have to pay them more than the score was worth just to get them. The counting guys would not be possible. The plainclothes guys would be a little easier. The uniformed guys have been with us the least time. Maybe them? Maybe find one who couldn't meet his mortgage. Maybe find one with a gambling problem that was getting over on him. Or a drinking thing he couldn't handle. Or a sick mother. Or something. You could probably find something, if you worked at it.*

Luckily, Mo knew from experience, most thieves did not. They were lazy—and not too smart—and usually had much bigger problems of their own than the ones they could exploit in others. Drinking and gambling and women and money problems and sick families, if

they had families, were all part of it. And the cops were always looking for them, for some little thing or other. That did not leave them
much time to calmly configure a foolproof scheme to steal Mo Weiner's money.

Maybe that's why someone who was only half smart, like Haney,
could wind up being in charge of cops. The guys in charge of catching the bad guys had to be only a little less stupid than the bad
guys were.

The hallway took Mo out to the street. It was two o'clock now, or
later. The night was still and hot. In the distance to his left, Mo could
see the seafoam green of the swimming-pool light rising up from the
ground. Overhead, the Starburst searchlights crisscrossed and waved.
Beyond, the lights of the Thunderbird rose into the dark sky. Cars
whined past on Las Vegas Boulevard. One with its radio too loud was
playing Rosie Clooney's "Hey There," but the speed and the distance
of the car distorted the sound. Rosie sounded like an angry old drunk.

Around the front of the Starburst the cars were coming in fast. The
parking-lot guys were keeping up, but barely. Men in tropical suits
and linen suits and Panama hats and fedoras sprang from the driver's
seats as women in floral prints and brightly colored pumps and fat
clumps of beaded necklaces extended their hands and were escorted
out the passenger side. It looked like some kind of casting call. Many
of the women wore hats, some of them big, sweeping jobs with things
that looked like birds and flowers and pieces of fruit attached. Mo
laughed. What a world! Women with animals and animal food on
their heads! Why? Why not cups of coffee and doughnuts? Why not
guns and ammo? Who decides?

Mo went across Las Vegas Boulevard into the Thunderbird parking
lot. Life was funny. Imagine not finding it funny! He folded a five-
dollar bill in his hand and duked the doorman as he went inside. The
man said, "Evening, Mr. Weiner." Mo said to himself, "Mr. Weiner!"
Life was funny.

The cop had waited until the patrol car drove away before he leaned
down and looked at the creep who had taken his gun. It was lying
on the pavement next to the creep's hand. The cop nudged it away
with his foot, then bent down and picked it up and stuck it in his

holster. A car went by but did not slow down. The cop took the handcuffs off the guy's wrists. Without even checking for a pulse, he knew the guy was croaked and gone.

The cop looked down the boulevard at the car lights coming and going. There was a fairly wide vacant lot behind him. The lights of the Strip itself were only half a mile away. Downtown rose in the other direction. Would anyone see him, passing by? What difference did it make? He grabbed the dead guy by the ankles and dragged him off the roadway. The vacant lot was mostly sand, and the going was pretty slow, but he slogged on. In another five minutes he had pulled the dead guy a hundred and fifty feet or more from the road. A clump of greasewood there was the cover he needed. He gave the guy one last hoist, and rolled him into the bushes.

He checked the registration on the Century, which was so new that it didn't even have proper license plates yet. The name was Ellen Glass, and the address was north of downtown. Stolen? Maybe. The guy driving, the dead guy, had been awful jumpy. Or awful drunk. Or both. He could have been just hopped up, or he could have been hopped up and driving a stolen car. Either way, the cop could not see any percentage in finding out. He did not like the idea that he was in uniform and driving a stolen car, one that might be reported stolen. Not when the guy who stole the car was lying dead in a greasewood bush with a hole from a police revolver through him. But that couldn't be helped. The cop started the car and pulled it onto the roadway. He drove into the West Side and parked it on a side street just off Bonanza. It was only a five-minute walk from there to Fremont Street, and a short walk from there to the station. He'd get in and see what Haney wanted to do with the junkie they'd been asked to pick up in the first place, and tell him about the guy driving the stolen Buick. And hope Haney was in a good mood. If not . . . well, there was no way to tell what kind of trouble that would be. The cop left the keys in the ignition and started walking.

Roland Sumner had grown up in an East Los Angeles neighborhood that was sliding downhill from middle-class black to lower-class Mexican when his folks gave up and moved to Watts. Sumner had gone to Dorsey High. He was a good boy—shy and quiet and determined.

He played the saxophone in the orchestra *and* the band, was a starting forward on the basketball team, and ran high hurdles and did the high jump in track. Did he have plans? He didn't remember much about them. He thought he'd go to Los Angeles Community College, or maybe Trade Tech, and try for an engineering degree. Lots of men seemed to be getting work in the aircraft companies or in those car plants out in the Valley. His old man talked about that, talked about how having a degree in engineering would get him off the shop floor and into an office. No more sweeping up. An executive position. The prospect of that seemed so remote that it made Sumner's head hurt to think about it.

In fact, his head hurt now. And the name of his headache was Worthless Worthington Lee. The man *would* insist on his Ivory Coast opening on the last Sunday in May. He *would* insist on everything being ready. And he'd made Sumner the man for the kitchen and the food and the dining rooms and the room service and the coffee shop. It wasn't a bigger job than Sumner was ready for, but Sumner wasn't ready for it to happen quite so fast. Right now, at two-thirty in the ante meridian morning, Sumner wasn't ready for anything at all to happen unless it included a highball or a bed.

He said, "Fix me another pot of coffee," to a light-skinned Negro standing in the doorway. "Let's go over the inventory list one more time. We *know* we can get that right."

Sumner was no fool. He'd got good marks in high school, where he was known among his friends as "the Professor." In his senior year he sent his applications off to LACC and Trade Tech. He got a summer job as an assistant in the metal shop of a factory that made parts for the airplanes. The shop was not air-conditioned, except for the three offices in the corner where plans were drawn and paperwork was kept. The shop itself was the size of a small airplane hangar and had a metal roof. By mid-morning the temperature was above ninety degrees, no matter the outside weather. By midday, it was above one hundred, and Sumner and two other colored men were the only ones left on the shop floor. All the other guys, which is to say all the white guys, saved their office work or their delivery work for the afternoon. Either way, they were in the air-conditioning or out in the air. Sumner bent flanges with a big hand-operated crank, crimping pieces of sheet metal, day after day after day. One afternoon, a big drop of sweat rolled off his forehead and down his nose and fell onto the piece of metal he was about to crimp. Sumner was sure he heard it sizzle. He set the sheet down, and went over to the air-conditioned office, and walked inside without knocking. A blond secretary looked up, her mouth agape, and two men with their feet on their desks took them down.

Sumner said, "Hey."

No one responded.

Sumner said, "Need a glass of water."

One of the men said, "Boy, there's water outside."

Sumner said, "I need a glass of *cold* water."

He didn't wait, but moved across the floor to the water cooler in the corner, an oasis glistening with beads of condensation. He snapped a paper cup out of the stack. A chair shifted on the floor behind him.

The man said, "Don't take a drink of that water, boy."

Sumner paused.

"It'll cost you the job, boy."

Sumner filled the paper cup.

"I ain't kidding now."

Sumner turned, and smiled. He raised the paper cup and winked, and said, "That's okay." And drank the water.

Out of work and without any good reference to show for his summer's employment, Sumner drifted for a week or two, thumbing the want ads and finding nothing. One afternoon there was a knock at his door. A slouchy kid he knew from the track team, a guy that everyone called Motor, stood on the other side of the screen, shifting uncomfortably from foot to foot.

He said, "Hey, Prof. How you doing?"

"Good, Motor. You?"

"All right. Listen, you still got that horn?"

"The saxophone?"

"Can I borrow it?"

"No."

"Why not?"

"Well, why?"

"I need a saxophone, man."

Motor had gotten mixed up with some musicians and then had

gotten a little combo together, and one of them had started booking work. Then their sax player had gotten a real job. Now they'd found a new sax player, which was Motor's older brother Marvin, but Marvin had hocked his instrument and didn't have any money to get it back.

Sumner said, "You can borrow the sax, but you have to take me, too."

Motor said, "You're on. I don't like Marvin anyhow."

At first, it was almost harder than working in the metal shop. Motor was a terrible organizer. He didn't have sheet music for half the stuff he wanted to play or half the stuff the people wanted him to play at the parties where he got the band hired. Sumner had a good ear, and he could sight-read anything, but Motor was also a terrible explainer. He'd say, "Do you know 'Fascination'? It's like that, but it's the *opposite* of that."

One afternoon, rehearsing in a club where they were supposed to play a dance that night, the stand-up bass player, a guy called Philly, said, "It's a four-four shuffle, in E, with a key change up after the break."

And suddenly Sumner *saw* it. He saw the song. He saw the *shape* of the song—where the break would be, and where the key change was, and what would happen to the solo. He said, "I got it." And then he played it. Then he soloed it. And he was never confused about music after that.

A year later he was playing the clubs on Central Avenue and had been thrown out of his father's house for being a no-good bum jazzbo with no future. He had started smoking cigarettes and taking the occasional drink of whiskey. He was quiet and studious about the music, and folks still called him "the Professor," but it was no longer the term of derision it had been in high school. It carried great respect, now, especially for a man who was only nineteen years old.

If he were telling his own story, he'd leave the next part out. He fell in love with a singer named Aileen. He was twenty-two. She was older. She belonged to a Central Avenue club owner named Leon Lincoln. Sumner paid no attention to that. He spent a month staring at her singing before he got up the nerve to buy her a drink, and then he spent forever buying her drinks before he got up the nerve to ask her to dinner. Everyone told him he was making a fool of himself, except the guys who said he was running the risk of having

Leon Lincoln run a bullet through him. He didn't hear any of it. He could hear Aileen sing in his sleep, and he didn't hear anything else.

Of course, his friends were right. Aileen was no good. She was a singer, first of all, which was always bad news. Plus she was a hype. Plus she had a man, who was both her *man* and her connection. She went to dinner with Sumner. He proposed marriage. She laughed at him and told him he was sweet. The following night Leon Lincoln and two huge men roared into the nightclub where Sumner and his men were setting up. Leon Lincoln came after Sumner with a knife and cornered him and held the blade close to his neck and said, "If I ever see you around Aileen again, I'm gone come back and ventilate you so bad y'own momma won't know you."

That night Sumner went to the club where Aileen was singing and begged her to run off with him to New York or Chicago. Aileen laughed at him and said, "You are so *cute*," and then said no. At precisely that moment Leon Lincoln came in through the back door of the club. He got a bead on Sumner talking to Aileen and came fast across the floor with his knife already out. Sumner moved up and away, because he did not want Aileen hurt, and was backing away for the front door.

There were two cops standing at the bar. They'd come in for the weekly shakedown. They shouted at Leon Lincoln to drop the knife. One of them pulled his revolver and repeated the order. Leon dropped the knife. Sumner hit the door.

Sumner found work in Las Vegas almost immediately. But not playing the saxophone. He found, to his dismay, that all he could hear in the music was the sound of Aileen singing. And he found that this distressed him beyond all measure. He started working in the kitchen at the Flamingo. It was 1953, and Vegas was booming. Sumner moved from joint to joint, getting better jobs and better wages with each move. By the time he hit the Starburst, he was almost making a good living.

He kept his head down and worked hard, and stayed away from music and women. When Worthless Worthington Lee bagged him for the Ivory Coast, he felt like he'd arrived. He was back working with his people, with *only* his people, just like he'd done on Central Avenue. There was more music, and more women, but he was cool. As the spring of the year turned into the summer, as Worthless's plans for opening in May got closer, Sumner felt himself starting to relax. He even started sitting in periodically with this combo or that. He didn't hear Aileen singing in his head anymore when he played.

He heard, in the spring, that Leon Lincoln had gotten drunk one night and in a jealous fit had cut his girl Aileen's throat, and then in shame had taken a gun and blown his own brains out. Sumner thought it was the saddest thing he'd ever heard.

Tonight, though, he wasn't in the mood. When the coffee came, he said, "Thank you, my man," and spread a printed sheet of inventoried items in front of him. The stage lights were off. The curtains were drawn. The roof above him did not glitter with a thousand stars, at the moment. The band that was not there right now was not playing beautiful music. The glamorous girls were not glamming. It was just the middle of the night, on a hot night in the city, on the job, anywhere in America. Sumner lit a cigarette and rubbed his eyes and said, "Sit me with and let's count. We'll do the cutlery first. . . ."

Waking up with Mr. Jones is bad no matter where you do it. Waking up jonesy in the police station is especially lousy. The door banged, and Deacon's head came up fast off the metal table and immediately started hurting. One of his hands was asleep. All he could think was, *Man, I need a* drink.

Possession and use made for a serious rap. If they looked, the cops would find tracks. If they went into his room, they'd find a kit. That would be enough to send him over. Guys on the circuit, guys who Deacon knew, had gone over for less. Art Pepper had done time. Chet Baker was in the jug right now, Deacon had heard, on nothing more than use. The cops had pulled him over in a car in L.A. and checked for tracks. They found them. For a guy with a narcotics record, that was enough. He got three months in the slams. And Deacon knew it was almost impossible to get good dope in the slams. Bad news for a guy with a habit.

That cop Haney was coming through the door behind two other cops in uniform. With him was a skinny guy in a dark suit. Haney looked horrible, like a man with a bad toothache. Deacon only *felt* horrible—but he felt very horrible. His stomach flopped and his heart was racing. One look at Haney and he thought, *I'm cooked.*

But Haney was quiet. He said, "You men, blow," and the uniformed cops left the room. As the door swung shut, Haney said, "This is Assistant District Attorney Filcher. He is preparing the paperwork on your case. You have no history of drug offenses in Nevada. I assume we will find your jacket in California and . . . where?"

Deacon stared at him.

Haney said, "New York? You look like New York."

Deacon stared at him.

Haney said, "Well, assuming it exists, and I *know* it exists, we'll find it. You'll be exposed on parole violations, if nothing else. I reckon that Filcher here will issue a warrant to search your room at the Starburst and find what we need to satisfy a possession beef. Am I wrong?"

Deacon looked at the guy Filcher. He was calm and opaque, and there was nothing to read there. Deacon felt his heart race. But he kept quiet.

Filcher said, "I say we sweat him for the guy he's buying his dope from."

Haney shrugged and said, "It'll turn out to be some beaner, running the junk over from Tee Jay".

"Let's find out," Filcher said.

"It's late," Haney said. "I'm tired. We have an officer nearly shot with his own weapon tonight. We have a citizen dead. We have a known addict here who saw the event. I think we can turn this thing over, now. What do *you* say?"

Deacon said, "I don't have anything to say." His mouth felt as if it had been soaked in coal dust.

Haney said, "Then let me talk. We could put you in the cooler until we get your paperwork from New York, or wherever. We could get you on the stuff in your room. We'll have you for use, and possession. That puts you in the can for a while. But you saw something tonight that we don't want talked about. That leaves us with a few alternatives. We can take you out into the sand with your friend . . . what's-his-name."

Deacon said, "Sloan. His name is Sloan. Was."

Haney said, "Yes. *Was*. We can take you out there with him, and drop you off in a similar condition."

Deacon gave it a moment. He regarded Haney, then Filcher. He saw Sloan fall, and the sick look on the pale Swede's face. He felt hot sudden rage rise in him. He turned his eyes back on Haney and said, "No. You can't do anything like that with me."

Haney was amused. He said, "Why's that?"

"Because you can't."

Haney's amusement increased. He said, "I *can't?* Why *can't* I?"

Deacon said, "Because . . . of a guy from Chicago."

Haney said, "What guy from Chicago?"

Deacon said, "You know what guy."

Filcher said, "This guy is really full of juice, isn't he? What the hell is this guff?"

Deacon said, "Maybe it's not something you want to talk about. There was this guy with a face like a rat and a bag full of pictures."

Haney's eyes registered, flicked to Filcher, and came back. He said to Deacon, "I get your point." Then he glanced back at Filcher and said, "Take off."

Filcher said, "What?"

"Take off. Go outside."

Filcher said, "Wait a *minute*, now. I'm not—"

"Go outside! Now!"

When they were alone, Haney said, "You are playing a very dangerous hand here."

Deacon kept his trap shut. He knew, just knew, he was cooked. With the D.A. out of the room, he had nothing. But the D.A. knew there was a reason he'd been given the gate. Maybe . . .

Haney said, "Where are the photographs?"

Deacon said, "I don't know. But if anything happens to me, they'll be all over this place."

The voice of Filcher said, over the intercom, "Haney, I think we need an officer taking a statement on this."

Haney turned, an insane look in his eyes, and said, "Turn that goddamn thing off."

Deacon had been in a few police stations. He knew that Filcher must have been listening to them speak, up to that moment. That meant he'd heard something about the photographs. That gave Deacon a little advantage. He sat in silence waiting for the next move.

Filcher came back in and said, "I don't even know what this is, but we have to get it on the record."

Haney did not move, or react, or respond.

Filcher said, "Or you can just explain it. What are these pictures?"

Haney said, "There aren't any pictures."

Filcher said, "I don't get it."

Haney said, "There's nothing to get. He's a junkie. He's probably gassed-up now. Get him out of here."

Filcher said, "What? Just like that?"

Haney said, "We get his papers from New York, we'll pick him up then."

Filcher said, "What if he skips?"

Haney said, "He won't skip. He's tied to the Starburst. He's Mo Weiner's boy."

Deacon saw the photographs again. He saw Haney in them. His head caught fire and burned, and his face got hot. He began to speak, then caught himself, and clenched his jaw tight. He said, finally, "Sloan was Mo Weiner's boy."

Filcher said, "Who's Sloan?"

"Sloan," Deacon said, "is the man you shot down on Las Vegas Boulevard tonight. That's gonna buy you a big headache with Mo."

Haney said, "You already bought a headache with *me*. Get out."

Deacon rose to his feet and headed to the door. He was so sick inside that, at that moment, he really did not care what they did with him. As long as they did it quickly. He wanted out of the police station. He wanted a cigarette. He wanted a shot of rye, or something stronger. He wanted especially not to look at either of these two creeps again. They were two scared, small men—bullies with badges who did not have a clue what to do next. That made him nervous. Nervous cops were dangerous cops.

The sun had come up. The desert was alive. Light was spreading over the sand, fanning out from the east, striking the mountains pink and setting little fires of color where the greasewood and the yucca grew, throwing bursts of purple onto the clouds that sat in front of the mountains. Deacon could not remember ever seeing anything quite so ugly. He hailed a taxi and told the driver, "Get me to the Starburst."

◆ ◆ ◆

Worthless Worthington Lee was just waking up. Or waking up for good, anyway. It had been another rough night. Sometime after two or three o'clock he had awakened to the sound of Dina crying in the front room. But when he got there he could not find her. She was not in the kitchen or the bathroom. Worthless got a robe and choked back a sense of rising panic, and went outside the little bungalow. Nothing. He could still hear the weeping, and he wondered suddenly if he was dreaming or losing his mind. He went back inside. The weeping continued.

Worthless found Dina standing inside the hall closet, her face buried in an old raincoat. She looked surprised then irritated, to be interrupted. Worthless, feeling worn down and broken and bone-tired, said, "Come on back to bed, girl." Dina had walked resentfully back to the bedroom and passed out again. He'd slept fitfully after that.

And now . . . Saturday. The sun was blowing over the desert like a breeze. In two hours it would be hot. In three hours it would be unpleasant. Right now, standing in his kitchen, watching the light spread out over the sand, Worthless thought it was unspeakably beautiful. The dawn did not break, in the desert. It blossomed. The whole world was a flower opening. The day was in bloom.

Worthless said, out loud, "Man, I surely *am* losing my mind. Chattering in my head like a schoolgirl. Let's get this day started, Lord."

With that, he put the coffeepot on and sat at the little card table in his kitchen and began to make notes. It was almost time. Two workdays remained. After Sunday night, everything would be . . . what? Well, it would be after Sunday, and it would be different. That's all he knew. That would have to be enough.

Nine

GRAHAM FILCHER ROSE and left his rented desert house earlier than usual, and drove toward Fremont Street. He had the top down and the windows down and a cap on his head, and felt he belonged in a motor rally, running the powerful Austin against a field of MGs and Jaguars. But he was only driving toward downtown Las Vegas, wearing a Brooks Brothers suit that belonged in, say, a Chrysler Imperial. Inside the car he might have looked like the assistant district attorney. Outside the car he looked like a young gent scooting off to his country estate.

He was running about ten minutes early for a handball date at the Y with a young Brazilian player—"built like a panther," someone had said—who he expected would give him a pretty good workout. He needn't have bathed and dressed at home, really, since he'd only have to shower and dress again at the Y. But entering the Y, as the assistant D.A., dressed in the dark gray suit, was like driving the Austin: it gave the right impression, and it made the right statement. He remembered the magazine ad that had sold him on the English sports car. It was in *Argosy*, or *True*. Two women, sharp-eyed and knowing, watched as a lithe young man dashed across the lawn of a big home. One said to the other, *"He's* the one with the Austin Healey." Just the right impression. The car had cost him a little over three thousand dollars, which was far more than he could sensibly have budgeted for an automobile. At least once a week, someone in traffic or on the street would slow and stare for a moment, and Filcher saw himself making that right impression. Men liked the car as much as women did.

He killed the extra ten minutes with a spin up into the West Side. With more time to spare, he might have driven through the mountains to Pahrump, or even all the way into Death Valley. He would stop at Amargosa for a cold soda, then run the car up as far as Scotty's Castle. He'd done that, the second or third Saturday he spent in the area, and every second or third Saturday he had meant to do it again.

That was when he had first arrived in town. He'd done all kinds of things that he did not do anymore. Sometime during the first month, he'd gotten a telephone call at the office from a man named Holbrook, who ran the Bank of Nevada and was the president of the chamber of commerce. He'd introduced himself and said, "We're having a little shindig this Saturday evening, me and the missus. Just a barbecue, very informal, y'unnerstand, over at our place on Rock Canyon Road. Put on your dungarees and come on over 'bout five."

Filcher had assumed Holbrook was kidding about the dungarees, so he dressed informally in Heller linen slacks that cost almost twenty-five bucks and a Sam Snead golf shirt that had cost him eight. He'd driven up in the Austin Healey, expecting to be received like the Prince of Wales. Instead, there were about sixty Cadillacs and Lincolns in the gravel parking lot. Behind the house, standing with cocktails and appetizer weenies, were a hundred or more guests. The men wore blue jeans tucked into or rolled over cowboy boots, Western shirts with pearl buttons, and string ties. Most wore large straw hats as well. The women were dressed the same way, some of them right down to the blue jeans. Filcher could not have felt more out of place.

Holbrook's "missus" was a tall, rail-thin woman who ran a foundation for orphaned children. She was Thomas Haney's sister. Filcher put that together and said, when they were introduced, "Of course, Mrs. Holbrook. I'll be working with your brother." Mrs. Holbrook appeared to blanch slightly at the word brother. Holbrook himself laughed and said, "Relax, Filcher. We're all civilians here. Haney's never invited to these dude rodeos. Let me introduce you around."

For the next eternity, Holbrook said, "Our new district attorney," and Filcher said, "Assistant district attorney, actually," while every blue-jeaned dude in the congregation stared at him. Later there had been pork ribs and big sirloin steaks served by Negro waiters in black trousers and white jackets, tagged like big game around the neck with red bandannas.

Filcher had not been invited to another dude rodeo himself.

This morning, with his ten minutes to spare, he tooled the Austin up to Bonanza and across to Jackson. The Ivory Coast was coming fast. The building was over. The construction trucks were gone. This Sunday, he believed, was supposed to be the opening. More headache for the cops. More headache for Haney. Filcher suppressed a smile. He did not mind more headaches for Haney. Haney *ought* to have headaches.

And he had one now over that addict they'd picked up the night before, after the policeman had shot that fellow resisting arrest. Haney had cursed a blue streak. *And* refused to say why. Interesting. Something to hide. Filcher loved knowing that someone had something to hide. Even when he didn't know what they were hiding. People with something to hide, and an active fear of discovery, could be made to do almost anything.

Filcher realized with a start that the lone automobile parked in front of the Ivory Coast had a man sitting in the front seat. He was a colored man, so dark that at first Filcher did not see him at all. He was so black, he looked as if he'd been carved from ebony. He sat motionless, eyes absolutely fixed on Filcher as he idled by. He was also extremely handsome, Filcher noted. And sitting in front of the Ivory Coast at 6:25 A.M. Was that suspicious? Was his own presence here suspicious?

Filcher decided not to find out. He gunned the English sports car around the corner and sped away, imagining the eyes of the black man following him. *He's the one with the Austin Healey.*

Twenty minutes later he was on the court, dressed in his shorts and sneakers. The Brazilian came down, accompanied by Rolf, the man who ran the gymnasium. Rolf said, "This is Joao. It means 'John.'" Filcher shook Joao's hand. The Brazilian had a face like a bowl of cereal—mushy, indistinct—and a limp handshake. He was powerfully built, but still. Filcher bounced the handball onto the glossy wooden floor and said, "Shall we warm up a bit?"

Albert Sherman sat in a cushioned lawn chair on the lush lawn in his own backyard, in front of a large square swimming pool surrounded by a jungle of trees that nature never intended to live in the same climate. There were date palms and Chinese pepper, eucalyptus and sequoia, night-blooming jasmine and wisteria, grapes growing on an arbor, and gardenia and carnations and lilies and giant Australian tree ferns and several huge cacti. Behind him, up a slight hill, was a sprawling home made of white adobe and red tile that was designed to look like one of the Spanish missions. Sherman had the telephone extension in one hand and a cigar in the other. It was nine A.M. on a Saturday morning. The surrounding hills of Bel-Air were quiet.

But his head was busy and thick as mud. Last night had been an orgy of bridge and booze and broads. Sherry felt like a Barrymore. But he did not drink and he did not chase women anymore, and he was an indifferent card player, and he didn't like the late hours. Today his hands shook and his brain ached. And for what? Because it was his business. Because he was trying to get a tired old actor, a has-been who probably wouldn't sell one single ticket at the box office, to agree to try a comeback. At the end of the night, Gable had said to him, "Put a cork in it, Sherry. I'll do your goddamn picture. Stop whining." Now he had only to get the right actress, and the right project, and the right director, and he would be set and would not feel that he had wasted an evening. And by then there would be a hundred other problems to solve.

This morning the problem was called Stewart Griffin and Eleanor Padgett. They had agreed to star in a picture called *Full House*. Then they had fallen in love. Then they had fallen out of love. The picture was two weeks old, and they both wanted out. Now they were coming for breakfast, and Sherry was going to talk them both back into the picture. He didn't care one way or the other about Griffin—people said he was the next Rock Hudson. Sherry had put Rock in *The Desert Hawk* and had let him out of a contract to do *Taza, Son of Cochise*. He didn't *need* another Rock Hudson. But Padgett was different. This was some girl.

Sherry had first heard about her from an agent named Alan Anthony, who had seen her in something in New York and was going on and on about getting her out to the Coast and getting her tested. Sherry said, "Shut up and deal," about three times before he'd realized the girl was not one of Anthony's clients. In ten years he had never heard Anthony even mention an actor who was not one of his clients. The agent said, "That's what I'm talking about, Sherry. I wish she *was* my client. She's that good." So Sherman had said, "Find out who represents her and get him on the horn. I'll see her. Then I'll make sure she changes agents."

Eleanor had come to the Coast and tested. It hadn't gone well. She looked frail and shy and injured, and her voice was weak, and she acted like she'd never acted before. And she was still the most captivating thing on film that Sherry had seen in years.

So far, he'd failed to find the right thing for her. Not for lack of trying. He'd put her in a Western and then in an epic with Greeks, or maybe it was Romans. It didn't work. There was something so modern, so 1950s, about her. She just looked wrong in gingham and in a toga. He'd put her in a movie about a swimmer, but she looked all wrong outdoors, too. She wasn't one of these robust dames, like a Jayne Mansfield or Marilyn Monroe. She was more like Grace Kelly, or Jean Simmons. She was beautiful, but brittle. Delicate. Too delicate, maybe. For a while he thought he'd found another Frances Farmer. "One of us is going to end up in the nuthouse," he'd told Anthony.

Then he'd read the script for *Full House*. It was a great yarn, really gripping stuff, *and* psychological, about a professional poker player down on his luck. The mob is wise and they're calling in his markers, and they're going to kill him and he knows it. Padgett was going to play the girlfriend, who sees the jam her poker player is in and decides to save him—by trading herself for his markers. Griffin would play the boyfriend. Sherry had struggled forever with the part of the mob boss who trades for the girl. It was a natural for Edward G. Robinson, but he was under contract to Metro and was too obvious, anyhow. Sherry had wanted someone a little smoother—someone who, when he winds up with the girl, doesn't make the audience puke. Stewart Granger? James Mason? In the end he'd settled on Tyrone Power, who he hoped would not drink himself to death before the end of production. And then the whole thing blew up in his face. Padgett one day did not come to the set.

Love. For Christ's sake. Sherry cradled the phone in his lap and felt his head ring. He shouted out, "Wilson!" A moment later a butler appeared out of the foliage, carrying a tray with glasses and a pitcher of orange juice on it. Sherry sighed and said, "It's about time," and took a glass.

Padgett when she arrived was contrite. She was wearing a very light, plain dress of linen, flat shoes, and a wide straw hat that hid her face. And sunglasses. All actresses in California wore sunglasses. Sherry embraced her professionally and removed the hat. He hated women in hats. Eleanor took the hat in her hands and stood staring at the pool, as if she had never seen one before.

Griffin did not come at all. He was taking the high road, his agent had said. He was not the one who'd refused to come to the set. He was not the one who'd halted production. He was not going to come crawling over to Sherry's house on a Saturday morning just to kiss somebody's behind.

Sherry said to Eleanor, "Sit in the shade over here. Have a Bloody Mary. No? How about some fresh orange juice then? Good. You sit. Excuse me for one moment."

He went back to the other side of the swimming pool and picked up the phone once more. He got Griffin's agent back on the line. Eleanor Padgett was positively shimmering in front of him. He said to the agent, "Your boy is off the picture and off the lot. Lose my telephone number," and hung up.

Then he went back to Eleanor. She looked like a small, wounded bird. He said to her, "I got a great idea. There's this nightclub opening in Las Vegas tomorrow, at a casino up there. We're going to go shoot some film, B-roll stuff to use for this musical we've been playing with. Come up with us. We'll have a few laughs."

And, to his surprise, Eleanor had smiled like a child and said, "Sure, Mr. Sherman."

"Sherry. We'll have a few laughs."

"Okay. Sherry."

Deacon had found Fatty late Friday night, or very early Saturday morning, after he finally got back to the Starburst. It was just after dawn. Fatty was in the lobby bar, more or less dozing, with his head resting on his hands. When Deacon drew close, Fatty's tiny eyes snapped open. He smiled instinctively and then, after he'd focused, said, "Dee-con. What's jumping?"

Deacon said, "I need it now."

Fatty said, "Hold on, tiger. And keep your voice down."

Deacon said, "I need it now. No joking."

Fatty said, "All right. Just go slow now."

Deacon moved forward on him. It was dark. The bartender was away. Deacon got so close to Fatty that he could count the threads in his seersucker jacket. He said, "I need it now. I'm not joking. And I can't slow down. Give it to me, and now."

Fatty laughed a high, nervous laugh and said, "Sure, Deke. Take it. On the house. Jesus. You're a regular Dennis the Menace."

Deacon took the envelope and shoved it in his jacket pocket. And was gone. He couldn't even remember, later, whether he'd given Fatty any dough.

But later it didn't matter. He'd gone back to his room and cooked it and then hit it. Then he'd run a bath and found a bottle of bourbon stashed in the back of his closet and filled a glass and gotten undressed and slid into the tub. The steam rose and the sounds squished around in his head. He saw Sloan go down, saw again that look of surprise and indignation on his face. Saw that pale swede with the gun in his hand, looking at Sloan, looking at the gun, looking at Deacon, hopelessly lost, for that one second, and scared. And then Haney.

Haney the pervert. Haney the freak. Haney with his power and his policemen and his black suits, his guns and his goons and his *orphans.* What was that woman's name? At the foundation? Had he known her name? He saw her face. Did she know the game? Did she know what Haney was, and what he did?

Deacon knew he was in trouble now. He knew it was serious trouble. Haney was not going to go away. Deacon had scared him just enough, and just long enough, to slip away from the station house and from Sloan's death. That was not going to hold. Guys like Haney, if they got spooked, didn't go away. And Haney, now that Deacon was away from him, was still plenty spooked. It would be only a matter of time before he came hunting, with Deacon in his sights.

Deacon drifted away. The tide of righteous indignation carried him off. His body went slack, and his head slid down onto his chest. The water in the tub was so still that little waves shimmered away from him when he exhaled. Deacon slept.

Not for long. An hour later he awoke, cold, slumped onto a bathtub filled with tepid water. There was half a glass of bourbon on the porcelain next to his head. He shot that back and waited for his head to clear. It cleared, a little. He thought . . . today? No. Today was Saturday. Tomorrow was the day. Today was no day. It was just a regular day. Deacon lifted himself from the water and toweled off and fell onto the bed. If he slept until noon, or two, or even four . . . Sound check at four? Something like that. Stella would be upset if he missed the sound check. Saturdays were big nights for the show. Stella would be upset. Deacon slept again.

Stella rose about noon. She drew herself out of bed and stretched, a royal among commoners, and went to the window. There were heavy shades there against the light, which she drew back just far enough to know that the sun was shining with its customary daytime vulgarity. Too much light, always, in the desert. She couldn't bear it. She said, "Jasmine? Coffee with cream, and some orange juice."

There was a ruffling and then the sound of feet on carpet in the other room. Stella went back to the bed and slapped at the lump next to her. An incredibly handsome boy named something like Clement shot up suddenly and said, "What?"

Stella laughed and patted him and said, "Nothing, dear boy. Time to wake up and have a little coffee with your aunt Stella. Clement, isn't it?"

"Clevon."

"Clevon. Divine name. How do you take your coffee?"

"Black, ma'am."

"How appropriate. Jasmine! One black, one white. No sugar."

Clevon said, "Can I . . . you know?"

Stella laughed, a music-hall laugh, and said, "Right over there, darling. Make yourself at home."

It had been a week since Stella hatched the only truly ingenious scheme of her adult life. And it had taken her a week to find the right way to put it into action. Now that she had, she felt very clever.

She had realized one afternoon that the reason she kept getting into trouble for bringing young men to her room was that the young men she brought to her room simply looked out of place at the Starburst. Why? Because the Starburst did not accept colored guests, and did not allow colored visitors in the guest rooms, and did not serve colored people in the bars or restaurants.

But the Starburst *employed* dozens of colored men and women. Stella had told Jasmine to steal a busboy's uniform from the locker room in the basement. She had told her to make it a *big* busboy's uniform. Jasmine had brought up pair of black pants and a white shirt with a bow tie and a red jacket with gold buttons. Stella had Jasmine get it cleaned. Then she'd started looking for someone to wear it. On Thursday night, over on the West Side, she'd met this young man Clement. Or Clarence? She had told him to come around to the back entrance of the Starburst on Friday afternoon, pick up a package, and then follow the instructions written inside the package.

And she had spent a lovely night with him. She wasn't sure exactly how she was going to get him to leave, wearing the uniform, and then get the uniform *back* from him. Lovely as he had been, she had no desire to see him another time. She never did. Somehow, a man who had been in her bed—no matter how much he had pleased her in bed, and this Clement, or Clevon, had pleased her a great deal— was never as attractive to her afterward as he had been before. And he was never as attractive to her as the idea of the next man she might meet.

When Clevon came back to the bedroom, she said, "You'd best put that uniform on again, darling. We wouldn't want to cause any trouble. The question is, how can you get the clothes back to me without arousing any suspicion?"

"I got something arousing right now, ma'am."

"Put that away. Jasmine's coming right now with the coffee. We don't want to frighten her."

"Yes, ma'am."

Stella smiled. He was very sweet. Too bad she already had him. How would she ever find another? She'd find another. After all, tomorrow night was the big opening night at the Ivory Coast. She'd have to ask Deacon, tonight, to take her over there. Or that boy Sloan. Or Mo? Maybe it would be more appropriate to go with Mo. That would make leaving with someone else a little sticky. But Mo would probably want to leave early. He never wanted to have fun anymore. If he ever had. He didn't now, anyway. She'd let him leave, and she'd stay on. They'd probably ask her to sing, which would mean she'd *have* to stay on. Mo would understand.

Jasmine came in with the coffee. Stella said, "Jasmine, this is the new busboy, Clarence."

Clevon said, "Clevon."

Jasmine said, "Busboy, my foot. Drink your coffee."

Anita could hear her uncle clanging pots in the kitchen. It was one way for her to gauge his moods. If he sounded quiet at this distance, from her cabin, while he was prepping for lunch, Anita knew she would find him moving quickly and efficiently when she got to the kitchen. If he sounded raucous at this distance, she knew she would find him violent and angry. That was the case today. Wally the bartender was standing outside the back of the café, one booted leg cocked against the side of the building, smoking a cigarette. He said to her, through the smoke, "I wouldn't even go in there, if I was you." Anita shrugged and went inside.

Her uncle said, "*Chingadera*," and hurled an omelet pan across the room, where it crash-landed on a rack of water glasses, breaking several in the process. Anita went past him toward the bar. He called her name and said, "Wait." She stopped but did not turn to him.

He said, "Are you sure this thing is all set?"

She said, "For the hospital? This girl is coming at two. Wally will be here all day and night. She'll be here all night. Everything is set."

He said, "I don't know."

She said, "What is there to know? You're going to the hospital. You're going to be fine. Let's finish with today first. Tomorrow will be here tomorrow, anyway."

With that she left him. She heard, behind her, the crash of dishes.

Wally came in ten minutes later. He said, "Can I get a cup of that coffee, Neeter?"

She said, "Serve yourself."

He did. She was busy at the counter, trying to clean up the dessert rack so that the slices of pie and cake on it did not look quite so poisonous. This meant trimming away the sides of the slices that had been there the longest. You could easily tell which ones they were, because the oldest ones had gotten this treatment several times already and were getting very thin. Anita reflected, not for the first time, how disgusting it was that people actually ate the food her uncle served.

Wally said, "Tell me again about this girl that's coming tomorrow."

"There's nothing to tell," she said. "I haven't met her. Alls I know is her name is Dot and she works at the Starburst."

"Man, she sounds like a real honey," Wally said. "You got a little cream?"

"You know where the cream is at."

"Yeah," Wally said. "You reckon she's been married before?"

Anita turned to him. He saw her face and said, "Okay. I'm sorry. I just wondered. It's just there's something about these divorcée women, y'know? They're all coming to Las Vegas and Reno for that quickie divorce. They get Reno-vated. There's just something *exciting* about that. Y'know?"

"No. Go away. Go mix a drink or something."

"You ain't no fun, Neeter. No fun at all."

She said, "That's right."

Saturday night was always crummy, and it always ran late. The crowd came from both directions. Some of them were all tooted up and ready for action, eager to drive the last piece of road and be in Las Vegas. They were loud and hungry and drank cocktails and coffee and ate steaks and chops. But some of them were going the other way. They had already been in Las Vegas and were going home. They were sullen and quiet, and didn't have much appetite. Most of them stopped in Shipton Wells only to buy gas and maybe go to the bathroom. The food and the coffee were an afterthought. They didn't drink much and never ordered dessert. Anita reckoned some of them didn't have any more money. She wondered where they were going back home to. These were the only people she ever met, ever, that made her feel good about her situation. At least, she could think, I am not going where *they're* going. 'Cause wherever they're going looks pretty bad.

The night was endless. Wally had all kinds of business. Groups of men in twos and threes and fours came pounding through the door and went straight to the bar. Some of them had a bite after they had a drink. Some stayed in the bar. There were couples, too, some of them looking like maybe they were off to get married. There was one single fella who came strolling up to the bar, a toothpick wedged between his teeth, patting his belly as if he had been served the meal of his life. He said, "D'y'all rent those cabins out back? 'Cause if you do, I'll take you out there and screw you *silly*."

Anita said, "I'll find out," and left the man there.

In the kitchen she repeated to her uncle word for word what the man had said. He grabbed a cleaver and went roaring into the other room. The man with the toothpick saw him coming and put two and two together and got four and was out the café door like a shot. Anita smiled to herself as she came back behind the counter. A couple who looked like newlyweds were standing by the door. Anita said, "Sit anyplace you like. Can I bring you coffee?" They nodded, and watched her uncle as he went back toward the kitchen, the cleaver resting on his shoulder, his face red and splotchy, the lump on his neck sticking out, shiny and white.

One more day. The thought of Deacon, and Las Vegas, and the nightclubs, and the dancing, and the casinos, and the lights . . . She got butterflies in her stomach and felt a little dizzy, just letting it all go around in her head. He was so handsome, and so sweet, and so delicate—so everything that men had never been to her, so every-thing that her uncle and the pharmacist and Wally and the men in the café never could be to her. Then the screen door slammed and there was another couple of knuckleheads, both of them wearing hats pushed way back on their heads, smoking cigarettes and smiling those expectant smiles. On their way to gamble it all away in Lost Wages, Nevada. Welcome to the heartbreak, boys. Anita said, "You fellas fixin' to eat something, you can sit anyplace you want."

One of them grinned and winked and said, "Where you want us, darlin'?"

Anita said, "Go sit. Take these menus with you." And the guy winked again.

Anita wondered, not for the first time, that thing that she had never said out loud: *If I were white, if I were all white, I bet men wouldn't treat me like that. If I were all white, they wouldn't dare. . . .*

Mo sat with his back to the pool, facing Dawson, the setting sun reflected in the big windows on the rear of the Thunderbird. Dawson looked bad, Mo thought, puffy and bloated and angry. He had said hardly a word since they sat. He sipped at his drink and behind black sunglasses stared at the swimmers, or the pool, or nothing. He did not appear to be looking at Mo at all, Mo thought. When he spoke, he spat, and the star over his heart that said DAWSON glinted sunlight. He said, when they first sat down, "Let's make this snappy."

"You got an appointment?"

"I got things to do."

"That's not what I hear," Mo said. "I hear you're not making your rounds, and that you've cut your onstage time down to nothing."

"What the hell, Mo? If we're going out of business, that don't make no difference a'tall."

"You let me worry about that. Making the rounds and doing a few numbers is part of your deal here. You've got to hold up your end of the deal."

"Who the hell wants to see an old cowboy sing?"

"Well, lots of people, Bill."

"The hell they do. They come here for a laugh—at my expense!"

"But that's not true, Bill. People get a big kick out of meeting you. They always say that. And then seeing you onstage. You're the biggest star most of them will ever see."

"Shut up, Mo. I'm not a star at all. I'm just an old lush, same as you said before."

Mo saw now that the tears were rolling down Dawson's cheeks.

He said, "I didn't mean that. And it isn't true. I was just trying to get you to let go of this place. You know it's going down anyway. I was just hoping to get you used to the idea faster. I'm sorry. We never could have a made a success of the T-bird without you. And I never should have said that."

Dawson pulled a bandanna from his pocket and wiped away his tears. A waiter saw the bandanna, mistook it for a cocktail order, and came scampering with a mixer full of tropical beverages. He glanced at Mo, who placed a hand over his glass and shook his head, and then poured for the cowboy.

Dawson said, "Killarney hasn't given me a figure yet."

Mo said, "He doesn't know the figure yet. It's big, though."

"How big?"

"Well," Mo said. "I don't know for sure, either. But . . ." He took a pen from his pocket, and a slip of paper, and jotted a number onto the paper, then slid the paper across the table to Dawson. Dawson looked at it and whistled. Mo said, "It'll be somewhere around that."

"My take?"

"Your take."

Dawson whistled again. Mo pulled the paper back and crumpled it up. Then he reached for a cigarette and, after lighting it, lit the crumpled paper on fire.

"Could almost retire to Beverly Hills on that."

"Speaking of which," Mo said, "There's this picture company coming up tomorrow to film the opening of the Ivory Coast. A guy named Albert Sherman."

"Sherry's coming here?"

"You know him?"

"For God's sake, I've known Sherry since he was Valentino's valet. I've known him *forever*."

"He was Valentino's valet?"

"Figure of speech," Dawson said. "I just mean I've known him awhile. He was a director, you know, before he became a studio man. He directed some pretty good stuff."

"Well, he's going to be directing the opening."

"Sherry. That old dog. Maybe it's a sign. I mean, if I'm a-leavin' here, maybe I'm supposed to be a-headin' there."

"Maybe so, Bill. Either way, why don't I put him and his people here, instead of the Starburst? Make it easier for you to get together on this thing."

"Mo, would you?"

"Sure. I'll tell 'em we were overbooked. Give 'em the big suites upstairs. They'll love it."

"Mo. I can't tell you how much I—"

"Forget it. I gotta go. I'm supposed to see the Ivory Coast tonight one last time before the big opening tomorrow." Mo reached across the table and touched Dawson's hand. He said, "I'm sorry this isn't working out the way you planned, Bill."

"Take your mitts off me, you big sissy," Dawson said. "This old cowpoke's gonna do just fine."

Mo rose and smiled, and said, "I'm sure that's true, Bill."

Going out to the parking lot, Mo felt almost overpowered. The resilience of the spirit never failed to amaze him. He had seen it in

Chicago as a younger man. He had seen it over and over again during the war. He saw it now in Dawson. So often people got to the point where you'd understand completely if they simply sat down and said, "I can't go on." But they didn't. They stood for a minute thinking that they couldn't go on, maybe. But then invariably they went on. They survived everything. Dawson was, in fact, gonna do just fine. There was no doubt in Mo's mind that the booze was going to kill him. But until it did, the old cowpoke was gonna do just fine.

Mo hailed a cab from in front of the Thunderbird. A driver he recognized pulled up and leaped from the car. He said, "Good evening, Mr. Weiner." Mo said, "Howzit, Sammy? You wanna run me over to that Ivory Coast?"

"Jackrabbit fast, sir. Ivory Coast." And they were off. The sun was fat and low in the sky, and the temperature had slipped back into the nineties. Mo was done with Dawson. It was almost comfortable again.

Worthless Worthington Lee sat at a banquet table in the main lounge, with Sumner and Mr. Peet and six other men from the Ivory Coast. There were papers scattered everywhere among the coffee cups and the overflowing ashtrays. Worthless looked a wreck—tired, worn, gray, and old. He said, "I'm just gone have to trust that you men get it right. I cain't watch all of this all of the time."

Sumner said, "We got it right, man. Don't worry. I'm gonna crack a head open if it *don't* go right."

Worthless said, "You do that, Sumner. But not on opening night. And especially not in front of the building. Let Rochester handle all that nonsense."

Mr. Peet said, "Who the hell is Rochester, and what's *he* got to do with any of it?"

"Rochester. Eddie Anderson. He's agreed to be our greeter."

There was silence. Eddie Anderson was maybe the most prominent Negro in America at that moment. He had been Jack Benny's radio sidekick for years, appearing as Benny's butler, Rochester, for a decade. But now Benny was on television. His Sunday night show was a huge hit, and Rochester, cringing, gravel-voiced, the picture and soul of strained Negro patience, was there for all America to see.

Sumner said, "He's gonna greet people *here?*"

Worthless said, "Yeah. He's an old friend of mine. Way back to my fight days, in Los Angeles." Worthless said *Angeles* the old-fashioned way, like *an-guh-lees*, and it sounded mysterious and strange. The fact that he knew Rochester was mysterious and strange, too.

Sumner said, "But he's coming *here*? How come?"

Worthless laughed and said, "Boy, this is the only place to be, come tomorrow night. I tole you about ten thousand times. This is the biggest thing that's ever happened to us since emancipation, man. Every Negro in America is gonna wish he was here. Eddie say he can't *wait* for it. So of course he's gonna be here. *Everybody* is gonna be here."

Mr. Peet said, "I can't wait to tell the dancers."

Worthless said, "Whyn't you tell 'em tomorrow? They got enough to worry about tonight, and I want them to get their rest. No sense riling them up any further."

Two of Worthless's men, Fidget and a tall, thin man, exchanged glances. Sumner watched through hooded eyes. Worthless seemed to miss it. Sumner said, "What?" and the men looked startled. They did not answer. Sumner said, "What? Out with it." Now the men looked nervous.

Sumner rose to his feet and said, "You better say something, fast."

The tall, thin man stood up slowly. He said, "It ain't nothing. He's just sayin' again how that police has been coming 'round some more."

Sumner said, "Which police?"

Mr. Peet said, "That man Haney."

The tall, thin man nodded, as did Fidget. Sumner said, "Whatchoo mean, coming 'round?"

Fidget said, "He's been h-h-here. Every d-d-day. Just snoop-snoop—"

"Snooping around," the thin man said. "Just snooping, asking questions, poking in and out. With two goons."

Worthless said, "Don't pay it no mind. We ain't doing nothing that's against the law. He cain't stick us with nothing if we ain't doing nothing."

Sumner said, "Sure he can. And he still thinking about Jeeter."

Worthless said, "Well, he's the only one who is."

Sumner said, "Maybe not. That district attorney man, that new one they say is a little light in his loafers, is on it, too. He was cruising by here this morning early. Driving around in his little sports car."

Worthless said, "Never mind him, either. Let's get back to it."

The group rose and began to shuffle away. Worthless checked his watch. It was almost morning. Tomorrow night, nine o'clock, and his world would be entirely different. For better or for worse. He said, "Eighteen hours to showtime, boys. Y'all get some rest, now. We got to look sharp tomorrow."

Hours earlier Mo had been over to see him. They met in the reception area, where Worthless was inspecting the cigarette girls. He was not happy with their uniforms. The skirts were so short that once they slung on their trays of cigarettes, cigars, and candy, they appeared to be wearing nothing but nylon hose. Plus the hats they were supposed to wear made them look like nurses. Worthless said, "We got to lose those caps, ladies. They stupid-looking."

Over his shoulder, Mo said, "Lose the gum, too."

Worthless turned and smiled, and said, "How come's that, boss?"

Mo said, "Can't sell gum in a casino, Worthless. Folks wad it up and throw it on the carpet, and it gets caught in the vacuum cleaners. Plus people will chew it up and try to jam it in the slot machines if they're losing too much."

Worthless shook his head and said, "That's the voice of experience, ladies. Let's toss out all that gum, too, soon's you get rid of them caps. What about the skirts?"

Mo cast an approving eye. There were six girls. All of them were over five foot six. All of them were black and bosomy and just beautiful, and they all had those fine showgirl legs. He said, "I think those skirts are just fabulous. Any shorter, and you'd have the law on you. But I think they're just fabulous. Make any man alive want to buy a pack of cigarettes."

"That's it then, girls. Y'all scat." Worthless turned to Mo and said, "Thanks for coming over so late."

Mo said, "Don't mention it. I'm glad to see it's all coming together. You ought to be proud."

"I be proud this time tomorrow night, if I ain't broke or in jail."

Mo laughed and said, "You won't be. This time tomorrow you're going to be a big piece of news. I think the Ivory Coast is going to be a huge success. Mind you, I am almost the only one that *does* think that. But I've been the only one right before. You watch. This joint is going to be number-one hot."

Worthless took Mo's elbow and gently steered him out of Reception, down into the pits. He wanted him to see the nightclub at the back, now that it was dressed and ready.

"You know we using white dealers?"

Mo was surprised. He slowed up and said, "No. Why?"

"Everybody else is colored," Worthless said. "All the waiters and the bartenders and the reception people and the hatcheck girls and *everything*. And the performers, of course. I got nothing but the best. We raided the hotels in Harlem, and the nightclubs on Central Avenue in Los Ang-uh-lees, and the black and tans in Chicago. Nothing but the best. We raided the Pullman cars. But there ain't no place in the world that gots colored dealers. 'Cause there ain't no place in the world that gots gambling for colored people. So . . . We got about ten men from around here that's going to be working the first couple of weeks, training colored boys to run the craps and blackjack and the wheel. I figure that much time, then we can put the white men upstairs to study the games while the colored men do the dealing."

Mo said, "If that's the only thing worrying you, you can rest easy."

"Well, it's that, plus it's that man Haney."

"He's been around here?"

Worthless pulled Mo out of the pits and said, "I haven't had much truck with him, but I keep hearing that he's been around."

"On that thing with Jeeter?"

Worthless nodded. "That and this place in general. He keeps talking about black men and white women. Seems kinda interested in that. Maybe too interested in that."

Mo laughed and said, "From what I hear, that is only a *professional* interest."

Worthless gave Mo a sidelong glance, studying his face. But Mo was staring at the ceiling. He said, "Is that all hand-painted?"

Worthless said, "Yassuh. Took forever. It's nice, though. This is the nightclub."

The room was splendid. The floor was raked and tiered. No one would get a bad seat. The tables were laid with fresh linen. Each had a silver flower vase and a matching silver ashtray with the Ivory Coast facade etched into it. Each ashtray held two packs of Ivory Coast matches and one Ivory Coast five-dollar chip. Mo said, "You know these ashtrays will all get stolen opening night?"

Worthless said, "I'm counting on that. Free advertising. Well, cheap advertising anyway. And I figure the chip ought to send most of them to the tables after the show."

"Almost guaranteed," Mo said. "It all looks right smart. I'm beginning to think my money's safe over here."

"I hope so." Worthless watched Mo with wonder. What a cool, cool customer. He had almost a million dollars riding on this thing, and he looked like a man who was thinking about buying a new pair of shoes. And not even in a hurry to make up his mind.

He said, "I'll leave you to it, then. Anything you want me to do for tomorrow night?"

Worthless said, "Nah. You just be here."

"I wouldn't miss it for the world, Worthless. Can't wait. I'll be over soon as things quiet down over at the Starburst."

Mo stuck out his hand. Worthless took it, as if he were accepting a gift, and shook it lightly.

Mo said, "Good night. And good luck."

"Night, suh."

When he was gone, Worthless went into the kitchen. There was just the right level of pandemonium there. He went back out to Reception. He had to talk with the bartenders one more time, and then he and Mr. Peet were going to meet with Sumner and some of the others. He was going to make a special effort to stop thinking about that white bastard policeman Haney.

Hours later, sitting with Sumner and Mr. Peet and his other men, Worthless felt . . . worthless. He was dog-tired and sore inside. He said, "Y'all git, now. You look beat."

Everyone but Sumner got up and shifted around a bit on their feet and mumbled good-byes and took off. Sumner just sat, looking at Worthless. He said, "You one tired old man."

Worthless had a sudden thought: *If I had a son . . .* And tears sprang into his eyes. He said, "It's a fact. I'm one beat old boy."

Sumner said, "Let it go, for today. I'll mop up here, and get things straight. And we'll start again in the morning."

"You a good boy."

"Ain't no boy."

"Then you a good man," Worthless said, and felt the tears well up again. "I'll leave you to it, and say thank you one more time. You a good man."

Sumner watched Worthless go. He said to himself, "I will never, never, never let anything make me look that beat-down. Old man shuffling off like he's been choppin' cotton his whole life. He *looks* like a field hand. I will never look like that."

Then he stood up and a wave of tired came over him. He went to the corner and took up a broom and started sweeping.

Deacon was standing in the ice-cold office. Mo had just come back from the Thunderbird, up from the basement, having crossed between the two buildings in the tunnel. Deacon looked mystified. He said, "How'd you do that?"

Mo said, "Do what, Deacon? You got a drink?"

Deacon waved his hand. He had a tumbler full of amber liquid and ice. He said, "How did you get up here?"

Mo said, "I came up in the elevator."

Deacon looked out into the hall. "Which elevator?"

"There's a second elevator, actually. A private car."

"That goes where?"

"It goes down to a basement office."

"And from there?"

"From there what? For Christ's sake, Deacon. What do you want?"

Deacon said, "Can I sit down?"

Mo waved at a chair, and went to his desk and opened the humidor there and took out a fat Cuban. He said, "Spill it. What's up?"

Deacon said, "Your bartender, Sloan, he's dead."

"What happened?"

"The police shot him."

"Why?"

"He was drunk. We got stopped. He got mouthy. And there was a scuffle."

"And he's dead."

"Yes."

Mo puffed at the cigar, watching Deacon, expecting something more.

He said, "And?"

"And what?"

"Is there more?"

Deacon said, "No. Just that he's dead."

Mo said, "Okay. Thanks for telling me."

"And that's it? That's all you've got to say?"

"Am I missing something? Is there something else here?"

Deacon said, "Well, yes. He's your guy, and the cops shot him for mouthing off, and they dumped him out in the desert."

"And what? Is there something I need to *do* about this?"

Deacon stared at Mo, then said, "No. I guess not."

"Then it's just another piece of bad news. I appreciate you telling me about it. I will make sure someone knows that he won't be showing up for work today."

Deacon rose from the chair and weaved slightly as he headed for the door. He said, "That's that, then. I'll be seeing you."

Mo said, "Yes, Deacon. You certainly will."

Haney had stepped from the tub, and dried and wrapped himself in a fine silk robe, and was moving to the front room when Willis appeared, snifter in hand, and gave him his cognac. He continued to the parlor. The lights of Las Vegas twinkled below. Haney sat in an armchair and fretted as he sipped the expensive French liquor, nosing deep into the glass and inhaling its perfume before each sip. It was a balm to him, like the bath, like the sounds of the Sons of the Pioneers and of Roy Rogers and Dale Evans. They soothed him. Tonight the guitars twanged and the honeyed voices sang, but Haney could find no peace.

Sometimes two and two did not equal four. Or, sometimes, just figuring out which two were which made getting to four impossible. Haney had known the shakedown was inevitable. He had been contacted by the man from Chicago, who had warned him about the man from Los Angeles. When nothing happened, Haney should have known better than to assume that nothing was *going* to happen. It never worked out that way, and it had been foolish to think it would this time. He should have been paying more attention. He should have been more vigilant. He should have been watching all the players, all the time, without rest.

He should have known something was wrong with that suicide in Shipton Wells, too. He had a policeman's nose, and to his policeman's nose, that one stank from the start. But it was not in his jurisdiction. Besides, it was just some creep from out of town. Besides, it was just a suicide. They got lots of those in Las Vegas. There was no reason to assume it was anything more interesting than that. On the other hand, he remembered his reaction to the details when he heard them, and the fact is—it stank. And he didn't do anything about it.

From that small mistake grew, now, the larger problem. Haney was pretty sure that Deacon was not the guy who had warned him from Chicago. He was obviously not the guy who was supposed to have the photographs. So where did he figure? Had he done the killing in Shipton Wells? Maybe. He'd done the beating on that crooked dealer. Or Mo Weiner *said* he did the beating on that crooked dealer. Either way, he knew about the photographs. Maybe he knew the person who actually *had* the photographs. But if that was the story, why no shakedown? Why was he sitting on the photographs?

And who else was involved? That nigger boxer Lee had made his little crack about the foundation. Could that be related to this? Was he connected to the bartender that got croaked in the desert? Or was that guy, in turn, connected to the little guy Jeeter?

That had been a mistake. Haney inhaled more of the cognac and felt his eyes burn. The Jeeter thing irked him. He'd sent two men around there to talk to Jeeter about his chippies. There was some friction coming from upstairs, directly from Haney's brother-in-law, Holbrook. He had a connection to Aunt Betty, who ran the city's highest high-end house of prostitution. It was strictly off-limits to Haney, and to his entire force. It was like the Vatican, or something. It had its own law. Holbrook was in charge of it. And somehow he'd got it into his head that Jeeter and his chippies were cutting into his business. Some of the high rollers were cruising over to the West Side and banging Jeeter's girls in some flophouse when they should have been going to Aunt Betty's and banging white girls.

So he had asked Haney to handle it. Haney had sent two guys over to Jeeter's to give him a message: no more white guys. Just that:

no more doing business with white guys. It should have been the simplest thing in the world, and Haney had no idea how it had gone wrong. The men had trussed Jeeter up like an Easter ham, and robbed him, and come back apologizing.

It made Haney's head throb. He had planned a little party for tonight. He could hear Willis, in fact, readying things. He called out to him, and when he came into the room, Haney said, "Not tonight, Willis. I've changed my mind."

There was a pause. He said, "Yes, suh. Not tonight."

Haney was alone again. He tugged at the snifter and felt the heat of his bath and the heat of the day leaving him. The night was cool and quiet. Las Vegas shimmered below. It was almost pretty, if you could forget all the sinfulness and evil that was going on, right now, where the lights glowed.

The trick would be to get Mo's horn player and the photographs in the same place at the same time and do away with them both. There would be a third party, presumably—the person who had the photographs when the horn player did not have them. But that person would not matter once the pictures themselves were destroyed. Provided Haney got all of them. How to do that, then? The horn player was a junkie. He was exposed there, legally, but that had not seemed to trouble him much. He would need money, because junkies always needed money. And he was a man, which meant you could get to him with pussy, but he was a single man, not a married man, so that reduced considerably the leverage you could apply.

And he was also, no doubt, one of Fatty's clients. Slip him some bad stuff? That would be a quick solution, if kind of indirect. But not one that would guarantee delivery of the photographs.

And there was the other question of Lee, the boxer, and what he'd said about the foundation. The two could be related. Though that seemed unlikely. Was there possibly a solution to both problems? Probably not. He could dynamite the Ivory Coast on opening night, and blow up half of Las Vegas. What then?

Haney, awash in his sea of troubles, sighed and contemplated the lights. What trouble! And why? For what? For nothing! For a little thing he liked to do in the bedroom! Maybe he could just let the photographs go public, call this Deacon's bluff, call the whole *world's* bluff, and let the photographs go public, then simply explain them.

What appeared to be going on in the pictures, he knew, was unsettling. What was *really* going on, though, was much different. Once he explained, people would understand. He could *make* them understand. And if they didn't understand . . . Well, he'd be finished. No. He'd be finished anyway.

He swore out loud. Willis came scampering and said, "Yes, suh?" and Haney quieted inside and said, "Nothing, Willis. Pour me another cognac, and then we'll call it a night. You can send all the others home."

"Yes, suh."

Willis poured a fresh snifter full and carted it back into the front room. In the rear of the house again, he rounded up the two men and two women there and said, "Boss say everybody go home." The two men grumbled. Willis said, "Don't start that stuff with me, little man. You take yo'self on out of here. You know he he's gonna want you back, and probably pretty soon. So go on home. You be back again soon."

The two men and two women moved away resentfully. Willis heard their car start a minute later, and the crackly sound of their tires on the driveway. He checked his wristwatch—a Timex that Mr. Haney had given him for his birthday. It was almost three o'clock. Way past time. He flicked off the lights in the kitchen.

Ten

THE SUN CAME up on the desert Sunday like a ball of fire, blazing heat and light and chasing the night away. Pieces of Saturday night still had not gone to bed. Two drunks wandered up Las Vegas Boulevard, heading somewhere but not getting there soon. A party of college kids drove by them, shouting obscenities and swerving into oncoming traffic. The driver whipped the wheel back and the car skidded sideways and slammed to a stop against the curb. One hubcap shot across the sidewalk and rolled into a sandy vacant lot. The car roared to life and was off again, the college boys shouting as it went. The neon above them began to pale against the light. Their roadster went on down the Strip, past the waning glitter of the Sands and the Sahara and the Desert Inn, the rising tower of the new Riviera, the new Royal Nevada, and the just-shuttered New Frontier.

Coming out the front doors of the Starburst, Fatty Behr saw the college boys fly by, past the two drunks wandering on and off the sidewalk. For an instant he thought the car would surely strike one of them. Then it was gone and the drunks stumbled on and the Strip went silent again.

Two carhops sat dozing in their cabana, waiting for the next load of suckers. They did not stir as the hotel doors swung shut behind Fatty and eclipsed the sounds of the remaining dusk-to-dawn gamblers. There were still fifty or more of them, slapping the slots, throwing chips into the craps table, laying 'em down and playing 'em down on the blackjack.

He had made a good night of it. The lounge had done very well, which boosted his cut. Stella had been terrific, and had done two encores, which was two more than she sometimes did, which meant that the crowd stayed on, had a couple more cocktails, and then went away happy. If it were up to Fatty, she'd do two encores every night. It was not up to Fatty.

The other stuff was up to him, though. He'd sold a little of this and a little of that. There'd been several couples who needed a room in a hurry and didn't mind how much it cost them, and Fatty had obliged. There had been a strange, hairy-looking brute from New Orleans who was just *dying* for a piece of tail. Fatty, disgusted though he was by the man's appearance, had made the arrangements. Before it was done, the man slipped him a one-hundred-dollar Thunderbird chip—the gorgeous dark blue one with the three brass-yellow side markings.

Very late, after Fatty had taken a second pill to keep him pepped up, a very normal-looking guy with a very normal-looking wife had approached him as he stood near the back lobby bar. The guy was nervous in the way that these guys are always nervous. Someone had told him Fatty was the man to see, and that *made* Fatty the man to see. So Fatty said, "Sure, pal. What can I do you for?"

The guy, with a quick, uneasy smile back at his wife, said, "We were just wondering. . . . Is there someplace around here a couple of out-of-towners could go for a little extra, uh, excitement?"

Fatty said, "Depends what you have in mind."

The guy said, "Well, something, uh, different. You know? Special."

Fatty said, "For you, or for the little lady?"

"Both of us."

"You want something for the both of you."

"Yeah. Another fella."

Fatty looked again at the little woman. She was trembling, and pale. Fatty could practically smell the pervert on this guy and it turned his stomach, plus, it was late, and he'd had a great night already. So he said, "Beats me, pal," and turned away. He thought he saw a look of relief on the woman's face.

In front of the hotel now, he was sure he'd made the right call. People wanted all kinds of things. Mostly he was happy to oblige, for a price. Something to ease their pain, or someone to share their loneliness . . . No harm in any of that. Sometimes they wanted a pill, or a fix, or a smoke of something to make their day a little less dreary or a little more remarkable. And why not? A white guy wants a colored girl. A white woman wants a colored guy. A man wants two women. A man wants another man. Fatty could help. But a couple like that, with the man wanting another man and wanting his wife involved? It made Fatty want to puke. He said to himself, out loud, "Go back to Akron, you creep." One of the parking attendants woke up and said, "Yes, suh?" and Fatty started laughing. He duked the guy a buck and said, "Go back to sleep, 'bo."

He'd planned to hit the T-bird and make one last swing. But the sun was coming up fast. There was no activity at the front door. The parking lot looked abandoned. The two drunks were wandering up and down the sidewalk, on and off, making their way slowly down the boulevard. Something in Fatty twanged with sentiment, just for an instant: he saw a pair of rummy old pals, out on the town, painting it red, having a hoot, away from their troubles and cares, just the two of them flapping around in the world. They'd go someplace now and flop and maybe have a nightcap at one of the dives downtown. One of them might get all mushy and tell the other one that he was the greatest pal a guy ever had. They'd clasp hands. They'd get teary-eyed and swear friendship for life. They might even hug.

It was the squarest thing in the world. It would never happen to Fatty Behr. He went across to the T-bird parking lot and around to the back of the building. There was a service entrance there and a service elevator that would take him directly to his room. It was 6:30 A.M. Enough already.

Gunfire woke Anita at dawn. She started and ran from her bed, and was cowering by the closet before she woke up all the way. Then she put on a robe and a pair of slippers, and peeked out the front door of her cabin. Her uncle was coming around the front of the café carrying the long-barreled pistol he used for target shooting. He'd been blasting at the coyotes that cruised the café's trash cans at night.

Anita had asked why he didn't leave them alone. At the very worst, they knocked the lids off the cans. Once in a while they tipped over one of the barrels. Nine times out of ten you'd never know they'd been there at all. Her uncle had said, "Because I hate them. That's why. Mind your own goddamn business."

It was his surgery day. Maybe he was nervous. She'd counted five shots or six, coming awake. Maybe he got one. That would certainly improve his mood.

Half an hour later she had dressed and done her hair and makeup and was making coffee in the big machine behind the café counter. Her uncle came in through the kitchen. He had the target pistol in one hand and was carrying a dead coyote, grasping it by the back of the neck like a house cat, in the other. He said, "Take a look, Anita. I got one."

The coyote's eyes were glazed but open, and his tongue hung out the side of his mouth. He seemed to be grinning. Anita said, "It's bleeding on the floor. Get it out of here."

He laughed and said, "I should get the bastard stuffed and mounted."

Anita said, "It's disgusting."

"Get *you* stuffed and mounted."

"Get it out of here."

The day dragged horribly. The customers came and went, and there were too few of them to make her hurry. She felt she'd been at work for ten hours when noon finally came. The midday bus was due from Las Vegas. There would be the usual collection of sad-sack losers; they wouldn't order much and they wouldn't tip at all, but at least there would be something to do.

Wally wandered over from the gas station about eleven, sucking on a toothpick, wearing a green suit. He said, "New threads. What do you think?"

Anita said, "Split-pea soup."

"Well, thank *you*, then. Square."

After the lunch rush came and went—Anita had gone into the kitchen three times to correct her uncle's mistakes when he got the side orders mixed up—and things were quiet again, she told her uncle, "You go and get cleaned up. I'll take care of the rest of this mess. That girl should be here soon, and Wally's here already. You get ready."

Her uncle said, "I'm ready now."

"You got your stuff?"

"What stuff? I got my pajamas and a stinking toothbrush. What else do you need for them to cut you open?"

"You could take my little radio, if you want."

"For what? I hate all that music. 'Hey dere, you wi' de starse in you ice . . .' I can't stand all that mushy teenager junk."

"Suit yourself. It was only a suggestion."

"Well, my suggestion is, shut your mouth and mind your own business and get this crap cleaned up before—"

"That's enough."

Anita and her uncle both turned, startled. Deacon stood in the café doorway, a shadow outlined in bright sunlight, a cigarette wedged between his lips. His hands twitched at his sides. He said. "Go ahead, sidewinder. Make your move."

Her uncle said, "What?"

Deacon said, "You heard me, hombre. I said, 'That's enough.' Slap leather, you yellow-bellied varmint."

There was silence, broken only by the hum of the burbling coffee-maker. Anita and her uncle stared at Deacon.

He said, "All right, then. Don't slap leather." He moved into the room. Anita saw that the lady from the Starburst was trailing after him. Deacon had his hand out now, and he was smiling. He said to her uncle, reaching to shake his hand, "How are you, sir? How're you feeling?"

Her uncle took Deacon's hand and said, "I'm fine. That was a stupid joke."

"You're right. This here's Dot. She's gonna cover for Anita tonight."

Dot stepped forward and had the uncle's full attention. She was tall and dark and had a big, bosomy figure that her dress did nothing to hide. Anita felt a twinge: *I will never be that much of a woman,* she thought. Her uncle shot forward two steps with both his hands out, reaching for Dot. He said, "How you do? How you do? I am the boss here. Let me get you out of that dress—"

Dot said, "Slow down, boss."

"Into a uniform, I mean," he said. "Let me show you a place to change."

Anita said, "Let me, *Tio.* My name is Anita. I'll show you a place to freshen up. Are you a size twelve or fourteen?"

Dot laughed and said, "Keep dreamin', kid. I'm an eight. A full-figured eight."

Deacon watched them go, and watched Anita's uncle watching them go. He had that hound-dog, horn-dog look, like he'd go for Dot in a big way. Like he'd go for his own *niece*, even. Deacon said, "So, you all ready for your date with the surgeon?"

He said, "Mind your own goddamn business," and followed Anita and Dot out of the room.

Fifteen minutes later they were ready. Deacon sat in the big Cadillac borrowed from the Starburst garage, waiting. Anita came out from her cabin, carrying a small wicker suitcase in one hand and a big cardboard hatbox in the other. Her uncle came next, clomping down the back steps of the café, carrying a dark overnight bag. Deacon saw, gulped, didn't believe, stared and then looked away; it was the same overnight bag he had taken away from the rat-faced man the first day he'd come to Shipton Wells. The first time he'd laid eyes on Anita. He said, "Anita! What's with the—" And then her uncle was upon them. He yanked open the front door of the big car and threw the overnight bag onto the seat. Deacon flinched, and the bag settled next to him. Uncle got in and slammed the door. He banged his elbow against the window, cursed in Spanish, and then furiously rolled the glass down.

He said, "Is this bag bothering you?"

Deacon said, "What do you mean?"

He said, "The bag. I'll put in on the floor."

Deacon said, "It's okay."

He said, "We'd better get going, no?"

Deacon said, "No. You're right. I mean, yes."

The Cadillac roared awake, and they were off. Deacon looked into the rearview once as they were coming out of the driveway. He could see Dot, through the screen door, standing and looking out at them, just as Anita had stood and looked the day he met her. The day that all of this started. It made his heart ache. He said, "Next stop, Las Vegas," and hit the highway.

Worthless had left the house early, and done his customary stroll past Garcia's store for his paper and off to the Hotel Apache for his coffee and eggs. He had returned to the house for an hour, trying to kill a little time, trying to burn away an hour without burning away an hour's worth of energy. Coming back he stopped again at Garcia's and bought a pack of Pall Malls. He had not had a cigarette in more than a decade. He felt that if he ever needed one, today was going to be the day. Walking back up Jackson Street, he filled his head with the tobacco smoke until he was dizzy. It was a long, long day ahead. He'd have slept later if he could. He had another cigarette while sitting in his makeshift office, watching the clock click forward.

Dina was rising as he readied himself to leave the house for the second time. She was shuffling around in the kitchen when she suddenly said, "You been smoking."

Worthless said, "Yes, I have. Bought a pack of cigarettes just this morning. First time in years."

"Don't be smokin' those things in this house," Dina said. "You know how I feel about cigarette smoking in my house."

For an instant, he saw her as she was when they met—free, righteous, fire-eyed, proud, very beautiful. It was right here, in the desert, here on the West Side. Her father had been a dentist, the only colored dentist in Nevada, and he kept her away from the kinds of places where people like Worthless were. She stayed out of the nightclubs and the bars and the juke joints and the roadhouses. Her father told her she was better than all that trash, and she knew it was true. Then one Saturday night, she and two friends had borrowed a car and driven into the West Side. Worthless had seen them park on Bonanza and walk up to Jackson Street. The three of them looked like fairy-tale figures, all crinoline and high heels and big hair, and they obviously had no business being on Jackson Street in the middle of a summer Saturday night. But they were bold as brass, and one of them, particularly, held her head so high that no one would dare tell her anything about being where she should not be. Worthless said to the man he was talking to, "Listen, if you want to go into that line of business, I'll lend you the money. Just don't let on where you got it. I'll catch you later." He left the man on the sidewalk and followed the three women.

An hour later they were all four drinking 7 and 7s in the Town Tavern, which at that time was the only joint on the West Side where a man could take a lady without apologizing to her first. Jukebox blues were playing. Worthless was ignoring the two girlfriends. He was staring at Dina, who had already had two cocktails and was asking for another. She was the most beautiful girl he'd ever seen. He made the decision right at that moment: *I am going to marry this girl and make her my own.*

He'd had to drive her and her friends home that night and take a tongue-lashing from Dina's father, a man scarcely older than himself, for bringing them home so late.

A month later they were man and wife.

By the following summer, it started to seem to Worthless that his wife was drinking quite a bit. By the fall, it was clear to him that she was having trouble with her drinking. Two years later, having had her in front of every kind of medical specialist the desert had to offer, he had accepted the fact that she was what they called an alcoholic— one of those hopeless drunks who can't drink right and who can't stop drinking. He'd accepted this the way he accepted all bad news. It was the Lord's will. He didn't question it. He did the best he could.

He said, "I won't do no smoking in the house, baby. But I may be home kinda late. You know, we gonna open that Ivory Coast hotel today. It's gonna be a long day."

"Thass no 'scuse for smoking in my house."

Worthless drew her close and kissed her on top of the head. She smelled like a bum from the street. For one instant he was washed over with a wave of self-pity, and tears sprang to his eyes. Why him? Why her? Why this? What in the world had either of them done to deserve this? What could an innocent like Dina have *ever* done?

Worthless said, "I see you tonight, baby." And left her there.

Outside the heat was turned up high. It was full summer, coming on, just the kind of hot, dry day it had been when he and Dina first met. Just there on Jackson Street. Just where his Ivory Coast had risen from the sand like some brave new beast. Just where he'd met this Anita. He realized suddenly that he'd had her somewhere in the back of his mind for a whole day. He'd been making little plans, seeing her move around the landscape of the Ivory Coast, as a hatcheck girl, as a cigarette girl, up onstage singing. He didn't know if she could sing, mind you. He didn't know anything. But he was thinking about her. A lot.

Moving down Jackson now, he watched a little wind blow papers against the curb. There was a fine grit of sand on the sidewalk. What *about* a girl like that? What could you do with a girl like that? Worthless felt all kinds of things, all at the same time, and not all of them seemed that they were supposed to go together. He wanted her, but he wanted to help her and he wanted to protect her. From what? From men like himself, he supposed. He wanted to give her something, to help make her something. *That is what's missing from my life,* Worthless thought. *With Dina, I never had the chance to do anything for her. I was going to take her to San Francisco, take her to Los An-gub-lees, show her the Golden Gate Bridge and walk with her on the beach. But her drinking got so bad, so fast, I hardly was able to take her to a goddamn picture show. . . .* Worthless had attended the funeral alone when her father the dentist had died. Dina was laying up, house drunk, and he couldn't even get her dressed.

Worthless felt his shoes gritting up on the sidewalk. He sounded like a soft-shoe dancer. He stopped to light a cigarette, and skidded his shoe back and forth across the sidewalk. A voice behind him said, "Hey, Bojangles."

Worthless stopped and turned. It was Haney, the cop. He was wearing a black suit and black hat, and a humorless face.

He said, "What a co-inky-dink. We were just talking about you."

Worthless glanced from Haney to the two big men, also in black suits, who stood behind him. They appeared to have just come out of Garcia's. One of them had a packet of Wrigley's spearmint gum in his big, raw hand.

Haney said, "This is your big day, isn't it?"

Worthless said, "Yassuh. It is."

"We were just remarking how fine it is that you are able to open such a splendid establishment. That the city will support such a splendid establishment."

"Yassuh."

"What with all the contracts and permits and bank loans and bank notes and all that, it must have taken a lot of cooperation."

"Yes, it did, suh. Folks been fine with me about that."

"Well, that *is* fine."

Behind the two black-suited officers Worthless suddenly saw that boy from the Ivory Coast, standing in the shadows inside Garcia's. What was his name? Midget? Widget? Whatever it was, he caught Worthless's eye and shot off into the shadows again.

Haney, watching Worthless, saw him see something. He said,

"We're just looking in on some of the local businesses. Making sure everything is working smoothly. We will be calling on you in the same capacity. Soon."

"Yassuh."

"You know about my foundation, don't you?"

Haney's voice had risen a pitch, as if he were speaking to someone half a block behind Worthless. This made the hair stand up on his neck. Who the hell was he speaking to? Worthless checked the impulse to turn around.

He said, "No, suh."

"It's a charitable foundation that cares for orphaned children," Haney said, in that same train-station voice. "Many of the local businesses have been helpful to us with donations."

"I'd like to help, too, suh."

"That's fine. I'll send someone around. Now get off the street."

Worthless left them there and went down Jackson. There had been no one standing around them. The shouting was for his own men, then. Worthless saw. They did not know that Worthless knew something he should not know. Haney was behaving in a way that would be natural to his own men.

Which did not explain Worthless and *his* men. If that boy Fidget had just been shopping in Garcia's, would he have jumped into the shadows like that? Most likely not. He had checked up on a lot of the men he hired for the Ivory Coast, because he didn't want anyone's police record to become the casino's problem. But he hadn't checked on Fidget. Maybe he had a warrant on him or something? He looked too frightened to be a dangerous boy. But you never knew. Human beings came in very strange packages.

Worthless took his busy head off the street and through the front doors of the Ivory Coast, determined to forget about Fidget. He had too many other fish to fry today to worry over a little fingerling like that.

Deacon had told Gleason, and now Gleason told Stella, that her favorite trumpet player would not be onstage with them tonight. Gleason said, "He had some personal business to attend to. He assured me it would not happen again."

Stella said, "Well, it had better *not*." Privately, she wondered. To-night was supposed to be the opening of that big Negro casino and hotel. Surely a man like Deacon would not miss a night like tonight, not with his connections to the West Side. She said to Gleason, "Dock him fifty dollars for missing a rehearsal and a show. We'll just work around him."

Gleason said, "You bet." He made a mental note to forget about the fifty dollars. A stand-up guy like Deacon? Forget it.

Gleason wondered what the personal business could be. He knew Deacon was a big hit with the ladies, but he never saw him around town with any of them, in the lounges and nightclubs where he and Andy went on their nights off. Maybe he had a special girl tucked away someplace. Maybe he had a special *boy* tucked away someplace. Gleason didn't think so. You could tell. With Deacon, though, you couldn't tell much.

One night he'd seen Deacon at the Dancing Waters show in the Royal Nevada's Crown Room. Deacon was smoking a cigarette and had a drink in his hand, and he was looking around the room with something on his face that was halfway between amused and dis-gusted. Gleason said, "What's wrong with *you?*"

And Deacon said, "Everything. I'm a two-four guy, man. Living in a one-three world."

Now Stella said, "Let's try that new tune. Without the dancers, please, Andy."

Gleason shook his head. He'd hear about *that* later on. For now, he faced the band, raised his baton, and said, "Places, now." And they swung into it. Nearing the break, Gleason pointed his baton at Springer. He took his clarinet to the solo Deacon would ordinarily have taken. Stella squinted at Deacon's empty seat.

Deacon got the big Cadillac off the desert and into town sometime after six o'clock. The streets were quiet. But it was Sunday; people were home, resting up, waiting for the heat to go down, getting ready to go out. Things would cook up again in an hour or two. Deacon drove halfway into downtown and then pulled the car to the curb. Anita's uncle had been dozing. He now shook himself awake and clutched the handle on the overnight bag. Deacon turned back to look at Anita. She was like a fairy princess, seeing her fairy kingdom for the first time. Her eyes were huge. She felt Deacon looking at her, and she said, "Oh, Deacon. It's just so beautiful."

She was looking straight up Fremont Street. Neon was already glowing in the late-afternoon light. Ahead of them, competing for attention, were the glittering garish marquees for the Hotel Apache and the Golden Nugget gambling hall and the California Club and the Lucky Strike Club, and right next door to each other the huge Westerner and the Pioneer Club, with the enormous Las Vegas cowboy rising into the evening sky. He was a vast neon fella wearing jeans and a check shirt and a cowboy hat cocked at a jaunty angle. He had a bandanna around his neck and a cigarette dangling from his lips, and his arm waved at you from three stories above.

Anita said, almost breathless, "It's not at all like in the daytime."

Deacon said, "You wait until midnight. It's like standing in the midday sun, it's so bright."

"I like how it is now."

"So where do you work?" her uncle said.

Deacon said, "I work up on the Strip, at the Starburst. This is downtown."

"Where's the hospital at?"

"Right around the corner from here."

"We got time to see the Starburst?"

Deacon, surprised, said, "Well, sure. I can drive you up there, if you like."

"It's prolly all the same junk, right?"

Deacon said, "No. Some of it's pretty nice. Anita?"

Anita looked positively spellbound.

Deacon said, "We'll take a spin up there, and I'll let Anita down at Dot's place so she can freshen up. Then I'll bring you back down to the hospital."

"That's good," her uncle said. "You do it."

Deacon fired the Cadillac back up and drew away from downtown. Anita turned as they left, and rested her head on the back cushions, staring dreamily at Fremont Street as it faded.

Deacon gave them the full treatment. He came onto Las Vegas Boulevard and let the big Cadillac almost idle along. He watched Anita in the rearview mirror, her head swinging slowly from side to

side as she gaped at the amazing excess before her. She was illumi-
nated. The sun was almost down now, and the light was long and
low coming from their right as they drove. The faces of the hotels
looked on fire. The El Rancho Vegas. The Western-themed Hotel
Last Frontier. The Flamingo, with its famed Champagne Tower. The
Desert Inn. The Sahara, with the cowboy-saddled camels out front.
The Sands, and the huge Riviera, with Liberace's name on the marquee. The brand-new Dunes, with Sinatra's name up in lights.

Anita said, "Oh, *Deacon*. They don't mean Frank Sinatra, do they?"

Deacon laughed and said, "Who else?"

When they got to the Starburst, Deacon slid the car right up to
the valet guys. One of them, a fella named Chuck or Chet or something, recognized Deacon at once. But Deacon winked at him and
shook his head slightly. Chuck said, "Good evening and welcome to
the Starburst, sir," as if he were any high roller.

Deacon took them into the lobby, just past Reception, and they
stood looking over the casino. The pits were humming and busy with
squares. The air was full of the jingle-jangle of money being lost. The
slots clattered and buzzed. They heard a pitman say, "Coming out!"
from a craps table. Anita looked transformed. Her uncle said, "I guess
there ain't time to do any gambling. Just as well."

Anita said, "Listen to you—and on your way to the hospital."

And he said, "I'm just saying . . ."

Deacon said, "Why don't you sit down and have a few hands of
blackjack? I'll take Anita back to her room."

"Well, I don't know." Her uncle looked around suspiciously and
held the overnight bag close to his chest.

Deacon said, "Come with me for a moment."

He steered Anita's uncle by the elbow, down into the pits. A dealer
he knew pretty well had an empty berth at a one-dollar blackjack
table. Deacon said to the dealer, "This here's a friend of mine. He
ain't no stiff and he ain't no garlic. Treat him good, will ya?" He got
a big nod back. Deacon said, "I'll be back for you in fifteen minutes.
Try not to break the bank."

"Sure. What's a garlic?"

"It's a square. Or a tightwad that won't tip. It's just casino jive. You
play and have fun. I'll be back."

He left him there, and took Anita off the floor and back toward the guest rooms. They caught the elevator down and went to the basement, then out the back hallway to the employee quarters.

Dot had given him a key with the number 107 stamped onto it. Deacon found the room. Inside it was musty and dark. Deacon found the light. Anita said, "Leave it off, won't you?"

Deacon felt itchy in the dark. This room smelled and felt like his own—not a home, but a temporary resting place, a hole you climbed in between rounds. It was a long night ahead, full of possibility but without any possibility of scoring. He wished he had a drink in his hand, or a bottle nearby.

Anita said, "I haven't had a chance to say thank you yet. Not proper, anyway."

Deacon felt her move toward him in the dim light.

He said, "I haven't done anything yet."

"You brought me here, in this room. You brought me into Las Vegas."

"You ain't seen nothin' yet, sweetheart. Tonight I'm gonna show you the whole world."

"I want to show you something."

Anita had him and held him. Deacon's head caught fire. She pulled him close, and she was impossibly soft and hot. Her skin was like wet fire. She put her lips on his neck, against his jaw, and kissed him there, her breath coming short and shallow. Deacon put his hands on the small of her back and drew her into him. They stood swaying for a moment. Deacon got stiff, and dizzy, and his head starting running: the drink that wasn't there. His kit. The line of dancers at the Ivory Coast. Dot, her big bosom heaving under him. Anita's uncle. The overnight bag. He broke away.

He said, "What's the deal with that overnight bag?"

"My uncle saw it in my room. He said he wanted to take it to the hospital. I took the other stuff out of it."

"And it's safe? The stuff that was in it?"

"Yes." Anita looked into his eyes. She wanted him to tell her what the photographs were for. She was afraid he would tell her what the photographs were for.

He said, "Good. I got to go see about your uncle."

Anita said, "I'm sure he's okay."

"Prolly. But it wouldn't do to have him blow all his dough on the night before his surgery."

Anita surged into his arms again. He held her for an instant, and they kissed. It was long and deep, and it was like the first time. Deacon's head swooned, went underwater, and he was gone. Anita simply melted, going slack in his arms. Deacon cradled her close to him. As the kiss ended, he lowered her backward onto the bed. Her chest was heaving and her eyes were glazed. Deacon could have done anything in the world.

He said, "I'll take him down to the hospital. You freshen up. There's a black dress for you, in the closet. I'll be back in an hour."

Her uncle was not at the blackjack table where Deacon had left him. After a panicky search of the adjacent tables, Deacon found him playing craps. He had the dice and he was throwing, a mad look in his eyes. He kissed the dice and blew on his hands and held the dice high and made the sign of the cross with his other hand and then hurled the dice onto the felt. Time stood still. The other players stared. The apronman said, "Winner seven!" and the players shouted. Deacon moved to the craps table, and pushed in.

Anita's uncle hit two more sevens coming out, and each time he made with the ritual: kiss, blow, cross, bless, and throw. The apronman said, "Five, a no-field five. The point is five." There was a collective whoosh of concern. Then chips started flying. One man said, "Fifty across." Another said, "Any C and E." Another said, "Press my six and eight." And Anita's uncle had the dice again. He threw a five. The apronman said, "And the five!" There was rejoicing.

He threw the dice and hit eleven coming out. He hit seven again, twice. Coming out again, he threw a six for the point. Then he hit everything on the board—fours and nines and eights, particularly— and made a little fortune across. Deacon leaned in close to him and said, "Now. Hit your six now." He rolled a six. Deacon said, "Cash me out."

And her uncle said, "What, now?"

Deacon took his elbow and squeezed hard, and said, "Don't chump yourself. Get off now."

Her uncle said, "Cash me out. Pass the dice."

Deacon got him cashed.

They got the car and got in it and moved down the boulevard. There was a bar on the way downtown, called Rick O'Shay's. The uncle said, "Let's stop for a drink."

Deacon said, "Not a chance. We're going to the hospital."

"I can't believe you made me give back the dice."

Deacon said, "You can thank me later."

St. Francis of Assisi Hospital was a flat stucco building south of downtown. Deacon parked the big Caddy out front, and the two men went through the revolving doors into the lobby. Inside, it was as quiet as a library. No sick people in Las Vegas—not on a Sunday night. A nurse behind the desk took the patient's name. She said, "Oh yes, Mr. Morales. We've been expecting you." Deacon couldn't tell whether she was joking. She said, "Sister Pritchard will take you up-stairs."

A nun appeared on silent rubber feet, coming toward them down a long hallway. Deacon said, "I'll have Anita here in the morning, when you wake up."

Her uncle said, "You didn't tell me it was a Catholic hospital. It gives me the creeps."

"It's just a hospital."

"Sure." He looked frightened. He said, "You think God gives more attention to Catholic hospitals?"

"I guess he probably spreads it around."

"You think I'm gonna be okay?"

"I'm sure you are."

"Sure." Sister Pritchard arrived and took him by the arm. He shook Deacon's hand and said, "Anything happens to me, you be nice to Anita. She's just a kid, you know?"

Deacon said, "I know," and the nurse took the old man away.

Haney wasn't at the station when Fatty tried him on the phone. So Fatty dialed a number Haney had told him was only for emergencies. He said, "Yes, it's important. Can you get him?" and then stood wait-ing, holding the receiver in one hand and cupping his hat over his ear with the other. The noise wasn't deafening, back at the public telephones by the men's room, but it was still too noisy to hear who was on the other end of the line. Fatty had no idea where it rang. He waited, holding his hat in his hand.

Two guys, clearly a little worse for their drinking, were coming toward him with expectant looks. They stopped when they saw he was on the phone. Fatty held one finger in the air and smiled his business smile, cupped a hand over the phone, and said, "I'll be with you fellas in a minute."

Then Haney came on. He said, "This better be good."

Fatty said, "Keep your hat on. You told me to call, so I'm calling. Your friend Deacon brought a girl to the Starburst. He parked her in one of the employee rooms. Then he left with some older man, a Mexican guy, I think. I don't know what it's all about, but the girl is not exactly Doris Day. If you see what I mean."

"No, I don't. What's the big mystery?"

"I mean, she's not exactly white."

"Is she still in the hotel?"

"Far as I know. Deacon went out and he hasn't come back."

"I'll be there in a little while," Haney said. "Slow him down, if you see him."

"Okay," Fatty said, and then nodded at the two hopeful men waiting for him. He said, "One more thing—" but Haney had gone.

He replaced the receiver and put his hat back on his head and said, "Now what can I do for you two gentlemen?"

Haney hung up the phone and said out loud, though he was alone in the room, "Get on the horn and have Harrigan come over here with another guy. And get me something to drink." Then he finished dressing.

This was a great opportunity, if it didn't bumble. Deacon and a nigra girl shacking at the Starburst would give him some leverage on Deacon and on Mo Weiner. And on the girl, although Haney didn't care about that. The girl never mattered. Why is that? The broad is often the cause of all the trouble. She's the reason for the fight or the double-cross or the murder. But she's never the one *doing* anything. And she's always the *undoing* of everyone. She's just there, in the middle, while the men slaughter each other. In this case, it didn't even matter who she was. Just another chippie, probably. Negro, though, or part. Which made it illegal for her to be shacking up with *anybody* at the Starburst, employee or not.

Willis, dressed in a butler's uniform, came in with an iced cocktail glass on a silver tray just as Haney had finished dressing. He said, "Thank you," and lifted the glass and drank it all away. "Don't wait up. It's going to be a very long night."

Deacon was back at the Starburst in no time. He showered and shaved and pomaded and dressed in his room and was back for Anita before eight o'clock. When she came to the door, wearing the simple black dress he'd bought for her at Gorman's, he thought he would faint. She had her hair up, and was wearing a single strand of small pearls, and was clutching a small black purse. Deacon said, "I've got a date with the most beautiful girl in Las Vegas. Just look at you." Anita extended her hand to him, as if she were a princess descending to greet her subjects, and then she laughed.

"You look marvelous. What happened to the hat?"

Anita bit her lip, like a baby, and said, "What hat?"

"Didn't you have a hat? You had a hatbox."

Anita bit her lip some more and said, "I forgot. Do you think I look bad without a hat?"

"Are you kidding? You look like a billion. Come on. Let's get atomic."

There was some confusion in front of the hotel. The valet guys had sent Mo's big Cadillac into the garage for the night. Deacon hadn't asked them to leave it up. He duked the guy five bucks and said, "Whistle me up a cab, will you?" While they were waiting for a Yellow to roll forward, Deacon wondered: *Why is Anita lying to me about the hat, and the hatbox? It was the most transparent lie—"I forgot"—but why lie about it at all? Women!*

His thoughts were interrupted. A big black sedan that reeked of policemen drew up in front of them. That Irishman Harrigan got out, with another cop Deacon didn't know, both of them dressed in funeral black. Then Haney got out after them. He came straight to Deacon and said, "Where are you going?"

"Going out."

"Out where?"

"Out, and about. What's it to you?"

He reached into his pocket and drew out a cigarette, and realized Haney wasn't looking at him. Haney was looking at Anita.

Haney said, "Just asking. You got a date, so I'm asking. Out where?"

Deacon said, "Like I said. Out, and about. Going around. See and be seen."

He lit the cigarette. Haney wasn't even looking at him. He was staring at Anita now, and smiling.

He said, "And who are you?"

Deacon leaned in to her. The valet guy had waved a cab forward, and it stood waiting now behind the black police sedan. Deacon took Anita's elbow and said to Haney, "She's with me," and took her into the driveway.

Haney said, "I'll get her name from the registration desk."

Deacon turned back and said, "She's not registered here."

"Then I'll find out which employee room she's staying in."

Deacon said, "Knock yourself out."

They left Haney at the curb. Deacon said to the driver, "Get us out of here."

Anita said, as they were going away, "Who was that man?"

"Nobody. A cop. Just somebody else's headache."

"I wanted to see where you work."

"The Starburst. Where the magic starts. Or where the paycheck starts, anyway. We'll see it another time. We got lots more to see tonight."

The sun had gone half an hour before, leaving the faintest of glows on the western horizon. The sky above was blue-black. The big criss-crossing searchlights in front of the Starburst cut a huge X. Across the boulevard, crowded now with cruising Fords and Chryslers, the lights of the Thunderbird rose into the night. Deacon told the driver, "The Riv, please."

They started there. The Riviera was the newest of the Strip hotels, and at nine stories the tallest. The lobby was big enough to put a place like the El Rancho Vegas inside of. There was no special act to see—Jeff Chandler was telling jokes and singing songs, for Chris-sakes—and the lounge was nothing special, but Anita was rapt. Deacon said, "They say they spent six million dollars building this pile."

Deacon knew the guy who worked the door at the New Frontier. They went there, and Deacon duked the guy five bucks, and they spent fifteen minutes sitting at a table in the back having cocktails and listening to the Dorsey Brothers do three or four numbers. Deacon did not get it. No one was dancing. They were listening like it was Carnegie Hall. Deadsville. He said, "Let's get some chow," and Anita nodded.

For dinner, Deacon tested his pull at the Flamingo. It worked. The doorman was a fan who knew Deacon from the West Side, from some of the nights at Mamie's Black Bottom. He dragged Deacon and Anita right up close. They were between sets. Deacon said, "We'll eat first, and listen later," and Anita seemed to find that funny. Deacon perused the menu with a detached eye, as if he were a regular, and said, "The lobster's not bad, if you like that sort of thing. They got oysters Rockefeller, too. And baked clams. They're known for the lobster, though. And the steaks."

"Are you going to have the lobster?"

"You have the lobster, or the clams," Deacon said. "I think I'll have the cow."

"I don't know," Anita said. "Lobster . . ."

Deacon realized that she'd probably never even seen a fresh clam—much less a lobster. What a kid!

The waiter came sidling up again. Deacon nodded at him. He bent low over Anita and said, "Has the young lady decided?"

Anita fumbled with the menu and said, "I'd like the . . . clamster, please."

"The clamster?"

Anita looked up, and began to color. The waiter turned slowly to Deacon.

Deacon said, "I want the clamster, too. With the drawn butter."

The light went on in the waiter's head. He said, "Yes, sir. With the drawn butter."

"And champagne."

Deacon did not know enough to request a special year or anything. He'd like to have been able to say, "If you don't have the '37, see if there isn't some of the '39," like he was Adolphe Menjou or something, but he wouldn't have known where to start. Not that Anita would have recognized the difference. She'd never seen a glass of

champagne in real life, any more than she had a lobster. Or a clamster. She thought Deacon was the most glamorous person imaginable.

Midway through their lobsters, Deacon said, "That's Eddie Fisher
and Debbie Reynolds over there." Anita turned to look. She did not
know who Eddie Fisher was, though she knew what his singing
sounded like, but she sure knew Debbie Reynolds. She said, "Oh my
goodness. It *is.*"

Deacon said, "Sure it is. In fact, don't look now, but about three
tables behind them there's Frank Sinatra and Keely Smith and Louis
Prima."

Anita laughed and said, "Sure. And President Eisenhower and
Mamie."

"I'm not joking."

"Right."

At that moment a voice said, "Deke, baby," and they both turned.
Joey Bishop was there, with Rosemary Clooney. Deacon stood up and
said, "Hey, Rosie. How's it going?"

"It's grand, Deke. We're over at the D.I., me and Joey here."

"Don't I know it? That's where we're heading right after dinner.
This is my friend Anita. Anita, this is Rosie Clooney and Mr. Bishop."

Anita half rose in her seat. Bishop got a look in his eyes that Deacon did not like. But Rosie crinkled up her eyes in that cute way she
did. She said, "Hey there," to Anita, who looked a little faint.

Deacon said, "You gonna make the West Side after the show?"

Rosie said, "Wouldn't miss it for the world. That's gonna be *something.*"

Bishop said, "Everything's something, sweetie. Let's eat."

The music blew, right then. Harry James and his orchestra were
on. Harry's trumpet came fast and clear, like a call to arms, as if it
were announcing a bullfight. Rosie gave Deacon a pat on the arm,
and crinkled her eyes again. Bishop left with a little forlorn look at
Anita. She turned to watch them go, and her eyes went to the stage,
then back to the floor, and she suddenly gasped.

She said, "You weren't joking."

Deacon said, "No? About what?"

"About Frank Sinatra. That's really Frank Sinatra."

Deacon smiled and said, "That's really Frank Sinatra. And Keely and Louis Prima. They're over at the Sahara. Not with Sinatra. He's not playing this week. So don't stare at him. Stare at me."

Anita said, "Oh, Deacon," and his heart melted. He turned his eyes back to the stage, and watched Harry blow.

After dinner—Deacon did not faint when the check came, but that was only because he'd had a couple more cocktails after the champagne and was anesthetized against the shock—they were on the boulevard again in a taxi. Deacon said, "We gotta go to the Sands first."

Pearl Bailey was headlining. It was nothing special for Deacon, but you never knew with Pearl and other people. Some folks thought she was hot stuff. Anita seemed bored. Or something. They stood at the back bar and ordered a drink. Deacon smoked. Pearl sang. Anita said, between songs, while everyone was clapping, "I didn't know she was colored."

Deacon said, "I don't think it's a secret."

Anita said, "Very funny, mister. If she's colored, how come she can sing here?"

"Well, she's very popular here. So is Nat 'King' Cole, over at the Riviera. So is Sammy Davis Jr."

"But I thought colored folks had to stay over on the other side of town."

"Sure, they've got to *stay* over there. They can't stay here. They can't eat here or drink here or gamble here, either. That's why this place is opening over on the West Side, tonight. That's where I want to go later. It's special, for colored folks."

"Colored folks *only?*" Anita looked alarmed.

"Naw," Deacon said, and laughed. "They'll let us white folks in, I reckon. I know the owners. We can pass."

Anita turned from him. For the first time, really for the very first time, Deacon saw what he had not been seeing. Anita was trying to pass. She'd probably spent her whole life trying to pass.

Deacon took her hand. As they were leaving the lounge and crossing the casino floor, Deacon pulled her a little closer. She looped her hand through his arm. Deacon felt, somehow, more loving, more protective, than before. He almost wished someone would say something. He wanted the opportunity to be brave and chivalrous for her, to throw down a gauntlet for her, to throw down his heart for her.

Instead he hailed a cab. He said, "Desert Inn, please," and then turned to Anita. She looked heavenly, still, and a little breathless. She lay back and looked out the window at the lights swooping by. Deacon leaned down and kissed her.

He said, "We'll just go by the Desert Inn for a few minutes, so you can see your old pal Rosie warble a few. Then we'll maybe go see this place across town."

"The colored place?"

"Yeah. It's going to be *the* place, tonight. Only place to be."

They blew by the El Rancho Vegas, with Joe E. Lewis's name on the marquee, and the Dunes, with its giant Caliph standing over it. In four minutes they were pulling into the D.I.

Deacon loved listening to Rosie sing. It was real singing. Most of the girls, it was just words and music. With Rosie, it was all music. She sang that goofy "This Ole House," which was turning into a big hit for her, and of course she did "Hey There," which of course made Anita think of her uncle. He always made fun of that song. For him, it was the epitome of stupid teenager music. He'd say, "Hey dere, jew wi' de starz in jew ice . . . ," and make her feel silly for liking the song. Now she felt silly for worrying about him. That was kid stuff. He was on his own, and she was on her own, and she was darned if she was going to spend this night worrying over him and his silly operation.

Deacon said, "What are you thinking? You look all funny."

She said, "Nothing at all. I need to go to the little girls' room."

Deacon stood, and together they left the lounge. Deacon waited while Anita crossed the side of the lobby to the ladies' room. She walked like a woman. She walked like she was *all* woman. Deacon felt light-headed.

He let himself worry about Haney for a moment. Should he worry? About what? If Haney found out which room, which was unlikely, and he waited there all night, which was unlikely, and if he saw the two of them coming in, which was unlikely, and if he could prove Anita shouldn't be there . . . It was all unlikely. Luckily, she did not look underage. Especially tonight, she did not look underage. He saw her now, coming back across the room, looking anything *but* underage.

Deacon checked his watch. It was coming on midnight. It was time to go to the West Side.

When Anita sat again, her brown eyes warm and bright, Deacon said, "Let's blow. I want to show you something really special now."

Anita said, "To me, this is all special. I can't believe a person could live here and really do this, every night."

"Well, sometimes we take the night off, you know. Sometimes we even work a little, just to remind ourselves how the other half lives."

"Don't be funny, Deacon. I *am* the other half."

"Me, too. But not tonight. Come on."

Going out the big swinging front doors, Deacon was sure for a fleeting moment that he saw Fatty Behr leave ahead of them. He saw a small man moving fast, from the back, away from him, wearing what looked like a seersucker suit and a snap-brim hat. The man glanced nervously behind him, but he was too far away and Deacon had had a few too many cocktails for him to know it was Fatty for sure. Deacon raised his hand to wave. A bellhop said, "Taxi here, sir."

They jumped in. Deacon said to the driver, "You know this new joint, the Ivory Coast?"

"I've hardly been anyplace else tonight, sir."

"No kidding? It pretty busy?"

"The place is on fire, sir."

"Well, let's go on back over there and put that fire out."

It was a twenty-minute ride. The boulevard was jammed up, and it was slow going through the center of the Strip. The cowboys on the camels were parading in front of the Sahara. Big neon was flashing around Liberace's name on the Riviera marquee. The huge searchlights crissed and crossed and rubbed against each other over the Starburst. Deacon lay back in the seat, and realized that Anita had gone to sleep. He planted a chaste kiss on her forehead and said, "Take your time, driver. No hurry at all."

Albert Sherman had driven up with a crew of nine and a panel truck full of equipment and a picture car, just in case. The convoy had left Hollywood at three o'clock in the morning, an hour when he preferred to be sleeping, and had rumbled through the desert as the sun was coming up. Sherry had been half asleep, but the sunrise over the sands moved him terribly. He saw great opportunity there—a *Scheherazade*, an *Arabian Nights*, an entire series of desert pictures. He had not read much about Arab life. There must be a million great stories, about Bedouins and caliphs and caravansarai and life at the oasis. Did Marco Polo go into the desert? What about Caesar? Didn't he go to Egypt? Or was that Anthony? Hell, Sherry would make the stories up himself. Look at the light and the way it plays on the dunes. Sherry was full of ideas. He fell asleep dreaming of camels and sandstorms and men with turbans and long knives.

His ingenue, Eleanor Padgett, had insisted on riding in the picture car. She was curled up there now, wearing one scarf around her head and another around her neck, and a big puffy sweater over capris, and huge black sunglasses. She looked like a street urchin, Sherry thought—a thought that made her insistence on riding in the picture car easier to bear. The early hour and his fuzzy state of mind had got him thinking about her, thinking about cuddling up in the dark for the ride into the desert. She had rebuffed him before he'd even made the offer, saying something about a late night and an awful headache.

Sherry had a sudden thought. If he were in the commercial advertising business, he'd create an entire campaign, aimed at men, designed to cure the headaches that women get when they don't want to sleep with their husbands. "Men! Has this happened to you? Get Bed-Zadrine! She'll never have a 'headache' again!"

By early afternoon the company was checked into the Thunderbird. They had planned on staying at the Starburst, but there had been a foul-up. It was booked. They moved across the street, where they were given suites on the top floor. *It pays to know people,* Sherry thought. He made sure Eleanor got the best suite—well, the second-best, actually, after his, but that was not negotiable—and made sure she had everything she needed. He had his man Fritz send flowers and champagne to her immediately, with a note. Then he took a shower and had Fritz lay out a fresh change of clothes. After barking some orders over the phone to Hollywood, and then barking some more orders at the crew, Sherry took a roll of fresh bills and went down to the lobby to check out the casino. Two hours and two two-dollar cigars later, he was up several hundred dollars. Fritz found him playing craps and said, "The men say it's time to leave for the casino, sir."

Sherry scowled and checked his watch. Then he said, "Color," and waited for the boxman to collect and exchange all his little blue-and-yellow and green-and-red chips for the more valuable mustard-and-white ones. He handed them to Fritz and said, "Get those cashed in while I go change, and then meet me upstairs."

A small crowd of darkies had already gathered outside the Ivory Coast. Sherry and the crew drew their three vehicles into the lot. There was a brief consultation with a huge, red-vested valet. Sherry said to his driver, "Tell Young Man River here that we need to get all this stuff inside." The valet waved the convoy around to a back service lot. Sherry told his men, "I'm going to find the top bwana here. You move on into the lobby with this gear."

Eleanor was wearing a fetching gown and an impressive rack of rocks around her neck, and a slightly smaller pair of sunglasses. Sherry knew it would be insulting to ask her to come in the back door of the casino with the rest of the group. He ordered Fritz to draw his car back around to the front of the casino. Eleanor stepped out there while Fritz held the door for her, as if she were arriving for the most exclusive of Hollywood world premieres. It was Graumann's Chinese, and every photographer and news-service cameraman was there. Eleanor alit from the car and shared a secret, shy smile with the world. *Like royalty, she walks,* Sherry thought, and complimented himself, again, on being able to pick 'em. She was nothing but a farm girl from Michigan when she got to Broadway, and she was nothing but a starving actress barely off the farm when he found her; now she was halfway to becoming a queen. He took her arm and complimented her dress, and they went inside. The crowd of darkies mumbled their approval.

Sherman found Worthless Worthington Lee, with two men Lee introduced as Sumner and Fidget, fooling with a slot machine. Sumner had a screwdriver and a pair of pliers and a rubber mallet, which he was using to smack the side of the machine. Fidget was staring at the panels on the front. Every time Summer smacked, Fidget called out a new combination: "Two ch-ch-cherries and a z-z-z-ero," he said. "A l-l-l-lemon, and t-t-t-two cherries."

Worthless said, "I told you to forget about it. Move this one out to the garage, and leave it alone. You got plenty other stuff to fuss with now."

Then he saw Sherry and Eleanor, and he said, "Mistah Sherman! How do you *do?*"

Worthless had made all kinds of plans, most of them smart ones. Sherry listened as he explained how one camera could be placed upstairs, on a balcony, to catch all of the arriving celebrities, while another could be set on the plywood platform he had built back near the bar, where the cameras could rest and swing and see everything that happened on the casino floor as well as in the registration and back bar areas. It was pretty smart planning. Sherry said, "Yeah. We can work with that. Course I'll have to let the cameramen make the final decisions."

"These is only suggestions," Worthless said. "I don't know nothin' about the picture business, 'cept what I see at the movies."

Sherry said, "If you'll keep Miss Padgett company, I'll see that the boys do it just the way you've set it up. Okay, Eleanor?"

Eleanor smiled at Sherry from behind her sunglasses, and then suddenly took them off and smiled at Worthless. It was dazzling. Sherry felt something cold drop in his stomach. He said, "Right, then. Back in a bit."

Eleanor put her arm out for Worthless Worthington Lee and said, "I think all of this is simply *thrilling*. You must be so proud."

Worthless said, "I *am* right proud, miss. And nervous as a Christmas goose, too."

"But you *mustn't* be. Your casino is going to be a huge success. I can feel it."

Eleanor squeezed his arm. She was the skinniest, tiniest, cutest little thing he'd ever seen. She was like a toy, like a little Hollywood doll, with her little feet stuck in her little shoes, and her little diamonds around her little neck. He felt he could encircle her waist with the span of one hand. He said, "How 'bout we get you a cocktail and a nice place to sit down? You know we don't open that do' until nine o'clock tonight?"

Eleanor said, "Couldn't I just tag along and watch you work?"

Worthless said, "Well, sho' nuff. If that's what you want, you just tag along with ol' Worthless and we'll work together."

"And I can have a little cocktail, too?"

Worthless said, "You can have all the cocktail you want. Hey, Sumner! Get this lady a liquor drink, will you?"

Sumner materialized from behind the slot machines. Eleanor thought he looked like chiseled stone. His eyes were huge. So was his smile. Eleanor slid onto a barstool and said, "I think I'll just sit here, for a while, and watch . . . Sumner, is it?"

Sumner said, "Sumner."

Eleanor said, "What a nice name. Sumner."

Sumner said, "That's right. What can I get for you?"

Eleanor smiled like a descending angel and said, "I'd like a Ramos fizz, please."

Sumner moved like black marble, across to her and then behind the bar. He said, "One Ramos fizz."

They had not learned anything at the front desk, even after Haney had badged the clerk and said, "Don't make me want to ruin you, kid. Just give me a room number."

The clerk was shaking like a leaf, but he didn't know a thing. None of the other front-desk people did, either. No one had seen Deacon come in with the girl, except Fatty, and Fatty wasn't around.

Harrigan said, "We shoulda followed them."

The other cop, a nasty brute named Clauster, said, "We shoulda decked him. Mouthy little creep."

Haney didn't say a word. He didn't look at either man. He had stopped looking at the clerk. Harrigan didn't know what he was looking at. The silence was making Harrigan nervous. He said, "We shoulda followed them."

"Shoulda decked him."

Haney said, "It's the girl from that café."

"What is?" Harrigan looked lost.

Haney said, "The girl with Deacon. I've seen her before. I couldn't place her. But she's the girl from that café, out in the desert. Shipton Wells. She works at the café in Shipton Wells, by the bus station."

"Where you went to look at that stiff?"

"That's it. When I went to look at that stiff."

Haney's face fell. Harrigan watched it going. He was lost, again. He said, "What's the matter with that?"

Haney didn't answer.

Harrigan said, "Was she connected to the dead guy?"

Haney didn't answer again. His face got darker and darker. Harrigan hated this.

He said, "Should we try and pick her up?"

Haney, finally, said, "No. Go and find Fatty. Leave me here. We need to find out what room she's in. Fatty will know. Go."

Harrigan and Clauster left him at Reception. He stepped off behind them, and walked down through the casino, moving slowly through the shouting, drunken gamblers. He emerged at the other side, and sat at the back bar there. He remembered, distantly, that there used to be a bartender here who got shot during a routine stop on Las Vegas Boulevard. It wasn't real to him. It was something he had read on a police report. That's all.

Except that was the night they'd picked up the guy Deacon.

And that was the night Deacon had let him know he knew about the photographs.

Which Deacon could know about only if he'd intercepted the guy from Chicago.

Who, Haney suddenly saw, must have been the guy that got croaked in Shipton Wells. Which meant the girl probably knew about the pictures, too.

It was like taking a shot in the head. Haney flinched with the sudden realization. The bartender, seeing Haney jerk, came over and said, "Something to drink, Lieutenant?"

Haney jerked again. He said, "Give me a cognac," without looking up from the bar. The bartender slid away from him, and slid back with a snifter. Haney took it in one hand and cradled it under his nose.

Deacon *wasn't* just a horn player, then. He had whipped that card dealer. He had gone out to intercept the guy from Chicago, caught him in Shipton Wells, and croaked him in the men's room at the bus station. And, of course, taken the photographs.

And was working with the girl from the café? And, now that he thought of it, the fat Mexican who ran the joint? Must be. Fatty had said Deacon left the Starburst earlier with a Mexican guy. He would bet on it.

Haney drained the cognac, and felt woozy and tired. He could be home, sitting in a bathrobe, listening to Bob Wills and His Texas

Playboys, sipping cognac and getting ready for a little something special with a special little friend.

That was over now, if he could not get to the photographs and destroy them. Which meant finding Deacon and the girl, and maybe the fat Mexican, whoever he was, and probably destroying them, too.

He saw Harrigan and Clauster bumping into each other in front of the reception desk. He nodded at the bartender and went away without paying.

Fatty came back down into the lobby, cruising. The last pill had not wound him up as fast or as far as he expected, which meant that the downer he had taken an hour before was working more powerfully than he'd meant it to. So he had taken another couple of uppers. Now his teeth felt tight, and metallic. That was one of the problems with him and his pills—every once in a while one of them didn't work right, and that messed up the whole formula. Maybe he shouldn't have had a drink. Maybe he should have eaten dinner? The faces at the bar blurred before him. Two broads Fatty was sure he had employed in the past walked right by him without even smiling. He said, "Hey, girls," but they had already moved on before he spoke.

Fortunately he had moved the junk, and the serious part of the night was done. The kid from the Ivory Coast had met him in back of the kitchen, just as he'd promised, and had the money, and he took the stuff. Where the money came from, Fatty didn't know. Or want to know. It was a lot of junk, so it was a lot of money. As long as Haney did not find out about either one—get a look at Fatty's bank account, or find out that someone was suddenly moving large amounts of narcotics—nothing could possibly go wrong. Fatty, coming across the casino floor, could not imagine anything going wrong.

Then he saw Haney waiting for him near the reception area. Two of his men, including that red-faced creep Harrigan, were sitting among the potted plants, smoking, while Haney stood with his arms crossed. Fatty cursed and hurried forward. Haney had probably been watching him weave his way across the entire casino. He'd have to straighten up fast.

Haney said, "We have a problem."

Fatty said, "Then we have a solution. Every problem has a solution."

"Shut up. And sit down."

Haney shoved him toward the potted plants. Harrigan stood up and pushed Fatty down into the seat he'd been in. It was unpleasantly warm through the seersucker. Fatty, for the first time since he'd met Haney at Hoover Dam, felt seriously afraid.

He said, "The horn player Deacon came in here with a middle-aged Mexican and an underage mixed-race girl."

"That's why I called you."

"Shut up. Now all three have gone. Do you know where?"

"No. I can guess."

"So can I. Can you find out what room she's in?"

"Well, again, I can guess. She is either shacking with Deacon—which, believe me, he is not that stupid—or I bet she's staying where this doll Dorothy stays."

"Who's she?"

"She's this doll that works in the gift shop. Friend of Deacon's. He took her for a ride this morning in one of Mo's Cadillacs. She didn't come back with him."

"But the Nigra girl and the Mexican did." Haney was thinking. Haney was thinking hard. Fatty could see Harrigan and the other guy sort of *waiting*. As though they didn't have to think now, because their boss was thinking. When he was done thinking, they'd learn what they needed to know. Cops.

Haney said, "That means something is going on in Shipton Wells. Here's what we need, then. Clauster, I'm going to need you to go up to Shipton Wells. There's a café there, and there's some cabins behind it. The Mexican guy runs the café, and the Nigra girl works there. I need you to toss their rooms, and find out what this broad Dorothy is up to. Don't let it get messy."

Clauster stood up and said, "You want me to go now?"

"Yes. And I want you to work fast, and come back quickly. And you," he said, and pointed at Harrigan's big red face. "I need you to go through the horn player's room and then this girl Dorothy's room. Again, no messy stuff. No guns. I'm going to find Deacon."

Fatty said, "What are we supposed to look for in these rooms?"

Haney's ice-clear eyes got cold. He said, "You? You are not supposed to look for anything. You are not supposed to know anything. And you are definitely not supposed to *ask* anything. You sit here and wait for me."

Harrigan and Clauster followed Haney up to the reception desk. Haney badged the clerk there again and said, "You got a house key for the employee rooms? I need it, and I need to know, right now, which room this girl Dorothy stays in. The girl who runs the gift shop."

The clerk said, "I'll have to speak to a manager about the room key."

Haney leaned across the counter and took the clerk by the necktie, and pulled it toward him without violence. He turned his empty eyes on him and said, "No, you don't. You don't have time to do that. You only have time to do exactly what I told you. Now, come out from behind that counter, with the pass key. Or I'll have these two men take you into the parking lot behind the building and beat you to death."

"Okay."

As the clerk was coming, shaking, around the side of the reception counter, Haney drew close to Harrigan and Clauster. He said, "I'm leaving you both now. You are looking for some reels of film, and some photographs. It's a blackmail job. The photos are a fake. Same with the film. It's a very big blackmail job, involving some very serious people. I would advise you, very seriously, not to even *look* at the material once you've found it. What you see could get you killed. I'm serious as a heart attack about this. Don't even look at it. Just find it, and then find me and tell me you've got it."

The two men nodded like machinery. Haney said, "Now go." They went.

Fatty was still sitting amidst the potted plants. Haney wondered: *If I didn't go over there now and tell him to get up, how long would he sit before he decided on his own it was time to get up? An hour? Four hours? Twenty-four hours? Good test for recruits, maybe.* He didn't think Fatty, with his pill problem, would last very long.

Haney checked his watch. Just going nine o'clock. The Ivory Coast would be warming up. The Strip would be warming up. By midnight it would be on fire. Then it would take seven or eight hours to get cool again. It must be the only place in the world where, right after the sun went down, the night came up. The lights shone all night, as surely as the midday sun did all day, and the night did not go down until the sun was almost ready to come up again. It was like two days in one—every day. *No wonder everyone up here is insane,* Haney thought. *There's no rest for any of them. For any of us.* He went out the front doors of the Starburst and into the bright night.

It was the first thing like a date that Mo and Stella had experienced in a long time. They were going to cruise down the Strip, watching the lights go by, just like in the old days, and then step out in front of the flashbulbs.

In the beginning, when Stella was new to the Starburst, Mo had taken her everywhere, squired her around the whole town, up and down the Strip, making her known to the people who made people. Making sure people knew that she was somebody to know. That was a long time ago. She was just a name from New York when she arrived. Mo made her a name in Las Vegas. Stella had been famous, a local celebrity. When people came to the desert for the first time, veteran players would say, "Oh you *have* to see Stella, at the Starburst lounge. She's the absolute limit."

Then, slowly, she wasn't. Mo didn't know how it had happened. Time passed. Stella started slipping. She drank a little too much. She spent a little too much time chasing men. She stopped making the scene. She never made the papers. Other singers came in. Guys like that Liberace started making a splash. People like Pearl Bailey started coming to the desert.

Mo didn't see it start, but he saw it end. Soon no one talked about Stella anymore as a performer. Some of them talked about her in other ways. But mostly people didn't talk about her at all. *Do they still talk about me,* Mo wondered? *Probably not. Or if they do, they probably aren't any nicer than they are about Stella.*

Mo sat now in the backseat of one of the Starburst's big Cadillacs, parked in front of the casino, waiting. He'd waited in the back bar awhile, then waited in the lobby bar, while being reassured repeatedly that Stella was on her way down. Now, at last, she came—all flounce and flair and feather. Mo couldn't have begun to describe the outfit she was wearing. He thought: *If I were a woman, trolling for Negroes, that's how I'd dress, too.*

He said, "Stella, you look like a million bucks."

She said, "I feel like a buffalo nickel. But thanks. Are we gonna be too late to make this shindig?"

"Not at all. Just be starting. Driver?"

Mo's doubts about Stella were nothing compared with his doubts about the Ivory Coast. He had become convinced, in the final hours, that it was the most foolish venture he'd ever backed and the most foolhardy investment of money he'd ever made. Who the hell did he think he was? Throwing hundreds and hundreds of thousands of dollars away on a Negro casino. He'd have to get his head examined, when it was over.

Going down the end of the Strip, the klieg lights and the searchlights and the neon foaming at the sides of the road, Mo began to relax. What difference did it make, anyway? Did he have some grand scheme for the money he'd make off the Ivory Coast? Did he have a retirement package in mind? Was it part of a master fifteen-year plan? No. It was all just what he was doing, and he could always start doing it again, someplace else, when it was over.

He said, "Any of your friends talk to you about this place?"

Stella narrowed her eyes and said, "What do you mean, 'my friends'?"

"I mean, people you know."

"People from where?"

"For Chrissake, Stella! People! People you know!"

"Sure. Some of the girls at the hotel. Some of the boys."

"Any white folks?"

"No," Stella said. "Gleason said something. Andy. Maybe Deke."

"That's it?"

"Yeah. But remember, Mo, I don't know anybody anymore. I don't get out much."

"Me, neither. Jumping Jesus, look at that!"

The driver had just turned the corner, off Jackson onto Bonanza. The Ivory Coast rose before them. And it was mayhem, a riot of color and light and noise and humanity. The street was full of standing, gaping people. There were cars lined up, halfway down the block, waiting to get into the parking lot. The hotel itself was ablaze in red and purple and gold lights. Mo could see can-can dancers on the balconies. Music came from there, too—New Orleans music, Dixieland maybe, with horns that sounded like men laughing.

Just at that moment there was a low, muffled explosion. To Mo's ears it sounded like a howitzer, or small mortar fire. A moment later the sky exploded in streams of yellow and gold fireworks. The street seemed to catch flame. The men and women below undulated in the sudden light. They gasped, and burst into laughter and applause, as moments later there were more fireworks.

Stella said, "God almighty. How you gonna keep 'em down on the farm now?"

Mo said, "It's something else, isn't it?"

"It's marvelous, Mo."

Mo began to sing, "I'm dreaming . . . of a black Christmas. Just like the ones . . ."

There were more bursts of light. From somewhere behind, Mo heard sirens, but they seemed to be going past Bonanza. Slowly the Caddy crept forward. The driver said, "I don't see no other way to go but straight in, boss."

Mo said, "That's fine, then. Just go on. We got all night. Stel, you want a cocktail?"

"Sure."

Mo opened a compartment built into the back of the passenger seat. It folded down like half an accordion to reveal a wet bar stocked with all the right stuff. With small, precise hands, Mo mixed a pair of highballs and dunked ice cubes into them. He passed one to Stella, and waved his own glass at the crowd pressing against the windows of the Cadillac.

"To the Ivory Coast," he said.

"Here, here," Stella said, and gulped at her drink.

Deacon had seen the crowd coming. With Anita curled up and sleeping beside him on the seat, and the fireworks exploding a few blocks ahead, he'd told the driver, "Why don't you skip Jackson Street? If you go over about three blocks, and then come back down Harding, you can pick up that street behind Bonanza. We can get in through the back way."

The driver nodded. The street wasn't called Harding, and the street behind Bonanza was called Winslow, but he knew what Deacon meant. There was a service lot behind the Ivory Coast. Deacon nudged Anita awake and paid the driver, and they both got out, blinking under the sprinkling fireworks.

Anita said, "I thought it was a fire. A real fire."

Deacon said, "The *real* fire's inside."

There was a cat Deacon knew standing guard over the back door, and he slapped Deacon on the palms and said, "Good to see you, man. Come *on*." He waved them through the kitchen, where black-skinned men in starched white outfits were slinging food and slamming pots and pans. It looked like a Broadway show, a minstrel kitchen. In the din of knives chopping and men shouting and plates banging, Deacon could pick up a beat and almost make a melody. He took Anita's arm and pulled her through the smoke and smolder and into another hallway. He didn't know where he was, but the main rooms had to be somewhere forward. Waiters in smart red jackets blew by them, carrying trays, empty and full. Ahead were swinging steel doors with big glass portals. Deacon could see no traffic through the glass. He pushed through. And he and Anita were there.

It was a huge, smashing, swinging success. The casino floor was jammed. The players were stacking the tables. The reception area was also full, a stampede of beautifully dressed men and women holding cocktail glasses and champagne glasses and cigarettes and cigars. The men were all wearing suits. The women were wearing evening dresses or gowns, and lots of jewelry, and quite a few hats. Most remarkably, Deacon did not see one single familiar face. The entire crowd was strange to him.

As he and Anita crossed, moving around the rim of the casino, heading toward the reception area, the crowd parted as if for passing celebrities. Deacon realized, quite suddenly, that people were staring at them. All of the women and all of the men were staring at them. No. Staring at Anita. He turned to look at her, just as they were slipping past one group of well-heeled white people. And Deacon saw her then as the others saw her. She was simply the most beautiful woman in the room—not just to him but *also* to him. She was the most beautiful woman in a room full of beautiful women.

He said, "Let's try and get a drink."

Anita nodded without looking at him. She was transfixed by the room. She seemed to be staring at someone. Deacon followed her gaze.

He said, "Wow. That's Spencer Tracy."

Anita said, "And Katharine Hepburn. And behind them, that's Ava Gardner. And Debbie Reynolds and Eddie Fisher."

"We saw them at dinner, remember?"

"She's changed her dress. And over there is . . . Oh my God. It's Cary Grant."

Deacon followed her eyes over. Cary Grant. Chatting with Nat "King" Cole and Edward G. Robinson. The men all had drinks. Nat was grinning that wide smile of his. He had a white woman on his arm, a singer from New York whose name Deacon suddenly couldn't remember.

Anita said, "I thought it was going to be all colored people."

"So did I."

"It's a lot of colored people. I've never seen so many colored people in one place, and all dressed up like this. With white people, too."

"That's Pearl Bailey, over there. And that's Frank Sinatra, at the bar, with that drunk Dean Martin. And Joey Bishop, who you met before."

"With Rosie Clooney."

"That's right." Deacon checked. Anita looked positively faint with enchantment. He said, "How 'bout we get that drink?"

Anita nodded. Deacon took her arm, and they began to move down onto the casino floor, across the casino floor, parting the crowd as they went. Deacon could simply not believe the men and women staring at Anita. Did she even notice it? She seemed not to. She seemed to be floating, right here and yet far away, somehow. She looked sort of cloudy. Deacon pulled her to the left and into the bar area at the back of the casino. He said, "What would you like?"

She said, "Very much."

He said, "Okay," and told the bartender, "Two Seven and Sevens, please."

Across the room he spied Worthless at last. He was wearing a suit, something Deacon had never seen him do before. He looked handsome and horribly uncomfortable at the same time. His smile was a big, toothy, gummy smile, a "yassuh" smile, a cotton-picker smile, pasted on his face as if stuck there with glue. He was moving through the crowd, shaking hands and bobbing his head and shuffling like a houseboy. Deacon felt shame for him. He could be standing tall and proud and strong like a man tonight. Like the guy behind Worthless, in fact. There was a man walking with him who had the right idea. He looked like a prizefighter going into the ring. He was standing tall and broad, pride in his eyes and the light shining on his skin. He looked electrified. Deacon realized with a start that it was Sumner, who used to work in the Starburst kitchen. He was like a new man now. He looked almost regal. And it wasn't even his joint.

Except it was. Deacon remembered again where he was. This was no white man's nightclub. This was a Negro man's place. His white face, and the other white faces, were the faces of the guests. The black faces in the room . . . This was *their* place, and their time.

He turned to Anita, her drink in hand, and said, "This is really something else, isn't it?"

She said, "It's not like *anything* else, Deke. It's just like magic."

"Cheers."

"Cheers."

Across the bar, Eleanor Padgett had removed her sunglasses and put them away for the last time right after her second Ramos fizz. The light was not so harsh now. And there was so much more to look at. She simply could not take her eyes off this boy Sumner, who looked to her like a statue—a statue made of hot, wet, black rock. All she could see of his skin was his face and neck and wrists and hands. But she felt he was almost naked before her. When he moved, she could feel him flex and ripple. So she ordered a third fizz and sipped at it, and waited. When he came back into her orbit and stood beside her, she said, "You're wrong about Hollywood, actually."

Sumner said, "Why?"

Eleanor said, "It's not a bunch of rich people sitting around swimming pools having wonderful lives. It's actually a lot of very insecure middle-class people, many of whom were very recently lower-middle-class people, desperately trying to hold on to their jobs. And petrified that it is all going to be taken away from them."

Sumner said, "Excuse me a minute."

The room was so full now that the noise was almost not human anymore. It was like standing in a waterfall. Eleanor had forgotten it was people making all the racket. She had sat with her back to the crowd, looking only at Sumner. Now, with him gone away, making a drink for someone else or doing whatever it was he was doing for someone else, she was suddenly aware again of the crush.

Over her shoulder she saw Sherry sucking up to Cary Grant, who was standing with Jack Benny, who was standing with that funny Rochester. Eddie? Was that his name? Willie? Something. Eleanor suddenly thought, *I'm drunk.* Sherry did not see her, and had not paid her any attention at all for an hour or more. Which was fine. She wanted to postpone for as long as possible—permanently, in fact, if at all possible—the moment when he would begin pawing her. It was coming, and she'd say "no" and "don't" and "stop," and she'd have to say why. Or maybe say nothing, and just go ahead and let him do what he needed to do. She'd done it that way, too. Desperately trying to hold on to our jobs and petrified that it is all going to be taken away . . . *That's the truth*, she said to herself. *That's me.*

Then Sumner was back, and smiling. He said, "This room is getting very small."

Eleanor said, "We need a bigger room."

"Or a smaller crowd."

"Do you have one of those?"

Sumner creased his brow. He said, "Yeah. We got both, in the same place—bigger room, smaller crowd."

"Maybe we should go there."

"Just you and me?"

Eleanor found herself melting. She said, "Yes. Just you and me." She rose from her seat at the bar, and Sumner was at her side, that fast. He took her elbow.

"Let's see what we can find."

Sumner steered her across the floor, around the edges of the casino, where a throng of white and black was throwing dice and catching cards and pulling on slot machines. They passed close to a craps table, where a very large Negro man suddenly shouted, "Up jumped the *devil!*"

Sumner caught sight of the man Fidget, wearing a waiter's jacket. He steered Eleanor over a step or two, and took Fidget by the arm.

He said, "Who's working Reception?"

Fidget said, "It's that K-K-K . . ."

"Kershaw?"

"Yes. K-K-K . . ."

"Thanks, man." He leaned to Eleanor and said, "Come on. I got a nice idea."

Fidget watched Sumner steer the white lady toward the reception area. He decided to tag along behind. Something was up. It might turn out to be a good thing for him to know what it was. Keeping back far enough not to be noticed, Fidget watched as Sumner shook hands with Kershaw behind the front desk. He could almost see the folded five-dollar bill enclosed in that handshake. Then he saw Kershaw pass Sumner a room key. Sumner put his head down, as if he were no longer able to look Kershaw in the eye. He turned away, and back to the lady. And they went over to the elevators.

Fidget said, "D-d-d-*damn*," and went off to find a telephone.

Harrigan went around behind the Starburst and came in again through the back door. He flashed a badge at a knot of Negro kitchen workers who stood beside the door smoking cigarettes. One of them said, "Aye-aye, sir." Several others said, "Oooh woooh," in an uppity way.

Harrigan smiled and said to himself, "Keep it up, you jig bastards. You'll get yours."

Harrigan went first to the room where the girl was supposed to be staying.

It was dank and smelled of concrete and cosmetics. There were brassieres and nylon hose hanging all over the shower stall, and dozens of bottles of creams and lotions and potions covering every flat surface in the bathroom. There was no place to hide anything like what Haney was after. A small wicker suitcase—it looked like something you'd take on a picnic—carried a pair of ladies' underwear and a pair of capri slacks, but nothing else of interest. In the bedroom he went under the mattress, checked the corners of the carpet, did the closet and the chest of drawers. There was nothing in the room that didn't belong in a young lady's room. A bundle of letters was stuck under the girlie stuff in the chest of drawers. The letters were tied together by a piece of silk or satin ribbon. They all bore a return address in Keokuk, Iowa. Farm girl. Harrigan stuck the letters back under the undies, then inspected the window coverings. Nothing. He then started over and did it more thoroughly. This time, he pulled the drawers from the chest of drawers, turned them upside down, and inspected the bottoms. There was nothing there but manufacturer's labels. He did the edges of the mattress with a pocketknife and found nothing inside but stuffing and springs.

Then Harrigan did Deacon's room. This was more interesting. There was almost nothing there, first of all, and that made it easy. No books, no magazines, no cosmetics, practically no clothing. The chest of drawers was almost empty. The closet held a couple of suits and a couple of pairs of shoes and one snap-brim fedora. There was an old cardboard-sided suitcase, which yielded nothing—or, actually, almost nothing. Harrigan ran his fingers through the base and came up with some marijuana seeds. Enough to get a warrant on, easy. He shook a few of the seeds and some of the leafy residue that went with them into a paper envelope, and stuck it in his pocket.

He needn't have bothered. In the bathroom again, having found nothing of what he wanted and having begun a second pass, Harrigan noticed a ceiling panel that looked out of place. It was loose to the touch. Harrigan stood on the toilet and pushed it up and away, and found a battered leather kit bag. He pulled it down and found every-thing he'd need to get a narcotics conviction. He grunted with sat-isfaction and tucked the kit bag away.

But there was none of what Haney wanted. No photographs. No film. No nothing. Harrigan went out to the lobby and found a phone.

He said, when he got him on the line, "No go, boss. Nothing doing. But there's a doozy of a narcotics beef for Deacon. Plenty of Mary Jane and the works for heroin."

"But no photos and no film."

"Nothing like that."

"And the girl?"

"Nothing doing there, neither."

"Then come on in."

Haney dropped the phone on the other end and cursed. This got worse and worse. It was bad enough that the evidence existed. It was worse that someone had it and that someone might one day leverage it on him. But it was much, much worse not to know who had it or where it was. That meant newspapers maybe, or grand jury, or who knew what. It didn't mean blackmail, or a shakedown, or anything else that a man like Haney felt he could handle. This was like a bomb that was getting more atomic by the hour. Something was circling, high above Shipton Wells, high above Yucca Flats, high above Las Vegas, carrying a big bomb that had Haney's name scrawled on it.

Haney went out past the frosted pane of glass that had his name written on it and said to the desk sergeant, "Tell Harrigan and Clauster to wait for me when they come in."

Haney did not like driving himself, but this evening he didn't want company. He took an unmarked police car and went downtown.

Deacon saw Mo across the casino floor. He was smiling, yet looked slightly ill at ease in his suit. He always looked like he was running a little late, and like he was on his way someplace else. Right now, with Stella on one side of him and some mug in a dark gray suit on the other, he looked even more restless than usual. Deacon said to Anita, "There's somebody I gotta say hello to. Come with me."

Halfway across the floor someone grabbed Deacon by the elbow. He turned. It was Satchmo himself—Louis Armstrong himself—saying, "Hey now, white boy," with his raspy voice.

Deacon jumped back step and said, "Satchmo! Is it shufflin'?"

"Man, it's shufflin' slow. What's up with these squares? Don't know how to have a party?"

"You got to show 'em. Get up there and blow!"

"We gonna blow in a minute. Who's your friend?"

Deacon pulled Anita close and said, "Mr. Armstrong, this is my friend Anita. Isn't she just something else?"

Satchmo gazed and rolled his big eyes up and down and back up. He said, "Just as nature intended, boy. Made for love."

"But not for *you*, now."

Satchmo laughed and said, "*You* the one for me, Deke. How 'bout doing a stretch with us here in a minute?"

"You say when."

"About five?"

"Yep."

Deacon took Anita across the floor. He was very aware of the men in the room, and some of the women, staring at her. He was thinking about where he could park her. Was anyplace safe, really? He came up on Mo just then, and said, "Mo. Good to see you here."

Mo smiled and said, "Hello, Deacon. Who's the friend?"

Deke pulled Anita forward. She stood eye-to-eye with Mo and extended her hand. Mo took it. Deke said, "This is my friend Anita. She's new."

Mo said, "She looks brand-new. I'm Mo."

Anita said, "Mo what?"

Mo said, "Mo' everything."

Anita laughed and blushed, and Deacon said, "Now, now."

There was a presence at his elbow and it got bigger and then it was the guy he'd seen in the dark gray suit. He shouldered in and said, "I'm Albert Sherman, from Monolith Pictures. Introduce me, Weiner."

Mo intervened. "This is Deacon. He's a horn player—the number-one horn player on the Coast. After maybe Chet Baker."

Deacon laughed and said, "Mo's exaggerating."

Mo said, "Okay. He *is* the number one horn player. Forget Baker. And this is Deacon's friend Anita."

Sherman, smitten, struck numb, said, "Um, dance?"

Deacon slid his arm into hers and before she could answer said, "She'll have to rain-check you. We were just heading that way."

Deacon pulled Anita away. She said, "I don't know how to dance to this music."

Deacon said, "Sure you do. Just follow me." He pulled her close, and they moved like water across the floor.

Mo was thinking, *No wonder Deacon's wandering around in Shipton Wells. Some piece!*

Sherry said to him, "Who's the girl?"

Mo said, "Who knows? Some chippie. Friend of Deke's."

"Is she colored?"

"Who knows?"

"She's a real beauty. Is she an actress?"

Mo said, "Isn't everybody? Where's yours?"

Sherman said, "I lost her."

"You can get another. Excuse me, won't you?"

Mo left Sherman to worry over his missing actress. To worry over getting another. To worry over his film crew. The room swirled and cooked. It was hot. More people were streaming through the door. Mo said hello to a couple of hard guys from Fremont Street, who looked out of their element in their square suits with the lumps under the left arms. Then in front of him was Sinatra's group, but not Frank. There was Dino and Joey Bishop. Joey was tipsy. Dino always made a big thing out of his drinking, but he never looked like he'd had more than a couple. He said, "Hello, lover boy," as Mo passed.

Mo said, "Dino. You look like a million tonight."

Dino said, "I *feel* like a million, Mo."

Mo kept going.

A cry shot up from one of the craps tables, and a drunken voice said, "Seven come eleven, baby!"

Stella had come into Sherman's orbit, and circled now to get close to him. She stopped by the bar and said, "Howzit going, Mr. Hollywood?"

Sherman made the connection to the Starburst, took in a yard of pale cleavage amidst the fur and feathers of her dress, and said, "Who knows? Stella, right? My camera guys are getting all of this. I have no idea what we could do with it. I got an idea for a film. And I wanna set it in a casino like this. But the pictures we're shooting tonight are impossible. All these stars! All under contract to different studios. Impossible. You'd never get the releases. Maybe I'll sell it to Pathe."

"Have you cast the casino picture yet?"

"No. I don't even have a script."

"I know all about casinos, you know. I can help you write the script."

"You can?"

"We can start tonight."

Sherman turned to look at her, just to be sure she was saying what she sounded like she was saying. Her eyes were cool, and direct, and hungry. Women! Sherry said, "I'm sharpening my pencil right now."

Stella laughed, a big, braying laugh, and Sherman suddenly lost interest. And Stella saw that happen. She said, "In any case, howzabout getting me another cocktail? I'm drinking whiskey sours tonight."

Sherman patted her on the arm and said, "You leave that to me."

The music was coming off the bandstand like Niagara Falls, swirling over the room and drowning conversations as it roared.

It took Mo fifteen minutes to fight the crowd and get to the door. What a crush. Every shoulder he bumped, every hat he ducked, said, *Money*. The Ivory Coast was going to be a smash. Mo had hit the number, this time, first time. The payout was going to be huge. In six months he'd never have to worry about Chicago or the Starburst or the Thunderbird again. In a year, he could be clear. In two years . . . well, two years was too long.

He made a note in his head to call Worthless. No. To send Worthless something. Flowers? No. A bottle? No. A broad? No. What? What do you get for the man who has . . . nothing?

Then he was out the front door and in the night air. The parking lot hummed with car horns and car engines and drivers and passengers shouting to one another. The valets came and went, fleets of them, fleet of foot, in their black-and-red jackets. What a crowd!

And Stella! Mo suddenly realized that he'd lost her. He looked back at the front door, over the heads and hats and shoulders. He couldn't spot her, or her feathers. She'd have to make it on her own. She'd make it fine, he reckoned. She was right where she wanted to be, anyway. Neck deep in Negro, on a hot summer night, in the hottest place in town.

Mo started looking for a cab.

Inside, a man was shouting at the bartender, "Gimme a goddamn liquor drink." Next to him, two sharps from Chicago were watching the women. "She ain't no oil painting," one of them said. "But I'd take her."

Stella had gotten her whiskey sour from Sherman and moved off, and right away had met up with a couple of fellas from Philly, or so they said, both of them musicians who had come up to the desert with Basie's band and then decided not to move on with the Count when his run was over. Or so they said. And they had some wicked reefer with them. One of them had gotten hold of a room key—he said his sister worked in the joint, but he said it in a way that Stella knew it was a lie—and the three of them had gone out of the casino and were walking the halls looking for the right number. Stella said, "If it's 203, wouldn't it be on the second floor?" And one of the guys from Philly said, "We on the second flo' now." And Stella started laughing and said, "You boys know I can't see a thing without my glasses." And one of the boys said, "I know one thing you be able to see just fine," and Stella started laughing again. Then they were in the room and smoking, and everything was going to be just fine. One of the men knelt down and started to take off her shoes. She thought that was so romantic. She said, "Why, that's so sweet." And the man said, "Uh-huh," and kept going.

The band jumped into a fresh number that put several couples on their feet at once. Someone from a blackjack table looked up at the stage just in time to miss the dealer draw an ace to his suicide king. When he looked back, his money was gone.

Deacon and Anita came off the floor as the other couples were coming on. She had a light in her eyes he had never seen before. She said, "I never knew dancing was supposed to be like that."

"Exactly like that."

"I like it. What was the name of that song?"

Deacon said, "That was called 'You Belong to Me.' "

Anita smiled and said, "Well, do you?"

And Deacon said, "Yes. Always."

The crowd was impossible now. Deacon looked for a way to get them over to the bar, or over to a table. But there were too many people. It was like Grand Central on a Friday evening, except nobody was going anywhere. Deacon, tall enough to see over half the heads in the room, still couldn't see anyplace to park his girl.

Then Satchmo's guys were moving onto the stage. One of them came over to Deacon and said, "Satch say he like to see you up there in five minutes, boy."

Deacon said, "Thanks, man," and then turned to Anita. "I'm gonna go blow a bit. You . . . Maybe if you . . ."

She said, "I'll be all right."

Deacon said, "Maybe if Mo . . ."

Anita said, "He left. I saw him go. But that's okay. You go and play. I'm going to stand right here and watch you. And you can stand right up there and watch me."

Deacon said, "Well, okay. I just don't like the idea . . ."

Anita said, "Of what? Your little Anita all alone with all these big Las Vegas men around her?"

Deacon laughed and said, "Well, yes."

Anita said, "Get up there, buster. I'll be right here, staring at you. You're the only one I see, anyway. You belong to me."

Deke left her. He had to shove his way to the stage, where a saxophone player he couldn't remember ever meeting said, "Hey, Deke. Come up, man. Got your axe all ready." He handed him a horn—not his own, but close enough. Deacon wiped the mouthpiece on his sleeve. He spat a couple of notes into it, then he shot a quick scale. Satchmo turned and smiled and said, "All right, boys," and without further notice the band jumped into "Stardust."

The room settled and heads started turning, and Satchmo got into the microphone and the band really got grooved into it. Deacon had trouble reading the charts, or rather had trouble *seeing* the charts. He was drunker than he thought he was. He swayed slightly, getting up to solo, but then he was on his feet and stacking notes and phrases and it was as smooth as Kentucky bourbon. It was just like blowing smoke rings again. He lit them up and let them go and they hung in the room like bubbles.

And time stood still. Deacon was on, and the room was quiet, and the music was like liquid amber. Faces stood still like faces caught on film. Deacon was in the room, but he wasn't in the room. He was over the room, sliding up and out, riding the ceiling and gazing down at the black and white and brown faces, smiling faces, grinning at him and Satchmo and Worthless's new Ivory Coast.

And then Deacon realized he could not see Anita. She was simply not anywhere to be seen. He knocked back the end of this solo and there was quite a lot of applause, and he smiled from habit, but she was not anywhere that he could see her. He felt suddenly, horribly, lost.

What if? What if?

Satchmo said, "That's nice, boy. You stay fo' another number?"

Deacon said, "Nah. You got lots of guys here to help you tonight. I wanna listen, man." And he left the stage in a hurry.

Haney was thinking, as he parked the car and started walking toward the Ivory Coast, *I got to get some niggers on the force. I got no business being here, at this time of night, on my own. Couple of big niggers with me . . . that would be different. If I can't shut this place down, I got to get me some big niggers.*

The place appeared to rock with noise and humanity. Haney checked his watch. It was two o'clock. Coming into the driveway, he could see maybe fifty to seventy-five people standing outside, drinking, talking and laughing, hollering at one another, smoking cigarettes, and waiting for their cars. Above them, can-can dancers swung and swayed on the balconies. Music poured from the building like smoke from a house on fire. Haney pushed through the crowd at the door, one hand poised to go inside his suit coat for a badge or a pistol—whichever he'd need first or fastest.

Inside, the heat and the noise were overpowering. It was like nigger soup. Black chowder. The air was thick with the smell of them, and of smoke and booze and sex and jazz. They were four deep at the bar and three deep at the tables. It was the first time he'd ever been in a casino when he couldn't actually *hear* the casino. No bells, no voices of the stickmen, no shouts of the players. It was just music and buzz.

And celebrities. Every name act from the Strip was here. Shooting his eyes around the room, Haney picked up Sinatra over there, with Dean Martin and that Joey Bishop, and Spencer Tracy with Katharine Hepburn. Over there, Edward G. Robinson, with . . . Ava Gardner? Yes. And Clark Gable. And Cary Grant. Sammy Davis Jr., that little one-eyed troublemaker, was with that singer with the eyeglasses named . . . ? What? Ella Something—Ella Fitzgerald. They were with a guy with a name like that, too. Ella Something. Elephant? Elefante? Belafonte. Harry Belafonte. And with them was Nat "King" Cole, the only singer of that type that Haney could actually stand. There was a broad Haney thought might be Dinah Washington. She sang a song called "Black Coffee" that confused Haney a little—it was very sexual and it was about black coffee, and that confused him.

He went across the bar area. He was looking for Worthless Worthington Lee, or Mo Weiner, or Fatty. Nothing doing, right now. Just the crowd. Most of whom he didn't even recognize. They didn't look like tourists. They didn't look like locals, though, either. They looked too rich and too well dressed. And too black. Did Worthless bring 'em in from Los Angeles, or Frisco, these high-tone coloreds? *They aren't desert niggers*, Haney thought. *Not from around here.*

There were too many of them. They were too big and too black, and having too good a time. Haney began to feel very small, and choked for air.

His mind was still stuck on the horn player and the girl. Harrigan had found nothing at all of the photographs or the film when he tossed the rooms at the Starburst. The narcotics kit would make for some leverage on the horn player, but that wouldn't help Haney if he didn't have the photos. Maybe Clauster had better luck in Shipton Wells. He hoped so. This was getting old. Haney was sick of it. He understood, suddenly, why fugitives get caught: it's exhausting to worry all the time about getting caught, and at some point you probably welcome it, just to have it over with.

Haney said, "It ain't happening to me like that." He shoved the man in front of him out of the way and pushed farther through the crowd. Across the room he could see the little weasel Fidget, one of the two guys he was paying to keep an eye on the inside of this joint. Fidget was waving to him from the reception area. Haney nodded his head stiffly. Fidget kept waving, then dove into the crowd. Haney kept shoving.

Inside the room on the second floor, Sumner was just getting the cork out of a second bottle of champagne. Eleanor was standing at the balcony, looking out into the night, over the pool. The music from below seemed to lift up and around her and into the room. She laughed a lovely light laugh and said, "Listen to the band." Then she sang along, "Sum-ner time . . . And the living is . . . easy."

Sumner laughed, too. It was too easy. The girl was standing there like it was nothing. She talked like it was nothing—like being here, in this room, with this man, was nothing. Or nothing *bad*, anyway. It made Sumner nervous. He poured the champagne and moved toward her. And she smiled again. Would he touch her? Would he touch her now? Or if not, when? Was she expecting that? If not, what in the world *was* she expecting? In Sumner's experience, white girls like this only ever went to a Negro man for one of two things: they wanted narcotics, or they wanted loving. And this girl did not look like she wanted either one. She looked so comfortable standing there with the glass of champagne—so close to him, he could smell the freshness of her. She looked like a Breck magazine ad, shimmery and perfect.

She said to him, "That must be rotten, not being able to play music for so long."

"It's just what it is, you know," he said. "It's not so bad."

"You *must* start again now, though," she said. "Let's drink to it."

Sumner said, "Cheers," and they clinked glasses. She was looking into his eyes, really looking *into* his eyes, and at that precise moment Sumner fell for her. It felt like falling. He leaned into her and pulled her close to him, and felt as if he were falling into her. They kissed, long and slow. Her small, tight body pressed into him. He said, "Give me your glass," and took it from her, and set it on the coffee table. Sumner went to the wall by the door and turned the lights down so low that the only illumination in the room was the glow of the swimming pool below.

He said, "Come here, now . . ." and moved to her.

Fatty saw Haney before Haney saw him, coming toward the Ivory Coast's reception area. Then Haney waved. Fatty cringed and waved back as if he were pleased to see him. Haney was shoving through the crowd, the black hat on his black square shoulders parting heads as it pushed through. Fatty thought: *Did he see? Does he know? Could he know?* He had just closed a sale to the little Negro named Fidget— the sale of a large quantity of exactly the kind of narcotics that Haney did not want being sold on the West Side. Fidget seemed solid—a nervous, jumpy little guy, but no squealer—but the sudden nearness of Haney made Fatty nervous, too. Christ, Haney was like a cockroach. Turn on the lights and there he was, every time you turn around.

Coming out of the crowd, Haney shook himself as if he'd been caught in the rain, and said, "Why aren't you at the Starburst?"

"Just checking it out. Just having a look-see."

"And what do you see?"

Fatty smiled and waved his hands before him. He said, "I see a lot of folks having fun, spending money, fixing to get into trouble. More business for you."

"I don't need that kind of business. And I don't want you doing *any* kind of business."

"You've made that perfectly clear, Thomas. Crystal clear. Understood."

"Where's the head jigaboo?"

"*Jigaboo?* Charming. You mean Worthless. He's around. He's wearing a tuxedo. It's a riot. He looks like he's catering a funeral."

"His own, maybe," Haney said. He was scanning the crowd. Fatty could feel the heat of Haney's attention moving away from him. Haney said, "Where's a phone?"

Fatty pointed.

Haney said, "Walk with me."

Back near the men's room they found a bank of telephone booths. Fatty stood and waited while Haney slipped inside and sat. He dropped a coin, dialed, and waited. The desk sergeant said, "We've been trying to reach you, Lieutenant. We have a code black in Shipton Wells. There was a shooting, and an officer involved. Two bodies. One of them may be Officer Clauster. We had a report from the scene. I've dispatched CHP."

Haney said, "I understand. No positive ID on the stiffs?"

"Not yet, sir. We have a line open."

"Keep it open. I'll check back."

Clauster dead. Which means Clauster wasn't coming back with the goods. Harrigan came out empty-handed, too. So, where were the pictures? Haney stood up and stepped out of the booth. Fatty could almost see the steam rising off him.

And this, now, would only make it worse. Fatty saw the nervous Negro Fidget coming toward across the room. Fatty waved once at him to get away, but Fidget kept coming. Fatty didn't see any graceful way to run. He flashed his eyes at Fidget as he got close, but Fidget had eyes only for Haney.

He got up close and said, "I n-n-n-need to t-t-t-talk."

Fatty said, "Not now."

Fidget said, "N-n-n-not you. You."

Haney said, "Spit it out."

"Something g-g-g-g-oing on. With th-th-th-th . . ."

"With what? For Christ's sake, with what?"

"With th-th-th . . . With that boy you asked me to w-w-w-watch. S-S-S-Sumner."

"And?"

"And a wh-whi-white lady."

Haney nodded and said, "Where?"

Fidget pointed straight up. "Room two-twe-twe-twe—"

"Never mind. Show me."

Stepping away, Haney said to Fatty Behr, "Stay out of trouble. I may need you later. Keep your eyes open."

"Aye-aye, Cap."

"Don't back-talk me. I'm not fooling around. Just keep your eyes open."

Deacon had come off the stage right into the arms of this big blond brute who said he was with Sinatra. He said, "Frank wants a word."

Deacon said, "Frank who?"

The blond guy said, "Very funny," and took Deacon by the arm. He had hands like hunks of meat, and the shoulders of a football player. Might have been a USC player, or UCLA, with those Nazi blue eyes and that blond hair. He said, "Follow me"—as if Deacon had a choice.

Sinatra was at a table near the edge of the stage. There were six or seven men gathered around him, dark men in dark suits, each one impeccably groomed. Deacon kept his eyes on Sinatra. He was smaller than Deacon would have thought, and when he spoke it was almost a whisper.

He said, "You blow nice."

"Thanks."

"*Real* nice. And I know. 'Cause I listen."

"Thanks."

"You make the scene in Hollywood?"

"Not too much."

"I'm making a suggestion. *Make* the scene in Hollywood. Call this number."

One of the dark-suited men reached out, a business card in his hand. Deacon took it and stuck it into his jacket pocket.

He said, "Thanks."

"You're welcome," Sinatra said. "You got the chops. You make the sound, and that makes the world go 'round. Duke him."

Another of the dark-suited men reached out and shoved Deacon a bill. Deacon stared at it. It was a fifty-dollar bill.

Sinatra said, "Take it."

Deacon stared at it and said, "No. Thanks, but no."

Sinatra said, "Take it."

Deacon said, "No."

Sinatra glanced around at his dark-suited companions, then back at Deacon, and then at the guy holding the fifty.

He said, "Get a load of this piker. I'm duking the guy fifty bones. And it's nix."

Deacon stared. Sinatra stared. Three of the men in dark suits stood up, silently, and shot their cuffs. Ready to rumble. Deacon's mouth went dry. Sinatra put his hands flat on the table in front of him and inspected his fingernails.

Then he said, "Dangle. But . . . keep the phone number."

Deacon nodded and withdrew. The three men in dark suits sat back down. Deacon heard Sinatra say, as he was leaving, "You believe that guy? Somebody get us some goddamn cocktails."

Deacon went looking for Worthless, or Anita, or someone. The music spun behind him. His head was light. He said to himself, "And get *me* a goddamned cocktail, too."

A little later, as he followed Fidget across the reception area, Haney spotted Worthless standing near the stage and talking with that horn player. There was something conspiratorial about the way the two friends were talking. Deacon looked excited, and Worthless was calming him down, reassuring him, or promising him something. The music was roaring behind them. Louis Armstrong was singing. "When you smilin', oh, when you smilin', the whole world . . . smiles with you."

Haney was watching Worthless lean down close and laugh at something Deacon said. Then he shook his head. Deacon was whispering low now. Worthless was reassuring him. He put his hand on Deacon's shoulder and squeezed. It was almost a caress, Haney could see—that warm, that close. Deacon laughed at something Worthless was saying to him. And they both looked up, together, to scan the room.

And it hit Haney like a heart attack. *This* was the shakedown. The whole problem was standing right across the room from him. Deacon had done the killing in Shipton Wells. He had gotten ahold of the photographs and the film strips. He and the nigger boxer were in it together—and sitting on the material, no doubt, as insurance against Haney doing anything to stop their Ivory Coast.

It was smooth. It was working. Haney's hands were tied. From across the room he saw Worthless suddenly see *him*. Worthless stopped smiling, and said something to Deacon, who turned to follow his look.

Haney said to Fidget, "Go. Go fast."

Then they were by the elevators and moving up to the second floor.

Haney had understood that the hotel wing of the Ivory Coast was not open yet. Fidget told him that only the main wing was finished and that not all the rooms there were ready. This satisfied Haney's concern about other guests. Fidget said there weren't many—maybe not any, in fact.

Haney said, "That's what I needed to know. Now get out of here."

Fidget said, "Don't you want me to-to-to . . ."

Haney turned on him, now with a small black revolver in his hand, and said, "Get out of here. And keep your mouth shut, you stuttering jerk."

Fidget went back down the hallway. There was no sound. Haney leaned in close to the wall and listened. Nothing. The door in front of him read 212. Hadn't the stutterer said, "Two-twelve"? No. Could have been saying, "Two-twenty," or for that matter, "Two-twenty-one," or "Two-twenty-two," or whatever. Haney moved down the corridor.

Wally checked his watch again. It was 1:45. It had been more than half an hour since that Dot had turned off the light in her cabin. He had stood outside the back of the café, smoking and waiting, smoking and waiting. Now it was time. There was no sound from the road. No sound from the cabin. Was she still awake? He knew she was. He knew that she knew what was going on. She had seen him looking at her, wanting her, waiting for the night to end. Every time she spoke to him, she had seen it. He was so hot for her that he was on fire. She saw that. She had to be ready for that. He chucked the cigarette off into the dirty sand and made his way around the corner of the café building until he could see her cabin in front of him.

It was dark. Wally stopped again and listened. Silence. He moved onto the little porch and stopped. Silence. He took the screen-door handle and pulled, and was surprised to see that the cabin door itself was open. The little minx! She *was* waiting for him. His heart raced in his chest. He stepped over the threshold. Inside, he pushed the cabin door all the way open. She lay on the bed in front of him. He said, "Hey, baby."

And mayhem. A man's voice said, "What the—," and there was a crash, and then the girl Dot screamed and there was a terrible noise and Wally saw the muzzle flash just as something fiery tore through his groin and leg. In the muzzle flash he saw a man crouching by the closet. Dot screamed horribly again. Wally tried to rise, and fell, and then the man by the closet was rushing by him. Wally caught him around the knees and the man fell and Wally was on top of him, clutching at his throat. The man swung at him, a heavy pistol in his hand, but missed. Wally grabbed at the man's arm, and caught it, and sank his teeth deep into the man's shoulder. He screamed, and the pistol fired again, and Dot screamed again. This time Wally felt something dreadful below his knee, in the same leg. The pain was excruciating. He bit deeper into the man's arm, and heard him scream some more, a weird animal shriek. The man dropped the gun. Wally's head spun with pain and rage as he scrambled his hands around on the floor, trying to grab it. He got it. He got it up into the guy's face. He pulled the trigger and the guy was gone.

Dot was screaming and the room was dark again and the man stopped squirming and Wally just lay down. The leg thing was horrible. It was hot and wet and felt like someone was jabbing him with a million boiling knives. He let go of the pistol. Then he let go of everything else. The last thought in his head: *Dot is standing there, screaming, buck naked and a real beauty, and there isn't one single goddamn thing I can do about it.*

Deacon could not find Anita anywhere. The crowd was too thick. The air was too thick. It was like walking through soup. Like pea soup. The fog in London is like pea soup. "A foggy day, in London town . . ." She was nowhere. The band had swung into "West End Blues," and it was just fabulous. He wanted to go back up there. He wanted to go home with Anita. He wanted to be clearheaded, and he also desperately wanted to be flying high. But now he was in-between, in a bad place. He was fuzzy, and he had lost his girl, and he wasn't playing, and it all felt bad. He pushed toward the bar and said to a guy there that he didn't know, "Give me a double shot of rye, man." When he got it he threw it down and felt it burn. His vision unblurred a little. He said, "Do that again, man," and the bartender did. The second one burned just right. He said, "That's good," and threw a five-dollar bill on the bar.

But no Anita was waiting for him when he turned and looked again. No Worthless. No Sumner. That movie guy was conferring with his cameramen. The little actress they'd had with them was not there. Well, it was late. Maybe she'd gone to bed. He wanted to go to bed. He wanted to find Anita and take her to bed. The thought roused him. He pushed back into the crowd.

Worthless had Anita. He was showing her the inside of things. They were in a room above the casino now, and Worthless was showing her how the "eye in the sky" worked. He said, "If you lean in close to that, you can read every card in that card player's hand." Anita did lean down, and stared. She suddenly said, "Oh, my. You could count the *hairs* on that man's hand."

She was just so achingly beautiful. She was like Dina had been. Worthless felt his heart swell and crunch in his chest. This was what he should have had. This was what he should have felt—should feel now. Maybe the biggest night of his life. Certainly the biggest success of his life. And he was going to go home alone at the end of it, and he'd be alone when he got there, and he'd be alone when he got up in the morning.

The girl said, "You know, Deacon likes you an awful lot. I think he'd rather work for you than work for that Mr. Weiner."

Worthless said, "Deacon, he's a good boy."

Anita smiled and her eyes crinkled. She said, "He's a good boy."

"You gone marry him?"

Anita gasped and said, "Gosh. I don't know. I sure hope so."

Worthless said, "That's fine. He's a good boy. Does he love you?"

Anita gasped again. She said, "I don't know that, either. I think he does."

"Well, does he *say* it?"

Anita said, "He's kinda quiet. He doesn't say it right out."

"Then he's a damn fool. Somebody ought to be telling you he loves you every hour of every day of the week."

Anita blushed and covered her face with her hands.

Worthless said, "Maybe that'll come. After you get married and start having chirren."

Anita buried her face in her hands now.

Worthless said, "How old are you?"

"I'm eighteen. Well, I'll *be* eighteen."

Worthless felt his heart crunch inside him again. He said, "Let me take you back downstairs. Get you back to that boy of yours."

"Thank you."

Worthless took her down the stairs they'd used to come up, stairs that came out the back of the room he called his office. The stairwell itself entered through a closet at the back of the room. Coming down now, he thought: *I could keep her up here and it might be days before anyone would even figure out there was a room here. I could keep her in here like a little doll.*

His head running on, Worthless said, "Take ahold of that rail going down. Them steps is a little steep."

Anita trotted on ahead of him. He felt his heart swell and crunch again, but with something new. Pride, maybe? For her. For Deacon. For the fact of them, together.

Downstairs, the volume came roaring back up to full. Peels of laughter and talk came off the casino floor. Worthless heard a man shout, "Big Dick from Boston!" and a lady screamed with delight. Two waiters carrying trays of empty dishes came by like camels to the oasis. Two others dressed just like them came from the other direction, carrying trays that were full. Anita turned and smiled at Worthless, and put her hands over her ears. She mouthed, "It's loud!" Worthless grinned and put his arm around her shoulder. He said, "It's the sound of people spending money."

They found Deacon standing in front of the stage. He was staring up at Louis Armstrong. He'd forgotten everything else. Satchmo was running a string of short, sharp notes into one another, and Deacon was shaking his head from side to side in time with the beat. Anita tugged at his sleeve. Without turning, Deacon brushed her hand away. When she tugged again, he turned, as if annoyed, and saw who was tugging. He pulled her into him.

Worthless left them there. His watch said 3:15. The casino floor was full, and it was full in a way that he had never seen—that no one had ever seen. There were black and white faces, cheek by jowl, jamming the craps tables, sitting at the blackjack tables, crowding around the roulette wheel. The bar was black and white and black and white, couples and singles and groups, all mixed up so you could not tell who was with whom. It might have been a white man's casino that had just let in colored people, or it might have been a Negro casino with a bunch of white customers. Either way, Worthless knew it was the first time it had ever happened.

And he had made it happen. It was his. Everywhere he looked, he only saw people laughing and smiling. This thing you couldn't do, because of the trouble it would cause, was doing just fine. And showing no sign of slowing down. People were *still* coming in the front door. Worthless could see, from the looks on their faces, that they were just coming in for the first time. He had a long night ahead of him yet.

Sumner kissed her again and held her close, and then felt her dress fall from her shoulders. It slid to the floor and made a whispering sound, and then she was naked. She was like ivory, so smooth and cool and pale in the soft light coming in from outside. It was like watching an angel materialize. He said, "My God, you're beautiful," and kissed her again, and she said, "No, you. I want to see you." And then her hands were on him again. His jacket came off, and she pulled at his tie. He kept kissing her, dizzy now, and pushed her hands away and worked at the tie himself. She started on his shirt buttons. Her hands were hot on his chest, and her breath was coming in sharp, short gasps. His shirt came away and she crushed herself into him— soft and on fire and trembling. He leaned down, scooped her into his arms, and lifted her off her feet.

Haney heard voices from where he stood in the hallway. Or rather he heard that low, buzzy sound that voices make. He had moved slowly from door to door, listening, feeling for sound. Now he was in front of Room 222. He could feel the noise from the casino in his feet, and the *bump bump bump* of the band, through the soles of his shoes. Beneath that, though, he could hear a fuzzy sound, intermittent, of talk in the room. Haney checked his watch, a cop's instinct to mark the time just before or after something important happens.

Then he took a deep breath and two fast steps and went shoulder-first through the doorway, smashing the jamb as he went and spraying splintered wood into the room.

No one there. What? His eyes caught the bed, unruffled, and the curtains, swaying. There were two figures there—a man carrying a woman in his arms—near the balcony. Haney said, "Hold it!"

Sumner had heard the pounding feet and the splintering wood. He turned and through the dim light saw the white man coming into the room with a gun just as he was lifting Eleanor from her feet. He spun now and stepped onto the balcony, swung her up to shoulder level, and shoved her away from his chest—off the balcony, straight out into the thin night air.

Eleanor screamed and waved her limbs about, and began to fall—and continued to fall, twenty feet straight down, to the shimmering swimming pool below.

Sumner did not see her land. He had turned back to the white man with the gun—boyfriend? husband? cop?—the moment she left his arms. Now he crouched and dashed forward. This surprised the white man—he saw now that it was Haney—who shouted at him to stop. They both heard Eleanor splash into the pool, and the sound of a woman screaming. Sumner saw Haney's gun hand came up, as if he would strike Sumner with it rather than shoot him. It was the only opening Sumner needed. He hurled himself into the policeman's chest, knocking him over backward and tumbling down with him. The gun went off. Ceiling plaster showered down on them. Sumner threw one punch into Haney's face and then was on his feet and going out the door. Sumner was gone before Haney could shoot again.

There were stairs at the end of the hall. He got there just as Haney came out of the room and fired again. The hallway shook with the sound. Sumner took the stairs five at a time and did the turn and took five more stairs and then hit a door and was outside.

Down the hall, Stella heard the noise and squinted up from her ministrations. The man she was working on said, "Damn! Don't stop now."

Worthless heard the shot, over the music, and grabbed Deacon's arm. Deacon had heard it, too. He pointed, with a question in his eyes: Pool? Worthless nodded. Deacon grabbed Anita's arm and said, "Stay here. Don't move." And he and Worthless pushed away through the crowd.

The crowd did not part. Had no one heard the gunshot? People were laughing and drinking and smoking. Worthless kept smiling that gummy smile, saying, "Excuse me, please," and, "Sorry," as he pushed through. Deacon rode in his wake. It seemed to take forever.

Then they were in the hallway and headed for the pool. A small crowd was gathering outside. A shape moving so fast that it seemed not to have features came through the door. Worthless said, "Sumner!" but the man did not even pause. He was past them, moving like a rocket, and gone. Deacon wasn't sure it was Sumner at all. Then they were outside and by the pool.

The policeman Haney was there, a revolver in his hands and a look of rage on his face. Albert Sherman's actress was standing there in front of him, soaking wet, dripping and crying and sobbing. And naked. Haney whipped around, turning the gun on Worthless as he approached.

"Get back. Where's that nigger bastard you were with?"

Eleanor said, "I don't know."

Haney said, "Where is he?"

Worthless said, "Easy, now, Lieutenant. What happened?"

"Shut up! Where the hell is he?"

Worthless said, "Easy, now. He's gone. He run right out and he is gone."

Haney said, "You are all under arrest. Especially you, you tramp bitch."

Eleanor sobbed a little harder. Deacon moved toward her. Haney said, "And you on a narco beef. You are all going into the hole. Get me a phone."

No one moved. No one answered. Haney stared around. He said, "Get me a goddamn phone. *Now!*"

No one moved. The crowd had swollen to thirty or more and it was getting bigger. It was mostly black. Haney felt surrounded. He was willing to kill them all, but how? The music poured from the casino every time the swinging glass doors opened. Worthless was watching Haney's face. He calculated: Haney—gun—bullets—six— one gone, at least—crowd of thirty.

He said, "Lieutenant? We got to do this right. Let me clear this crowd."

Haney said, "Get me a telephone line."

Worthless said, "I will. But let me clear this crowd first, or someone is going to get hurt."

Worthless moved off. Deacon took off his suit coat and put it around Eleanor's shoulders. The pool water had gotten still again. The wind was still. The music was distant, and the jazz sounded soft and easy now. It wasn't "Summertime" anymore. The palms swayed above them, and the light breeze ruffled the fronds.

Worthless said, in a voice that meant business, "I want all y'all off this patio now. *Right* now. Go inside. We gone settle this up."

The crowd murmured, mulled a moment, and began to move inside.

Worthless said, "I mean *all* y'all, now."

The patio got quiet. Haney said, "Move over there," and jerked the gun toward the other side of the pool. Deacon backed up a step or two, trying not to look at the gun as Haney moved it back and forth between him and Worthless. Haney was pale and his eyes were like rocks. But Worthless, moving slowly across the patio, looked very calm. *That old man has seen a lot of stuff,* Deacon was thinking. *The girl looks like she's preparing to meet her maker. Me . . . I'm just a horn player. I haven't seen anything.*

Deacon said, "How about putting down the weapon?"

Haney said, "How about shutting your mouth?"

Worthless said, "Easy now. I don't know what this's about, but I bet we can work it out just fine without anybody getting riled up."

Haney said, "Too late. I'm already riled. You bastards have something that belongs to me. I want it back. This is not police business. This is personal business. That means I will kill all of you, right now, if I don't get what I want."

Worthless said, "Well, that sounds easy. If you—"

"Shut up!" Haney turned on him, vicious, and spat the words. "Shut up! No more talking. I got another man dead in Shipton Wells. A *police* officer. I want those pictures now."

Then there was silence, but for the little breeze in the palm fronds and the distant sound of the band. Worthless waited, and watched Haney watching Deacon. After what felt like an eternity, Worthless said, "I don't know what pictures you are talking about."

Haney said, "Not you, then. Him. He knows what I'm talking about."

Deacon waited another moment. His mind was racing. It was coming up blank. All he could think, right now, was whether Haney had Anita. Whether Haney had connected him to Anita. If he had not, then what happened in the next few minutes did not matter that much. *If Worthless gets shot . . . If I get shot . . . so what?* But if he had a cop dead in Shipton Wells . . . then he might have hooked it all up to the café and Anita and her uncle.

Deacon suddenly became aware, in the stillness, of the girl standing silently and shivering. He said "How 'bout leaving her out of this?"

Haney looked as if he had forgotten about her. He gave her a glance, and then said, "Go."

Eleanor dashed away in Deacon's suit coat.

Deacon said, "And how 'bout leaving everyone else out of it, too?"

Haney said, "Just me and you, then. You're the one I'm gonna kill first if I don't get some answers *fast*. Where are my pictures?"

Deacon said. "They're gone."

"Gone where?"

"I destroyed them. And the movie film."

"When?"

"Right after I got them. The guy came out from Chicago. He killed himself. He left the stuff behind. I didn't know what to do with it. So I burned it."

"All of it?"

"Yes," Deacon said, and began to feel relieved. This was going to work. Haney was buying it. Deacon said, "I burned the whole thing."

Haney wanted to believe it. Deacon wanted him to believe it. All the power went out of the photographs if Haney believed it. All of the power went out of Haney, in fact, if he believed it. His arm sagged slightly, and he lowered his pistol. He was about to speak.

And there was suddenly a woman there, moving silently out of the shadows and across the patio. She was ghostly and black, and wearing a dress that had to be thirty years old. Her hair looked as if it had not been brushed in years. She was carrying a highball glass in one hand and some kind of a Japanese fan in the other. She drifted to the edge of the pool, and said, "Congratulations, dear."

Worthless, moving to her, said, "Dina?"

"It is a big, big success. I came to tell you congratulations."

The woman swayed slightly and stopped beside the pool. She waved her fan at Haney, and said, "Who is this man? He doesn't belong here."

Worthless said, "Get inside, Dina," and reached for her arm. But Haney was there first. He shoved Worthless away with one hand,

and crooked his elbow around her throat. Dina dropped her Japanese fan, and the highball glass shattered at her feet.

Haney said, "This is the famous Dina."

"Easy, Lieutenant. She got nothing to do with this."

"Shut up, Lee."

"She don't got nothin' you want, Lieutenant."

"Shut up. And get away from me. One more step—"

The casino doors blew open and Fidget raced onto the patio, waving a gun and shouting, "Th-th-th-that's not the g-g-g-g-guy—"

Haney spun and shot him. Dina screamed. Fidget dropped to the patio.

Haney cursed viciously and turned his gun back on Worthless and Deacon, and began backing toward the casino building. Dina hung slack in his arms, as limp as old clothes.

Worthless said, "Dina got nothing to do with this. Fact is, *I* got nothing to do with this. It don't involve us."

"It involves you now. You and the junkie are going down. You're going to tell me where the photographs are. Or I'll shoot this woman right now."

Worthless started forward, his big fighter's hands in front of him, death in his eyes, moving like machinery.

Haney said, "I'm not kidding. I'll kill her."

Worthless continued forward. He said, "You let her go."

"Stop now," Haney said. "Or I'll shoot her."

Deacon said, "Go ahead and shoot. That woman's dead."

Haney knew it the moment Deacon said it. The woman felt like a sack of grain. Haney loosened his hold on her neck and she slid away from him.

Deacon saw his opening and took it. He leaped forward and took two fast steps and was inside Haney's reach before Dina hit the floor. The two men tussled and spun and Haney shoved Deacon away from him. Falling backwards, he swung his pistol hand and smashed Deacon hard in the face with his gun. Deacon went over sideways and crashed through a glass tabletop going down. He hit the patio in a pile of shards and felt some of the glass go into his hands. Haney kept coming. Deacon lifted a hand to protect his face and cut himself with a piece of glass that had stuck in his palm. Haney kicked at him and said, "You lying bastard. You didn't burn anything. Where are the pictures?"

Deacon said, "I don't know."

Haney hit him on the side of his head with the pistol. Deacon saw stars and then his head hit the concrete and a loud thump went through his skull. Haney loomed over him. He said, "The pictures, goddammit. Where's the pictures?"

"Don't hit me again. I'll tell you." Deacon clutched at his head. Haney moved the pistol off him, for a moment, waving it toward Worthless. Deacon said, "I'll tell you."

Haney leaned down close to Deacon, so close Deacon could smell his hair tonic. Deacon whispered, "The photos, and the films, they're—"

Haney leaned closer still. Deacon sprang at him. He sank his teeth into Haney's ear and grabbed his pistol with one hand and jabbed a thumb into Haney's eye with the other. The cop shook his head fiercely and roared with pain. Deacon bit down harder, tasting metal in the blood that spurted from Haney's ear. Haney cursed horribly, and Deacon felt hot breath on his neck.

And then the gun went off, close to his head. The sound crashed around him like thunder, and chips of concrete and glass blew into his face. Another bullet came right away, shattering glass somewhere farther off. Deacon bit down harder and flailed around reaching for Haney's gun hand.

Then Worthless hit them both hard, a football tackle from behind. He had Haney in a bear hug that somehow had encircled Deacon, too. The ex-boxer's huge arms enveloped them both, crushing them together as he lifted them from the ground. Haney's pistol hand thrashed around. Somewhere a woman screamed, and a man's voice said, "Get away from that fight!"

Then they broke apart. Deacon spun away wildly. Worthless clutched at Haney, and got him around the throat, but the policeman's gun hand was still waving around. Another bullet went—Deacon could not have said where—and then Haney was free and Worthless had dropped to one knee, near where Dina had fallen. Haney rose over him and lifted his gun and it went *blam!*

Deacon saw Worthless fall. He thought of Anita. Then Haney turned the gun on him and one last time it went *blam!* Deacon went black and it was all over.

Eleven

WORTHLESS WORTHINGTON LEE'S funeral was the largest public gathering the West Side had ever seen. More than six hundred mourners drove in the motorcade from Jackson Street to Woodlawn Cemetery, where they watched the Reverend Clayton Usher preside over Worthless's journey home. Three hundred more crushed into the Ivory Coast to drink away his memory.

There had been rioting the night after his death.

The afternoon newspapers reported that the ex-boxer "Worthless" Worthington Lee had been shot and killed by police the previous night during a gunfight at the Ivory Coast Hotel and Casino—only hours after it had opened to the public. Lee had been questioned during the investigation into the murder of Carl "Jeeter" Ross, a prominent West Side businessman. On the night in question, Lee had resisted arrest, drawn a weapon, and begun firing upon police, and upon his own patrons, at the Ivory Coast. Before police officers arrived on the scene, Lee had shot and killed an Ivory Coast employee and an unidentified Negro woman. Police had returned fire.

Lee had died at the scene. So had an employee of the Starburst Hotel and Casino, a trumpet player known as Deacon Davidson. Police Lieutenant Thomas Haney, himself wounded in the ordeal, had arrested several of Lee's accomplices. Haney appeared in newspaper photographs wearing a big white bandage over his left ear. A loose round from the ex-boxer's gun, it was said, had grazed the side of his head.

In a related event, police had arrested a casino gift-shop employee, Dorothy Beeman, in connection with a shooting in Shipton Wells. The café bartender and Las Vegas police officer Victor Clauster were killed during the Shipton Wells shooting, which was under investigation. Police had not said how the Shipton Wells incident was related to the violence at the Ivory Coast Hotel and Casino.

The West Side exploded. There was one night of rioting, which Haney's men ignored because it did not leave the West Side. They were poised to pounce if it moved toward downtown or the Strip, but it did not. Negroes marched down Jackson Street and gathered in front of the Ivory Coast, where they made speeches and declarations of war. Then they burned a car on Bonanza. Someone threw a brick through a shop window. A beauty operator named Selma Pringle was injured slightly and hospitalized when two youths accosted her outside Garcia's store. Garcia was injured when he attempted to detain the two youths.

The police dispatched to the West Side watched with amusement and waited for things to return to normal. But things didn't return to normal. There was a town-hall meeting in the parking lot of the Ivory Coast. Solid West Side businessmen were calling for an investigation into the shootings at the Ivory Coast. Filcher, smarter than Haney, felt the pressure building.

He said, "We've got to do something."

Haney said, "You're goddamned well right. As soon as they move off of the West Side, we got the license to slaughter them all."

Filcher said, "No. We've got to get something in the newspapers."

The following day both the main desert dailies ran extensive and entirely positive obituaries on Worthless Worthington Lee. Filcher had a man ransack Lee's little house, where he found a good photograph of Lee in his boxing days. Filcher made sure both papers ran it.

He also made sure that the news accounts contained conflicting information about the funeral. One said that services would be held at Spirit of the Valley Cemetery, at eleven o'clock on the morning of Wednesday, June 2. A reception would follow at the Spirit of the Valley Memorial Hall. The other said that services would be held at twelve o'clock on the afternoon of Wednesday, June 2, at Woodlawn Cemetery, with a reception immediately following at the Ivory Coast. Neither piece of information was correct, but he had representatives of the two cemeteries phone the newspapers with the erroneous times.

In fact, there had been no funeral arrangements made for Worthless. There was no one to make them.

306 ♦ Charles Fleming

So Mo Weiner stepped in. He called someone who knew someone at Spirit of the Valley, who told him there was no possibility they could be ready for a burial on Wednesday. Mo had someone else who knew someone else call Woodlawn. He made it financially imperative that they *get* ready for a burial on Wednesday.

That day, a motorcade of automobiles collected at the Ivory Coast and made the drive out to Spirit of the Valley. By the time the mourners arrived and discovered that no services were planned for that day for anyone named Worthless Worthington Lee, it was almost too late for them to make the drive to Woodlawn. But not quite. The motorcade returning from Spirit of the Valley met up with the motorcade moving toward Woodlawn. They merged. An enormous snake of automobiles drove the nine miles north to Woodlawn.

As the service was ending, someone pointed out that they had gathered to honor the memory of Worthless Worthington Lee and they ought to be celebrating at the Ivory Coast—the palace that Worthless had built for them. The motorcade motored back to the West Side, where a few men from the crowd kicked in the front doors of the Ivory Coast and got the bars open. For the next ten hours, until the free liquor ran out, they danced to a makeshift orchestra and held their own private service in the late boxer's name.

Mo didn't stick around for that. He and Stella, walking from the grave site at Woodlawn, saw the growing energy, the anguish that was setting in and turning sour. Mo said to the driver, "Is there a way to drive back so that you bypass the West Side? Go that way. Go out by the airport." He and Stella rode in silence, watching airplanes float down onto McCarran Field.

At the Ivory Coast, a squad of police waited across the street, checking in with Haney regularly, and let Worthless's funeral party unfold. It went on until the small hours of the morning, until the booze ran out and the musicians went home.

Filcher said, "I told you."

Haney said, "I'd rather have slaughtered them all."

They were sitting in Haney's dim office, surrounding by the graphic evidence of Haney's long and illustrious career. There were two new "exhibits." One featured Haney's photograph in front of a jewelry-store. The owner lay dead on the ground behind him. The other was a postcard from the Ivory Coast, next to a restaurant menu marked

May 29, 1955, pasted next to a black-and-white police camera's photograph of the Ivory Coast swimming pool. Haney, his left ear wearing a huge white bandage, stood on the patio over the bodies of two black men bleeding into dark puddles beside the swimming pool.

Filcher said, "We never would have heard the end of it. Look at what's going on in the South."

"I'd rather have shot some of them."

The one lucky draw in the whole thing—for Haney—had been the death of the horn player Deacon. Or rather, what happened after that. He was a pretty popular guy, evidently; moreover, he was white. Haney said he wasn't worried, but Filcher expected to hear some real noise. He expected Morris Weiner to *make* some of that noise. He was Deacon's employer, and he might have been able to figure out, or find out, what had actually happened that night by the Ivory Coast pool.

Not that Filcher knew what had *actually* happened. The jacket on the incident left several questions unanswered. There was no explanation for what Clauster had been doing at the café in Shipton Wells when he died in the gun battle with the bartender there. There was no explanation for the death of the "unidentified negro woman" included in the body count. In fact, there wasn't even a cause of death listed for her. Filcher knew, independently, that she was the common-law wife of Worthless Worthington Lee. Haney had told him that the woman had simply dropped dead at the sight of her husband being shot.

It stank. It all stank. Haney had interrogated both the dead horn player *and* the ex-boxer less than two weeks before the shootings, questioned and released them without charges. That stank, too. It was clear to Filcher that Haney was running something beyond the scope of police business. Filcher knew already that Haney ran some guys who ran dope and women. He imagined that had something to do with the violence on opening night at the Ivory Coast. What, exactly? Filcher was sure he could find out, but he could not see a way to make it his job to find out. Not for now, anyway. And for now it didn't matter.

Especially because it was so quiet. After the initial ruckus and riot, the West Side went back to business. The Ivory Coast opened back up, a week or so later, under the care of a scrawny little nut named

Peet. The activity at the Starburst and the Thunderbird went back to normal. Mo Weiner never said a word. Perhaps, as Fatty Behr had suggested to Haney during one of their weekly chats, Mo was distracted.

As usual, Haney had insisted they meet out in the sticks. This time it was at a roadhouse in Pahrump, dozens of miles from town, halfway to Death Valley. It stank of beer and was not air-conditioned. Fatty sometimes felt that Haney chose places like this just to keep everyone off balance. Since he himself was not human, Haney would not be bothered by things like the heat and the smell, as someone like Fatty would be. This gave Haney some invisible advantage. *As if he needed any leverage over a guy like me,* Fatty was thinking.

Fatty explained that after the blow-up at the Ivory Coast, Mo had lost his main nightclub singer, Stella. She was spending all of her time smoking marijuana with some boys from the West Side. They were the kinds of colored boys she used to smuggle into the Starburst. Now she went to them, and stayed.

One rumor going around was that she and the horn player Deacon had been lovers. Another said that she and Deacon and Mo were *all* lovers, in some kind of sick three-way romance.

Haney said, "That's disgusting."

Fatty said, "I'm just telling you what people say."

Haney said, "It's still disgusting. Is it true?"

Fatty said, "Who knows? But Mo's not letting any grass grow. One broad I got working at the Starburst says Mo's got some new chippie stashed away somewhere. Either he had her all along and was hiding her from Stella, or she's new."

"What do we know about this one?"

"Nothing. Just that he leaves the casino every night around midnight, and doesn't come back for a couple of hours. No one knows where he's going."

"So, find out."

Fatty said, "I'll do what I can."

"No," Haney said. "Find out."

As a further break for Haney, Deacon apparently had no family. There was no funeral, no service, and no obit. Filcher did not even know what had happened to the body.

Sitting in Haney's horrible office, Filcher reflected that the photograph of the shooting scene by the Ivory Coast swimming pool had two black bodies in it, and no white ones. He'd love to know why that was—and what happened to that guy Deacon during the shootings, and what happened to him afterward. Maybe Deacon had gone the way of that *other* guy from the Starburst, Filcher thought, the bartender that Harrigan had killed. Gone out to the desert, into the sand.

Filcher stood up and said, "There is some paperwork headed your way. It has to do with permits for this movie company. They want to film at the Thunderbird and the Ivory Coast."

"They were up here before."

"They were filming the night there was that trouble at the Ivory Coast. Now they want to make their movie."

"I met one of them."

"Sherman. He's the head Jew. You must've mentioned your favorite charity. He wants to make a donation."

"Smart Jew. Sign the papers."

Filcher stood up and said, "Is there anything else?"

Haney said, "No. I have something planned for tonight. I'm going home."

At home, two hours later, Haney cinched the sash on his bathrobe and said out loud, "I'll be in the front room. Bring me a brandy."

He was exhausted, but excited about what lay ahead. It had been arranged, then canceled, then rescheduled, and that had cost plenty of money. This stuff did not come cheap. Nothing good did, though. You want it done right? Spend the money.

The Negro butler came in bearing brandy on a silver tray. Haney met him halfway across the room and took up the snifter. A Roy Rogers record was going on the Victorola. Haney said to Willis, "Is everything ready?"

Willis nodded and said, "Yes, suh."

Haney said, "I'll be along in about ten minutes, then. Have everything in place."

Willis said, "Yes, suh," and left the room.

What a summer! It wasn't even Labor Day. The city had seen records broken left and right, for crowds, for hotel occupancy, for gaming revenues, and for criminal activity. Haney and his crew had been run ragged. Domestic disputes. Fights in card rooms. Drunken driving. Several incidents involving men who did not want to pay for the broads they'd agreed to pay for. A couple of robberies, even. Haney had gotten some good ink off a jewelry-store heist that had gone bad. Three men from Phoenix had tried to knock over a joint just off Fremont. The owner was a tough little guy who had a pistol taped to the bottom of the cash register. He'd blown a big hole through one of the men from Phoenix and thrown the switch on his alarm system. That cost him his life. But it also brought the cops down. Haney's men had captured the other two crooks and charged them with a host of felonies, including murder. They'd stand trial in the fall. Haney was almost certain they'd get the chair.

That didn't quite make up for the Ivory Coast mess, but save for a few loose ends, that was pretty much tidied up as well. The nigger boxer was out. His wife was out. The trumpet player who did the guy in Shipton Wells was out. But the photographs were missing. Haney had made Harrigan go through the Ivory Coast one room at a time, then go back and finish searching the café in Shipton Wells. The stuff just wasn't anywhere.

Neither was the girl from Shipton Wells, the one Haney had recognized as the girl from the café. She had simply disappeared. That troubled Haney a little—but just a little. She had been one shaky leaf when Haney had questioned her the night after her boyfriend was killed. She wasn't going to turn into any kind of threat for anybody, whether she knew something or not. Still, Haney didn't like not knowing where she was. It suddenly occurred to him: was she the chippie Mo Weiner was visiting after hours? That didn't smell right. She was barely of age and she was mulatto, and he was a sixty-year-old Jew from Chicago. Did that match make sense?

Did any match make sense? Could you read, off of anyone, the face of their secret desire? Could you see, on anyone, what would be, unfettered, the true shape of their lust? Haney could only hope not.

Perhaps it was all over. Haney stuck his nose deep into the snifter and took a long swallow of the brandy, and waited. Roy and Dale crooned.

♦ ♦ ♦

Going out the back entrance of a little downtown bar called Eddie's Sandbox, Filcher caught Thornton's elbow and said, "Are we crystal-clear on the Thunderbird thing?"

Thornton, a nervous, wire-rimmed C.P.A. from Cincinnati, said, "Absolutely. It's airtight."

"I'm not going to wake up and find my name plastered all over these documents?"

"Impossible. It's all confidential stuff. Unless you or Dawson suddenly die, there is no reason anyone would ever see the paperwork at all."

"No insurance issues, or permit issues, or gaming license issues?"

"Nothing. Airtight."

They were in the parking lot. Wind was whipping sand around their ankles. Filcher saw the eagerness in the little accountant's eyes. He'd told Thornton he was married, but he'd acted like he was available. He'd had to.

Thornton moved toward him and said in a breathy voice, "So . . . how about it?"

Filcher said, "David, you know I can't. With my wife at home and all . . ."

Thornton groaned and said, "Forget her. Just for tonight."

Filcher said, "I can't. Maybe later . . ."

Thornton groaned again. "Call me."

Filcher got into his car and sped away without looking back.

It was a pretty sweet deal. He'd come away with controlling interest in the Thunderbird. Dawson, that Hollywood homo, was the front, but the real investment was coming from a group of Los Angeles businessmen who were tied up in all kinds of bad things—bad things that would make it impossible for them to hold a gaming license. Dawson could hold it. Filcher could finesse the commission. He'd have to keep wearing the assistant D.A. hat for a while. But it got him closer to the action than he'd even hoped. Morris Weiner, seeing which way the bread was getting sliced, had come to him like a real gentleman.

Weiner had said, "I know what gives. There's no reason to make a federal case out of it, though. Why don't you join the old boys for the next monthly meeting?"

As simple as that. He'd sat at the long table with Holbrook and

Seligman and Marquez, between Weiner and Truxton, right across from Wingate and Hackberry. Right before the meeting started, Truxton said to him, "So you're the fag that bought the Thunderbird from Mo?"

Filcher said, "No. That's Dawson. My name's Filcher."

Truxton said, "You're the patsy, then. You made Mo a happy man."

Filcher said, "What are you talking about?"

Truxton said, "Relax. Have some breakfast."

The principal order of business that morning was not the Thunderbird but the Ivory Coast. It had been opening and closing since its gala premiere. Even with the events of the opening night, and the irregular schedule after that, the place had been a sensation. The after-midnight action, especially, was huge. Worthless Worthington Lee had cooked up this idea of a "third show." Unlike the hotels on the Strip, which had ten o'clock and midnight shows, the Ivory Coast also had a two o'clock show. When folks on the Strip were supposed to be hitting the casinos, filled up with food and music and booze and ready to lose money, the folks at the Ivory Coast were just sitting down to dig a third helping of music. Since that was the only place to hear music anywhere after the second show ended, people started flocking over to the Ivory Coast after the action ended on the Strip.

At first it was just the coolest cats from the Strip, white and black, that headed over to the Coast after the last shows at the big hotels. They went to gamble, to suck down some juice, to beat their feet and jam with one another. When it was hot, it was red-hot. Its reputation spread so fast that pretty soon even the squares were lining up to get in.

Filcher had not been there that first night, but he'd been there on many occasions since. It was something to see. There were actors from Hollywood and singers from New York and rich white men and women from all over—whooping and hollering like animals. Actually, like Negroes. Even the white people were acting like Negroes. And this was something brand-new.

All his life Filcher had seen colored people trying to act white. They tried to talk white and look white and dress white, and do their hair white, and live and work the way whites did. The lighter-colored ones even said they *were* white, and managed to pass.

This made sense to him. Being colored was tough. Being white was better. Who didn't want to be better?

But now, for the first time in his experience, there were white people trying to look and sound and act like Negroes. He heard young men, young *white* men, say things like, "What's happening, daddy?" or "Slip me some skin." Their voices became like colored voices. They sounded like field hands. And they dressed colored, some of them, wearing outrageous clothes, bright things that you'd never see in Hart Schaffner & Marx or Brooks Brothers or any other decent clothing store.

In the clubs, they snapped their fingers and "grooved" to music they could not possibly like. Boys and girls who Filcher just *knew* had been listening to Patti Page and Pat Boone—kids whose idea of a wild song was probably Rosemary Clooney's "Come On-A My House"—were suddenly stomping around and singing along with "Shake, Rattle and Roll."

Onstage, some of them sang like Negroes, too. There was a local band called the Freshaires, a group of white boys who did some very melodic lounge performances, singing things like "Sincerely," and "You Belong to Me." But one night Filcher had seen the main singer from the Freshaires, up onstage at the Ivory Coast, swinging his hips and yodeling like a possum-fed darkie. You could close your eyes and almost not know the difference.

Filcher had also been part of the crew that had mopped up after the opening-night mess at the Ivory Coast.

There'd been quite a lot of mopping up. Haney had really got his tit in the wringer. There was gunplay and there were dead bodies, and even though it was the West Side, that required some explaining. Filcher had not seen any advantage in not helping Haney get out of the jam. Haney was still the one with the connections. Haney was still Holbrook's brother-in-law. Filcher knew only a little about Haney's network of women and dope. He decided not to make Haney's life any more complicated than it already was.

Holbrook, chairing the breakfast meeting as always, said, "It seems to me there are two questions that we need to resolve here. First: Do we want a colored casino on the West Side? Second, depending on the answer to that: What do we do about ownership on this Ivory Coast?"

The men grumbled a moment before Houck said, "I think propping this joint up and keeping it open is a good idea. I don't want the coloreds coming down the Strip. And I don't want them marching, like they're doing in Alabama, for their *right* to come down the Strip."

Truxton said, "Hear, hear."

Holbrook leaned over to listen to something Seligman was whispering to him, and said, "Anyone disagree with that?" When no one answered, Holbrook said, "Then we're agreed. Sponsoring some place off the Strip for the colored crowd is good for all of us."

Truxton said, "Hear, hear."

Holbrook said, "For God's sake, Truxton, be quiet. Now, what about the second part?"

Half the men at the table didn't know and didn't care and couldn't be bothered to find out what that second part meant. They began to drift, and talk among themselves. Filcher watched Mo, who was not distracted at all.

Wingate, who ran the Desert Plaza, said, "I don't care what happens, either way. But that third-show crap has to stop."

Houck said, "I second that. I can't afford to lose any more business than I'm already losing to the strippers and the hookers. And I certainly am not willing to lose it to some colored casino."

Holbrook said, "Maybe we can make that part of the deal. No more shows after midnight. Just gaming and drinking."

Wingate said, "I'd support something like that. Either that or close it down."

Seligman, who rarely spoke, said now, "Closing it down is not an option. We can't be the bad guys on this one. When the colored people in this town get ready, they're going to march down Las Vegas Boulevard and take away everything we have. They're going to march through the doors of the big casino-hotels and burn them to the ground, and you sons of bitches are going to swing from the lampposts like Mussolini."

Houck said, "There ain't no lampposts on the Strip."

Truxton said, "We'll *build* 'em."

Seligman said, "Shut up. This is the rising tide. It cannot be resisted or beaten. But it can be ridden. If we don't keep this joint open, or get another one open, I promise you, we are asking to have our throats cut in our beds while we sleep."

The men sat silently for a moment. Mo Weiner said, "I think Pinchus is absolutely right about that. And I think we ought to either find a buyer for the Ivory Coast now or create a consortium to prop it up and keep it open until a buyer comes along."

Marquez, who had kept quiet through the whole thing, now said, "I might be the buyer. I like the odds on this. But isn't there some legal complications?"

Mo said, "I think our district attorney can answer that to your satisfaction," and fixed his gaze on Filcher.

Filcher got Mo's look and said, "Assistant district attorney, actually. And there *are* some complications, but nothing that can't be worked out."

Marquez said, "Like what?"

"There is some confusion about the title," Filcher said. "This old boxer held the papers. He had no heirs. But he had a common-law wife."

"The one he was strangling when the cops showed up," Truxton said.

Filcher thought about that for a second and said, "That's right. That's what started all that mess. As usual. It was a domestic disturbance, which I know you men know is the policeman's worst nightmare. This one happened to take place in a casino. Anyway . . . She's dead, and she was just an old lush, so it should not be difficult to clear the title."

"Is that all?"

"Pretty much," Filcher said. "I think the gaming commission will play ball with us. I've been in touch with the Ivory Coast's financial backers, in fact, and I think I can broker a deal—if you're sure you want in and if there's no one competing."

Marquez said, "There'd better not be anyone competing. Or I'll come down and cut their throats myself, in their beds, before the niggers get there."

Holbrook laughed uncomfortably, and Marquez guffawed. "It's just a joke, gentlemen. Just a joke. But what gives with these 'financial backers'? I thought that old boxer was on his own."

Filcher blushed slightly and fought the impulse to glance at Mo Weiner. He said, "Some money people from out of town. Harlem, or someplace. They just want out. They're not interested in any more trouble."

Marquez said, "There's always more trouble."

Several men who knew this to be true nodded their heads in agreement.

Holbrook said, "On that note, if there's no other business today?"

Houck said, "What was the name of the shine that opened that place?"

Mo said, "Worthless Worthington Lee. May he rest."

Outside, while they were waiting for their cars, Filcher said, "Gotta hand it to you, Mo. That was real finesse."

Mo said, "That wasn't finesse. That was just good timing. Someone was going to go after the Ivory Coast, soon as they smelled a bargain."

"After I set the deal up, for Marquez, you're going to owe me one."

Mo smiled at Filcher and waved at the valet as he drew the big Starburst Cadillac into the driveway. Mo said, "Don't kid yourself about that, Filcher. I did not put as much money into the Ivory Coast as you may think. I'm not a moron."

"I didn't mean to suggest that."

"And I'm not going to owe you anything. I know what happened at the Ivory Coast. I can probably prove it. And I've got the pull to convene a grand jury if I want to prove it. I see you jockeying here— which, by the way, is fine with me—and I see you setting your boss up for a good old-fashioned necktie party—which, by the way, is also fine with me. Haney is one of the great creeps of the Western world. If something awful should happen to him, well, it couldn't happen to a more deserving guy."

Filcher said, "You have the wrong idea about me."

"No," Mo said. "I have just the right idea. You're a cheap, conniving weasel. You make me sick. And you'll do just fine here in the desert. Just stay off my toes."

Mo gave the valet guy a buck and shot Filcher a wave as he drove off.

The Greyhound bus exhaled sharply as it stopped, blasting fumes across the parking lot. Deacon got a whole lungful going down the steps. He was still weak. He walked the next few feet with halting, jerky steps. It was more walking than he'd done in weeks.

His wounds were mostly healed. His strength was mostly back. He felt pretty good, most of the time, as long as he was lying flat on his back in a hospital bed.

This was different. Getting to the bus station had been a long, slow, sweaty nightmare—all clammy hands and white knuckles and sick stomach. The driver knew every pothole between Las Vegas and Shipton Wells, and he managed to drop a tire into every single one of them. By sundown, when Deacon got off the bus, he was wrecked.

And what he saw did not lift his spirits. The neon sign was off. The café was boarded up. The windows on the main dining area had been smashed in. There were no cars around. It was desolate. Deacon knew, coming out here, that his chances of finding Anita were slim to none anyhow. But he didn't expect there to be *nothing*.

That's what it was. He took a slow stroll past the café, out to the cabins behind. He pushed open this door to the cabin where Anita used to sleep. There was nothing inside. No hint of her. No trace.

Deacon went back around to the front of the café, and over to the gas station that stood next door. A guy wearing greasy overalls was fixing a flat tire. He had the tube inflated and was slowly rotating it through a sluice of water, trying to find the leak. Sitting in the gas-station office was a man in a slick dark suit, thumbing through a magazine. Deacon went past him and into the repair bay.

He said, "Hey," but the mechanic did not look up.

He said, "Slow leak, huh?"

The mechanic looked up but did not speak.

He said, "I'm looking for the girl that used to work in the café."

"You and everybody else."

Deacon said, "How do you mean?"

The mechanic looked up. He said, "You a lawyer?"

"No," Deacon said. "Just a friend."

"You don't look like a lawyer."

"Well, I'm not. I'm just a friend. Do you know where she is?"

"Nobody does. Nobody 'round here, anyway. You buying this place?"

"No. I'm just looking for the girl."

"Good luck, then. All these lawyers have been around here. They're looking for her, too. She owns this café now, I guess."

"What do they want with her?"

"Want her to sell it. Plus the cops wanted her to testify or something."

"About what?"

"I don't know. They came out and had a warrant and searched the place. They didn't say what they were looking for. Offered me money if I told 'em where she was."

"And did you?"

The mechanic eyeballed him, and glanced into the office where the man in the suit still sat. He said, "What's it worth to you?"

"It's worth a lot," Deacon said. "But I'm broke-ass broke."

"Well, I don't know where she is, anyways. She took off from here one night and left that Wally in charge—same night her uncle was going in to the hospital. I never saw a single one of them again. Not alive, anyways. They took Wally out in a box."

"Yeah. I heard."

"He was my cousin."

"I'm sorry."

"Yeah."

Deacon leaned forward and tapped the inner tube. He had been watching little bubbles form on it. He said, "That's your leak, man. Right there."

The mechanic looked down and said, "Damn. You're right. You got good eyes."

Deacon said, "Thanks," and turned to go.

The mechanic said, "You want a job? I need a guy out here."

"No, thanks."

"It'll get busy again, once they open the café back up."

"Is the uncle reopening?"

The mechanic gave him another look and said, "Not likely. He died in the hospital. He never made it off the operating table."

There was that 7:50 bus, the same one the rat-faced guy had been on in the beginning. Deacon got on it, heading west. It was almost ten o'clock before he was in downtown again, walking from the station under the hailstorm of neon back to the Fremont Hotel.

Mo had broken all the news to him—two weeks or more after he'd gone into the hospital. For that first week, they told him later, he'd been unconscious. There had been two gunshot wounds. Either one was serious enough to have killed him. Both together were deadly serious. The surgeon told Deacon that if his friend had not gotten him out of the county hospital and into the private one he would not have made it.

If the doctors knew about Deacon's heroin habit, they did not say so—or not when Deacon was conscious. He had writhed and sweated and choked and clenched his teeth, and ached in every muscle. And he wasn't even there to feel it. The surgeon told him later that he had been in a coma for a full week. Time enough, then, for cold turkey.

That night, when he woke up, Mo was sitting by his bed. It was late, way past midnight. The hospital was silent as the grave.

Mo said, "Well, a lot happened. What do you remember?"

"The Ivory Coast. I was brawling with Haney. Worthless got shot."

Mo said, "That's right."

Deacon listened to the fluorescent lights crackle. He watched Mo, trying to read his face, not wanting to ask. He asked anyway. He said, "Is Worthless dead? And his wife?"

Mo said, "Yes. Both of them."

"What about the girl?"

"The actress? She's fine. She didn't even catch cold."

"What about Sumner?"

Mo shrugged. "Dunno."

"And Haney?"

"Haney's fine."

Deacon closed his eyes and thought of Worthless. His last sensation, the night of the brawl, was of the ex-boxer's big arms encircling him and Haney. The last thing he remembered was Worthless falling to his knees, and then the sound of a gun going off. Deacon caught a sob in his throat.

Mo said, "I know. I'm sorry."

"Will there be a funeral?"

Mo sighed and said, "We had one. Almost two weeks ago. You've been out."

And Deacon went out again, sliding away from consciousness and into sleep. When he awoke, it was daytime. A nurse was smiling at him. He fell asleep. When he woke up again, it was dark, and Mo was there.

Deacon said, "Worthless was the only one, you know. He was the only good one there was, out here."

Mo said, "You're right. But we're moving. Do you think you can get up?"

"Maybe."

His chest was agony, and it took ages to get out of the bed and wrapped in a robe and onto his feet. He was beat before he started. Mo said, "This isn't going to work. Sit down, and I'll get a wheelchair."

Deacon slept while Mo rolled him out of the room and down the hall and out the rear entrance of the hospital. There were about a dozen black men sitting there on upturned apple crates and oil drums, smoking and laughing. Three of them were singing some kind of old spiritual.

Mo said, "It's a short drive. You lie down in the back and rest."

A few minutes later, Mo drew the car up behind a dark, quiet house. He tooted the horn, and a band of women appeared. Deacon passed out again.

When he awoke again, it was a different day and it was daytime, and he was sitting up in a warm, well-lit, pine-paneled room. The walls were bare, and the air smelled of lemons. There was nothing in the room to indicate where he was, or how long he had been there, or what was supposed to happen next. Some time later, a very small Negro woman came tentatively through the door and said, "Oh!" as if she'd seen a mouse. She went away, closing the door behind her. Twenty minutes later a young man in a white lab coat came through the door. He said, "Don't worry. I'm a doctor—well, almost a doctor." He gave Deacon an injection. It was dark when he woke again, and Mo was there.

It took Mo several evenings to tell the whole story. Deacon could only stay awake for a few minutes at a time. He'd be awake, and alert, and then he'd simply disappear. Then it would be the middle of the night, and he'd be alone, and he'd wonder where Mo went, and then he'd be asleep again and then Mo was back. The first few nights, Mo had to start over at the beginning.

Mo told him about how Worthless died. And Dina. And Fidget.

And, almost, Deacon. Mo told him how Haney wrapped it up, and about all the arrests. Deacon understood.

All but one or two things. "Why am I okay, then?"

Mo said, "Well, you're dead. In the technical sense. That's the way it had to play. If Haney thought you pulled through, he'd need to do something about that. So, you had to die."

"How come I'm here, if I'm dead?"

"I know a few doctors," Mo said. "I pulled a string or two. It was really just a matter of paperwork. There was a body they'd found in the desert, John Doe, adult male, about your size. They didn't have a positive I.D. on him. I convinced them that was you. They filled out the death certificate, and destroyed the papers on the John Doe. I got you into a private ambulance and put you in the hospital under another name."

"What name?"

"You remember Sloan, the bartender? You're Sloan."

"That was the body in the desert," Deacon said. "And where am I now?"

"You're in a whorehouse. Aunt Betty's place. I know Betty from way back. She's okay. She keeps her mouth shut. And she's off-limits to Haney."

"I see."

Then he asked what he'd been afraid to ask. He said, "What about Anita?"

Mo stared at his shoes. "I don't know. She took off. I never saw her again. I can ask around for you, if it's serious."

Deacon said, "It's serious."

But Mo had been able to learn nothing. And there was no one to ask. Worthless was gone. Anita's uncle was gone. Wally was gone. There might be something at Shipton Wells, something, or someone, that would point the way.

Deacon couldn't go to Haney. Not as Deacon, and not as Sloan. Even for Anita.

Deacon lay in the whorehouse for a week, in and out of the consciousness, boxed in by pain. Someone would give him a shot of something, and he'd sleep again.

As his head cleared, his future darkened. Mo made it clear there was nothing for him at the Starburst. Too risky, for everyone. He said, "I can set you up with a little dough and help you get out of town. You could go to L.A., or Havana, and really disappear. I know some people in Havana. But you can't stay in Las Vegas. You're too easy to recognize. Somebody would put two and two together and get four. And then Haney will have to kill you all over again."

Deacon felt chumped. He burned, when he was awake, for some kind of revenge. He cooled off only when he slept. He'd slip out of consciousness as if he were sliding into a pool of water, slipping down, slipping out, easing out of his head.

He'd come out of dreams so fiercely real, sometimes, that he literally thought he could see and feel Anita in the room with him. Then he'd wake up, and be in the quiet, pine-paneled room. Once he shouted out in his sleep, and when he awoke his room was full of women—all kinds of women. There were women in lingerie. There was a woman in pigtails and a hoop skirt. There was a woman dressed like a ballerina. It looked as if they were all going to a costume ball. Then he remembered he was in a whorehouse. The very small black woman he'd seen on the first day came sliding between two very large-bosomed blondes and said in her high, squeaky voice, "You girls get back to your business. I'll handle this young man." The girls scattered, and the tiny woman said, "Now, what business you got scaring up my girls like that?"

One day Mo said, "Doc says you can start walking tomorrow. It's been six weeks."

"Six weeks? It's been six weeks?"

"Yeah. A lot of that time you were in a coma, though."

"I don't remember it."

"No. You don't remember all kinds of things. I heard that a nurse tried to find out whether you were in a coma down there, too." Mo pointed at Deacon's crotch.

Deacon grimaced and said, "Did it work?"

"No."

"Someone really *did* do that? Isn't that a little creepy?"

"Not really," Mo said. "You're a good-looking guy. And it was a male nurse."

"Very funny. When do I get out?"

"First you start walking."

One bullet had pierced Deacon's left lung. A little higher and it would have been his heart, and Mo would not have needed to shuffle any paperwork. As it was, the doctor said, the lung was pretty scarred.

He said, "No more horn playing, I'm afraid."

Deacon said, "I'm a bartender."

The doctor said, "Must've been another guy I saw, over at the Starburst."

Deacon said, "I'm a bartender."

The other bullet had gone into his chest close to the shoulder and had hit the shoulder blade and ricocheted into the muscle. There was a very nasty scar where they'd had to go in and dig around to get the bullet out.

The track marks on his forearms were all healed. Maybe that was over. Deacon did not feel the weight of the monkey on his back.

He felt the weight of everything else, though. Winded even by the short walk from the bus station, he got a cab in front of the Fremont. He told the driver, "Starburst, please."

He napped a little on the drive over. Or passed out. He came to, and lit a cigarette, and gave the driver his last five-dollar bill. He waited for the change, and did not give the man a tip. That was how tight it was now, on the dough. The doorman who stood waiting for him to exit the taxi was not known to him. He said, "Thanks, man," and went past him into the hotel.

It was like stepping into an avalanche. The slots whirred and buzzed, and the noise from the casino floor rose up and crashed. Deacon headed down into the pits, the cigarette wedged between his lips, trying to walk right and smile at the people he knew.

He needn't have bothered. Six weeks was an eternity in Las Vegas. With all the traffic, all the new faces, night after night, and all the drama at the tables and in the rooms, six weeks is a lifetime. No one even looked at him. He saw faces he knew, some of which he had names for. But no one was waving, or even looking. Across the room, he saw a cocktail waitress he'd taken to bed, talking to a bartender he'd played cards with. He raised his hand to them. They nodded, blasé and indifferent, and went back to their business.

One man looked, though, and saw, and understood. Fatty Behr was standing with his back to the lobby bar, watching the action, making his plans. He saw Deacon come through the front doors, unsteady on his pins, and make his way slowly across the casino floor. Fatty was in the business of guessing what people wanted before they told him. This guy was walking far too slowly, and looking around the room like he was planning to rob the joint. He had something on his mind. It took a minute or two before Fatty realized who he was looking at. This was a dead trumpet player, moving across the Starburst, headed for the elevators. Not back to the employee residences, but over to the elevators.

That meant a call to Haney. Fatty checked his watch. It was just after ten o'clock. Haney would be at home, probably, and Haney had made it clear that he'd take a call at home only under the direst circumstances. Fatty thought he'd find this pretty dire.

He found a phone and rang the house. After an impossibly long wait, Haney's valet or butler or whatever he was answered the phone. He said, "Please hold the phone." After another impossibly long wait—Fatty watching as the trumpet player got into the elevator and disappeared from view—Haney was on the line.

Fatty said, "It's me. You know that trumpet player used to work at the Starburst? The one that got iced the night the Ivory Coast opened? He's not iced anymore. He just walked into the Starburst. Looks like he's calling on Mo."

"That son of a bitch is dead."

"Not anymore he's not."

Haney cursed into the telephone, then said, "Could you be wrong?"

"Not on this one," Fatty said. "I used to sell him a lot of junk. I know him."

Haney cursed again. He had a lot on his mind. He had big plans for that night. He checked his watch. The men from the foundation would be arriving shortly. The others were here already, he knew.

Was this important? Was it urgent? Haney weighed it against what lay immediately ahead for him. He decided it was not important enough. Not as urgent as some other things were. He said into the phone, "I'm calling Harrigan to take care of him. Keep him there."

Fatty said, "I'll try."

"Don't try. Do it. Or answer to me if you don't."

Fatty went over to the elevators and stood waiting.

Deacon got off the car when it stopped two floors up. Mo's secretary was gone. The outer office was empty. Mo himself was nowhere in sight. Deacon slipped past his secretary's desk and through a doorway into Mo's office. It was cold there, and still, and so silent.

The distant afternoon he had spent up there with Mo, the afternoon that Mo had stared down Haney and got him to back off on the issue of that crooked card dealer, Deacon remembered Mo opening a desk drawer as if he were reaching for a gun. Which drawer? Deacon opened two and got nothing but stationery. He hit pay dirt on three. He took a little blue-black snub-nosed .38 out of the drawer and put it in his jacket.

Mo came in just then, from a back door that Deacon always forgot was there. He said, "You're an idiot to come here—an irresponsible idiot."

Deacon said, "I'm sorry. I got no place else to go."

Mo said, "Haney finds out you're here, you won't need anyplace else to go—ever."

"I know. I'm sorry. And I'm not staying. I need some dough, and then I'll scramble."

Mo said, "You've been to Shipton Wells?"

"Yeah. I got nothing. How'd you know that?"

"Where else would you be? I knew you'd left Betty's, without saying good-bye. I knew you got no place to go. I figured if you're not there, and you're not here, and you're not dead, and Haney hasn't got you yet—well, where else? You're not smart enough to leave town. Obviously."

Mo went to the wet bar and started mixing a drink. He said, "You want a whiskey?"

"No."

"I'm having one." Mo came back across the room and sat in the big leather chair behind his desk. He said, "Sit. What about Anita?"

Deacon sat across from him and said, "I got nothing. She's gone, and there's no way of knowing where."

Mo regarded him for a moment and said, "I think I know where."

"Where?"

"Hollywood. You remember there was a film crew up here the night the Coast opened? It was a guy named Sherry—Albert Sherman. I don't know it, but I asked around a little bit. My partner at the Thunderbird—you know Dawson—is pretty sure that she went off with Sherman. After she heard what happened to you."

"Why would she leave with *him?*"

"Why wouldn't she? Big Hollywood noise like that. He might have told her he'd make her a star."

"And just leave me? Just leave her uncle?"

"You and the uncle were croaked. Why should she hang around?"

"Just like that?"

"A girl's gotta eat." Mo threw off the last of his drink. "You sure you don't want a whiskey?"

Deacon shook his head. "I should go."

Mo said, "You'll need some bullets for the gun." He opened a drawer Deacon had not checked and pulled out a box of ammunition. He tossed the box across the desk, and Deacon caught it. Mo said, "How you fixed for greenery?"

Deacon said, "I'm busted. I got about three bucks."

The phone on the desk rang then. Mo glanced at the door, then at Deacon, and reached for the phone. He said, "Yes," and listened. He said, "Thank you," and hung up.

"You'd better go, and now. Two of Haney's men just barred in downstairs. They're looking for you."

"How did—?"

"It doesn't matter. You have to go. Walk with me."

Mo reached into his jacket and pulled out a clutch of folded bills. He peeled away several and handed them across to Deacon as they started out the door. He said, "This guy Sherman runs an outfit called Monolith Pictures. He draws a lot of water down there. You can't expect to just waltz in."

"Thanks, Mo. You are the man."

"That's what they say."

In the hallway Mo turned right, away from the elevators, and beckoned Deacon to follow. Deacon said, "I have to ask you one thing."

Mo said, "What?"

"Haney, and the guy from Chicago. What was that?"

Mo said, "I heard this guy was coming in with something for Haney. I knew it was something Haney was going to pay a lot of money for. I didn't know what it was."

"Why didn't you tell me to bring it to you?"

"I didn't know you. I didn't have anybody here I could trust—at least not with something that could backfire on me like that. And I didn't know whether the stuff was valuable or not. If it was, and I asked you to get it, you'd just have run off with it. If it was something really serious, you might have gone to Haney first. So, I thought I'd just let it play out. I figured it was narcotics, or stolen property, or some kind of blackmail thing. And I'm not a dope dealer or a fence. And blackmail isn't my game. So . . ."

At the end of the hallway, Mo pressed a button that looked like a light switch. A door opened.

Deacon said, "What is this?"

"Private car. Come on."

They stepped into a small elevator. Mo mashed a button inside, and the door closed.

Deacon said, "But why?"

"My only interest was in knocking Haney back. If it was a ton of money or something, it wouldn't have been a single guy, a stranger, coming in on a bus from Chicago. If it was anything else, well, it didn't interest me. I just wanted Haney nervous."

"If it was blackmail, didn't you want to know what he was being blackmailed for?"

"No. Why would I? I'm not a blackmailer. I got a business to run. It keeps me very busy. I'm running two joints. I was getting ready to open the Ivory Coast. I didn't have time for this, beyond sending a guy to intercept a guy. It cost me nothing, and the net result was the same. Haney's world became unstable. So I got what I wanted."

"Well, yes. But . . . look what happened."

"A lot of that was going to happen anyway. I don't feel responsible. Beyond looking out for you."

The elevator opened onto a hallway just like the one they'd left on the second floor. There was a door at the end. Mo opened it. A plain hallway ran beyond that. Mo said, "Go that way. At the end, there is a small room. On the other side of the room, there is another door, and on the other side of the door is a stairwell. It leads to the parking lot behind the Thunderbird. The doors have handles on the inside only. They open out, but they don't open back in. You won't be coming back here."

Deacon said, "What about you? Will you stay"

Mo said, "For now," and extended a hand. Deacon took it, and they shook. Mo's hand was cool and dry. Deacon realized it was the first time Mo had ever touched him. He said, "I'll be seeing you."

"Stay in touch. And think about Havana. There's plenty of action down there. And it could be, a couple of years from now, this will all look cute. And then you can come back."

"Thanks, Mo."

"And remember, you're dead."

Deacon went through the door, and it closed behind him. He went down the passageway.

Harrigan braced the front desk clerk, two pit bosses, and a bartender before he bullied his way to the second floor. That little rabbit called Fatty had insisted that Deacon was in the building. Harrigan wasn't taking no for an answer from anyone. He pushed his way right to the boss's office. But he found him sitting alone, going through papers, and he looked like he'd been alone all night. There was one dirty glass. There were no dirty ashtrays. The man looked surprised when Harrigan burst in. There was nothing to suggest he hadn't been sitting there, quietly cooking the books, all night long.

Harrigan muscled back to the lobby. Stanfill, the daft bugger they'd partnered him with, was standing by the slot machines with a notebook in his hand. He said, "I couldn't get nothing out of no one."

Harrigan said, "Where's that little dope peddler?"

They found Fatty by the hatcheck. "Alls I know is, he was here, boys," Fatty told them. "That's not my department, but I was doing your boss a favor. Don't get pushy with me. I already gave at the office."

Harrigan said, "You know this rat, doncha? Where would he be going?"

Fatty thought: *Where indeed?* Everything he knew about Deacon's world was gone—Worthless, that mulatto girl who went to Hollywood. . . . He said, "He'd be headed for the West Side. If he's holed up somewhere, it might be Aunt Betty's. Or he's left town."

Harrigan and Stanfill hit the parking lot and ran a squad car down Las Vegas Boulevard to Bonanza and then under the tracks to Jackson. It took Harrigan twenty minutes to get there and find the whorehouse known as Aunt Betty's. He'd never been in—never had cause to go in, seeing as how the joint was off-limits to law enforcement, owing to some deal the owner had made with Holbrook—and he didn't know the building at once even when he parked in front of it. He checked his side arm, then gave his partner another visual inspection. Unsteady, he thought. He said, "You stay with the car. If that little bastard comes running out, you tell him to halt, once. And then shoot him."

Harrigan went in. The front door was unlocked. A huge Negro was on him at once. He said, "Good evening, suh. How can we help you?"

Harrigan waved his service revolver at him and said, "Shut up, ya big darkie. And keep away from me." A quick glance around—two "parlor" rooms off to one side, hallway down the other—told Harrigan his man was not on the ground floor. He hit the stairs. A tiny Negro woman was just coming into the foyer as he went up. He gave her a wink and put a finger to his lips as he hit the top of the stairs.

Deacon heard the commotion downstairs. He'd hardly had time to get in himself and was sitting on his bed, trying to formulate a plan. *Must leave town,* he was thinking, *and must leave now. Must take the Greyhound for Hollywood. Must get a taxi over to the Greyhound station. Must ask Aunt Betty . . .*

Then he looked through the curtains at the street, and saw the squad car parked at the curb.

So it really *was* time. Deacon put his jacket back on and hit the door.

Harrigan was at the top of the stairs. He heard a door swoosh open behind him, and turned. The back of someone who might have been Deacon was going through another door at the end of the hall. Harrigan raised his service revolver and said, "Stop, there," and then fired two shots. Wood splintered, and the door popped off its hinges and creaked inward. Harrigan was on it and through it. A pair of very young women, one dark haired and one light, stood cowering in the corner. Harrigan roared at them, "Where is he?" One of them glanced instinctively at a door in the opposite corner. Harrigan hit it running. Another stairway. He was on the steps, going down four at a time.

It landed back in the front foyer. And that room was empty. Harrigan ran out the front door. His partner was sitting in the squad car, with the engine running, examining his fingernails. He didn't even look up when Harrigan came outside. And there was no Deacon in sight. Harrigan slammed back through the front door. He went down the hallway to the left. Another set of doors. A kitchen and a toilet. A back door on the kitchen. A yard. A fence, and a gate, and the gate was swinging. Harrigan got there and looked out over the sand beyond. It was just desert, with no one moving on it as far as the light would carry. Harrigan cursed and came back around the building to the front of the house.

Deacon, watching from a corner in the backyard, held his breath and waited. His chest ached. He wished he had gone ahead into the desert. Harrigan had decided not to follow there. He would probably search the house and grounds now. Deacon cradled the snub-nosed .38 in his palm, and hated the feel of it. His hands were sweaty and slick, and his breath came in raspy gasps.

And Harrigan was leaving. Deacon watched him go. He heard the squad car growl up and move off. He sat for another fifteen minutes or more, waiting. He thought: *This, from now on, is my life. I'll have to run like this every time I see a cop.* He got onto his feet and walked to the front of Aunt Betty's.

The tiny Negro woman was standing on the sidewalk, her eyes on the street. She didn't turn until Deacon was almost on top of her.

She said, "Boys like that gonna give the cops a bad name."

"I'm sorry, Betty. It's all my fault, and I apologize."

"Blasted up my bedroom door."

"I'm sorry about that, too. Anyone hurt?"

"Naw. Still . . ." she said, and spat on the sidewalk. "I know they only God's chirren, like everyone else. They know *not* what they do. But Lord help me, I wish the devil would take them now."

"I'm going."

"I think that's best, son," Aunt Betty said. "You watch yourself. And don't hurt nobody else, neither."

"Yes'm."

It was nearly midnight at Haney's place when the first of the two foundation cars arrived with the little ones. Many of them had fallen asleep on the drive from town. Some of them were crying. It took

Willis and the two drivers half an hour just to get them all into the big playroom and quieted down. Some fell asleep again right away. Others had to be given bottles. Two of them needed fresh diapers. Willis said, "I don't do no diapers," and left that to the two foundation drivers.

Haney had come in at midnight. Willis said, "We not quite ready, suh."

Haney said, "I'll have another brandy, then. You'll let me know?"

The babies were all dressed now in their little suits and gowns. The little boys had their hair greased up and slicked down. Some of them had little mustaches painted onto their lips. The little girls had bows in their curls and were wearing lipstick and eye shadow—courtesy of Haney's sister at the foundation. The two foundation men had arranged them in the playroom, settling them down into the pillows, on the sofa, on the floor. Willis had told the foundation men, "I'm bringing in the others. You gots to leave now."

There were five others this time. Three men and two women. Haney had found three of them through a contact in San Francisco. One man and one woman were married and had been circus performers. The third was a friend of theirs. They were small. The other two were from a connection in L.A. Willis didn't know whether they knew the other three, or even each other. But they all came in like professionals—dressed and polished and beautifully made up. The two women carried cocktail glasses that were enormous in their tiny hands. One of the women looked a little tipsy. Haney would not like that. He didn't like them to drink. Willis didn't care. None of this was for him. Haney, whatever else he was, never ever asked Willis to participate.

Willis went to the wall switches and the room went dim. The big windows that looked down the valley into Las Vegas went black. Beyond, the lights of the Strip twinkled.

Willis said, "Ya'll get started. The man will be along in a minute."

In the other room, Haney was already on a slow boil. The third brandy was going right to his head. He felt pleasantly warm, and loose, and outside of himself. What with the ugliness of the summer, and the persistence of it all, he had not been able to arrange an evening for himself in four or five months. Bringing the three in from San Francisco, and even finding the two from L.A., had been such a headache. The three from Frisco had been here for a month already.

Haney had not seen them. He wouldn't see them until the night itself and until he had found at least one more, and preferably two or three more, to go with them. They'd been staying in a hotel downtown, waiting, at great expense to Haney, waiting and not being told what they were waiting for. Haney had found that there was no real point in doing it with less than four, and that took time and it cost more, but there wasn't any reason not to do it right. Even if it meant waiting.

The phone rang then. Haney cursed under his breath and heard Willis pick up the receiver and speak into it in the other room. Willis came slowly forward and said, "They's a call for you, suh."

Haney said, "I'm not available. Tell 'em it will have to wait until morning."

Willis looked pained, but he turned and went back. Haney heard him speak, and the click the phone down. What would the call be? Nothing but Harrigan telling him that creep trumpet player was dead. Again. Or lost. Either way, the news could wait until morning.

And now all the other waiting was over, at last. Willis came into the room and said, "All ready, suh."

Haney said, "Thank you, Willis. You can go now."

"Thank you, suh."

Haney put down the snifter and cinched his robe tight again as he rose, and moved slowly and with great pleasure toward the playroom.

The front room was lit, but empty. Deacon had left the taxi a quarter mile away, and waited until it was gone before he set out walking across the sand. It was dark, without a moon, and after the lights of the taxi had gone, he saw the house glowing before him and beckoning like a log fire. There appeared to be a man sitting, alone, in an armchair.

But when he got close to the house he saw that the room was empty. The man in the armchair had gone.

There were two panel trucks in the driveway. Deacon went around to the front of them and felt the hoods. They were warm, but not hot. The windows on one were rolled down. There were keys in the ignition. He checked the other and found keys hanging there, too.

There was more light, glowing dimly, at the other end of the house. Deacon went there. The sand scrunched under his shoes a little. There was the faintest of breezes. As he drew close, he could hear the buzz of music playing softly inside. He scooted close to the big windows that looked down over the valley.

At first he saw nothing at all. Then he noticed a figure. It was Haney. He was wearing a bathrobe, which was hanging open, and standing with his hands on his hips, staring down at something. Deacon could not see anyone or anything else in the room. Then something moved, on the floor. Deacon squatted down, shifted position, and moved over one window. The light was better there. The glow coming from another room fell now on the floor and on the sofa. Deacon could see that there was a door at the other end of the room, leading out to a patio. Deacon moved as quietly as possible across the sand, toward the door.

He got on his hands and knees, and raised up just enough to see inside.

Then there was a sudden loud noise and the room went bright. Deacon hit the deck. But the noise was from outside. One of the panel trucks had started up. Its headlights swept the room now as it swung backward out of the driveway. Deacon stayed on the ground as the truck shifted out of reverse and into a forward gear and ground across the driveway. Deacon waited until the sound of the truck got dim before he looked through into the room again.

The view, now, was quite clear.

There were babies there. Babies in makeup, dressed in grown-up clothes. Five or six of them were slumped onto the sofa—boys and girls, the boys wearing tuxedos and the girls wearing gauzy dresses and strands of pearls. The baby boys had mustaches painted onto them. Several of them appeared to be asleep. There were several more on the floor.

In fact, there were two of them on the floor right in front of him. One of them was making love to the other. They were on their hands and knees, half clothed, and going at it like dogs. And there was another pair of them, farther back in the room, lying down and doing exactly the same thing. They were swaying and doing it in time with the music, which Deacon heard now was a Gene Autry record. The voice said, "Give me land, lots of land, and the starry skies above / Don't fence me in." There were babies making love on the floor and listening to Gene Autry.

Deacon felt his brain catch on fire. It was as if his head were about to explode. And then he realized what Haney was doing.

Another baby, a girl baby, wearing some kind of tiara on her tiny head, was standing up with her face in Haney's crotch. Haney was moving his hips slowly back and forth, also in time to the music. He reached down now and took the baby's head in his hands.

Deacon took the snub-nosed revolver out of his pocket and came into the room shooting. He fired one shot straight up and then two shots into the big windows facing the valley. Glass shattered with a terrible noise. Some of the babies started crying. A woman's voice, horribly high-pitched and barely human, screamed. Then there was silence.

Haney, as if coming out of a reverie, looked around in a panic. It took him a moment to find Deacon in the dark. He reached into his bathrobe as if he were going for a weapon, but came up empty. He said, "Stop! Don't shoot that thing! There are babies here!"

Deacon moved forward on him. The babies on the floor grabbed at their clothes. The baby girl wearing the tiara started buttoning up the front of her gown. Something was desperately wrong with the way they looked. Warped. Old, and wrinkly, and freakish.

They were midgets. Deacon suddenly saw that they were midgets. The ones on the sofa, the ones sleeping and the ones crying, were actual children. The ones making love on the floor were midgets. But the one who came into the room now, behind Haney, was not. He was a full-size Negro man, and he was holding a gun. He said, "Drop it, mister, or I'll shoot you right now."

Deacon said, "No."

Another baby began to cry. Haney said, "Willis? Put the weapon down."

The Negro set the gun on the floor.

Haney said, "What do you want? We're not hurting anybody."

Deacon just stared, and waited. The room was terribly cold, air-conditioned hard against the desert heat. Deacon came awake in the chilly air, and his head felt clear for the first time in days. He glanced around as if awakening from a bad dream. Awakening, though, into a nightmare. Babies and midgets!

Haney said, "Ask them yourself. We're not hurting anybody. This is what they do for a *living*."

Deacon did not speak.

Haney said, "Is it money? Willis, go and—"

Deacon said, "Shut up. If you move again or talk, I'll kill you."

The room was very still. The Gene Autry record had come to an end. The needle skipped and seemed to wheeze, and skipped and wheezed. No one moved.

Deacon said, "This, after all . . . *This* is what everything is about? You and some midgets?"

"It's not what you think."

"Never mind what I *think*. Jesus! This is what everything has been about? The photographs, and the film, and the guy in Shipton Wells? And everything at the Ivory Coast? About you and some midgets?"

"Not just me. I was trying to protect my sister. She runs the foundation, you know."

"So?"

"It's the babies, you know? I couldn't let anything happen to my sister, or to the babies. I can imagine what you think about the photographs. I suppose you find it repulsive."

"It *is* repulsive," Deacon said. "It's pathetic. All of this death is about nothing more than you and—*this*."

"You don't understand. It would *kill* my sister if she knew. I had to protect her. You can see that, can't you?"

Deacon said, "No. I can't."

Haney eyed Deacon, and the pistol. Off to the side, Willis tilted his head at Deacon and raised his eyebrows in question. Haney shook his head slightly. Deacon, temporarily deranged by the scene before him, saw none of it.

Coming back to himself, Deacon said, "What happened to the girl from Shipton Wells?"

Haney said, "She went back to her job at the Starburst."

Deacon said, "Not her. The other girl. The café waitress."

Haney said, "The Negro gal? She went off with the movie guy."

Deacon said, "Went off where?"

"Who knows? She just left town."

"When?"

"Right after," Haney said. "It was the day after."

"The day after you killed me."

"Yes."

Haney's face showed not the slightest emotion.

Deacon said, "The doctors said I was shot twice."

Haney nodded.

"They said I was shot twice, while I was lying on the ground."

Haney nodded.

"They said I was already unconscious when I was shot."

Haney said, "What do you want from me? An apology? I'm a cop. I was trying to kill you."

"All because of the photographs . . ."

"That's right. You *were* trying to blackmail me, weren't you?"

Deacon thought for a moment. He said, "No. I was just trying to get along. The pictures were an accident."

"Then where are the photographs now? Does the girl have them?"

Deacon shrugged. He saw, from the corner of his eye, the Negro butler moving sideways on silent feet. He said, "Stop moving, you." And the man stopped. Haney stood still, too, his hands smoothing the silk of his robe, his limpid, empty eyes studying Deacon. The midgets stared up at Deacon as if he were the ringmaster.

Deacon said, "The truck that started up a minute ago. Where did it go?"

"The drivers leave the babies and then come back. They'll be back here soon."

Deacon nodded. He was trying to think. His head felt like muddy sludge. His tongue felt like muddy sludge. One of the midget ladies was now smiling at him and clasping her hands as if she were praying. The babies had all gone back to sleep. Deacon said, "What about the foundation?"

"It's legit. I support it. I collect money, and I make contributions. I never touch the babies. You have to understand that. I never, never touch the babies. They're just, like, scenery. I only go with grown-ups."

Deacon, disgusted, stared at him.

Haney said, "See, it's not illegal. I never broke *the law*. Nothing I have done is against the law. But the pictures made it look that way. That's why I had to have them."

"Who's the other guy in the pictures?"

Haney thought for a moment. He eyed Deacon, and the snub-nosed pistol. He said, "It's Holbrook. My brother-in-law."

Deacon smiled—a sick, stomach-turned smile.

Haney said, "It's not funny. Imagine what it would do to him. And my sister. It would *kill* her. And it would ruin me. I'm the *law* here. Imagine what the pictures would do to my reputation."

Deacon began to laugh. The babies were crying, and one of the little people, a man in a tuxedo that wouldn't have been too large for a house cat, was crying, too. Haney flushed bright red. His empty eyes were like burning jewels. His *reputation!* Deacon laughed and could not stop.

Haney said, "It's not funny."

Deacon, laughing, said, "Of course it's funny. Look at you!"

Haney shouted, "It's not funny! What if it was you? What if it was pictures of *you?* How about that? What if it was pictures of you and that little black bitch? What if she was crawling around on the floor, sucking—"

"Shut up, you rat," Deacon growled. His fingers tightened on the pistol and he stepped forward and pointed it at Haney.

But Haney laughed, and then shouted, "Willis!"

Deacon turned. The Negro butler was moving again. Deacon pointed the revolver at him and said, "Stop, you." He took a step toward Willis to show he was serious.

Haney dove onto the floor, going after the weapon the butler had dropped. Deacon heard the policeman move behind him, and turned just as Haney was getting his hands on the gun. He was a swath of dark silk robe and pale, buttermilk-colored skin. Deacon felt they were both moving underwater.

Haney clutched the weapon and raised it.

Deacon fired first.

Haney clutched his stomach and raised his gun hand. Deacon shot again. Haney doubled over and dropped the gun.

Behind Deacon feet were scampering. When he turned, Willis and the midgets ran for the corners. Some of the babies woke up and began to cry. Haney started moaning, low and mournful. Deacon, dizzy, and light-headed, leaned down and picked up the gun Haney had dropped, and stared into Haney's face.

The policeman was clutching his stomach. His robe was going dark red, fast. His face was ashen and his teeth were clenched tight.

He said, "You bastard. I'll kill you." His hand shot out and snatched at Deacon's ankles.

"You did that already," Deacon said. He shifted his foot away from Haney's hand, and then kicked him, hard, in the gut. "That's for Worthless."

Haney crumpled up. "Oomp. Jesus. It hurts."

Deacon kicked him again hard. "And that's for me."

Haney groaned. "*Jesus*. It really hurts. I've never been shot before."

"High time, then."

"I need a doctor."

"No, you don't."

Haney's eyes flashed, and then dimmed. He was losing ground fast. Deacon could see him going. His teeth clenched, and relaxed, and clenched again.

He said, "But . . . I'm going to die."

"Die, then."

Deacon stood up. The midgets cowered. Willis raised his hands and covered his face, and said, "Mister, please don't hurt them babies."

Deacon suddenly felt the smallness of it all—of Haney, and his ridiculous desire, and the wretched creatures who fed it. He felt the smallness of himself, standing in a dying policeman's house, holding a gun on a defenseless Negro and a room full of crying infants and terrified midgets. Worthless dead, his wife dead, Anita lost, and for what? For this? Because of this? It was a great, black joke that wasn't funny, a pathetic joke that had been played on them all. By what? By a world that itself was so terribly small—filled with small people, all clinging, desperately clinging, to the few small things that gave them joy or made them feel not afraid.

Deacon was not afraid. He had no joy. But he was done here. He walked away from Haney, out of the house and into the dark outside. The heat came up and wrapped around him like a mist. The air was full of sage, and so dry that Deacon's face burned.

Behind him someone was screaming in the house. Deacon kept moving. He threw Haney's gun out into the desert and stuck the snub-nose into his pocket. The keys were still hanging in the panel-truck ignition. He got in and stamped on the starter, and the truck growled to life. He threw it in gear and headed down toward the valley.

The lights from the Las Vegas Strip winked below. His ears were ringing and his head was light. The night felt airless. Deacon rolled down the window but it didn't help. The heat of the day had not even begun, but already he could feel it building. He glanced over his shoulder and watched Haney's house recede.

Halfway down the hill there was a stop sign. Deacon pulled the hand brake on the panel truck and took his hands off the wheel. The engine idled and was the only sound across the desert floor.

Deacon lit a cigarette, and watched his hands shaking. He waited for a moment until they got still.

The Strip was north from here, farther down the hill and to the left. Straight ahead, over the desert floor, the sun would come up soon. To Deacon's right was darkness, and the south.

Deacon knew he did not have much time. Haney's house would have a phone. The butler would already be on to the cops—Haney's own men—maybe after straightening things up so it wouldn't be so obvious what Haney was doing when he got shot. Or maybe the foundation drivers would be back. Someone would give the cops a description of the truck, probably within an hour or less. By the time Deacon could get to Las Vegas, and ditch it, and get another one, they'd be on to him.

If he headed south, which was the obvious direction to run, the Las Vegas cops would radio the highway patrol to look for him going toward Los Angeles. He could go east, maybe, into the desert, on one of the farm roads. When the sun came up, he'd be the only thing moving for miles and miles around. If the cops put a plane up to look for him, he'd be cooked. If he hooked around and drove west, there was only Death Valley ahead, and the great Mojave Desert beyond. There was no place to hide.

There were clouds in the east. The first rays of light were beginning to light them from below and behind. There wasn't much darkness left.

Deacon released the parking brake and put his hands back on the wheel and turned it to the right, heading south. He'd drive down toward Baker, or Barstow, and decide later what to do. He couldn't get a bus, probably, because they'd be watching the bus stations. But he could steal a car, maybe, or hitch a ride somehow.

For now, anyway, he had to move. He eased the panel truck up to fifty, and slipped down the hill and out of sight of the ranch house. In another twenty minutes, Las Vegas had disappeared behind him. His hands slacked on the wheel. Somewhere, ahead, was Anita. He drove on.

ACKNOWLEDGMENTS

The author would like to thank, for their encouragement and support, Karl Fleming and Anne Taylor Fleming, John and Sandra Malone, Sid and Toby Singer, David Vigliano, Joshua Kendall, Jack Langguth, Vincent Castellanos, and Julie Singer. Without them, nothing.

The author would also like to thank Trish Geran, Katherine Duncan, Jonnie Kennedy of the University of Las Vegas's Lied Library Special Collections, and the Las Vegas African-American Cultural Society.